THE
MARRIAGE
TREE

THE
MARRIAGE
TREE

A VINCENT CALVINO NOVEL

CHRISTOPHER G. MOORE

Heaven Lake Press

Distributed in Thailand by:
Asia Document Bureau Ltd.
P.O. Box 1029
Nana Post Office
Bangkok 10112 Thailand
Fax: (662) 260-4578
Web site: http://www.heavenlakepress.com
email: editorial@heavenlakepress.com

Heaven Lake Press paperback edition 2014

Jacket design: K. Jiamsomboon
Author's photograph: Ralf Tooten © 2012

ISBN 978-616-7503-23-3

For Daniel Vaver

This novel is also co-dedicated to the following individuals in recognition of their financial contribution to support a one-year scholarship for disadvantaged children living along the Thai-Burmese border: Mike Herrin, Kevin Cummings, James Gulkin, Michaela Striewski, Jarad Henry, Keith Bacon, and John Bright.

"Men are not gentle creatures, who want to be loved, who at the most can defend themselves if they are attacked; they are, on the contrary, creatures among whose instinctual endowments is to be reckoned a powerful share of aggressiveness. As a result, their neighbor is for them not only a potential helper or sexual object, but also someone who tempts them to satisfy their aggressiveness on him, to exploit his capacity for work without compensation, to use him sexually without his consent, to seize his possessions, to humiliate him, to cause him pain, to torture and to kill him. *Homo homini lupus* [man is wolf to man]."

—Sigmund Freud, *Civilization and its Discontents*,
trans. and ed., James Strachey
(New York: W. W. Norton, 1961)

ONE

From: Vincent Calvino
To: Dr. Apinya
Confidential: Patient/Doctor Privilege
Date/Time: 25 April, 20:37

Fifteen days have passed since I found Ploy's body. I should buy a lottery ticket ending in the number fifteen. As I sit here staring at the empty page in my typewriter, I realize it's been almost two weeks since the start of Songkran. And eight months and ten days have come and gone since the first arrival of the visitors. My words appear in one color ·· black. Empty containers on a dark, moonless night, stacked at a port, waiting to be shipped. No one comes for them. No one wants them.

As a private investigator, I have a one·man Bangkok office. It has been temporarily closed because of the health of the one man. Since

1

I returned from Rangoon, I've been picking the lock on a secret door. Why would I do that? On the other side are people banging to get out. Some of them are strangers, but some of them I know, some I loved, and all are waiting. You are going to ask me, "Waiting for what?" And I am going to tell you, that's what I want to find out. But to unlock that door requires a special key.

Care must be taken in speaking the word "key" in Thailand. If the wrong tone is used, it sounds like the Thai word for shit. Pick your metaphors with caution. Pick your dreams with care. Pick your beliefs or they will be picked for you.

Hallucinations. People look away when you tell them you see things they can't. Madness is what they call such reports. What I experience is the sight, smells and sounds of the dead, who come as visitors. They come almost every day. Sometimes they appear more than once or twice.

The plight of Sisyphus comes to mind as I watch the visitors. Technically they aren't hallucinations. I know what I see comes from my head, though it makes little difference. Everything we witness comes from inside our minds. How can I say my computer is real and the visitors are illusions? The Romans handed down the ancient Greek story of Sisyphus. My Italian grandfather taught me all about the old gods. He thought they were the way to unlock the secret door. That they were the key.

Sisyphus was an ancient reality show about the meaning of hell. He cheated death and in doing so swindled the gods. Sisyphus wished for eternal life ·· but his immortality came with a condition. As a penalty for his sneaky behavior, Sisyphus was given a job for eternity. His task was simple ·· he had to roll a boulder up the side of a mountain, but each time, just before he reached the top, the boulder would break free of his grasp and roll down to the bottom of the mountain. It wasn't a great job, but he did have great job security. He realized his dream of living forever.

Every day, forever, Sisyphus climbed the mountain, pushing the rock, and each day it rolled back to where he'd started. The next day, more of the same. Eternity measured out one day at a time, always with the same outcome. His story is a bit like that of the Bill Murray character in the movie Groundhog Day, but without the Hollywood ending.

Our hell isn't just a physical place; it exists also in pointless, repetitive, mindless and meaningless activity. To live without purpose or meaning is worse than death. Everywhere I look I see the mortal clones of Sisyphus -- a lawyer at his desk, a secretary in her corporate cubicle, an Indian nut vendor walking on Soi Cowboy, a plastic surgeon, a yoga master, a bargirl as she clutches a chrome pole. These are the boulder pusher's bastard children, each dwarfed behind his or her own high stone. These mountain climbers work without ropes. Each day they face the same version of eternity as the day before and know that when tomorrow comes, it will be waiting for them again.

My grandfather's lessons in mythology failed to teach me, though, that in Thailand the likes of Sisyphus climb not mountains but sword trees. The daily life of Sisyphus was sweet compared with the fate of adulterers condemned to climbing one of those trees for eternity.

Imagine a forest of sword trees stretching as far as the eye can see ·· an infinite number of trees and an infinite number of men standing naked before each one. The men, all adulterers, were living and breathing one minute, dead the next. Each one has woken up in the forest in front of a sword tree. The branches consist of millions of small, sharp knives that glimmer in the light. The adulterer climbs to the top of the tree, lured by the sight of a seductive beauty perched at the top. As he climbs, his flesh, shredded by the tiny knives, flies loose from the bone. Bleeding from the punishing wounds, he finally reaches the top ·· only to discover that the naked woman is now at the bottom of the tree. She passionately begs him to climb down and experience her fleshly pleasures. On the journey down the sword tree, his flesh is once again ripped and torn until he is nothing but bloody, raw bones. But as he reaches the ground, he finds the temptress vanished once again and reappearing on her perch at the top of the sword tree. She howls for him to hurry up the tree to satisfy her lust.

Sisyphus got boulder duty in return for immortality. The Thai adulterer is filleted like a snow fish, and his punishment continues for eternity. Rolling boulders = An elusive, meaningless expenditure of time. Chasing women = Shredding flesh and never appeasing one's sexual hunger.

Behind the locked door are boulder rollers and women chasers, all longing to step out of the bargain. They no longer wish for immortality. They pray for death. When the visitors appear in my room, they are refugees from the mountain and the forest. They wish for peace and so find their way to me. I feel that they are waiting for me to unlock the door. To set them free. Why do they believe it's within my power?

I don't. I tell them they've come to the wrong place and person. I tell them to go away and leave me alone. They always return. Boulder rollers and sword tree climbers are programmed for repetition. Like most people who have no choice, they are desperate. The dead are more desperate and persistent than the living. Never mind. I will continue to send them away, even though they will continue to appear. We are of a kind -- the living and the dead. Entangled in our daily climb.

Early on the morning of April 10, I found myself standing at the base of a sword tree. A seductive young woman was dead in the tall grass. Only I didn't recognize her or the role she would come to play in my life over the following days and weeks. I saw only what was in front of me at that moment. I didn't look hard enough. I missed the Agni icon on the ground. One of those small ceremonial figurines normally found in prayer rooms, on yoga tables or in spirit houses was on the ground in front of me, waiting for me to notice it and pick it up. I missed the Agni. I missed a number of things that morning.

But I had found a girl who had magically flown from the top of a sword tree to the bottom and back again, ad infinitum, so I started looking for the man who'd grown tired of climbing that tree. I figured he'd be the killer.

I knew that, more likely than not, the sword tree man I was searching for was a coward as that describes all men who accept intolerable conditions in return for immortality. He wouldn't have had the guts to kill her himself. That in itself doesn't make him abnormal. Killing another human being is an extreme, unthinkable act. Buying a sex slave is permissible so long as no big noise is made. My grandfather believed that Sisyphus was punished not for wishing for immorality but for cheating the gods to obtain it. Sisyphus was a cheat. The man on the sword tree is another kind of cheat. Cheats hire a sword tree gardener, someone with the experience to prune, not the tree, but the temptress forcing her man up and down it. I'd found a dead woman. The hard part was to find the man the real killer had found to free him from his daily climb.

This fragility of life disturbs me. The flame of faith in eternity isn't the key.

I am searching for words to tell the story of the hardest of all missing persons cases, the case where the private investigator has gone missing and doesn't know how or where to find himself. That kind of search tests the strength of a man's faith -- his belief that finding what has gone missing is worth the effort.

TWO

MONDAY, APRIL 8, five days before the start of the Buddhist New Year. Walking along Soi Cowboy, Vincent Calvino was greeted by the joyous buzz of a street celebration with girls, punters, tourists, voyeurs, nut vendors and food hawkers. It had the look of a medieval town square as the first news that the Black Death had ended brought everyone into the street to party. Soi Cowboy—the epicenter, where the contemporary equivalent of plague survivors gathered—had rows of bars dedicated to a permanent victory celebration. Each bar Calvino passed had a version of the same laughter, dancing, drinking, whoring and singing, as if the plague had ended just hours ago. Let the good times roll. Death had been defeated.

Calvino had survived being shot at in Rangoon. But like all survivors, he still felt the cold steel blade of fear in the knowledge that he'd only been lucky, and in the fact that those who hadn't made it out alive had been near.

Calvino glanced into a couple of bars like a man on the prowl. Patterson Roy waved, holding a whiskey sour in one hand and a cigarette in the other. He called Calvino over to his bar, Mama, Don't Call, which had a dozen Isaan dancers who'd slipped their chains in the rice fields but continued to shuffle on stage as if the memory of those restraints had never left them.

"I thought you'd be back," said Patterson. "Nui's inside."

He shook his head, tonguing an unlit cigarette.

"Damn, if she wasn't right. The girls know when someone's got the sickness, Calvino."

Nui, a twenty-six-year-old from a village near Roi Et, had entered her third month at Mama, Don't Call and had collected three marriage proposals, two offers to be someone's *mia noi* and four opportunities to be a steady girlfriend. She had a poker hand with nine cards and was eyeing one of them, one of the girlfriend customers, when Calvino walked in. Nui finished her lady's drink, slid off the bar stool and gave the customer a hug. Then she walked over to Calvino and hugged him.

"I miss you too much, Khun Vinny."

With a girl like Nui, if she liked you, she'd throw away a girlfriend card. But then, a girlfriend offer was like drawing the two of diamonds. It wasn't a card that made for a winning hand. Besides, Nui liked Calvino.

"You pay bar," she said.

Calvino nodded, pulling out his wallet. She waved the thousand baht note over her head and did a little dance for the benefit of her friends seated on the backbench, like hockey players who never got much ice time. Now a high-stick pro, Nui had come a long way in three short months, from high school to a post-doc in what made men tick.

"You okay tonight?" she asked, pouting her lip as she tried to read his mood in the dim light.

He looked happy enough, she thought.

"Never felt better," he said.

With that confirmation she hugged him again. Her smile reappeared as she ran his thousand baht note under her nose, closing her eyes and sighing. The scent of cash made her light-headed. But she still hadn't totally made up her mind. She wanted the money, but she didn't want trouble.

Money. Trouble. The competing ideas circled like vultures as she sipped her lady's drink.

"Sure?" she asked, squeezing his hand.

Calvino's crooked smile was enough. She squeezed him tight and ran off to change out of her bikini and into her jeans and T-shirt. Patterson Roy slipped onto the stool beside Calvino.

"Second bar fine in a week. The third bar fine upgrades you to boyfriend class," he said. "That means you are automatically on the no-fly list for other girls in the *soi*."

Patterson thought of himself as running a luxury private airline in the business of booking private hostesses. When Nui bounced out of the back in her street clothes, the first thing she did was run up to Calvino and wrap her arms around his neck.

"You still okay?"

After he nodded, she said, "We go now."

"Don't keep her out too late, son," said Patterson, winking. "She has school tomorrow."

Patterson's lower lip extended like a rubber soap dish.

"What are you studying?" Calvino asked her.

"Facebook 101 and Skype 303," she said, grinning.

"She's nearly earned her master's degree for Skype financing," said Patterson, before walking over to another customer.

They sat in the back of the taxi, and Nui told him how she was thinking of accepting one of the marriage proposals. It was from a German, thirty-two years old, who ran his own import/export business and promised to buy her parents a house and a pickup truck.

"You'll like Germany," said Calvino.

"You won't miss Nui?" she asked.

"We can Skype each other."

She liked the sound of that. The rest of the short trip, she showed him pictures of the German, his car, his dog, his house, his mother and father, two sisters, a brother and someone she thought was the German's uncle. A box of condoms fell from her purse and onto her lap as she shifted through the photos. With a single graceful movement she stuffed the condoms back in without any sign of embarrassment. The problem with boyfriends, thought Calvino, is that they can't add two and two to see what's before their eyes. They lie to themselves about what they see and what it means.

Calvino said, "Why are you marrying the German?"

"He's a good man."

Gut instinct, stripped clean of doubt.

Nui knew the layout of Calvino's condo. After slipping off her high heels, she made for the bathroom, singing to herself. Calvino figured that someone like Nui should be miserable and angry. Instead she was happy—to be out of the bar, to be in a condo rather than a short-time hotel and to be with someone she knew paid well and expected little in return. Calvino's home was familiar, and she could relax. She took her time in the shower.

Calvino waited for her in his sitting room with a glass of wine. When she padded barefoot out of the bathroom wrapped in a towel, she spotted him in light reflected from the cityscape outside the long bank of windows. As she'd done at the bar, she wound her arms around his neck and kissed his cheek. Unlike at the bar, Calvino's skin now felt clammy. She rubbed his sweat between her hands and dried them on the side of the towel. He no longer looked like the man who'd bar-fined her. She felt uneasy, frightened by the vacant look in his eyes. He didn't seem to see her.

One of the first lessons that a bargirl learns in her job is that once a new customer wants to pay a bar fine, she should ask herself where on the one-to-ten scale of sanity and insanity he belongs. Is she getting into something ugly?

After three months Nui had taught herself how to read a customer and decide where he fell on various scales—sane or insane, depressed or happy, stupid or clever, rich or poor. The sanity scale, she'd learnt, was the most important.

She let the towel fall to the floor and leaned forward, pressing her breasts against his neck, expecting him to turn around and grab her. Instead she felt him trembling against her.

Nui reached down and picked up the towel and wrapped it around herself.

"What's wrong with you?" she asked. "Are you sick? Do you need to see a doctor?"

He inhaled deeply and turned his head slightly toward her.

"Do you smell the wet ashes?"

The smell, repugnant and vile, clung to his nostrils, and he tasted it when he swallowed. These weren't ordinary ashes. He breathed them into his lungs—crematorium ashes that monsoon pellets of rain had made into a fine paste, to remind the living of the nature of fine dust mixed with water.

She sniffed the air and shrugged her shoulders.

"I smell wine."

He was just as she'd found him on her first visit, a few days earlier. Sweat bubbling on his forehead, eyes staring straight ahead in the darkness.

"Do you see them?" he asked.

She strained to see what he was looking at in the dim light but saw nothing.

"No."

"The woman, that's Mya, the Black Cat. She's a singer. And Rob, he plays guitar. And Yadanar, he's the one on the piano."

She stroked his hair.

"We make love now, okay?"

"They play jazz. But sometimes the music is delayed, and it makes listening distracting. Do you like jazz?"

"I don't like crazy talk."

She looked at the clutter in the room—a heavy debris of photographs, newspapers, files, artifacts, and old Remington typewriter—and started to show her fear.

She pointed at the typewriter, "Is that your computer?"

Calvino smiled, pressed a couple of the keys that struck the paper. "This is Apple's grandmother."

Her eyes narrowed as stared at the typewriter. Slowly she shook her head, hands on hips and clicking her tongue. "I no like crazy customer."

He pulled out his wallet, and she watched him remove three thousand-baht notes and hand them to her. He might be insane, but he paid well. She looked at the money, returned to the bathroom, dressed and, as she'd done the first time, let herself out without saying goodbye.

THREE

EARLY TUESDAY MORNING Calvino woke up to witness three ghosts standing on the balcony outside his bedroom window. They stared at the lake across the road. What were they looking at? In the past they had never ventured onto the balcony. They never seemed to focus on anything in particular. He rubbed his eyes and looked again at the balcony, but the ghosts were gone. Sometimes they stayed for hours; other times, less than a minute. But one thing was clear—the ghost visitations always returned like a bad penny. He'd lived for decades in a culture where the number of people who believed in ghosts approached a dictator's percentage of votes in an election. It was one thing for Thais to subscribe to ghosts as real, but when a *farang* started seeing ghosts, even they assumed he had gone mental and needed psychiatric attention. Calvino was faced with a dilemma—who had the strength, resources and time to constantly resolve such contradictions? Many a farang had gone crazy trying.

Calvino's sightings created a wrinkle in his perception of time and space. If he didn't believe in ghosts and still saw them, what could he do? Who could he turn to? And would it make any difference? His friend, Colonel Prachai Congwatana, who was a member of the Royal Thai Police, deployed Shakespeare and jazz as his assault troops to conquer the world of ghosts.

"It's unpatriotic for a Thai not to believe in ghosts," Colonel Pratt had told him.

The Colonel believed that finding the right combination of pitch and tempo for a John Coltrane piece sent a signal for ghosts to gather and to perform for the living. The kicker was different for every person. A ghost suspends itself inside the shell of a person, he said. He used his saxophone to burrow inside and release the ghost trapped within. Jazz sets ghosts free. For Colonel Pratt jazz was more than music; it was a telecommunication system. Dudes like Dexter Gordon and John Coltrane created a common language linking life and death. The right sax player had the talent to coax the ghosts back to the other side.

Calvino's problem was he hadn't been listening to jazz before the ghosts' arrival. On the contrary, the music only started when the ghosts gathered and started performing themselves. Colonel Pratt had suggested therapy, and Calvino had grinned in response.

"So when a farang reports a ghost haunting, it means he's mentally ill?"

Colonel Pratt had said, "Farang are non-believers. One who sees his first ghost in middle age should be viewed with suspicion."

Calvino couldn't argue. Belief in ghosts, he knew, is an essential part of Thainess. A farang by definition lacks Thainess. Of course this was an illogical loop, an eternal circle, but Calvino accepted that logic had nothing to do with who fit in the loop and whether their mental world made any sense.

Colonel Pratt decided against allowing Calvino's PTSD to slide under the Thai door of ghosts. He'd been a few meters away in Rangoon the night Calvino had killed two men. They'd held Calvino's client hostage in an SUV. And, again, he'd been with Calvino the night in Bangkok when Mya—the singer known as the Black Cat—and Yadanar, the piano player from a wealthy Rangoon family, had been killed in a car bombing.

Together they'd circled the wreckage of the Benz and the crater the bomb had left in the street. That night, Colonel Pratt felt that something snapped inside Calvino's head. Some internal mental switching system had swung open a gate, and for the better part of a year now, Calvino had been reporting visitations by ghosts. Putting them back in the bottle had become a full-time job. Calvino had tried yoga and meditation before moving on to drinking and bar-fining. None of the self-help remedies had exorcised the visitors.

As the first hint of sunlight leaked into the room, Calvino kicked back the sweat-soaked sheets and rolled out of bed, his mouth dry, and slipped into his workout clothes. He downed a glass of orange juice before leaving the building and crossing the road to jog on a two-kilometer track that circled Lake Ratchada. The ghosts so far had left him alone on this excursion. Jogging seemed to be the one way he could lose himself and forget the hauntings. As he began to run around the track, it occurred to him that the place would never make it onto any list of the top 100 places to jog before you die. There were thousands of places like this one in the world, though here it was possible to rent a two-seater paddleboat in the shape of white swan for 100 baht.

He wondered whether the earlier risers he was joining on the track were also running from ghosts. The shallow-breathed joggers, their sweaty faces flushed and eyes bugged out, ran past the swan paddleboats without noticing them. Men and women, young and old, were out before eight in the morning, racing against the clock, against the thermal boost that kicked in late each morning, suffocating the city as if with a pair of hot, sweaty hands. Joggers lost in thought or in the music playing on their iPhones kept up a steady pace around him. Calvino understood he was running among people haunted by many things other than ghosts.

As April turned a hairpin corner and roared toward the Songkran holiday—the annual water festival that marks the start of the Buddhist New Year—Calvino was finding that a cool breeze was as rare as a white hair on the head of a Chinese leader.

Beads of sweat rolled down Calvino's neck as he slowed his pace to a fast walk. If a car leaked oil at the rate he sweated, even a large bribe wouldn't buy a roadworthy sticker from the Motor Vehicle Division. Even corrupt officials have their limits, just as human bodies have theirs. His lungs heaved. Coming to a halt, he leaned forward, trying to catch his breath. Other joggers passed him on the track. He watched them disappear into the shimmering heat haze. He walked along the edge, waiting to find another jogger to use as a pace car. Joggers, he thought, belong to the tribe trying to escape the snare of old age. They share a delusion that the impossible is possible. It reminded Calvino of Bangkok's expat community, which subscribed to a whole catalogue of delusions to use as a shield against the brutal truths of their situation.

Calvino had started jogging on his doctor's orders. He had no illusion it would make him immortal. The idea of immortality made him snicker. Dr. Apinya made him grin, too, with her insistence on his writing down his inner thoughts, fears and anxieties and then sharing them with her. She read his feelings like inkblots or tea leaves.

On his second lap around the Lake Ratchada track, Vincent Calvino wiped the sweat from his face with the hand towel he'd wrapped around his neck. His speed slowed for a moment before he found the energy to pick up his pace again. A memory flashed through his mind. He was on a Rangoon street. It was night, and he was hunched down in the driver's seat of an SUV. Behind him two men held guns on Rob, his client's son. The image vanished as a passing jogger brushed against him.

The interior of the SUV had smelled of cordite and blood. Sometimes that mixture of smells came back to him as he ran in the early morning.

But he wasn't in Rangoon; he was in Bangkok, running around a lake, enveloped in the heat, Ratchadapisek traffic on one side, the water on the other side and blue sky clouding up overhead. Morning, not night. What is "real"? Isn't that what Morpheus said to Neo, Calvino wondered. He saw himself hovering above the lake in a hot air balloon. Lake Ratchada from a hundred meters above looked like a wading pool for one of Goya's giants. The water had shed its soft blue of a newborn's eyes, replacing it with the dull green stare of a reptile. Calvino wiped his face again. On the surface of the reptile's lidless eyes floated a pair of swans.

He watched as small wakes formed behind the aimless glide paths of two swan boats crossing the lake. The people inside the swans sat under blue and red umbrellas. As the hot air balloon inside his mind drifted down from the sky, Calvino felt a sudden, inextinguishable trace of regret just as one of the swans changed course, exposing its profile. A pearl-shaped teardrop rolled down its face like a stone and splashed into the lake. The single tear seemed to turn the color of the lake to amber and then a roiling, hot red, as if grief had ignited the water.

Seen from ground level, the vast circular track appeared to collapse into an arrow-straight line. The early morning sun penetrated Calvino's sunglasses as he climbed to his feet again to rejoin the others jogging round and round. They ran as if there was a finish line, but none was to be found. Instead for each runner there was an endurance limit, the unmarked place in the circle where he or she slowed to a jog and then further to a brisk walk before collapsing onto a bench. This was Bangkok, a city that set its men and women on an endless track that inevitably defeated them. The track stretched ahead, never-ending. Calvino glanced at the blue sky. There was no balloon. For Calvino, Bangkok realities flashed in and out of existence like rare subatomic particles.

The rising heat was now leeching the life out of the older runners. Middle-aged office men and women, already on Songkran holiday, discovering that bodies stationed at desks for hours day after day will suffer on the track—huffing, red-faced bodies, shiny with perspiration, perched atop aching, trembling legs. When Calvino had run a 10K marathon in Rangoon a year before, he'd finished dead last. Watching the others on the track, he saw a mirror image of himself back then. After Rangoon he'd vowed to get into better shape. He didn't want to end up like the old men he spotted now, sitting on a stone wall under the shade of a palm tree, talking into their cell phones, with stork legs dangling under large stomachs. He knew that a private investigator had to stay fit or he wouldn't survive. Passing the old men, he saw their defeated look—another mirror image, he thought. The tropics had etched deep line drawings on their faces, drilling under the skin as if the muscles and bone couldn't stop that drill bit from plunging to the bottom.

He found his pace car—actually two pace cars. They hadn't taken notice of the farang shadow on their tail. Calvino hung back a few meters and then closed the distance slowly. The two Thai-Chinese men in their late forties ran side by side. The early morning light turned their skin the color of an unripe pumpkin. Their faces were gnarled and slack, like those of drinkers and smokers. Calvino let them set the pace. He recognized them as the kind of men who had come on a rescue mission, hoping to save their bodies by jogging around a lake. He thought of them as kindred spirits, men who still believed that staying healthy remained possible despite the blow torch tropical heat of April burning through the heart of men.

One runner's calves, wrapped in sinews and veins like double helixes, had hatched blue snakes breaking through the surface. Pacing himself with these runners, younger than him but in worse physical condition, allowed Calvino the luxury of feeling he'd improved since his Rangoon run. The doctors had told him that someone was always in worse shape, mentally and physically, and he tried to remember that advice in the face of overwhelming evidence that in his case the doctors were wrong. Keep the faith, they'd said.

It occurred to him that faith is like bubble gum—you have the choice to chew, swallow or spit it out. It's only a matter of time before your aching jaws force you to make a choice.

Running alongside the two men now, Calvino overheard their conversation. Government offices had shifted gears to a downhill coast for the Songkran holidays. The joggers were government officials who talked about Burma. A spirit house war had erupted between the Thais and the Burmese. A Thai company had built spirit houses inside Burma, and the Burmese had burnt them down. The problem had ricocheted like a stray round hitting a flat surface as it bounced among various ministries. The joggers were on one of the negotiating teams.

"The Burmese are agenda throwers. No good. At our meeting yesterday, they want to talk about refugee camp policy. What do refugee camps have to do with spirit houses? Nothing, but he insists on talking about refugees. I say it's not on our agenda. It's in another committee. He says, throw out the agenda. We talk about it on this committee."

The other jogger listened and added, "The Cambodians are much worse. I really hate the way the Khmer kidnap agendas. They come into a conference and talk about Khmer

21

King Jayavarman VII and how we steal their heritage and disrespect their culture. They never listen to anyone. No one sees what's happening until it's too late. Then they use a temple to steal Thai land! The Khmer are stupid like water buffalo."

"The Burmese are evil, which is worse."

The fatter jogger with jelly legs answered his cell phone, panting as he pressed it against his ear.

"Why can't the Burmese and Cambodians understand us?" his friend asked before noticing the phone call had taken him away.

"*Chai, tilac,*" the one with the phone said—Yes, darling— in a toy robot voice.

After the call had ended, he shook his head and without breaking his stride said, "She makes my life a misery. Have you ever lived with a woman who made you wish that you'd been born gay?"

Calvino laughed as he passed them.

"Thanks for making my day," he said to the jogger with the woman problems.

In the past he'd happened upon joggers discussing astrological charts, auspicious dates and advice from bosses, patrons, parents, monks and gurus. A wish for sexual realignment was something new. It seemed that any reality that could be imagined could be found in Bangkok.

He ran with them until they reached the park side of the lake. The 130-rai Benjakiti Park had been carved out of a vast tract of government land. As large as the park was, it was no more than a tiny razor nick on the huge face of the Tobacco Monopoly Land, with its low-rise houses, factories, warehouse, offices, green space and treed spans. Enclosed by the spiked, whitewashed walls of an earlier age, the area stood firm against the invasion of the modern Bangkok that engulfed it.

At the far end of the track, with the Queen Sirikit

Center ahead, Calvino waved goodbye to the two Thais and jogged up the path to a gate of the parking lot. He stopped as a Honda Accord and a Toyota pickup negotiated the speed bumps and drove to the guard station. As he waited, Calvino thought about walking back to his condo, showering, dressing and writing down his thoughts to be delivered at his doctor's appointment the next day.

The two Thai joggers had given him material to write about for Dr. Apinya, but he wanted more time outdoors. So rather than turning left and following the way back to the MRT and the underground passage to the opposite side of the road, he turned right and jogged past a security guard in front of a kiosk. He crossed the road and jogged along a lane that led to the interior of the vast area. The buildings had the look of the 1970s shophouse culture of Bangkok—low-key, no more than a couple of stories tall, with no space between them. Like all tightly gated communities, the locals looked at everyone who wasn't working for the company with suspicion.

FOUR

THE BACK STREETS were deserted on the Tobacco Monopoly Land. Though Songkran didn't officially arrive until Saturday, for most Thais the holiday had already started. Offices, factories and warehouses were all closed and shuttered. The parking lots were empty except for one crammed with heavy trucks, light pickups and forklifts parked in neat rows. The city had gone quiet with the absence of half of its population and the remaining half sitting in their living rooms, watching TV. As Calvino jogged along the back lanes, the grounds appeared deserted. In the windows of houses and offices he saw no movement. He saw no one as he made his way through the area. No security guards, no workers, no bosses. Silence and solitude wrapped the buildings and the street. He could hear the beat of his own heart.

Calvino sighed with one of those pent-up, long exhalations that come when at last a man can breathe freely, with no wet ashes, and enter a secret place abandoned by its gatekeepers and staff.

Running off-track had become an article of faith for Calvino. With some clever planning, a 10K circuit could be traced inside the grounds. The land ran for a couple of kilometers behind the lake. He had to remind himself now and then that this quiet piece of paradise wasn't in the boondocks but smack in the heart of a city of over ten million people.

The people who worked on this land brought billions of baht a year into the coffers of the Ministry of Finance. Tobacco, Calvino knew well, was a cash cow for Thailand. A government monopoly over cigarettes was like owning a big herd of cash cows. The milk poured continually from their multi-tits, an image Calvino conjured for himself as he turned off the lane and jogged through a narrow grassy area, some of it overgrown with tangled tropic plants as strong as bamboo and as thin as string, shoots climbing toward the sun. He ran beside a small canal with wildflowers sprawling along the banks, finding himself glad to have gone exploring. His doctor had said that departing from routine would speed up his recovery.

Without warning the toe of Calvino's running shoe hooked into a cross-stitch of thick green vines that had feelers snaking into the canal. Rather than preparing himself for the fall, he let his momentum carry him forward toward the ground. At the last moment he braced himself, but it was too late, and he hit the scorched earth with a thud. For a few seconds he lay on his stomach, dazed. Raising himself on his elbows, he noticed for the first time, no more than half a meter away, a woman stretched out on the ground.

He closed his eyes, hoping the image would vanish. Eventually the visions of the dead always faded to static in his head—faded to sky, buildings, grass, palms or cars—and the world would rush back, embracing him with a mother's comforting touch. Eyes still closed, he rose to his knees and opened his right eye just a slit, then his left eye. Now with both eyes wide open, he gazed at a woman in a blue tracksuit with white piping, still motionless. He crawled closer, reached out and touched her neck for a pulse.

Calvino sat back on the ground, staring at the body. She couldn't have been dead for long. In the tropics bodies decompose quickly. The heat changes the color of the skin, bloats the stomach and chest cavity, and turns the face into a shrunken horror mask. This woman—she was more a girl, no more than eighteen—might almost have been sleeping. Calvino stood up, looked around the area. In the near distance were a couple of houses. They appeared empty. There was no one around.

He leaned close to the body and noticed that the woman's hair, long and black, was flayed outward across the grass. No one fell to the ground with hair ending up in that position. Someone had made a point of spreading her hair out like a peacock's tail feathers. She had an uncommon beauty, with a perfect nose, full lips and eyes, still open, that had been reshaped from Asian to farang. For someone so young, she'd had a lot of plastic surgery. But dead people with perfect features, it occurred to Calvino, have no more future than dead people with malformed ones. She could have been a movie or TV star, or one of the "pretties" who work in auto shows. Calvino carefully reached inside one of the pockets of her tracksuit. Nothing. He slipped his hand out and tried the other pocket, turning it inside out. Again it was clean. Not a scrap of paper, no cell phone, credit card or Thai ID. Ordinary pockets are never that clean, he thought. He sat back, staring at the body. He studied the dead girl's perfect face, incongruent in this remote overgrown area of the Tobacco Monopoly Land, her unblinking eyes staring up at the sky. Who was she, this girl with the clean pockets, the sleeping beauty with no means of identification?

"Who are you?" Calvino said aloud.

Her face and swan-white neck showed no cuts, bruises or scrapes, no marks of any kind. It was as if the young star had emerged from the makeup department and taken her place on a film set. Murder victims in real life are never beautiful, Calvino knew well. They've been knocked around, shot, stabbed, strangled or poisoned, and each method of death leaves a calling card on the body. Calvino continued his search for evidence of a struggle. He checked her hands, examining the fingernails, none of which were broken, and there were no signs of someone else's skin or blood there to suggest a struggle against an attacker.

The tracksuit was expensive. The logo on the left hip had a silver anchor embedded in a spray of ferns. One of those imported $300 designer suits that hi-so women wear, he decided. It wasn't the usual knockoff he saw on women joggers circling the track around Lake Ratchada. He checked the label. Juicy Couture. The dead girl had a taste for high fashion and a budget to go along with her taste.

How could someone that beautiful and young be dead, with not a scratch on her? Next to the small canal he stared at a face sculpted into absolute perfection. A great deal of time and money had been invested in that face. A face that appeared as if touched by an angel, a face of symmetry and balance not known in nature. He expected her at any moment to sit up, stretch her arms, smile and say in an easy voice, "Hello. Who are you? Where am I? Did you bring me here? Have I been sleeping long?"

"You're dead," he said to the body.

"Please don't say that," he could almost hear her reply.

"Can I take a closer look at your throat, your chest?" he asked the corpse.

"If it makes you happy," the voice in his head told him.

He zipped the front of her tracksuit down far enough to examine her throat and the top of her chest. She wore no bra under the tracksuit top. As with the face, her breasts appeared to be the product of plastic surgery, though again without telltale marks.

He couldn't control his pounding heart. He dripped with sweat and felt short of breath. Her skin was cold to the touch.

"No... no..." he repeated to himself.

"What natural cause could have taken your life?" he finally asked the girl.

This time no voice responded. Rising to his feet, he walked a few feet down to the edge of the canal. The water ran slowly. In the weeds he discovered a small shrine—a wooden spirit house—half hidden, tilted to the side. Its little figures of soldiers, mythic gods, costumed dancers and elephants spilled onto the canal bank. A water glass held half a dozen burnt incense sticks. The stubs of yellow candles as narrow as a pencil were mixed in the debris. Calvino picked up one of the melted candles and smelled the wax. Not long ago it had been hot. He dropped it back on the ground.

This new discovery was disturbing and reassuring at the same time—disturbing as he'd found evidence that someone had been making an offering, and that person must have seen the body; and reassuring in that it confirmed that what he was seeing was real. It wasn't just his mind projecting images.

FIVE

IT WAS 7:45 A.M. and still cool. He glanced back at the mysterious body in the designer tracksuit; it would need to be removed to cold storage. Calvino was in running gear— off the rack of a Sukhumvit street vendor. He had left his condo without a cell phone, money or any ID save for his plain-white condo security card.

Calvino always advised clients never to leave their offices or homes without ID; complacency, he'd learned the hard way, was the major long-term enemy of an expat. Assuming there is no danger, letting one's guard down and thinking that everything will always continue to be normal: he knew that these are the habits a fool allows himself. You might, for instance, stumble upon a body. Only a fool ignores the possibility of a man's normal world flipping into abnormality in the blink of an eye. Move off the normal path and the odds against you increase. Calvino hadn't followed his own advice. A flash of anger and self-hatred bent him forward and left him breathing slowly. His lungs full, he took off in a full sprint, running back through the grounds toward the lake and the track.

He reached the track as the 8:00 a.m. playing of the national anthem blared from the loudspeakers. Everyone in the park and on the track came to a complete stop, observing a moment of silence until the music finished.

No one moved. The security guards stood at attention as Calvino ran past. The anthem created a cone of silence, and for that brief time the dead and living observed the same stationary speechlessness. The sight of a farang running through the park and onto the track during the national anthem drew hostile stares. Calvino kept running until he saw the two Thai government workers, who now stood still on the track.

As the anthem ended, Calvino *waied* the senior Thai.

"I need to use your cell phone. It's an emergency."

This was the same jogger who'd taken the call from a woman who'd made him regret not being born gay. He hesitated.

"It's very important. It's about a woman."

The Thai smiled, handing him the cell phone, a gesture as if to say he understood the role of women was to cause emergencies.

"Thanks," said Calvino. "I'll only be a minute."

The other jogger said, "You should stop when the anthem is played. What you did is very disrespectful. You could be arrested."

"This is an emergency."

The two joggers watched as Calvino phoned Colonel Pratt.

"Pratt, I've found the body of a woman on the Tobacco Monopoly Land. Yeah, just a few minutes ago."

The eyes of the phone owner widened.

Colonel Pratt replied, "This isn't your phone."

"I'm on the track at Lake Ratchada. I left my phone at the condo, so I've borrowed one from a jogger."

"What's his name?" asked Colonel Pratt.

The government officer shook his head, his face gone pale.

"What's your name?" Calvino asked him.

"Who wants to know?"

"The police. I've reported a body."

The blood drained from the jogger's face. Calvino handed him the phone.

"Here, talk to the Colonel."

The jogger, wild with disbelief, stared at the phone before slowly putting it to his ear. He gave his name and address and explained that he had nothing to do with the body. After the call with the Colonel ended, he collapsed against his friend. This hadn't been a good day for him. He'd received an annoying call for money from a minor wife, and then a crazy farang had run through the playing of the anthem to use his phone to report a death. Jogging was supposed to be good for a man's health. That notion was obviously bogus, a lie.

"The Colonel asked me to go with you to view the body," said the jogger, "and to call him back with what I find."

"Why doesn't he come himself? What's this have to do with you?" his friend asked.

They stared at Calvino, waiting for him to answer the strange request.

"The Colonel wants confirmation," said Calvino.

Both joggers looked at Calvino as if he were crazy. In the last year Calvino had come to recognize that look. He'd been getting it a lot.

"But why?" the jogger pleaded.

"He wants you to confirm that I didn't imagine a dead body."

"Do you imagine finding dead bodies?"

Looking away at the road, Calvino shrugged his shoulders.

"I have a history of seeing ghosts. This isn't a ghost. I saw a real body. Come, I'll show you."

The two joggers exchanged glances. The cell phone rang. Calvino could tell it was Colonel Pratt on the other end from all of the "*khrap, khrap*" that came from the jogger's end of the conversation. Sir, sir, sir—like a needle stuck on an old LP repeating a single lyric in a perpetual loop.

SIX

THE NEXT DAY, Thursday, April 11, Calvino made his way to Silom Road, where Dr. Apinya's office was on the seventh floor of an old high-rise office tower. For years there had been a wedding planning business on the ground floor. White gowns, veils, bouquets and smiling couples in cinema-poster-sized poses. The business had vanished long ago. The ghosts of all the happy couples are all that remain, Calvino thought as he walked through the ground floor. Taking the elevator to the seventh floor, Calvino walked into the office. He felt as if he'd stepped into a Chinese opium den with the soft lighting, lava lamp and new age music. A receptionist sat at her desk, wiggling ivory chopsticks above a plastic container with eight slices of salmon lined up in a neat row. She looked up as Calvino came in.

"Can't make up your mind?" he asked, looking at the sushi.

"I never know whether to start at the bottom and work my way to the top, or start at the top and work my way to the bottom," she said.

"I thought Thais started in the middle and worked both directions at once."

Without replying to his observation, she said simply, "The doctor will be with you in a few minutes. She's running late."

Half an hour later, Calvino walked into the office of Dr. Apinya, a woman in her late thirties with long hair tied behind her head. Her glasses had thick black rims that gave her a serious academic appearance. Her Chinese face, large and oval, was soft, gentle, caring. Her eyebrows had been carefully sculpted, rising over the glasses as if indicating perpetual interest or surprise. From each of Dr. Apinya's pierced ears, gold earrings, small, rounded like a matching pair of wedding rings, fit snug against the lobes. On her tailor-made baby blue silk blouse, her name on a name tag pinned above her left breast.

She looked up from a file with Calvino's name on it.

"Vincent. Sit down. Would you like coffee?"

Every session she asked the same question. He shook his head, sitting in the chair opposite her desk.

"How have you been doing?"

"All right, I guess."

"You guess?"

Do I tell her or not, he asked himself.

"We talked before about holding back. There is no reason for you to. You need to feel comfortable enough to tell me anything."

"I passed a restaurant on the way here that sells shark fin soup."

"You found that disturbing?"

He nodded.

"Yeah, I did. I saw your receptionist eating sushi. And I asked myself why that wasn't disturbing but the fins were."

She made notes in his file, her glasses pushed forward on her nose. He watched her write with her left hand in slow, careful strokes.

"What feelings do you have about shark fin soup?"

He explained that one day it had dawned on him what chain of events had been set in motion each time the soup appeared on his table. The degree of coordination and

34

cooperation, from the moment a fish trawler left port to the time it caught the sharks, cut off the fins, threw the live sharks back and returned to port. Then the packing, the cold storage, the loading and driving of trucks, the unloading, the storage again, the loading of the fins on smaller trucks and the fins' arrival, crated, through the back door of a restaurant kitchen.

The image of bleached out fins in the window of a Chinese restaurant in Siam Square flashed through Calvino's mind. He had stopped and examined them—the shape, texture, size and placement—thinking about their source. He wouldn't eat the soup anymore, nor could he bear watching anyone else slurp it down. He told Dr. Apinya that he wanted to shout from the rooftops about the murder of sharks.

"It's too bad that sharks have so few friends," she said.

The chatter took on an aimless quality bouncing from subject to subject, violence, alcohol, hookers, murder victims, until abruptly he asked, "You know the Tobacco Monopoly near Rama IV Road?"

She smiled, waiting for more shark fin observations.

"I jog around the lake most mornings. Yesterday morning I made a detour through the grounds. I was jogging along an open area near a canal. I stumbled and fell, and when I started to get up, I saw a body."

"One of the same bodies you've told me about before?"

Calvino had expected the reaction, but it didn't stop him from shaking his head in frustration.

"No. This was a real body."

"Okay, it was an actual body."

"A young woman's body."

"Have you seen her body before or was this the first time?"

"Dr. Apinya, I am not talking about a body out of my head. I called Colonel Pratt. He had the same patronizing bullshit reaction: Vinny's crazy again, seeing things, making stuff up. When he showed up and saw the dead body, secretly I think that maybe, in a strange way, he's relieved."

"Why would the Colonel have been relieved, Vincent?"

"Because he saw I was telling the truth. I had found an actual, real dead body. A young woman."

For the first time in a couple of months, Calvino noticed that Dr. Apinya looked uneasy, off-balance.

"How did you feel when you saw this body?"

"I asked myself if I was crazy."

Colonel Pratt, Calvino added, had also been unprepared for the reality of Calvino's discovery. They'd stood together at the scene with the two Thai joggers and a platoon of cops. A police forensic team had arrived and worked the crime scene as anonymously as the waiters who cleared the dishes at the Last Supper.

He told the doctor what the Colonel had said to him: "Vincent, I don't want you to get involved any further. You'll be asked to answer some questions. That's routine. After that go home, go back to getting better."

She leaned forward, touching her left gold earring. Calvino read that tell like a professional poker player and anticipated the card that would be played next.

"You feel that you have a right to some control of the investigation? Like control over a restaurant that serves shark fin soup?"

Calvino was disappointed.

"Everything comes back to that, right—control? I'm having problems because of losing control in Rangoon. The kid getting shot in the space I controlled. His girlfriend blown up in Bangkok, a place where supposedly I'm in control. We've talked about nothing else the last three months."

He looked at his watch and pushed back into the chair.

"What I do best is find people who've gone missing. The girl I found is a missing person. The police have her body. They don't know who she is. When they know that, when they know what happened to her, I'll be happy to go back to my usual ghosts. Have the regular conversations. Right now, I'm not trying to control anything. Or anyone. I just need to know who she was."

"Are you self-medicating?" she asked.

He thought about whether to tell her about the two fumbled attempts with Nui but couldn't bring himself to utter the name of Nui's bar, Mama, Don't Call.

"Do wine and whiskey count as medication?"

He realized his session was coming to an end before he'd read his latest journal entries.

"Is that the purpose for drinking, Vincent?"

A flicker of genuine concern crossed her face.

"It's the only purpose for drinking."

He found himself grinning at her.

"You kept your journal?"

"Never missed a day. I was going to read to you about finding the body, but..."

"You're right, our time is up. But since you seem to be in crisis... I have an opening later today if you'd like to come back, and we could start with your journal."

"I could do that. I promise I'll leave shark fin soup off the menu."

He smiled as he closed the door behind him. The empty plastic container with the chopsticks folded inside sat next to the computer keyboard.

"The doctor says she'll see me again later today."

He found himself staring at the tiny grayish piece of ginger wedged like a tiny body between the receptionist's teeth.

"Try the California roll next time," he said, looking away.

Six months of therapy before he was allowed to get his gun back from Colonel Pratt. There was one other small detail—Dr. Apinya, the Colonel's recommendation—had to sign off that he was "of sound mind." Even the receptionist had power over his future.

Back on the street he made a point of walking by the Chinese restaurant with the shark fins in the window. A group of Chinese businessmen occupied one of the banquet tables. A waiter served them bowls of the soup. If anyone needs a little more control of their lives, he thought, it's the sharks, who continue to swim in the waters controlled by the Chinese. He recalled an old Chinese saying, to the effect that when you don't control where you swim, look for a safe harbor to escape and hide.

Dr. Apinya had been nagging him about trying to control outcomes. She didn't understand that he was merely trying to find a safe harbor in a land where all waters were patrolled by powerful predators and even they weren't safe as bigger sharks preyed on them.

SEVEN

CALVINO CLEARED HIS throat, looked up at the doctor, locked eyes with her and looked down again at the short stack of typed sheets on his lap.

"Why don't you just finish reading it yourself?"

She smiled.

"I want to hear you read it."

Of course she was right. The tone and emotion were as important as the words. The personal landscape stripped of its voice was dead as ash and tar on a hot summer evening. Calvino sucked in his breath and resumed reading his entry for Tuesday, picking up after his call to Colonel Pratt.

> I called Pratt, and he said to wait for him at the scene and that he'd be there shortly. I checked the time. I figured I had thirty, forty minutes before he arrived. I jogged back to my condo, changed clothes, unplugged my cell phone from the charger and found my digital camera on the bookshelf. As I returned to the crime scene—I was assuming it was a crime—I saw the two Thais awkwardly waiting some distance from the body, whispering and throwing me heavy, dark stares.

They weren't happy to see me dressed like a lawyer, the suit and tie, watching me standing near the body, taking photographs. I moved in for a closer look. The Thais also inched closer. I turned around and took their picture, with one of them fingering an amulet on a chain around his neck. Two frightened, bugged-eyed civil servants who suddenly wished they'd paid the money to join a gym. Free jogging tracks come with some hidden costs.

Two things were clearly bothering them. It was hard for them to know what was more disturbing ·· the dead body in the designer jogging suit or me, the live farang, transformed in appearance. Dealing with the dead was a piece of cake in comparison. Here I was, no longer the farang jogger in baggy shorts and a T·shirt, but a man dressed in a suit during the hottest month of the year, and that made me either a very powerful individual or a crazy and dangerous farang. Whether I liked it or not, I was asking them to make the kind of choice each of them made every day as civil servants surrounded by those asking for favors. They'd had a lifetime of reading the social position of Thais in their fashions and accessories, but with farang, making a status call made them feel like an illiterate asked to sign something they couldn't read. They looked insecure, anxious. I paid no attention to them, and that no doubt added to their troubled state.

Most farang have no obvious alphabet that spells out their social status or rank. To the Thais we are more like those ancient cave paintings. How to translate a farang into the Thai context? It's a risky business. The rule of thumb is that a farang can be safely ignored, but now and again, one of the bastards makes a Thai official's life miserable. Making the wrong decision about that black swan carries the potential to be a career killer. Near a lake with white swan paddleboats bobbing on the shoreline, could I be the dreaded black one, gone onto land? They weren't sure.

Fear in their eyes. Scared and silent. Both men stood waiting for the police. Not that they had any choice. A police colonel already had their names and cell phone number. I could see how much they wanted to run away, but they couldn't. Frustration, annoyance and fear, like fruit on an Atlantic City slot machine, had lined up perfectly, showing them to be losers.

If they bolted, then what? What excuse would they give when the cops finally caught up with them? "I had an appointment to throw water on the weekend, and needed time to prepare my water gun"? Their big mistake was letting a farang borrow a cell phone. Regret etched sharp lines in their faces. I snapped another couple of photos of the Thais just to remind myself how regret furrowed a face like a rice field ploughed by an ice addict.

I squatted down and took close-ups of Jane Doe's face and neck, her hands and fingernails, and the silver anchor logo on the hip of her tracksuit. When you're photographing a Jane Doe, you don't think about her being dead. You think, do I have all the angles covered?

Colonel Pratt and a squad of uniformed men came up from behind, fanning out around me, leaving me in the middle of a semi-circle. No one smiled or said anything. They stared at the body, waiting for someone to make a decision about what to do first. A forensics officer pressed the neck for a pulse. He looked up and gave the obvious verdict: "She's dead."

Brilliant, I thought. But then I decided to cut them some slack. Don't be a smart-assed farang, I told myself. Give them space. I moved away from the body.

The forensics guys arrived, shouldering their own bags of misery. Turmoil over changes among senior positions in their department had caused them to wonder if their careers still had a pulse. Two of the officers knelt down and inspected the corpse, pointedly demonstrating that no one was going to rush them—not the cops, not these civilians. One member of the team measured distances with a surveyor's tape, and a colleague wrote the numbers in a notebook. The forensics team came alive once one of them discovered the small shrine, ten meters away in the tall grass. They smiled and joked as they bagged the incense sticks, the candles, the spirit house, the tiny toy·like elves, demons, soldiers, elephants and dancing girls made of plastic, clay and porcelain. It looked like someone had pillaged a child's dollhouse.

I walked over to Colonel Pratt. Seeing me approach, he shook his head.

"Vincent, why did it have to be you?"

And I said, "That's a question for the gods. What should I have done? Walked away? Fled the scene? Pretend I didn't see the body?"

Pratt fell silent and after a moment recovered his thoughts. Then

he was back to business, asking me,
"Are these the two joggers who helped
you?"

Two cops were taking their
statements. Nodding, I said to Pratt,
"I borrowed the phone of the taller
one."

Pratt sighed. "You got them
involved."

There was no good way for him to say
I'd ruined his holiday. Songkran—one
of the most important family holidays
in Thailand—starts this weekend, and
like every other Thai, Pratt had
been planning to take off mid-week,
ahead of the rush, and settle in for
quality time with his family. He
wasn't the only one who was going to
feel disappointed. This new case had
the elements of a big story in the
press. In the heart of Bangkok. Dead,
beautiful girl. Police believe the
girl was killed over a personal or
business conflict. Blah, blah, blah.
Soon there'd be a reenactment of
the crime in front of the assembled
press. The problem was the cops had no
murder suspect. That fact led to the
ugly possibility that their holiday
leave would be cancelled.

All the cops around the dead girl
shook their heads, saying among
themselves that they saw nothing but
trouble, paperwork, long meetings and

reports converging at a point beyond the time horizon and approaching infinity.

I told Colonel Pratt how much I wished someone else had called it in. After a while he seemed less upset, adjusting to the situation. That was his nature. Accepting that he has a problem is his first step in dealing it. Determining whether the death was by homicide or natural causes would require an autopsy and lab work and a report. For now, an hour filling out paperwork and he'd be back home. He'd deal with the rest once the holiday had come and gone.

So it was a real body, and I hadn't been hallucinating. That was the bright side. The upside. And I could see he was thinking that maybe, just maybe, the old Vincent was coming out of the dark tunnel of wild half·lit dreams.

One member of the investigation team—who had the look of a Muay Thai boxer storming out of the corner as the bell rang for the first round— asked me questions and then asked if I'd mind going to police headquarters to talk. No surprise. The cops would naturally have questions for any person who found a body. The surprise was Colonel Pratt's attitude—his official Thai cop expression. He said, "Vincent, go with these two officers and give them a statement. I'll come along later."

I was thinking that it wasn't that long ago that Pratt had stared down uniformed men, pulled rank, told them he'd handle it, and they'd slip away like hungry ghosts who'd been exorcised.

"Talk to them, Vincent. I'll follow after I finish up here."

The first thing a criminal lawyer advises is <u>never</u> talk to the cops. Boldface, underscore, italicize "never" and then blow it up to size 24 font: <u>Never</u>. There was no percentage in ever talking to them. Don't try to explain or to justify. It is futile. Keep your opinions to yourself. Keep your mouth shut except to demand a lawyer. I am a lawyer. I know all of this. So what did I do? I talked to the cops. I violated Calvino's Law because I had this urgent need to talk to somebody about the dead girl. That's what I've been doing for nearly a year since I came back from Rangoon: talking about dead people. It was a natural extension to talk about this dead girl. The fact that my conversation partners were cops didn't enter into my decision.

Big data, small data. We swim in a vast sea of data. The best you can hope for is to keep your head above the surface. But there's no shore. Only sea and sharks circling. You drown or get eaten. That's your choice. It's like that in a police interrogation, when they want to squeeze data from you in the old-fashioned way. Inside an interrogation room you are attuned to the smallest details. Everything in that room has the potential to hurt you, cause you to doubt yourself, force you to confront the fact that nothing is under your control. They have you by the balls.

I'll paint the interrogation room for you. The walls are a smoky green like a house lizard's tail. Inside, it's hot. It feels like a sauna laced with the smells of garlic, cigarettes, coffee and stale food. The air hangs heavy, so that it feels solid enough to touch. Air isn't supposed to feel like anything. Everything about the room screams at you that your plane is about to crash. Pull the rip cord on your parachute now. Get out before you crash. But you can't leave. They won't let you. The cops take you to places like this because they want to let you know you're in a place that belongs to them. No one is going to come into that room and say a stern word to them, no matter what they do to you. That piece of metadata is transmitted through every detail in the room.

> There was no table. Or chair. I
> sat on a stool. The kind of plastic
> stool that costs ninety-nine baht
> and that food vendors slide under
> foldup tables along Sukhumvit Road.
> I look up. Above me a naked light
> bulb hangs from a moldy old cord.
> This is a room designed to extract
> data in the form of a "confession,"
> and these data collectors have no
> computers or keyboards. What they
> have is vast experience in opening
> suspects like data files. They break
> down the suspect's login and password
> and help themselves to what's inside.
> The room itself is their algorithm.

Calvino looked up from the paper. First at Dr. Apinya, who wondered why he had stopped. He looked around her office. How could she have any idea what he was talking about? Her vase of flowers, the coffee table, the comfortable chairs for clients, her teak office desk, its top as clean and innocent as a newborn baby's head... The bookcase was filled with rows of books. Her diplomas were framed and hung on the wall. Framed photographs of her family stood on a side table behind her. This was another confessional room, one designed for the private confession that he was paying to make.

"You've not finished, Khun Vincent," she said. "Is there a reason you've stopped at this point?"

She glanced down at the stack of paper.

"You were about to talk about the actual interrogation. How did you feel when the police officers asked you questions about the dead girl? Or would you rather continue reading? The choice is yours."

The only difference, thought Calvino, was her office was designed to make him feel comfortable enough to confess his feelings willingly. He had a choice. He could leave at any time, even if he refused to cooperate. A police interrogation room, he thought, is a rabbit hole that swallows a man, stoking his feelings of dread until he admits to a crime. In such a room, as in the afterlife, there are no good choices. You can never break free. Never wake up.

Calvino looked down at his journal pages and continued reading.

For three hours the two cops interrogated me. They said that I was the prime suspect. They worked well together, dropping hints about how nasty things could become if I didn't give them some straight answers. That meant telling them what they wanted to hear. Cooperating by confirming their story of what happened. That's the job of interrogators.

"If you were jogging, why did you wear a businessman's suit?"

"I changed after I found the body."

"Because you wanted to destroy the evidence?"

It looked bad even in my own eyes. I went quiet, but it was too late for silence.

"Who was she?" said the other cop in an ice·cold voice. He was late· twenties but a veteran. The interro·

gation room was his ring. Thin, fast, tight-lipped, Ice's large eyes tracked me like a cat's eyes track a mouse.

"I have no idea," I said. With cops it's best to keep your answers short. Embroidery is good for old ladies making doilies; in a police interrogation long answers stitch up a blanket they'll later use to suffocate you.

The second cop was lugging an extra layer of fat that bulged at his waist, opening the bottom of his T-shirt like a window blind. He looked a few years old than the Ice boxer. He stood like an anchor in front of me, sending the message that he wasn't going anywhere and neither was I. He wore a black T-shirt and jeans and a knockoff Rolex. Or it might have been a real one. I couldn't tell in the dim light. The two cops' clothing shared something—no nametag. No cop ID. No bullshit.

The fact is, neither of the two cops liked my answer. Thais have a way of disguising anger with a smile. These two guys—Ice and Fire—weren't bothering with the formality of a smile. That's a commodity used to milk tourists for cash. Cops have other ways to extract what they want. Police departments should make their interrogations a spectator sport. It's nothing like the movies. Thai cops are old-fashioned data collectors who only know how to use analogue methods, well-suited to medieval training.

The two cops closed in around me. It was showtime, and I was their audience. Fire had mastered the hostile, aggressive, threatening posture. Ice's expertise was in the clenching of teeth and fists. He weaved and bobbed. I was an eyelash away from a kick to the head or chest or groin or stomach. He left all of the options open to my imagination. All actors, if you look long and hard enough, have a tiny residue of boredom on their faces. After all, they are only acting out a script like any actor or bargirl. The bored faces I remembered from the police at the crime scene had vanished. But these faces displayed the low-heat simmer of disgust. This wasn't an audition for an angry cop role. This was the real thing. Resentment worked into their voices, bodies and clenched fists, setting the stage for escalation to the next round.

"You think you're somebody special because you know a colonel? That means nothing. He won't help you. He can't help you. You can only help yourself by telling us why you took her to the park."

"I didn't take her to the park. I don't know her. I saw her for the first time exactly where you saw her. She was already dead when I found her."

"What's her name? Tell us. Get it over with. You had a fight. She insulted you. She refused to let you touch her. It happened fast. You didn't mean to hurt her. We can understand that."

"I don't know her. Never met her."

Short and to the point, the kind of answer guaranteed to ramp up the pressure to make me crack. Have you ever wondered how the police get false confessions from innocent people? Civilians can't stand up against the emotional terror that is the main purpose for enhanced interrogations. Ice and Fire had changed out of their uniforms into street clothes and put me in a room they controlled. That's a situation no one teaches you how to handle when you're in school.

By the time the second hour had passed, their hostility level had ramped up another peg as they started in on the subject of human sacrifice. How did they come to that conclusion? One of them had seen a farang movie about sacrificial killings, and there was evidence at the scene of the crime of some kind of ritual with the spirit house, burnt candles and incense sticks. Photographs of the scene were slapped down on the table in front of me.

"Look at these. Tell us about the ritual you two made at the spirit house."

I could read their game plan easily. One of the officers, Ice, leaned over me, flexed his jaw, his eyes narrowed, his mouth firm, and asked me to repeat again why I'd unzipped the track suit top.

"It was sexual, wasn't it?" he asked.

"I made a mistake," I said.

Both cops liked the sound of that admission.

"Now we're getting somewhere. Tell us about your mistake, Mr. Calvino," said Fire.

"I shouldn't have stopped. Colonel Pratt was right. I should have just kept on running in a giant circle until I returned to the track around the lake. I should have left it to someone else to phone the police. I'd say that was a serious mistake."

"I think you made a big mistake killing the girl. But you don't want to talk about it," the tough cop said.

"There wasn't a mark on her. How did you kill her?" asked Fire, who did most of the talking.

"You are going to tell us," said Ice, just to remind me not to forget him.

There's no need to caricature cops like these two. I'm reporting straight up what they said, how they circled me on the stool and how they reacted in their dramatic cop-show way. They were derivative of someone's movie or TV script. I saw that they were real men, but I also saw that they were hollow and a whole world had been poured down their throats.

Ice raised his fist to provoke me and expected me to flinch. I'm from New York. I've seen fists before. I sat calmly, hands folded on my lap. I gave him no hint of a desire to fight back. Passive resistance inflamed Ice, who was hoping for the natural reflex reaction of blinking, ducking or raising a fist in return. He got none of that out of me. He'd given his best interrogation shot and I'd absorbed it, shaken it off.

They lit cigarettes, put their heads together and spoke their Thai laced with police slang, glancing over at me. One of Calvino's Laws is never cause a cop who is interrogating you to lose face. I could see that Ice was thoroughly upset and could have cut my throat and written up the death as a shaving injury. There is no good cop, bad cop routine in those circumstances; there's only bad and worse. They were getting set to cross the boundary into the worst things in their repertoire. This was the time-tested way to extract data—brute force, then guile, then brute force.

Ice assumed the Muay Thai part, the intense, pissed-off, menacing cop devoid of sympathy, but keeping open a small window of hope that he might be persuaded to ease off. Fire got typecast as the psycho, violent buddy who looked like he was about to crack a head no matter what I said. Nothing about him suggested persuasion would do any good. Fire slammed a thick telephone book against the wall. In that small room it was like a sonic boom three feet away.

"Next time, your head gets in the way, understand?" he said.

Imagine a tick finding itself on a bloodless carcass. Fire's frustration hadn't eased. He was just warming up.

He'd seen that the loud smack against the wall had made me duck like I'd done in the front seat of the SUV in Rangoon. I'd shot two men dead in the backseat. For a moment I wasn't in the interrogation room; I was back in the SUV and thinking I was a dead man. Ice pushed me in the chest, knocking me off the stool.

"I thought the physical stuff was your buddy's job," I said. "Good cop, bad cop. Good cop doesn't push the suspect around."

They dragged me off the floor and sat me back on the stool. I no longer looked like a downtown businessman in my suit and tie. They'd messed up my clothes to take me down a peg or two.

"Tell us her name, and how you knew her."

After two hours we'd come full circle with the line of questions being repeated. The technique is to get you to say something inconsistent or add a new detail, or better still, give in and start making shit up as the telephone book is raised level with your head.

"Who helped you kill her? Don't tell us you acted alone. What's the name of your accomplice? Tell us and we'll let the court know you cooperated."

Hour three is when they hit you with one of their best gambits—the Prisoner's Dilemma. The idea is to get you to rat out someone else, so that guy goes to prison and you walk away free. They never said who this mysterious accomplice was. I was supposed to tell them. Later, it was clear that they had a particular person in mind.

Fire swung away and hit me in head with the telephone book. The force of the blow knocked me from my stool. This time I got up on my own and sat back on the stool.

"No need for a translator. I understand telephone book in multiple languages."

I thought about the two Thai joggers who'd let me use a cell phone to call Colonel Pratt, but I knew those weren't the accomplices they wanted to hear about. And playing smart with them would give them a good excuse to use their second data extraction tool, the thicker yellow pages listings of all of those businesses run by corporate generals and politicians, and Ice would use it to smack me even harder without leaving a trace. I stared at each one of them, keeping my thoughts to myself. Such as how I couldn't remember ever reading how the advent of new technology was killing off the yellow pages, making an essential instrument in police interrogations difficult to find.

At the three-hour mark I told them that if they took me to the morgue, I'd show them why I zipped down the dead woman's top. Both cops looked worn down. The fury had gone out of their questions. They hadn't eaten lunch, and the heat of the day blasted through the interrogation room. For a lot of Thais, missing a meal sends them to the edge of hypoglycaemia, blood sugar levels plunging. They'd started to sweat. Anxiety and nausea had kicked in, slowing them down. Sweat poured down my face. My suit jacket had big wet patches under both arms. My tie hung unknotted around my neck. We'd reached a point in the interrogation where their physical resources had been exhausted. It was a question of whose body would give out first. The two cops left the room, talked, had a smoke and returned to tell me that we would be meeting with Colonel Pratt at the morgue later that day.

I smiled, nodded my head. The cop threw the telephone book against the wall.

"We're not done with you, farang."

The problem with interrogations is the cops fall into one cliché after another. The last bit of dialogue came from a crappy daytime soap opera where a Thai cop says to the street tough, "We're not done with you, Lek."

And Lek's eyes would be wild with fear, the right side of his mouth quivering, as he tries to decide whether to laugh in their faces, shout that he wasn't done with them either or just display the hot-white glow of wordless hatred. I didn't like any of those script options. I gave my best Forrest Gump smile, the unsettling one that makes people who see it think you are "simple," a moron or mentally unstable. Ice picked up the phone book and handed it to Fire. I regretted my visual wisecrack. This was another rule not to violate. Don't wisecrack with the police. Ever. The second smack from the phone book caught me over the right eye. This time Fire put some real arm into it. The blow knocked me off the stool and sent me sprawling. As I started to get back to my feet, Ice laughed as Fire, snarling, gave me a kick in the ribs. The two cops pulled me to my feet and pushed me back onto the stool.

I was getting worn out from these trips from the stool to the floor and back again. One cop pushed a photograph into my face.

"This is your friend," he said. "You know him, right? You two did this together."

"Did what?"

The telephone book hit me at the kidney level on my back as Ice circled around. It was a foul move. Ice was supposed to be the good cop. Obviously they weren't playing by the rules. Again the picture was shoved in my face.

"Who is this?" asked Fire.

Ice continued to stand behind me. I could hear him breathing down my neck. I looked at the picture.

Tuole Sleng in Phnom Penh had a wall of photographs of men who'd stared into the lens of a Khmer Rouge photographer. The man in the photo had that desperate, hopeless expression, a man defeated and ready to accept his fate. The features of the man in the photograph weren't Thai. He had dark skin, a long nose, his face blackened by the stubble of a beard, his thick eyebrows knitted and his hair black as night.

I stared at the photograph. Studied the face. The funny thing was it looked familiar, but I couldn't place where I'd seen it. You sometimes pass someone on the street and you recognize them, but the context is missing—a bank, a health club, a restaurant or a bar—and the frustration sets in because outside that one place they don't exist for you. It was a face out of context. The man in the photograph gave me that feeling.

"Don't recognize him," I said.

"He said he recognized you," said the cop.

"Farang all look alike. Isn't that what Thais say?" I said.

"He's not Thai. He's an illegal from India."

Calvino looked up from the journal. He'd come to an abrupt halt, leaving his doctor wondering why. Calvino sat across from her desk, looking at her attempt to disguise her feelings of disappointment. Calvino waited, letting the silence expand in the doctor's office.

"Did you know him?" she asked.

Calvino smiled, "Aren't you supposed to ask how I felt about the interrogation?"

Dr. Apinya recovered her composure with a little cough.

"How did you feel?"

"You don't care how I felt. You want to know what happened next. How am I here and not there, in prison?" Calvino said.

He'd caught her off guard, and she blushed.

Calvino watched the tide of red wash from her cheeks to her throat, leaving a strange map on her skin.

"A few hours later I walked into the morgue, where Colonel Pratt and others were waiting for me. The cops had taken my handcuffs off, but why are you smiling?"

"I remember feeling good, knowing they were going to let me go."

He had a great deal more to say. He thought about telling Dr. Apinya about how frail and vulnerable the terror had made him feel—the terror he couldn't show to the cops in the interrogation room.

The timer binged.

A police interrogation might continue for hours and hours, but therapy is a controlled data search and works on a different timetable. He left his narrative hanging at mid-sentence and left.

"See you next week, Mr. Calvino."

Dr. Apinya was incredibly polite in her greetings and leavings behavior; it was only in between that she pumped her clients for information. Calvino thought of her as not that different from a cop—a specialized detective, trained to search the psyche of a patient and disarm any intruders found lurking inside. Unlike his recent session with the cops, he had to pay for Dr. Apinya's interrogation and keep an appointment for more. He started to miss Ice and Fire, who took no money and threw him out once they couldn't break him.

On the way out of the office, Calvino wondered if his doctor had any idea that solving a murder depends on exploiting a small window of opportunity. Catch the killer in forty-eight hours, or chances are he won't get caught. Calvino knew well that homicide detectives will push themselves into exhaustion trying to find a suspect within hours of a murder because they'll never have a better chance to nail the killer. Failure to extract a confession will look bad on them. For a good investigator the failure would feel still worse—like a gangrenous leg that needed amputation, but with no one available to do the job.

A young, beautiful woman had been murdered, and the uncaught killer was wrapped around the necks of the cops like a python. The lack of a suspect was about the worst message a police department could send to the public. That message would be screamed from every media source, online and offline—we know you're corrupt and don't give two shits about us, but when a young girl is found dead, it's time for justice.

Calvino walked away having left behind a variety of powerful emotions—in Dr. Apinya's office as in the police interrogation room. This was how the cops interrogated the working class. Their method was meant to terrorize them, make them miserable and hopeless. Leaving the room with a smile on his face had insulted them. He'd bottled his feelings and refused to show them to the cops. What he showed and what he felt were as different as a bottle of Mekong whiskey and a twenty-year bottle of single malt.

EIGHT

IT WAS COLD in the morgue. Calvino felt the chill against his skin as he was frog-marched into the room by Ice and Fire, who had changed back into their uniforms. Three other officers wearing jackets followed the parade. They crossed the uneven, cracked tiles between three stainless steel autopsy platforms whose liquid-retaining rims, once shiny, had gone monsoon morning dull. Colonel Pratt, like the other officials in the morgue, wore a coat against the chill. Standing before a wall lined with drawers, he'd been talking with a white-coated medical examiner who was flanked by two assistants.

"Midnight at the Oasis" played, not the original but Renee Olstead's version. Calvino shivered as the cold seeped through his sweat-soaked clothes. His teeth chattering, he looked around the morgue for a set of old speakers. They must be cleverly hidden, he thought. Olstead's mellow, heartfelt voice belted out, "I'll be your only dancer ... and you can be my sheik." Had the music been chosen at random? What were the chances of that? The Black Cat had loved that song. One night while on a case in Rangoon, Calvino had ended up inside a bookshop below where Mya lived, and she had sung that song for him. Colonel Pratt was the only person that Calvino had disclosed that piece of information to. Life and death had come and gone since then. Too many things had happened, one after another, since Rangoon, and listening to the song, Calvino caught a glimpse of the Black Cat in the corner of the room, smiling, drawing on a cigarette, keeping beat to the music.

"Pratt, listen—'Midnight at the Oasis.' You told them about it?"

Colonel Pratt looked at the medical examiner and the cops around Calvino.

"Vincent, there's no music."

"You're sure about that, Pratt?"

"You look cold," the Colonel said, rubbing his hands together.

He lifted a jacket from one of the tables and draped it around Calvino's shoulders.

"I am cold. It doesn't mean I'm not hearing that song. You're telling me that there's no music?" asked Calvino. "I get it. Cold, beatings, morgue... It's a mind game to keep the suspect off-balance."

He looked at Ice and Fire. They had no idea what he was talking about. The others in the room stared at him. Talking in Thai, the doctors discussed possible diagnoses for someone hearing phantom music.

"Trust me, Vincent. There is no music in the room."

Then why can I hear it, he asked himself. Why can't I stop shaking?

"We haven't identified the body," said Colonel Pratt.

"Your colleagues thought an appointment with the yellow pages might jog my memory. Instead they managed to open the jukebox inside my head. They shouldn't be disciplined, though. They tried their best."

The warmth of the jacket dulled the ache of the cold. Calvino took a deep breath and, looking at the two men who'd interrogated him, held out his hand to shake. Checking first with the more senior officers, who gave a nod, they shook hands with Calvino.

"Nice grip," said Calvino.

He walked across the room and joined Colonel Pratt, who had opened one of the drawers and rolled out the metal frame with the young woman's body on it. Jane Doe's body was fully covered. It looked childlike inside the body bag.

"Where's she from?" asked Colonel Pratt. "Bangkok? Upcountry? Japan? China? She could be from any of a dozen places. We've run her fingerprints and found nothing on file in Thailand. We've passed copies of the prints on to Interpol. We might get lucky. They might come back with a match. But I doubt it. The report on her DNA sample won't come back for a week. Again, we might get lucky."

In Colonel Pratt's experience the unspecified dead turned up in canals, on beaches, in fields, in parks, on roadsides and in back alleys in Thailand by the hundreds every year. Unclaimed, unconnected to any evidence supporting identity, whether they'd died of natural causes or had been murdered, they were all victims with a shared destiny—to wait for a piece of luck to turn up a connection.

Calvino had taken more than his share of missing-person assignments. Looking for the lost was bread-and-butter business, ensuring a steady, reliable number of new cases every year. Thailand was a sort of hub for people who had disappeared—or had gone into hiding, avoiding relatives, ex-wives and defrauded employers. The lucky ones had a worried parent or spouse anxious about their well-being. Some of those had someone willing to pay a private investigator to find them. In the world of money, using it to find another person is an investment, one that someone believes is eventually going to pay off financially or emotionally.

"Anyone file a missing person report?" asked Calvino.

"No. That was the first place we looked," said the Colonel. Turning to the medical examiner, he asked, "What killed her?"

"Hypoxia."

She'd stopped breathing, but there wasn't a mark on her.

"A drug overdose?" asked Colonel Pratt.

The medical examiner shrugged.

"The toxicity report will give the details," he said, "but that's one possibility."

Everything in the universe is possible according to the laws of physics, Calvino thought, but what is probable is another matter. Calvino looked at the woman's young, unlined face, thinking, why did you stop breathing?

"Anything else?" asked Colonel Pratt.

"The deceased was six weeks pregnant," replied the medical examiner. "It will be confirmed in the autopsy report. What I'm giving you are my preliminary findings."

"Looks like you may have found a motive, Pratt," said Calvino.

Sometimes a body is physically present but its identity isn't traceable. Technically this Jane Doe was a missing person. A body with a fetus inside and no ID attached. Death without identity seemed to Calvino to have an unsettling finality, especially when the body belonged to a young woman.

Colonel Pratt nodded as one of the medical examiner's assistants unzipped the body bag to expose the entire body. Her designer tracksuit had been removed and sent to the lab for processing: prints, DNA, hair, stains, blood—the full schedule of keys that might unlock the mystery of who this woman was and how she died.

Colonel Pratt and the medical examiner had a private moment in the corner. Calvino stood in front of the tray with Jane Doe's remains.

Someone is waiting for you, thought Calvino. Missing you, wondering where you've gone Someone who will grieve for you.

Another thing about the body had caused some confusion.

"It looks like she was sexually violated," said the medical examiner. "Our preliminary examination found tears inside her vagina, consistent with rape."

"Drugged and raped and pregnant. The press won't find this of any interest," Calvino said, joining their circle.

Colonel Pratt sighed and shook his head as he looked at the body.

"You understand the situation," he said.

Calvino understood, for example, the extra juice he'd received during the rough-and-tumble interrogation. A young, beautiful, pregnant woman raped and killed would have the reporters circling police headquarters asking why the police hadn't arrested the culprit.

Calvino's eyes stopped at the right ankle of the deceased. A small blue tattoo of three capital letters spelling "JAI." She'd had running shoes and socks on when he'd found her body.

"Pratt, you see the tattoo on the ankle?"

Colonel Pratt leaned over and examined the slender ankle.

"It means heart in Thai," said the Colonel.

"Why would a Thai use the Roman alphabet for a Thai word?" said Calvino.

"You're assuming she's Thai."

"You're assuming it means heart in Thai. If she's not Thai, why those letters, and could they mean something other than heart?"

"Farang know '*jai*' means heart," the Colonel said.

"In all-capital letters?" asked Calvino.

"What do you think the tattoo means, Vincent?"

"I hear music in a morgue that no one else hears. I wouldn't be asking what I think J-A-I means."

"A crazy idea can turn out to be the most sane explanation," said Colonel Pratt.

Calvino had begun to adjust to the cold. He rubbed his hands, blew on his fingers.

"Her boyfriend's initials. That's what I'm thinking. Look at her. Someone's been paying a small fortune for plastic surgery. You put that much money into creating a woman who has no flaw, maybe your next step is to have your initials tattooed on her ankle. A reminder each time she puts on her shoes that she is owned."

"You think the tattoos are the initials of her patron? A branding like the American cowboys did in the nineteenth century?" said Colonel Pratt. "It might have a double meaning."

"The word 'patron' has a funny ring, looking at her. Where is he? Does he know his treasure is in the morgue with his kid inside? Or was he the one who made the arrangements for her to end up here?" asked Calvino.

He's definitely warmed up now and no longer heard the music.

"There are many questions. We can't answer them now. All we can do is wait until a suspect we have talks," said Colonel Pratt. "And he will."

One by one Calvino's police officer escorts slowly drifted out of the morgue—the last place anyone wanted to celebrate Songkran. Two senior officers nodded at Colonel Pratt as they passed. It was one of those gestures exchanged by brother officers. Calvino watched them, standing tall and proud and certain in their rank and authority. Not one of them acknowledged him on their way out. Their minds were on Saturday, the first day of the Songkran water festival celebration of the living, of family and of friends. A time of "water heart"—the little gestures to ease a stranger's life. Colonel Pratt said nothing as the last officer left. The initial investigation had wrapped up.

While one of the assistant medical staff zipped Jane Doe's body back into the body bag, another one helped her push it back into cold storage. Jane Doe vanished into the closed drawer.

Calvino and Colonel Pratt were now left alone in the morgue. Each waited for the other to say something first. The Colonel started but then stopped before he had uttered a sound.

"You had to let them do it," said Calvino. "You didn't have a choice."

Colonel Pratt worked his hands into a fist, clenching the handle of the drawer. Calvino's words made him uneasy.

The truth was Calvino understood why Colonel Pratt had been forced to stand down. The Colonel was his friend, and Thai friendship came with a promise of protection, but it could never be absolute. No shield could ever be impenetrable. Over the years the Colonel's protection had been sufficient to ensure that Calvino avoided the worst abuses of authority. There had been a time when a farang who was a close personal friend of a Thai police colonel had some leverage. But now the old agreements and ways were fading away. The old relationships were dying too. In the new reality Calvino's interrogation was bound to run its normal course despite his friendship with the Colonel. That would have never happened a decade earlier. The new regime in the department expected Colonel Pratt to change with the times and show that his first loyalty was to the force. No shield would be allowed to protect a foreigner. Outsiders could no longer rely on such shields and had to fend for themselves as best they could.

If the Colonel had tried to intervene, Calvino realized, then the two of them wouldn't now be standing together in the morgue alone.

"The good news is no more small interrogation rooms and telephone books," said Calvino.

"We've arrested a suspect, Vincent."

Calvino raised an eyebrow.

"Yeah? So why the batting practice with me for the last three hours?"

"They had information that connected you to the suspect."

Calvino, caught off guard, wrapped his arms around his chest.

"Who is he?"

"An Indian national found hiding at the scene. An illegal migrant who sells nuts on Soi Cowboy."

He showed Calvino a photo of the suspect.

Calvino cocked his head to the side, looked at the face. Now the face suddenly had a context. Calvino recognized him. He'd seen the face walking along Soi Cowboy with a tray of nuts, stopping at each bar that had customers out front, trying to make a sale. Calvino had once paid him for information in a missing person case.

"You've got a confession from him?"

"Not yet, but it's a matter of time. We believe he was camping out not far from where you found the body. He admitted to knowing about the spirit house next to the canal."

"You're saying the case is already closed, is that it?"

"We have some solid evidence."

"Did this Indian tell you the dead woman's name?"

"He said he didn't know it. But he knew your name."

"My name? Did he really? Or did the cops tell him my name?"

Calvino looked at Colonel Pratt for a full minute, trying to read what was going on behind the official policeman's expression. They'd been friends for years, but that never stopped them from hitting a wall that protected suspicions, uneasy feelings and doubts. The cops would have put the Indian through a process that made Calvino's interrogation look like a walk in the park.

"Why would he use my name?" Calvino said, testing exactly how much Colonel Pratt knew.

"He says you paid him for work on a case last year. Akash Saru."

Calvino looked away, closing his eyes, trying to see past a lot of wreckage that the last year had left. Paying informants was like buying a lady drinks—a man lost track after a year.

"And he's right. I did pay him."

"So why were the two of you on the Tobacco Monopoly Land together?"

"I was jogging. Pratt, the question is, what was Akash doing there at that time of morning?"

He hadn't remembered the nut vendor's name. The bargirls had shortened Akash Saru to Ack, a guttural, half-spit sound.

"Going for a walk. That's his story," said Colonel Pratt.

"Finding Akash in the area doesn't mean that he killed the girl."

"Forensics lifted a set of his prints from her body."

"I'm sure they found a set of my prints too. And I sure as hell didn't kill her."

He'd hired Akash Saru one night on Soi Cowboy. Calvino had been looking for a twenty-two-year-old man named Chuck who had gone missing in Bangkok. He'd been last seen with a dancer who worked at the Midnite Bar. He'd not been the first twenty-something to vanish into thin air after his first bar fine. Five days later, after the dancer slipped back from a cozy little holiday in Koh Chang, the Indian nut vendor had phoned. Calvino talked to the girl. That evening he took her back to her room in an old building filled with service girls. Chuck was watching TV in his shorts and eating popcorn when Calvino walked in. He wondered how many other missing persons were sitting around in their underwear in a squat on Petchaburi Road, waiting for their loved one to return from her last short-time.

The name of Chuck's bargirl had been Pizza. Calvino smiled now, remembering how he'd told Chuck's father he'd found his son living with Pizza. It had taken a couple of minutes to clarify that Pizza was her name and not to be confused with the food. And no, he'd told McPhail at the time, she didn't come with double cheese, and no, she wasn't necessarily two slices short of a super deluxe. Ed McPhail was one of the survivors of the scene at Washington Square, now demolished, and one of the few old-timers that Calvino could rely on to watch his back or find information no one else could. Over the years, their two livers had become best friends.

Calvino needed to know who she was, this pregnant dead woman he'd found on a Wednesday morning. The name Jane Doe didn't suit her. Had his nut vendor informant raped and killed a stranger? In Bangkok it seemed that, unless the laws of physics were violated, if it could possibly happen, and it was plausible, then it must have happened somewhere.

"After you finish with Akash Saru, I'd ask one favor."

"Name it, Vincent."

"While the cops were putting me through the wringer, the Indian was in the next room getting the work-over, right? They must have broken him. That's why I'm here and he's in the lockup. Let me have a talk with him, Pratt."

"You've got nothing to say to him. And he's got nothing to say to you. Listen to me, as a friend. Don't get involved in this case. This is an active investigation that will be all over the papers by tomorrow. How do I explain allowing a foreigner to talk to the accused?"

"He did me a favor a year ago. I owe him. He's entitled to hire an investigator who is also a lawyer to advise him. It's called access to counsel. He has a right."

"And he's going to pay you in peanuts?"

"He wouldn't be the first client to shell out in nuts."

"Why get involved, Vincent?"

"You said yourself that I should get back on the job, that I've had too much time to brood, and I'm thinking you're right. A new case would be good therapy."

Colonel Pratt sometimes forgot that Calvino had been a lawyer. Sometimes he filed things away in his memory until the right moment presented itself. This was one of those moments. The Colonel felt the trap of logic catch both legs.

"Do you ever think about going back to New York?"

The Colonel asked Calvino this question a couple of times a year. It was his signal that he'd run out of ammunition.

"Yeah, Pratt. I'd like to go back to my old New York every day if I could—for two hours," Calvino said, smiling, and Colonel Pratt tried unsuccessfully to suppress a grin. "We could go back together. See a Yankees game. Sit in the front row at the Blue Note. Breakfast at a diner in the East Village."

"That's more than two hours," Colonel Pratt said.

The Colonel paused, shook his head.

"Find another case, Vincent."

"I like this one. It's a puzzle. It has a mysterious woman. She's a fairy-tale princess, young and beautiful. No ID. How is it that a pregnant teenager is raped and killed and dumped in the middle of Bangkok, and nobody sees anything? And she doesn't have a scratch on her—not a mark anywhere. Her fingernails are clean. No evidence of a struggle tells me there was no physically violent sexual assault. And the killer took the risk of dumping the body on the Tobacco Monopoly Land? What the fuck is that about? Why there? There are thousands of places to hide a body. That's not one of them."

Colonel Pratt smiled.

"If your Indian informant drugged her and she was unconscious during the act, she wouldn't have been able to resist, would she?"

"You'll have to wait for the toxicity report," said Calvino. "If she has no drugs in her blood, you've got nothing to hold my client."

"His fingerprints. And there's the matter of his culture. Indian men's attitudes about women differ from ours. Rape is tolerated in India. We can't let that happen in Thailand."

Emotions can lead even the best cops to ignore solid evidence that doesn't support a gut feeling of guilt. Colonel Pratt had a wife and a daughter, and every day for weeks Thai newspapers had hammered the public with a series of stories of rape victims in India. Graphic stories detailing gang rapes by small groups of Indian men. One woman had been gang-raped on an Indian bus after her boyfriend had been beaten unconscious. A week later another woman had been brutally raped and murdered. The press had the ability to turn two unrelated cases into a vast, out-of-control crime spree of rapists waiting for victims on every corner. It didn't take much imagination to find a link between the dead girl found on the Tobacco Monopoly Land and an Indian nut vendor who'd been living there illegally. The public would accept the police's case as it fit the profile—all Indian men were dangerous rapists, and their evil would infiltrate Thailand unless stopped by the firm, quick action of the Thai police.

NINE

ONE OF THE worst sins in Calvino's world was to act out of sentimentality. It blurred judgment and made men stupid and women careless. Calvino hadn't insisted on seeing Akash because of some misguided sentimental attachment. Akash had been compensated for his information about the bargirl named Pizza who'd slipped back to her spot on the stage, clutching the chrome pole in a Soi Cowboy bar. Sooner or later Calvino would have tracked her down on his own. How many Pizzas worked on Soi Cowboy? Unlike other fast food commodities, Pizza had been consumed but reassembled and was back on the shelf for a new customer. She worked at one of the largest takeout menu joints in the world. Akash's report that she'd come back only accelerated the inevitable. The two men had been square. Neither owed the other anything. That said, they had a history, a connection, enough thread for the police to weave into a conspiracy story.

Calvino had no illusion about the risks an outsider faced in Thailand if he involved himself in a murder case. There were other illusions he had yet to deal with, but understanding what he was up against wasn't one of them. He knew that parking himself inside an open murder investigation was a little like walking into a dark room with a dozen cobras, stretching out and spending the night on the floor. The cops had decided Akash was the guy to take the fall. They wanted the Indian's blood. They needed to wrap up the case before the press played up the race card. Even Colonel Pratt was circling wagons with his colleagues and soon the majority of the population would join them. The hounds would bay for blood, and the cops would give them what they wanted. Anyone who piped up asking about human rights or evidence would find the wrath of the mob turned on them.

Given a library's worth of reasons to let the police deal with Akash in any way they chose, Calvino decided to help Akash. He doubted the Indian had killed Jane Doe. But he might have. Calvino's motive was less about Akash than it was about the dead girl he'd found. This wasn't some newspaper report he'd read. He'd found the body. He wanted the killer caught and castrated, if possible by a mean street dog. But there was more to his decision to investigate the murder. Another murdered woman floated into his consciousness—the one called the Black Cat, Mya. She had died in Bangkok seated next to her cousin as a bomb exploded under their Benz. That murder case had never been solved. Jane Doe was a surrogate case for the one that had defeated him.

It was now Friday morning, the day before Songkran. Akash sat with his legs shackled. The chains looked huge around his skinny legs, while handcuffs bit into his skin on his wrists. The Indian looked dazed, dejected, his head lowered. He slowly lifted his head, his watery eyes staring into the middle distance. The guard nudged him with a baton and said in Thai, "Someone is here to see you."

A look of amazement flashed hot in Akash's large brown eyes—puffy and bruised. He looked like he might cry.

"Khun Vinny!" he said. "You remember me, my friend? I am so happy to see you. This terrible thing has happened. They say I murdered a young woman, that I had sex with her."

"Did you?" asked Calvino.

Akash's face clouded, his teeth biting his lower lip as he shook his head—a performance Calvino suspected had been used on the police.

"No, of course not! I did not kill her! I did not have sex with her!"

His excited voice echoed down the noisy corridor.

"The police took a set of your prints off her body. Why would they have found your prints there? Tell me the truth or I can't help you."

Akash reached out in supplication, tears running down his cheeks.

"Please, Khun Vinny, you must believe me. I would never harm a girl like that. I saw her in the grass. I was camping nearby. I thought it strange that a girl would be sleeping with the sun already bright. She lay beside a path I used to walk home. I swear, I touched her only to find a pulse."

"Did you find one?"

Akash shook his head, rattling his chains.

"She was dead."

"Why didn't you phone the police?"

Akash shook his head again.

"I have no papers. I am what the Thais call a *khaek*, a visitor. The Thais look down on people like me. Dark skin, no good, they say. We smell bad, they say. Every day I see disgust on their faces as I pass. We are repulsive to the Thais. How can a poor man like me report the death of a beautiful girl to the police and not have a problem?"

He searched Calvino's eyes for an answer. He didn't anticipate what was on Calvino's mind.

"Why did you tell the police that I was at the scene? You told them that I'd I vouch for you. Put things right."

"Mr. Vincent, the police told me you also saw the dead woman and then asked me whether I knew you. I was very much relieved to learn this. I said, 'Yes, Mr. Vincent is my friend.' You look angry. Why? Did you wish for me to lie to the police?"

Calvino finally had his answer about the size of the wall Colonel Pratt had hit in trying to stop the cops from interrogating him. There was no way the Colonel could have done anything but stand aside and wait.

"If you're lying to me, Akash, you will have big trouble. Do you understand?"

Akash's head, bobbing like a pendulum in an overwound grandfather clock, said, "Mr. Vincent, I swear what I've told you is true. What I told the police is the truth. Akash is a truth teller. Ask anyone. Finding that girl was Allah's will. And I pray that it is the Prophet's will for you to rescue me from prison for something I did not do. This is a truly terrible deed. I give you my solemn oath, in the name of the Prophet, that I did not kill the girl."

TEN

LATER THAT FRIDAY McPhail walked along a narrow clear path inside Calvino's office. Calvino's back was turned to the door. He'd been expecting McPhail, who was an hour late for their appointment.

"You should fire your maid," said McPhail. "You're working in one of those Bangladesh fire hazards. One lit match and whoosh, baby, everything goes up in flames."

He looked at the long ash on his cigarette and smiled.

"You'll find an ashtray under the stack of newspapers on my desk."

McPhail lifted the newspapers, tapped the ash into the glass ashtray and then looked around for a place to sit.

Calvino stood up, gesturing toward the next room with a newspaper clipping. The photograph showed uniformed police beside the burnt-out hulk of a Benz.

"Ratana, I found it," he shouted to his secretary.

Ratana had searched for the clipping earlier in the morning, before he'd arrived.

"I knew you would," she said.

She walked in carrying a lacquered tray with Chinese fire dragons. It held two glasses of ice water.

"The fire department's emergency response team has arrived. And just in time," said McPhail, taking one of the glasses.

"Sit down, Ed."

"Sit where?"

Ratana removed a stack of file folders from a chair.

"Thanks, Ratana," he said.

Calvino watched his friend puff on the cigarette as he sat down.

"You want a little pick-me-up with the water?" he asked.

McPhail smiled.

"I wouldn't mind."

Calvino walked behind his desk, sat down and, leaning forward, opened a desk drawer. He removed his bottle of Johnnie Walker Black, unscrewed the top and poured a long shot into McPhail's water glass.

McPhail sipped the water and whiskey and smacked his lips, still eyeing the clutter of the office.

"All you're missing are thirty feral cats."

"It's called research, Ed."

"What happened to your right eye?"

"I was looking up cat shops when the phone book suddenly slapped me."

McPhail shook his head and lit another cigarette.

"The cops worked you over pretty good."

Calvino handed him the newspaper clipping with its photograph of two uniformed police officers. The story underneath explained how they'd been disciplined for misplacing evidence in the bombing case.

"They got some payback."

It was the same two officers, Ice and Fire, who interrogated him about the dead girl.

"You hit your head on that wall for months," said McPhail. "No wonder it made you crazy."

McPhail looked around the office again, shaking his head.

"But from what I can see, nothing's changed."

Calvino decided not to mention the music in the morgue. Only crazy people heard music that no one else heard. Were you crazy if you questioned your own sanity? Calvino worked through an answer as McPhail drank his whiskey.

Ratana appeared and hovered around Calvino's desk. She looked nervous, as if her boss might still be unwell. She'd had no warning. He'd phoned just half an hour before he'd showed up, saying he was back on the job. That he'd just left the prison and had found a new client there. His decision to accept a new case had confused her. As far as she was aware, he had no active clients and had informed everyone he was taking on no new cases.

She looked him over without making it obvious and waited for him to ask for messages. Well, not messages, as people had stopped calling him at the office. There could be something that he wanted. He looked normal enough, sitting his chair, the computer on, checking his email and telling McPhail that he'd run into a phone book. She didn't fully understand, but that was often the case when she attempted to track the conversation between McPhail and Calvino.

She cleared her throat and sighed.

"If you need anything..." she said, pausing.

He raised an eyebrow.

"I'll let you know."

"That's good. You'll let me know. You can phone or just call out. Whichever works."

She lingered a moment longer before slipping out of the office.

"I'm fine, Ratana," he called after her.

After she'd left, McPhail finished his whiskey and water.

"That was good."

He surveyed the stacks of papers piled in neat rows.

"What are you going to do with all of this shit?"

"I'm organizing it."

He followed McPhail's gaze around the office, trying to see it through a different set of eyes.

"It doesn't look like you're using the Dewey Decimal System."

The office walls, Calvino's desk, the table and the floor were exactly as he'd left them more than three months before—blanketed with photographs, some he'd taken himself, and newspaper clippings from the *Bangkok Post*, *The Nation*, *Matichon*, *Thai Rath* and half a dozen Thai crime magazines. It was the longest stretch he'd ever spent away from the office. He'd followed Dr. Apinya's order for a furlough, and her order had remained in force until he'd decided an exception could be made for Akash, as he wasn't a new client. It was a lawyer's distinction. Every so often the old instinct for splitting hairs became irresistible.

What really mattered was the fact he'd returned to his office, a place he'd avoided for months. He had work to do. Akash's case would distract him from the wreckage he still carried around from Rangoon. Looking around his office, Calvino felt in a perfect state of harmony as he took in his entire body of material evidence, random clues, speculations and wild imaginings—it was a space where all of these possibilities combined into half a dozen plausible explanations to account for the car bombing. How things had happened the way they had, who had ordered the hit and the reason for killing Mya and Yadanar, two musicians from Rangoon, on their way to perform in New York.

On every surface—tables, desk, chairs and floor—he'd stacked hard copies of data, graphs, charts, information and more information connected to the car bombing. In his mind he saw an organic beauty unfolding like a film that came alive from his day-to-day storyboard, drawing on news sources, handwritten interview notes, digital photographs Ratana had printed out on A4 glossy paper, police photographs from the crime scene and so on.

Every high-profile murder had an MO. The cops had sifted through the debris, trying to make sense of what had caused the Benz to be reconfigured in that particular arrangement of pieces. Some of the pieces had been tampered with. Some had disappeared. The results of the official investigation had left the main questions of motive and opportunity inconclusive, and the case had been quietly shelved. The unofficial investigation had pointed a long-nailed finger at one influential figure named Thanet, chief executive officer of the Diamond Flagship Import and Export Ltd. This CEO sat atop a powerful family empire, with substantial business interests and high-level political connections. He'd come up the shady backstairs of the system two steps at a time, as if he'd been a New York investment banker in his last life.

Thanet was forty-two years old and enjoying the fruits of being on top of the mountain.

Nearly a year had passed between the murder of Mya and her cousin Yadanar and the dead girl he'd discovered on the backwater patch of the Tobacco Monopoly Land. Nightmares, delusions, voices—visitations, he called them—had gradually left him stranded in a no man's land where real and unreal boundaries dissolved.

Calvino had memorized the elaborate timeline from the moment the two musicians had left the stage of the jazz nightclub on Sukhumvit Road to the time of the explosion. Now it was as if some stranger had drafted the timeline. As if Calvino were seeing something new in it.

"What are you staring at, Vinny?"

Calvino's eyes glazed over as he stared at a series of A3 color photos of what had been left of the blown-up Benz. Every angle of the wreckage. The broken glass, twisted metal and human body parts with numbered tags as they lay in the street. He'd seen the same image a hundred times on the TV news, a hundred more times in newspapers and thousands of times on the Internet. There were other photos of the emergency team who'd arrived on the scene of the blast and filled half a dozen body bags, stuffing in a leg here, an arm there, a foot and Mya's head. The dual killing had been major news for a week, with brief reports on progress for another few days.

Calvino thought of crimes as time sequences, blocks of time populated with conversations, telephone calls, whispers, planning, secrets, cooperation and opportunity. But usually, unless someone broke down and supplied the missing links, or there was CCTV footage, filling in the timeline was an exercise in frustration.

"Sometimes," he said aloud, "when you get stuck figuring out a problem, you set it aside and find a similar one and see if you can learn something new. You ask yourself, 'What am I overlooking?'"

"What *are* you overlooking?"

Calvino smiled.

"If I knew, I wouldn't be overlooking it. I'm thinking about the young woman I found on the Tobacco Monopoly Land. She was dead, but she looked like an angel sleeping. So beautiful you wanted to weep. Not anything like what happened to Mya."

"Man, you've got to let go of the Black Cat."

Calvino nodded, thinking everyone said the same thing—McPhail, Ratana, Colonel Pratt... Even old man Osborne, who had sent Calvino to Rangoon to find his son and now lingered on, fighting cancer in the final stages, made a daily ritual of "letting go." The father no longer mourned Rob, his son who'd died in Rangoon. Osborne had slipped into the space of mourning for himself.

"Forget about the dead, Calvino," Osborne had said. "The problems of the living are enough to keep anyone occupied."

Calvino had spotted the old man standing on a corner, smoking, holding a glass of single malt in the other hand and shaking his head in disapproval.

"You can't forget the dead," said Calvino. "They won't let you."

McPhail looked around.

"Man, who are you talking to?"

"I'm thinking out loud."

Ratana rushed into the office.

"Let me drive you back to your condo."

"The Thais believe that when someone is violently killed, their spirit hovers in the air at the crime scene, waiting for justice," said Calvino. "Ask Ratana. Isn't that right?"

Her hands rose to cover her mouth. She lowered her eyes and nodded.

"I know," said McPhail. "Thais think ghosts of murdered people stick around like they're in a first-class Thai airport lounge waiting for their flight to be called. Only their flight is delayed, and they get upset and they want revenge. Right, Ratana?"

"Like most things you say, Ed, there's a fingernail of truth chewed off and spit on the floor," said Calvino, answering for his secretary.

McPhail was happy Calvino had intervened.

"But I know for a fact, Vinny, that you don't believe in ghosts," McPhail continued. "You told me so years ago. You don't just one day wake up and say you've converted to the church of ghost believers. You gotta believe that kind of shit from the time you're a kid or you never will. Right, Ratana?"

"You need to grow up with it," said Ratana.

"See, what'd I tell you? You didn't grow up believing in ghosts."

"New York is nothing but ghost believers," said Calvino. "My grandfather was a high priest of ghost believers."

"Ratana, now he's lying."

"Are you ready for another shot?"

Calvino unscrewed the whiskey cap and leaned forward to refill McPhail's glass.

"Okay, you can give me a shot," McPhail said, using his finger to measure along the side of the glass. "But way, way above the line, if you don't mind."

Ghosts or no ghosts, the fact was that no one had been arrested for the killings of Rob Osborne in Rangoon or Mya and Yadanar in Bangkok. The police spokesperson in Bangkok had issued a press release that translated into the banal—our investigators continue to examine leads into the car bombing. If there really were leads, no one mentioned what they were. Once the public were assured the crime hadn't been politically motivated, interest quickly faded. In reality the evidence was inconclusive, except to confirm it had been a professional job; there were no loose ends, no leads that led anywhere. No magical Phillips screwdriver that the police could use to reassemble the steel, glass and limbs.

"Look at this," Calvino said, handing McPhail a photograph of Jane Doe.

"She's dead?"

"Dead."

McPhail showed the photograph to Ratana.

"She was killed? Who could have done something like that to this girl?" said Ratana.

"The police say a man named Akash killed her."

"An Indian did this?" said McPhail.

"I hope they execute him," said Ratana.

Calvino held up his hand.

"Wait. The suspect didn't kill the girl. He says he's being framed."

"If the Indian didn't do it, who did?" she asked.

It was hard to know how any justice system ever worked when most people, including the cops, shared Ratana's point of view—if not the *khaek*, then who could have done it? Calvino had a list of names.

"My job is to show there is no evidence that Akash killed her."

McPhail said, "Then you'd better find someone to take his place on the ball-cutting bench."

Defending a murder case usually meant exactly what McPhail said—you found someone else to put in the murderer's chair. To get your client out of the chair, you'd better bring a replacement. That had been the problem in the car bombing case: the chair had remained empty, falling into a shadow and disappearing into a warehouse of forgotten furniture.

Murder cases tended to end up in cold storage, like the young woman in the morgue. After just a couple of days, the local newspapers already had a couple of murdered farang stories to sell and more would follow. A Jane Doe could have come from anywhere. Mystery, beauty, youth and pregnancy would have staying power for someone with an identity, but Jane Doe was nameless, stripped of family, region and education. Her death would easily be bumped as old news, one more unsolved Bangkok murder case that had held people's interest for forty-eight hours. Afterwards, she'd be forgotten as attention switched to the latest kidnapping, rape and murder charges filed in separate cases involving foreigner victims. She'd been found early Wednesday; by Saturday the news of Jane Doe's death would be fading. The police hadn't released the fact she was pregnant. Their excuse was that the autopsy report was needed to confirm the medical examiner's finding. By the time that emerged, Jane Doe would be old news.

And so it went. Jane Doe's murder didn't make the cut when it came to the news-value rankings. Competition against the latest victim was always tough. It was the same for a private investigator. But for Calvino this new case imparted the passionate feeling he might unlock the world of ghosts and find a way to be rid of them. His mind had been laboring to match the initials JAI to any foreigners working and living in Thailand. A Thai would have likely used Thai script but a smart, rich foreign educated Thai might have used the Roman alphabet. Calvino concluded the clue to solving Jane Doe's identity was locked in her ankle tattoo.

ELEVEN

THE FIRST PERSON on Calvino's list whose initials were JAI was an American lawyer named James Arthur Innes. Innes was from Chicago but had been in Bangkok for eight years. McPhail tagged along with Calvino as backup. They arrived together for the appointment at Innes's office in a modern high-rise off Silom Road.

Innes opened the door to his office himself. He had no secretary. He wore a tan suit jacket.

"Mr. Calvino, I've been expecting you."

As Innes reached out to shake hands with Calvino, an exposed cufflink displayed his initials. McPhail looked him over. This guy, he thought, is the first on Calvino's list to interview? It could get interesting.

"This is Ed McPhail, my associate," Calvino said.

"You have an associate?" said Innes. "The private investigations business must be doing well."

He showed them into his office.

"I work cheap," said McPhail. "Not for nuts, but cheap."

"Life doesn't always work out the way we wish," said Innes.

"We won't take much of your time," said Calvino, moving inside the office.

Innes occupied a stylish setup, an elegant package wrapped in chrome and glass that reeked of money. Innes slipped behind the bar, positioning himself in front of his notebook computer and a stack of IPO listings. Another computer was on his office desk at the other end of the room.

"That's good. I have very little time."

"The demands of work," said Calvino, taking a stool at the bar opposite Innes.

"I was told you were once a lawyer."

He'd Googled Calvino's name. The desired knowledge was never more than a couple of clicks away.

Calvino leaned forward, elbows on the bar.

"That was a long time ago. New York still had the Twin Towers."

"Those good old days are gone."

"They weren't all that good," said Calvino.

Innes raised an eyebrow.

"At least we can agree that, whatever they were, those days are behind us."

They circled around each other, buying time, sizing the other guy up like a couple of prize fighters in round one.

"On the phone you said you had contacts in Rangoon who might be useful for one of my clients," Innes said.

Innes ran a one-man Bangkok consulting operation. Calvino had seen his type of expat businessman before. He might not understand a lot about Thai culture, but he got one thing right—in Thailand appearance is substance. What you see is all there is. Nothing behind the mask but another mask, so what would be the point of ripping off the mask? Innes's office was big enough to house half a dozen lawyers. All that space for one man—that was a message. In the hyper-dimension of business, power needed lots of room.

Innes's personalized style had the look of a private members' club designed in the minimalist tradition—sleek, opulent, polished designer furniture with surfaces as slick as a candy apple. Cherry wood bookshelves that rose from floor to ceiling against one wall were filled with leather-bound law books that looked untouched. Another wall displayed one of those museum-sized Burmese canvases of hill tribe people working the land. A full wet bar with stools and glass mirror was on the left side, and opposite the bar was a sitting area that featured one of those ten-grand sofas that looked like it had been looted from a Middle Eastern palace. The office was his personal signature, each detail confirming the status of Innes as a substantial person.

He grinned as he watched Calvino and McPhail drink in the fine details of their surroundings.

"Hey, I know the guy who painted that," said McPhail, walking up to the huge framed oil painting. "How'd you get something that size out of Burma?"

The question gave Innes an adolescent's joy that his efforts were appreciated, perhaps even envied.

"That's confidential," he said.

"Lawyer's talk for getting away with a crime," said McPhail. "I never seen anything he painted this size."

"A one-off commission," said Innes. "The original buyer had a sudden financial problem and needed money."

In Bangkok, unless a man's showcased possessions removed all doubt about his success and wealth, he had no entry to the backrooms where the deals were made, no important friends in high places—and that meant he existed in perpetual orbit, ringing around but never quite landing inside the network. Calvino had checked out James Arthur Innes and found that he had received large retainers from resource and energy companies doing business in Canada, the United States, Burma, Malaysia and Indonesia. Hiring a lawyer like Innes was useful for big foreign corporations, which coughed up large fees for his access, negotiation skills, monitoring and reporting on the shifting power arrangements inside the Thai business and political system. He delivered the important stuff that couldn't be found online or done in backroom offices of legal drones working in Bangalore.

Innes was sitting pretty. He had the smug confidence of a middle-aged white man gone soft at the waist, the flesh on the face going slack around the jawline, with strong shoulders under the tailor-made suit. Calvino scanned the framed photographs perched in front of the law books on two of the bookshelves. Four of them were of Thai women, smiling—one in a nightclub, another on a beach, the third at an exclusive restaurant and the fourth, a younger woman, sitting on the ten-grand sofa, legs stretched out, throwing the photographer a kiss. Jane Doe wasn't among them.

McPhail poured himself a scotch from a bottle of fifteen-year-old single malt whiskey.

"The minister of natural resources is an old pal of mine," said McPhail.

He mentioned a name.

"I've played tennis with him," said Innes. "But that's not the reason you want to talk to me."

Calvino pulled a photograph of Jane Doe out of his briefcase and slid it across the bar.

"She's the reason."

Innes slipped on a pair of gold-framed reading glasses. He picked up the photograph, studied the face and removed his glasses. Calvino watched the expression on his face. The photograph of a woman you know, someone you've slept with, someone you've kept, who is now obviously dead, will cause the hardest face to flinch. Nothing registered on Innes's face as he laid down the photograph.

"Who is she?"

"I was hoping you might be able to tell me."

"What makes you think I know her?"

Calvino gave him a second photograph with a close-up showing the tattoo on her left ankle.

"Same girl, different angle."

Innes again examined the photograph as if it were a footnote in an IPO offering and then looked up.

"Take a look at the tattoo on her ankle," said McPhail.

"With your initials," said Calvino.

"She wasn't much older than this whiskey," said McPhail, lifting his glass in salute.

Innes broke out laughing.

"You come to my office with pictures of a dead girl who has the word 'heart' tattooed on her ankle, and you think we have a connection? I should throw both of you out."

Calvino glanced over at the bookshelves.

"Before you do that, I see you keep pictures of your women. Collectors are in my experience proud of their possessions. Your outrage isn't all that convincing. Before I go, I'd like to ask if any of the ladies in those pictures have your initials tattooed in private places?"

"Get out!" Innes said.

"No way I'm leaving any fifteen-year-old whiskey behind," said McPhail, draining his glass. "And I do know Mr. Big in the mining business in Burma. If you want an introduction, we can work out a commission."

"Out!" said Innes.

Innes came around from his side of the bar with a Glock and waving it like a magic wand or a baby rattle—the way a man flashes a gun when he doesn't have any experience in handling one. He was acting like a man whose knowledge of guns came from TV.

"You can take a man out of Chicago, but you can't take Chicago out of the man," said McPhail, shaking his head as he stared at the weapon.

"One last question: where were you on Tuesday night?" asked Calvino.

Halfway surprised the sight of the gun hadn't triggered a hallucination, Calvino decided that, if nothing else, this stagey threat suggested that maybe he was getting over his ghost problem.

Innes lowered the gun.

"You don't know when to stop, do you?"

"Just answer my question, Innes," said Calvino, making no effort to get up from the bar.

"I pulled an all-nighter to meet an important deadline," said Innes.

"You were in your office alone?"

Innes clenched his jaw, shaking his head. It occurred to him that Calvino wasn't someone he could easily throw out of the office, close the door on and have the problem go away.

"I was with that one," said Innes, pointing the barrel of the Glock at the last photograph on the bookshelf.

It showed a twenty-something Thai woman in a tight red dress with bee-stung lips, narrow hips and a smile like she'd been plugged into an electric circuit board.

"Her name is June. She spent the night."

Calvino climbed down from the bar stool, walked over to the bookshelf, pulled the frame off the shelf, turned it around, opened it and took out the photograph. He looked on the back. Innes was the meticulous type—IPO work required a certain mentality about information—and he'd written June's name, phone number, date of birth, address and breast, waist and hip dimensions on the back.

"You can print another one. I'd like to take this one."

McPhail said, "Man, he's gonna shoot you if we don't get out of here."

"Mr. Innes would only pull the trigger if he could bill for it. Otherwise, no, he wouldn't shoot anyone. This isn't Chicago. Isn't that right, Jim?"

Calvino had walked back, stopping a couple of inches from Innes, crowding him, the intimidation of physical proximity that people from New York taught people from Chicago.

A man who lavishly furnished an office might have the temperament to redesign the women in his life. Plastic surgery was another form of art appreciation.

In the elevator ride down to street level, McPhail said, "A nasty bastard, even for a lawyer. Because he's loaded, he thinks he can pull a gun. What the fuck was that?"

"He's operating in a tough world. So he thinks he has to act tough or he's gets eaten before breakfast. And what is his one brilliant idea? Wave a gun. He's a two-bit actor who wants to be taken seriously as a performer," said Calvino. "He's been lucky so far to play before amateurish audiences. Innes is a cheerleader pretending to be a quarterback."

Lighting a cigarette, McPhail countered: "Wrong. He's like the team owner. That painting from Burma is worth at least a couple of hundred grand. Think about it, Vinny. What's in it for Innes to kill the girl? He can buy, trade, exchange or throw away any woman he wants."

McPhail had an insider's logic and experience. Either way, from what Calvino had seen, Innes didn't have the stuff of a murderer. Posers, he knew, are cowards underneath, covering their fear with masks of bravado, afraid someone might discover the truth and humiliate them. Also, Innes had an alibi, and Calvino would check it with his girlfriend named June.

"Akash didn't kill the girl," said Calvino. "But the difference between Innes and him is Akash is in jail. He's a nobody without a wall to hang his shirt on."

McPhail took a long pull on his cigarette.

"Why do you give a shit about the *khaek*?"

As the doors opened, Calvino walked out first.

"I'm thinking about Jane Doe's family. Do they even know that she's missing? If that were my daughter, I'd want someone to tell me she's died."

"When Innes pulled the gun, did you have one of your hallucinations?"

Calvino shook his head.

"No flashback. No nothing. A middle-aged guy in a suit, his hand shaking as he held the gun... No, all I felt was contempt. I don't think anyone has ever hallucinated on contempt."

"That's good, or you'd be lost in a permanent state of delusion."

With McPhail, Calvino found he either laughed or cried.

"Ed, if truth were an economy, the trend line would be clear. We're in for a major depression. Separating people from reality is all there is left."

"No wonder you hallucinate, Vinny."

"Ain't it the truth?" said Calvino.

The elevator door opened and they stepped out into the corridor filled with people going about their business.

TWELVE

A FEW MINUTES before four on Friday afternoon, Mon Hla strolled the grounds outside the family hut in Mae Hong Son, shading her eyes against the bright blue sky and trying to avoid staring into the blinding, fiery ball of the sun. She'd heard something coming from the direction of the mountains. She searched the sky for the source of the growing sound of a roaring engine and beating blades.

Their hut was the odd one out in the camp. The others were hunched and weathered like a group of old women; they'd been built from bamboo stripped from the nearby forest, capped with corrugated roof sheets and supported by thick poles they'd cut from trees. Shoots of green grew from some of the bamboo poles, smearing the line between the living and the dead.

Mon Hla's family hut was made of more substantial stuff, materials that cost a lot of money—red bricks, concrete bricks, cement and a foundation. Their hut was the only one like it in their row, a cause of resentment from the bamboo hut people. The camp was isolated from the nearest Thai village, and Mon Hla's family lived an isolated life within the camp. Living like turtles, her family tried to ignore those who ignored them except to ask for a loan. Mon Hla had never thought they were better than those in the bamboo huts, but what she thought hadn't changed anything.

She walked toward a winding, muddy stream and a terraced hill that sloped down to the edge. From their hut they had the best view of the blue mountain ridge hugging the sky, warming its shoulders against the sun. Her thoughts drifted from the mountains to her sister in Bangkok. She remembered her sister's face, smiling and laughing. Mi Swe had a child's face.

Two days earlier the members of her family had been stirred from their daily boredom by the turmoil and worry of an unannounced visitor. The man's appearance had scared them. He'd arrived wearing an official uniform, walked directly to their hut and demanded that her mother and father tell him why Ploy had run away. No one in Bangkok could locate her. The uniformed official demanded to know where she'd gone. The family's eyes were blank as they stared at this stranger. His uniform had gold buttons that caught the sun. Her mother and father glanced at each other, confused by his presence and his question. Each sought comfort in the other, neither had any to give.

Their eyes blinked with frightened ignorance.

"You must find Mi Swe and return her immediately," he said.

"How can we find our daughter? We can't leave the camp. It's not allowed," Nang, her mother said.

The official looked angry.

"You will contact your daughter. If she doesn't return in two days, there will be a big problem."

Her father, Sai, shook his head, shrugged.

"There is no problem. Our daughter knows her duty. We raised her to believe in the Buddha."

The official calmed down, his face less flushed, and he attempted a tiny smile.

"Then we all understand each other," he said. "But if Mi Swe doesn't return, the Buddha won't be able to help her or you."

The father remembered the face of the official. He was the one who had brought a stack of money and given it to him the day his daughter left. With it they had built a fine hut from bricks and concrete. Even Buddha would have understood why they'd been forced to accept the money. They breathed a sigh of relief when the official left the second time, but they couldn't ignore his threat.

Now, a couple of days later, the outline of a helicopter was taking shape against the blue sky. Sunlight hopscotched off its windscreen. In months past Mon Hla had watched helicopters dusting crops far away. Like tiny metal windmills flying through the air. But she sensed this one had another mission. She couldn't figure out where it was going or who the men were inside. She wondered what it would be like to look down on Mae Hong Son from the sky. What would the world look like from up there? Would it be cooler in the sky?

In the mountains it never got as hot as it did in Bangkok. Mon Hla's sister, Mi Swe, wrote letters saying how hot the city was and how lucky her sister and brother were to be in the north. She signed them with her Thai nickname, Ploy. New identity, but the same sister, the same Mi Swe who had walked to the small river to haul water buckets to the family home when it was just another bamboo hut like those that everyone else lived in.

Songkran heat had crept up like a mugger and hit the north with both fists. Two scorching hot days had come and gone since the official had visited their hut. Mon Hla knew her father was worried. No one had heard a word from Ploy or her friends; they had no idea how to contact her.

The helicopter turned from the mountains. The bird's altitude dropped as it approached the camp. It was difficult to judge the speed. The engines screamed like an angry hawk. Other people, old and young, emerged from their huts, shading their eyes, staring at the object coming toward them from the sky.

Heat had drained the energy of both her parents, who stayed inside the cool brick hut. Her shirtless father lay on a cot watching her mother in front of the gas stove, cooking a special treat, rice cakes. Mi Swe had sent them money from Bangkok every month, but it was "Ploy" who had more recently been sending them twenty thousand baht each month. No one in the camp had that kind of money. Even the doctors, police and officials earned less. But now their family lived in a brick and concrete hut and had lots of money. Their neighbors whispered how the family had sold their daughter for gold. They grinned at the family like the village idiot stroking a pet rabbit. True, it was a great deal of money, but most of it was being spent on her brother, Swe Thaik, who suffered from a rare kidney disease with a long name. He needed daily medicine, the camp doctor said, or he would die. Most sickness in the refugee camp was treated with a couple of aspirin. No one wanted Swe Thaik to die. True, Mi Swe had gone to Bangkok to work, and money had been exchanged.

"What is it?" her mother shouted from inside the hut.

"It's a helicopter," Mon Hla said, turning back to shout her response.

Mon Hla's mother stood in the door watching her daughter and many other children and young people laughing as they ran toward the river, waving their arms to attract the pilot's attention as the furious sound of rotating blades reached their ears. In the past, an important visitor had arrived by helicopter and handed out small gifts to the children. Maybe that nice man was inside with a new round of gifts. Every day in the camp, children and adults drank down hope—as empty as dreams—filling their bellies until they were fat with sensual desire.

She saw the faces of the two men inside the helicopter suspended in the air over the camp. The helicopter tilted, then banked to the side as it entered Zone 1, heading in a straight line toward their hut. It was easy to spot—brick in a row of bamboo. Mon Hla thought the men inside had found Ploy and were bringing her home. She raised both hands as the helicopter passed.

One of the men leaned out of the helicopter and tossed a flashing object. For a second it was framed against the sky, exploding like a Chinese firework. A rain of white sparks fell on the roof of their hut. Circling around, the helicopter dropped more sparkling objects in Zone 4 and along the perimeter of the camp where people lived in tents. In moments flames leaped from the bamboo huts, long tongues of fire licking the jaws of the sky as if seeking to submit. The helicopter circled one last time before gaining altitude and disappearing beyond the mountains.

Mon Hla ran back from the river. She couldn't get close to her hut. A wall of fire and dense black smoke stopped her. Everyone was running, screaming, crying—men, women, children, everyone fleeing the flames. Some people ran with their clothes burning on their backs. Some lay still on the ground with their skin black and burnt. Hundreds of huts in the camp gathered like a giant lantern with an enormous orange flame. Within minutes the camp was no longer recognizable as a village where people had lived. That camp was gone, replaced by bamboo kindling feeding a huge bonfire. If there is a hell, the camp door had opened on that place and the devil himself danced in the flames. Mon Hla cried, her body shaking, her face covered in sweat, screaming the names of her mother, father and brother. And Mi Swe. The only reply was the cries of neighbors and the crackling of the bamboo on fire. The smell of wet ash clung heavy in the air.

THIRTEEN

SATURDAY AFTERNOON, THE first day of Songkran. At a table positioned on the far side of the bar inside the Beer Garden, McPhail watched Calvino sketch from memory the anchor logo he had seen on the hip of the dead girl's tracksuit. When Calvino finished, he slid the paper over to McPhail, who looked at it the way a Bangkok taxi cab driver might look at a map. He turned it until it was upside down, then considered it sideways. Finally he shook his head.

"I give up, Vinny. What's is it?" asked McPhail.

He took a long drag from his cigarette and then, tilting his head upward, exhaled.

"An anchor," said Calvino.

"Man, that doesn't look anything like an anchor. It's looks like an octopus crossed with a gecko crucified on a swastika. You sure this is what was on her tracksuit?"

Calvino nodded. A television set was suspended over the bar. Calvino watched video coverage of a fire from a refugee camp.

McPhail tried to kick-start the conversation again.

"What if she was involved in some kind of cult?"

"The anchor's a designer label, McPhail."

"That company will go out of business unless a bunch of skinheads win the lottery and decide to take up jogging."

He looked over at the TV.

"Another factory up in flames."

"Refugee camp," said Calvino, reading the caption under the video.

"Smoke 'em out," said McPhail. "No more refugee problem."

Calvino studied his drawing of the anchor logo and wiped a rim of sweat from his upper lip. He scooped the paper from McPhail, crunched it into a ball and tossed it on the empty tray of a passing waitress. It hit her on the forehead and she stopped, surveying the source of the attack.

"Three points," said McPhail.

"Bring another round," said Calvino to the waitress, "and a drink for yourself."

"You have a real talent for throwing wadded-up paper. It's big league next to your ability to draw," said McPhail.

Calvino watched as McPhail lit another cigarette and waited for someone to come and tell him to put it out.

"She was one of the most beautiful women I've ever seen."

"She was dead, Vinny."

Calvino cocked his head to the side.

"The cops have no idea who she is. None. They've got nothing but a designer tracksuit to track her down. And it's likely a fake from the Weekend Market, where they sell hundreds every weekend."

"If her name had been tattooed on her forehead, they'd have missed it," said McPhail. "Come on, Vinny, I'm joking. They've got DNA, fingerprints, so the forensic guys will ID her. Bet on it."

The next round of drinks came. After the waitress left, McPhail, who'd palmed his cigarette, took a long drag.

"What did Pratt have to say?"

Calvino shrugged.

"He asked, 'Why were you running through restricted areas of the Tobacco Monopoly?'"

"Good fucking question. And you said, 'Sir, it will be Songkran this weekend. And I was looking to meet someone to play water games with,'" said McPhail. "He probably was happy there was an actual body. You've got a record of seeing bodies that aren't there."

He dropped the cigarette and ground it into the floor with the heel of his shoe.

"Sorry, cheap shot."

It seemed to Calvino that cheap shots defined a class of expats with nothing else to do but pass the endless hours in a shallow ditch of knowledge, gliding through another day of non-stop happy hour. Calvino didn't want to think McPhail had become one of them. He looked at the dozens of men sitting around the bar. One of them had asked the cashier to switch the TV coverage of the upcountry refugee fire to a football match. Men preferred to watch sports while choosing one of the freelancers. The hookers hovered at their elbows, doing their job—waiting, smiling, flirting. The flow of time was measured in timeouts on the TV and the speed of wallets opening and shutting.

Until one morning, each of those men would wake up, see the hooker next to him and understand why bars always had the TV turned to sports. The patrons were like midget basketball players who pushed an eight-foot ladder under the hoop, climbed up, dunked the ball and then smiled as if they were pros. The hoop was the pro. The hoop didn't care whether the player cheated. It only cared whether the player scored.

Calvino had his own set of net and hoop delusions. That made him no different from the other guys at the bar. He'd accepted that he was the same. There was no high horse to mount. As McPhail drank his gin and tonic, Calvino withdrew deep into an internal space where he'd fled, a mental safe house he'd used since the Rangoon killings.

McPhail lowered his glass, seeing that Calvino had spaced out into some other place.

"Man, it's my fault. I should have gone to Burma with you. If I'd known it was gonna fuck you up, I would've gone. You've been in the shit before. How was I supposed to know you'd get PTSD? It's like the clap. You can bang a hundred women, no problem, then number 101 gives you a dose."

Calvino nodded, drank his Mekong and Coke.

"You're on the pills the doctor gave you?"

"Morning is a red one. Nighttime I swallow two blue pills."

"Ask for a white one. That way you can pretend you're swallowing colors to make a happy flag in your head."

"Okay, okay, it's not funny," McPhail continued. "But you've got a loose screw. Those pills are like a Phillips screwdriver tightening up what's rattling around in your skull. They are working, right?"

"I'm trying. But the threads are stripped. Let me get back to you on my brain carpentry."

Calvino had learnt that in the land of mental disturbance, everyone had a theory, a remedy and easy cure. The Internet had made everyone an expert. His secretary, Ratana, had arranged for private meditation. Once a week he sat in front of a robed meditation master, breathing deeply for forty-five minutes. Once a week he saw a therapist. These carpenters had the job of rebuilding his mind. It had been a slow process. Calvino practiced his breathing exercise as the waitress came to the table and set down the beers. Calvino slipped her a hundred baht tip with the quick flip of the wrist used to pay a bribe to a traffic cop. She smiled, a cop's smile, and Calvino watched her as she walked back to the bar.

"Pratt phoned you," said Calvino.

There was no point in making it a question.

McPhail rolled his eyes.

"What if he did?"

"Innes complained, right?"

"We should've thrown the fat little fucker through his office window."

Calvino saw McPhail squirm in this seat.

"Pratt asked for your help to pull me off the investigation. Am I right?"

McPhail, an uneasy grin crossing his lips, drank from the fresh beer.

"The dead girl has nothing to do with you. Why would you want to get involved? What's the point? You go around Bangkok finding bodies and pretend the dead person is a client? That's nuts, Vinny."

Calvino shifted in his seat, hands clasped around the beer bottle. He raised it and took a long shot against the back of his throat.

"When you find a body, you are involved. I had three hours of getting knocked around by the cops. If that's not involvement, we need a new definition."

McPhail shook his head as he stubbed out his cigarette.

"You found a body and the police gave you the third degree. So fucking what? Let it go. The police are handling it. That's why the Thais have police. In between shaking down people for bribes, the police spend some of their time investigating murders."

"How do you know she was murdered?"

"Okay, she had a teenage heart attack and croaked in some secluded part of the Tobacco Monopoly. The point is, after the autopsy the cops will know if she died of natural causes or was murdered. If someone killed her, the cops can find out who it was. It could be that Soi Cowboy nut vendor you think is innocent. Prepare for that. You can follow what they're doing in the newspapers like everyone else. Finding the body doesn't give you any special right to stick your nose into a police investigation."

McPhail's little speech sounded as if Colonel Pratt had written it. The words he'd chosen, the stringing of the phrases were a police colonel's mind in action. Calvino would have bet on it.

"The police stuck their nose into my life. The cops, when they weren't swinging the yellow pages, told me that ninety percent of the time, the person who finds a body is the killer."

"And you're drinking with me this afternoon because you convinced them you are in the ten percent."

"Actually, they said that after the autopsy report they wanted me back for another round."

"With your DNA on the body, you better hope they find someone else's genes."

"I couldn't walk away," said Calvino.

"Calvino, as long as I've known you, I've never seen you walk away from a woman's body, dead or alive."

A customer and two hookers walked past on their way out to a taxi and a short-time hotel.

"Sometimes it's not about walking away—you need to run away. Get the hell out. This is why you've messed up your head, Vinny. You know what I'm saying?"

Calvino knew exactly what McPhail was saying and had heard it already from Colonel Pratt and Ratana. He'd told himself the same thing as well, for all the good it had done. Who is in control of how the mind registers a close-range shooting? Who could understand why in the past the rough stuff hadn't troubled him? He'd been through plenty of those times. He'd been lucky and got the drop on two thugs who'd drawn on him. He was sure killing the two men wasn't what had pushed him over the edge.

"You're trying to control what the police decide to do about this dead girl like it's your case, Vinny."

"I want to know what happened. Is that wrong?"

They looked at each other, then away, drinking their liquor, watching the farang at the bar making deals with freelancers, climbing the ladder to make their winning dunk shot.

"There's more wrong than right in life. Are you just finding that out?" asked McPhail.

One of the football teams scored a goal, and a couple of the punters watching the TV roared with approval. They ordered another round of drinks, and the hookers gathered in to help them celebrate. Somewhere in the back of Calvino's mind was smoke and fire. Ice and Fire. A Jane Doe with an ankle tattoo and, on her designer tracksuit, a logo that looked like an anchor, the kind that keeps a ship from drifting into the shoals.

FOURTEEN

SHE WAS RUNNING late for their appointment. Calvino sat alone near a window at a coffee shop with a view of Sukhumvit Road from three stories above. As he waited, he passed the time by watching the street. Gone were the long lines of tinted-windowed cars waiting for the traffic lights to change. Gone too were the cops and security. In the void the water throwers set up their ambush points. Sukhumvit Road was a no man's land, with roving bands standing in the back of pickups, searching for targets. Songkran was urban warfare with water guns. Every small band bonded by looking out for their own and attacking everyone else. It was the Thai version of *Lord of the Flies*, a descent into a state of nature, red in tooth and claw. People had forgotten how much fun it is to organize and send out raiding parties on the street.

One group of Thais and foreigners, hunting together like a pack of lions, cornered a motorcycle driver dressed in a pizza delivery vest and hat. A large carrier box rested on the tail of the bike, the takeaway phone number in large black letters. Squeezed between the driver and the warm box, a young woman rode pillion. A Thai no more than fifteen years old, wearing designer sunglasses, ran alongside the motorcycle and tossed a bucket of water at the driver. The water caught the driver on the shoulder and he braked hard. Turning his bike around as a second band charged in, shooting high-powered water pistols, the driver searched for an exit. The driver started out and then braked and turned his bike around again as yet another group with high-powered water pistols opened fire. Another exit blocked.

When a man is trapped on all sides, in that moment of truth he discovers something about himself. Like a squirrel cornered by a pack of dogs, the driver and the woman riding pillion tried one last time to escape, only to lose control of the bike as another bucket of water scored a direct hit to the driver's head. Bike, driver and passenger skidded across the slippery road. The first water pistol brigade marched forward, shooting from the hip as the driver limped back to his bike. The woman passenger lay still on the road. One of the teenagers ran up to her and dumped water on her head. He and his friends laughed and danced around the woman on the street until she rose to her feet laughing too.

Late in the afternoon of Saturday, the first day of Songkran, Calvino waited for Judy Alice Ibsen at a local coffee shop. From above he watched from his water gun-free zone. The traffic had dwindled to a few cars and buses. People who could leave town had left. Calvino had sought refuge for his meeting at one of the dry zones offering a ringside seat to watch water throwers terrorize the diehards who remained. Songkran acted as an annual test run of what urban rebellion and anarchy would look like if the weapons fired only water ammo. Sukhumvit Road teemed with irregular water fighters from around the world linking up with the local slum dweller militias. Water thugs, like all armed bullies, owned the streets for three days.

She came up from behind him.

"You must be Mr. Calvino," she said.

"You recognize me from the back?"

She blushed.

"My English isn't so good."

He turned around and looked at her.

111

"I recognize you, too."

He'd gone through lists of NGOs, and an inside person at the airport had given him access to the immigration database for the previous year. Her initials, JAI, put Judy on his list of people to interview. He'd then received a substantial bonus—he found that she was in Bangkok and willing to meet him. Neutral Ground ought to have been the name for the coffee franchise, rather than Starbucks.

From the moment he saw her, Calvino knew she was regretting agreeing to meet him. Her hair and clothes were dripping.

"You got caught," said Calvino.

A waiter brought her a hand towel, and she wiped her face.

"That's better," she said.

Opening her iPad, she checked the screen and then Calvino.

"You are Vincent Calvino."

"You can never be too careful," he said.

She sat down.

"If I were careful, I would not have come to meet you."

"Nothing wrong with your English."

The days when someone couldn't recognize someone were over. Most faces were by then just a Google image search away. Though young and dressed for the part, Judy lacked the attitude of the foreigner who might seek thrills in chasing down strangers with water guns. Judy had a weary and anxious look as she sat at the table. A waitress brought her coffee. She parked her roller bag against the wall and collapsed the plastic handle flush with the top.

Her hands tapping against the side of her coffee cup, she listened as Calvino asked, "What it's like working with refugees in the North?"

She'd been asked the same question dozens of times, and each time she wanted to scream, "Go outside and look in the gutter, then sit in the gutter and stay there overnight and the next night. Wait for food to be given to you. Be grateful for scraps."

She wore no makeup. A few lines, the beginning of a spider's web, had formed around her clear blue eyes. Thin-lipped, she had blonde hair cropped short to her head. An earring dangled from one earlobe, and she wore faded jeans with holes in the knees, dusty sandals with worn straps and a T-shirt with Che Guevara on it—bearded, black bereted and eternally young. She looked down at her iPad, switching between Skype and her Gmail account. She performed the anxious digital finger dance of someone waiting for a message.

Calvino patiently waited until she glanced up. Was she going to disappear into the cliché of the overworked NGO? Or would she stick her head out of the shell—her real self, not the one buried in the iPad.

Finally she relaxed and looked up to meet his eyes with the beginning of a smile.

"If you want to know the truth, it's depressing. With the fire at the camp, how else could I feel? I should have been there. Instead I was in Bangkok."

Any true human connection between two strangers starts with an expression of their state of mind. In Judy's case, guilt whorled inside her head, fed by heat, smoke and fire.

Who wouldn't feel depressed working inside a refugee camp along the Burmese border? One that had been destroyed by fire, he thought, remembering the smoke and flames on the TV. No one could ever imagine what another person might feel in circumstances like those. Witnesses to destruction and death can find themselves cut off, Calvino knew, isolated from others who haven't shared the experience. In the presence of others Judy tried to shake off her feelings of estrangement and guilt, or least not to show them to a stranger like Calvino.

"You look troubled," he said.

Watching her twist the ring on her right hand, he couldn't decide if it was a wedding ring or a birthstone.

"I can't stay long. I must leave for the airport soon."

She glanced at her wristwatch.

"Going back to Oslo?"

He looked at her bag.

"No, I'm going to Mae Hong Son," she said, expecting a reaction.

When she saw a blank look on Calvino's face, it was clear that the name of the province hadn't registered any emotion.

"You may not have been following the news," she said.

"I saw the fire at the refugee camp on the TV news," he said, leaving out that the TV hung above the bar at a beer garden.

"Then you know."

She pressed her fingers together, making a bridge with her hands.

"One moment there is a community," she said. "The next, ashes and death."

He shook his head, sipped his black coffee.

"Watching TV news doesn't tell you much about what really happened," Calvino said. "The official version is what you're expected to believe. News is sorted into three letterboxes in your own personal post office—false flags, disinformation or misinformation. After a while you get pretty good at spotting the sleight of hand. You know the tricks, the fades and the misdirection. You learn how it works, and once you know that, you see through the act. After the performance, you can figure out who wrote the script. So to answer your question, yeah, I saw the news about the fire at the refugee camp, but I don't know the real story. Maybe after you go back, you could let me know what really happened there. Because I'd like to know."

The beginning of a smile bloomed into a full one.

"Thank you for that."

Calvino shrugged. Part of his therapy was to avoid watching or reading the news. The doctor had ordered a mental rest from the constant barrage of violent images that the news delivered.

"I can understand why you're in a hurry to get back. You knew the people."

The undercurrent of distrust she'd felt upon her arrival at their meeting shifted somewhat. She thought Calvino might be open to listening to what she had to offer.

"It's true. I knew them by name. I wouldn't be here now if I could have caught an earlier flight."

Being aware of what had happened the previous day and being there on the ground were two different states of being.

"A refugee camp burnt to the ground," she said. "No one has a confirmed count. The numbers might reach a hundred dead. Hundreds more burnt. Many more are in a state of shock. The survivors have all lost loved ones. Children..."

She paused and couldn't finish the sentence.

"More than two thousand people have nowhere to sleep or cook. They have nothing but the clothes on their back. Everything was destroyed. Everything, Mr. Calvino."

He watched as tears clouded her eyes.

"I'm sorry."

"'Sorry' is a small English word. And small words like 'sorry' are sounds that disappear into the noise of an ordinary person's day. For the people in the camp, they are burying their dead."

She stopped talking and concentrated on opening a new email. She toggled through a dozen attached photographs.

"Give me a moment," she said.

Calvino watched as she sipped her coffee, looking at the photographs of flames, billows of thick, black smoke, masses of people dressed in sweatshirts. A young, thin father wearing a gray baseball cap holding his baby, its head covered with a pink hat. Hundreds of people behind them.

"I've been getting pictures since last night," Judy said.

"That explains why you look like you haven't slept."

It also explained why she'd been absorbed by what was on her iPad screen—a feed of images had been coming through as she sat across from Calvino.

"How does anyone sleep?"

She hadn't looked up. Shaking her head, she scrolled through the latest batch of photographs from the camp.

Calvino knew that volunteer refugee workers experienced the front lines, bumping up against misery without escape, the desperation of people whose lives were in free fall. They burnt out after a few months, a year or maybe a couple of years. It was only a matter of time. One day they found they couldn't stop crying. They saw things that weren't there. Heard things underneath the silence. Calvino understood that empty space, a place without enough kick room to break free from the wide-open jaws of the dark whale.

"You asked me to meet you about a missing person," she said.

"I want to show you a photograph. Tell me if you recognize the woman."

Calvino took his iPad from his briefcase and opened up the folder with the photos of Jane Doe. He slid the device across the table, lining it up next to Judy's. Calvino thought about the old days when he had showed people actual physical photos. Now it was a file with dozens of scans. To survive, a Bangkok private eye needed to adapt to the times. He'd known that when he slipped into the anonymity of a coffee shop, most of the customers would be hunched over their tablets and smart phones. A private eye could blend right in using his own electronic device, showing photos of a dead woman without raising an eyebrow from someone at a nearby table.

"Why would I recognize her?" she asked, her eyes narrowing as she stared at the folder and looked up at him.

"Scroll through the pictures. Then I'll take you to the airport."

She stared at him for a few seconds.

"Okay, I'll have a look. But you don't need to take me to the airport."

"I have a car. It's Songkran. You won't find a taxi. You're almost dry. You should try to stay that way for your flight."

Judy looked at the pictures of Jane Doe. Calvino set up a facial recognition test. Anyone looking at a photograph of someone they recognized reacted by sending a set of visual signals that translated as *I know that face; I know this person.* Liars who denied the recognition counted on others not picking up the signals. Like most skills, the reading of reflex reactions could be learnt. With someone like Innes it might be possible, with years of training as a high-level hired gun negotiator, to control the automatic responses, override the built-in giveaways in the subtle changes in the position of the eyes, the jaw and the lips, and the movement of the whole body.

Calvino carefully studied Judy's face as she looked at the headshot of Jane Doe. What he hadn't expected to find were signs of personal recognition.

"Do you recognize her?" asked Calvino.

She puffed air into her cheeks, exhaled, repeated the process, scrolling through more of the JPEGs.

"She might be a girl from my camp, called Mi Swe," she said, looking away from the iPad, her eyes drawn to the water throwing in the street below.

Calvino followed her gaze. A pickup in low gear prowled the street, the back loaded with barrels of water and a half dozen soaked kids with white-powdered faces, targeting anything that moved. Water shot from the back of the pickup, hitting men, women and children, and the bands on the street returned fire. Ice water with chunks of ice hurled through the sky. The escalation of the Songkran water war began with ice and ended in the fire of Mekhong whiskey.

"Might be? You're sure that you don't recognize her?"

"It looks like..." she said, her teeth touching her lower lip as she paused. "There's something strange about the face. When someone is sleeping they look different. But like I said, it might be Mi Swe."

"You're going back to the camp. You'll need to tell her family."

"If it is Mi Swe, her mother, father and brother were killed in the fire at the camp. Her sister's alive. That's how I know."

She sought to read Calvino's reaction as he stared at her, not knowing how to play it forward.

"The girl in the photos isn't sleeping. She's dead."

Judy touched the bridge of her nose with her right hand as her eyes filled with tears.

"Dead?"

She left the thought hanging and looked away to the street below.

"How did she die?"

She sipped the coffee and reopened her iPad. Having found what she was looking for, she turned the tablet around for Calvino to look at the image on the screen.

"This is Mi Swe's sister."

Calvino saw a face that looked very much like Jane Doe.

"They look like twins."

Judy swallowed back a sob, shaking her head and laughing and crying at the same time. People at other tables stared at her, wondering what the farang had said to cause such suffering.

"Mon Hla is a year older. Is, or was. I don't know what tense I'm in. It's like a nightmare. Look behind Mon Hla. That's the refugee camp in Mae Hong Son. That's what it looked like before the fire."

The camp, Mi Swe and most of her family had all ceased to exist. All that remained to clutch onto were a few memories—a mental photo album of a smile, laughter, the small acts of kindness and grace. Death and fire had closed the album, leaving images frozen in the past like flies in amber.

Calvino touched her hand.

"Are you okay?"

"I am not okay," she said.

The grief swelled inside her. He'd seen this expression of sorrow a hundred times before as a relative, a spouse or a friend felt the sudden jolt that death left behind as a calling card.

"You wanted to meet me and tell me Mi Swe was dead? How did you know she came from my refugee camp?" she asked, using a paper napkin to tab her eyes.

Calvino opened another JPEG on his iPad.

"I didn't. But I had this," he said.

On his iPad screen, Mi Swe's blue JAI ankle tattoo appeared.

"Did Mi Swe have a tattoo on her ankle?" he asked.

"She might have had one. Tattoos are a new fashion. Old people don't get it. Why are you asking me?"

She sat back, arms folded, shaking her head.

"The initials in the tattoo match the first letters of your three names."

Her head snapped up from the screen.

"So you didn't know she came from my refugee camp?"

"I had no idea. The police have no idea who she is. Or that she came from a refugee camp."

"Do they know who killed her?"

Calvino shook his head, noting that he hadn't said Jane Doe had been murdered.

"They're investigating a few leads," he said, looking at the photo of Mon Hla. "To answer your question, they don't have a clue."

Her head bent at a slight angle, and a shaft of light streaming through a window highlighted her blonde hair. The Skytrain ran past in a blur outside the window. She watched till it disappeared from view.

"Are you the man in Bangkok who bought Mi Swe?" asked Judy.

"What makes you think that?" asked Calvino.

A crooked smile made him look, in that instant, like a stroke victim. He'd been accused of many things, but buying illegal immigrants for sexual slavery had never been on the list of his crimes of passion and profit.

"That you set this meeting up. You have Mi Swe's picture. You want something. The way you looked at Mon Hla. The way men look at a woman they're involved with or want to buy. I saw you staring at Mon Hla's photo. Men can't help give themselves away when they look at a woman."

"I had no idea Mi Swe was Burmese from one of the refugee camps."

He looked up from the photo.

Judy studied his eyes, and said, "Not just one of the camps. The one in Mae Hong Son that's completely destroyed."

120

Her tone had turned harsh, judgmental, and caused Calvino to wonder what he had done, if anything, to set off her sudden burst of hostility.

"Did I say or do something?" he asked.

"It was the way you looked at Mon Hla. The way men look at beautiful women. Disgusting," she said.

"She reminded me of someone I knew in Burma. Nothing more. Tell me about Mon Hla's family and the fire."

"Mon Hla helped out at the camp clinic. She told one of my colleagues from Holland that a helicopter dropped a phosphorus bomb. They were attacked. Someone started the fire deliberately."

"Maybe they're related?" asked Calvino.

An impatient expression crossed her face.

"I already told you that Mi Swe and Mon Hla are sisters."

"Not that connection. This is something different. Might there be something to connect Mi Swe's murder and the fire?"

She searched his eyes to see if he was being serious or playing a game.

"What kind of connection?"

"I don't know. People, events and things can have all kinds of invisible wires connecting them in strange, non-obvious ways. I'm asking you for your opinion based on what you've seen, heard and read. Like you asked me if I 'bought' her. You were making an association. Not the right one. A minute ago, you thought you'd found a link that might make sense of why I stared at your photo of Mi Swe's sister. Like you I'm trying to make sense of Mi Swe's world. We share a common purpose. From what you've told me, she was sold to someone in Bangkok. Maybe a farang, maybe a Thai. But that's a good start. It would be better to wind back to the beginning. Tell me about her family. How old was Mi Swe?"

"She's eighteen, nineteen."

"Her sister, Mon Hla, how old is she?"

"Twenty."

"The family didn't try to sell the sister to someone in Bangkok?"

"No."

"Was there a reason one sister was sold and not the other?"

"I don't know."

Short, clipped answers. Calvino recognized them as the same order as the ones he'd spit out during the police interrogation. He decided to roll the conversation back to confidence building.

"You've volunteered at the camp for how long?"

"Six months. Not that long. But long enough to know most of the people living there."

She hated the word "volunteered," as if what she did was just show up and supervise. She worked as a nurse, one of two for two thousand people. No one volunteered for living in the middle of that scale of misery.

"You met Mi Swe?"

He was asking to see if she'd lie.

"Never. Mon Hla showed me pictures of her sister and the family."

Judy nodded, sipped her coffee, holding the mug with both hands.

"Mi Swe left two years before I arrived at the camp. I know her family and her cousins. I think that's her picture. I can't remember. At least, not a hundred percent."

He liked her honesty about the past. Most people were dead certain what had happened in the past even when they weren't present. For them it was enough to believe the stories of those who had been there.

Earlier she'd had tears welling in her eyes as she'd looked at Mi Swe's photos, her face shaped in the pattern of someone who grieves upon seeing the body of someone they know. A few minutes later Judy wasn't sure if the girl in the picture was Mi Swe or some other girl who looked like her. Calvino's frustration deepened.

"When you get back to the camp, talk to Mon Hla. I'll email you some photographs. Ask her to confirm that this is her sister. Will you do that for me?"

"You're asking a lot," said Judy.

"Wouldn't you want to know if your sister had died?"

"It's chaos at the camp. You don't understand the situation."

Calvino slowly shook his head.

"It was a long shot, my asking you for some help in finding the person who killed Mon Hla's sister," said Calvino, softly. "But you're too busy. That's okay. It happens."

"I'll ask Mon Hla about Mi Swe. That's all I can do."

"And ask if she knows anything about the tattoo on the ankle. I'll email a photo of it to you."

Judy raised an eyebrow. He opened the Jane Doe photo folder and dozens of other tiny JPEGs appeared on the screen like tiny lights side by side in infinite rows.

"You didn't see all of the pictures," he said.

He opened another photo of the JAI tattoo.

"Ask her about this."

On the drive to the airport Judy talked about her training as a nurse in Norway. Medical careers ran in her family—her father a doctor, her mother a nurse. She had witnessed her first autopsy at ten years old. Her mother supported her decision to volunteer in a refugee camp in Thailand. As Calvino parked at the old Don Mueang Airport, she reached back and lifted a small carry-on bag from the backseat. She opened the car door, stopped and looked back.

"One thing I wanted to ask you."

"Ask."

"You found me because of the tattoo?"

Calvino looked at her as the door opened and she moved to get out.

"One with your initials—J-A-I," he said, punching each letter.

"It means heart in Thai," she said with the newcomer's confidence, hinting that she had something to teach Calvino.

"That's good to know," he said.

She looked at him, trying to see if he was mocking her.

"I will phone you tonight," he said.

"I can't promise anything."

Calvino understood the hedge. Judy was going into something like a war zone, not knowing the circumstances.

"Tell Mon Hla I feel *hen jai*," he said—Thai for give her comfort and compassion. "And ask her one question: does she know the girl in the photograph? I've attached a couple of photos in an email. Is that her sister? And if it is, I want to know who bought her sister. I want that man's name."

"Mon Hla's lost her family. Don't put me in a difficult position."

"The Thais say, *lam baak jai*. It will be uncomfortable to ask her. But wouldn't you want to know if that loss included a sister? Even if it tore my heart apart, I'd want to know."

She closed the car door and walked away with her carry-on. She didn't look back. Calvino wondered if that was the way she dealt with disturbing, conflicting emotions. And it might point to the cause of his own troubles. He'd been unable to stop himself from looking back at the murders in Rangoon, the bombing in Bangkok.

Nothing was more confused in Thailand than the heart, a torrential storm of hearts, good ones, black ones, hot ones, cold ones. *Jai* pointed in one direction—to matters defined by the heart. And in Thailand that was everything.

FIFTEEN

JUDY DIDN'T PHONE. Instead she sent an SMS: *Mon Hla says photo is her sister, Ploy. More later.*

Calvino typed a reply: *Tell her I am sorry.*

He stared at his message. Not Mi Swe, but Ploy, a Thai name. He tried to make sense of the names. His message seemed too much and too little. He deleted it and typed again. *Phone me. Sao jai*—Sad-hearted. He sent it.

Twenty minutes later she replied: *She's lost her whole family. No time. Maybe later. Sia jai. Judy.*

She'd nailed her sadness perfectly in Thai, thought Calvino. Not too bad for six months in the country.

When was this time called "later"? Calvino asked himself this question as he sat alone, waiting for another message. Several minutes passed, and Calvino eventually busied himself. He used the time to download dozens of images from what was left of the smoldering Mae Hong Son refugee camp. Fire cleanses, they say. Fire clears away the undergrowth and renews the soi with ashes.

He closely examined each of the photographs. The images had been taken by reporters, NGOs and locals who'd gone to witness the devastation. The age of digital cameras and cell phones had made "what happened" a matter of record. Why it had happened and who had caused it to happen remained as much mysteries as they had since the beginning of time.

Not a single hut had survived, leaving behind a ghostly outline drawn with gray mounts of ash. He thought of the ground zero moonscapes of World War I battlefields, with the trees stripped of branches and leaves, some of them no more than skinny, shattered poles. A shirtless man in black baggy trousers and sandals standing in front of corrugated sheets, leaning at odd angles, stacked in piles, the intense heat of the fire having twisted and bent the sheets into objects of utter desolation. The computer screen filled with an aerial shot of what was left of the camp. From a thousand feet above, it didn't look like anyone had ever lived in that place. What remained was a uniformly gray fine powder, like the contents of a giant ashtray. One official said a helicopter had dropped a spark on the camp. He was quickly transferred. After that the authorities reported no contradictions of what had caused the fire; they said the preliminary investigation produced evidence that the fire had resulted from the careless use of a gas cooking stove. A cooking accident had caused the firestorm.

The bamboo huts, the two clinics, the camp hospital, the warehouses—a community for Burmese refugees seeking shelter from political forces larger than themselves—had all vanished. Not a single bamboo structure remained, and scattered among the ruins was a lone brick dwelling. Why hadn't someone noticed that one of brick structures appeared to have been specifically targeted? Or had it been incinerated in the firestorm? He wondered. He looked out the window at the traffic jammed in front of Queen Sirikit Center. People in the cars were returning to their homes, families, dinners, TVs and beds. Could they imagine returning to find all they possessed and loved reduced to rubble? A cooking accident, the authorities said.

Looking at the photos, Calvino thought about the refugees who had died at the camp. The refugees had lived no better than herd animals. Livestock fenced in, largely forgotten, waiting for a future elsewhere. They had found their future in fire and ash. Now they were news, where they'd remain until the next disaster flung them to the back pages and finally out of the press altogether.

He created a slide show on his computer and sat back, letting each frame freeze and change after a minute. After a photo of Mon Hla, Calvino inserted images of Mya Kyaw Thein, Rob Osborne and Kati, sweet Kati. A strong scent of cordite filled his nostrils as he stared at Kati. He wrinkled his nose and drank some wine, but the stench of cordite wasn't easily defeated. It was as heavy and strong as the night when a round from a long-barreled Colt .22 crashed through Kati's skull just above her right eye. In the next frame Mon Hla appeared, and next showed Mya with her signature Black Cat smile. He stopped the slide show and stared at Mya's photo, clicked back to Mon Hla, and then back and forth. When he looked up, he saw the twisted wreck of what had been a car scattered in pieces over a hundred-meter range along Ratchadapisek Road. Inside, two bodies charred beyond recognition—and then Mya and Yadanar reassembled into flesh and blood, breathing human beings.

There they were, in the sitting room on the sofa, talking to each other in low tones. They paid him no attention.

"I can't hear you!" Calvino, sweating, his head pounding, shouted at them.

They gave no indication of hearing him.

"You aren't real. You're from my head."

Mya Kyaw Thein turned away from Yadanar and smiled at Calvino, her head tilted to the side. She sang "My Man." It had become her theme song, the one he remembered from the first night he'd seen her at the club. Such illusions are as fragile as cut flowers, and umbrellas, rain and whiskey can't stop the inevitable withering and dying process at the heart of the impossible. The death of illusions, he thought, must be nature's way of establishing the boundary of where truth and lies meet.

He covered his ears, closed his eyes and said, "I can't hear you."

She stopped mid-song and returned her attention to Yadanar, who had opened a copy of Henry Miller's *Tropic of Cancer*. Yadanar giggled as he read a graphic passage with a vividly recalled sex scene. Rob Osborne appeared on the balcony, staring in through the window and then beating his fists against it. But Yadanar continued his reading. Disturbances between Yadanar and Rob had happened before. Mya showed no expression as the two men threatened, taunted and insulted one another in their ritual of hatred.

Calvino's heart pounded as a panic attack made his breathing shallow, irregular and rapid. He felt like he might black out. The shouting in his head then increased as if the volume had been turned up, and no amount of covering his ears could disguise it. He slowly found the strength to lift his computer and carry it across the room. One step at a time, he tried to control his breathing, using the exercises his therapist had taught him. Sweat dripped from his face onto the computer. The air conditioning made no discernible difference. It was as if his body were on fire. He told himself to keep on moving, that whatever he did, stopping wasn't an option.

He'd turned his back on the visitors, leaving them in the sitting area. They hadn't followed. That much he was grateful for as he walked across his loft to position himself as far away from them as possible. He sat on the edge of an elevated platform and stared out at the traffic, the lake, the Tobacco Monopoly grounds. Then he realized he'd forgotten his cell phone back in the sitting area. Going back to retrieve it seemed like a physical impossibility. Something very bad would happen if he went close to the visitors. He couldn't explain the feeling, but it was overpowering.

When would Judy's "later" arise? It no longer seemed important. Staying away from the visitors was all that mattered.

Calvino told himself to ignore them. Those people were dead. Gone. Buried. Nothing he could do would change that. What they were doing now was trying to change him, control him. His mind tried but couldn't control the place where he lived. They had taken over his sitting room, made it their environment. They had chased him away from the interior place where he lived and worked. Calvino returned to his computer screen. His hand shaking, he furiously sorted through a file with hundreds of photos. He found Ploy in her designer running outfit. The woman he'd found in the high grass, the woman he'd seen at the morgue, was no longer a Jane Doe.

He added her photographs to the slide show, next to the one photo Judy had given him of Mi Swe's sister, Mon Hla.

"You have a name. A Burmese name, Mi Swe. And a Thai name, Ploy," he said. "You have a sister. You had a family."

A huge sense of sadness enveloped him as he stared at her picture. He changed it for Mon Hla's photo. That didn't resolve anything as Ploy and Mon Hla could have passed for twins. Sisters in Thailand—hill tribe, Thais, Khmer and Burmese alike—could bear an uncanny resemblance. Ploy and Mon Hla had faces that were nearly interchangeable. Only Ploy's features had been shaped, modified, enhanced. The natural beauty of Mon Hla had been heightened in Ploy, as if an expert had been hired to perfect a work of art. When he saw the next photo, it was Mya in her stage clothes—black leather pants and a tight-fitting black T-shirt.

Calvino refused to run or back away. He sat on the platform near the bank of windows. He shifted his weight, trying to get comfortable, sweating inside the air–conditioned room. He breathed through his mouth. He fought against the presence of the phantom visitors. He fought the smell they trailed in with them. The pizza deliveryman who'd been attacked on his motorcycle, his girlfriend on the back, had been in the street below. Protected by the glass window, the distance to the street, he could observe and stand separate from the violence. In his loft he had no such protection. The visitors had plans for an attack. He felt they were biding their time, waiting for the opportune moment.

He prepared the only way he knew how; he slipped on a set of earphones and listened to his best friend Colonel Pratt playing John Coltrane's "My Favorite Things." It had been the song he'd played that last night at the Living Room. Mya had been on stage performing beside the Colonel. Yadanar played the piano as she sang. She owned the audience. The two of them were booked on a New York flight for their gig at the Blue Note. Nero, Calvino's cousin, had pulled off the impossible, calling in a favor, and the impossible became a three–night gig. Nero had come through big–time. They were going to the Big Apple, where Mya would take ownership of one of the toughest audiences in the world. She never got there. The audiences that never gathered to hear them went on with their lives and would never know what they'd missed. Calvino listened to the music and remembered. The experience was forever lost except for a handful of people who'd heard Mya perform in Bangkok and Rangoon.

Listening to the Colonel playing Coltrane pushed the timeline back, taking the moment back to a celebration of life, a pre–death moment, one Calvino clung to. Colonel Pratt's saxophone set up shop inside Calvino's head as he scrolled through the digital photos. He found himself looking at a continuum of one woman with slightly different expressions—but three women, who were one woman. And the visitors appeared at the opposite end of the room. He cranked up the sound until the Colonel's sax drilled deep into his brain, inhabiting it, throwing out the ghosts who sat an arm's length away. He could reach out and touch them if he wished.

An hour later, after the visitors had gone, Calvino checked his phone—he'd had four missed calls. None of them were from Judy. The first two calls were from McPhail's number. Call number three was from the Soi Cowboy bar owner Patterson Roy. And the last call was again from McPhail.

Calvino dialed McPhail's number. Before he could say anything, he caught a blast from the voice on the other end.

"Hey asshole, I thought we had a meeting tonight. Who am I talking to? It's fucking McPhail you're talking to. So where are you?"

He looked at his watch.

"I'll be there in twenty minutes."

"It can't be that important if you forgot."

"I didn't forget."

He heard McPhail arguing with someone. Another voice came on the phone.

"You are an asshole for not letting me know you're running late. McPhail said you'd clear his bar bill. I want some comfort, Calvino. He's got six chits in the cup."

"Who is this?"

"Who is this? It's Patterson. Who the fuck did you think you had a meeting with?"

"Happy New Year to you, too," Calvino said.

"Everyone is throwing water, and no one but McPhail is drinking."

"Twenty minutes," said Calvino. "I'll pay McPhail's bill."

"Don't forget your umbrella."

Patterson hung up a happy man. His main worry had been money. Calvino had eliminated his anxiety about getting paid; he could take as long as wanted.

SIXTEEN

POOLS OF NEON washed over Soi Cowboy in a continuous rainbow of dappled light, spilling into the shadows in the narrow soi and illuminating touts, enforcers, bargirls, coyote girls and a throng of farang showing up like a herd of wildebeest on a steep river bank, contemplating whether to cross. Bargirls ran water gun patrol missions, ambushing strangers on organized hit-and-run operations. With predators lurking along the fringes of the neon, the sober passersby looked nervous, but the drunks, as always, were ready to splash in and swim for it. Calvino avoided two drunks, faces caked with white talcum powder, stumbling toward him, hair dripping. A group of Chinese in cargo pants and polo shirts rushed past him like a precision team on a mission, running from a three bargirl hit squad who fired their water guns as they ran. One of the bargirls shot him in the back with a water rifle. He'd dressed for the water gun battlefield in shorts and a New York Yankees T-shirt, securing his wallet in a plastic zippered pouch hanging around his neck, thus blending in with the other members of the Songkran red-light tribe.

For the duration of Songkran the whole street converted into a hot and wet-bodied tribal zone, expanding the scale of public lewdness and drunkenness, and escalating water gun massacres to epic proportions. Lost in the Soi Cowboy mayhem was the seed of a Thai tradition—splashing water to wash away sins to celebrate the Buddhist New Year. The thrills of the water battles were intense enough to let them forget about the sin-cleansing part of the festival.

Most of the bars on the street had gone corporate. Patterson Roy ran one of the last of old-fashioned Soi Cowboy watering holes, where a handful of long-term expats dropped enough cash to support the bar on the understanding that outsiders weren't welcome.

McPhail sipped on his seventh gin and tonic as he sat on a stool outside Mama, Don't Call. The name had come from one of Patterson's old girlfriends, who always hit him up for a loan that would never be repaid. He believed it was pressure from the mother. They'd fight, she'd say, "Mama, don't call," and he'd give her money. He figured the expression helped her rake in the dough, so it might help him to do the same. McPhail had been watching the action on the soi. Next thing he knew, Calvino materialized in front of him, coming in on his blind side. McPhail jumped as if someone had taken a swing at him.

"Where've you been, Vinny?" he asked.

"Easy, Ed."

Calvino lowered himself onto the stool next to him.

"Where's Patterson?"

"Inside. It seems Mama calls his new live-in girlfriend all the time. He fucking regrets the bar name. It's come back to bite him in the ass. I told him to rename it Knuckles—The Place Where Knuckle Draggers and Knuckleheads Exchange Bodily Fluids."

A waitress took Calvino's drink order.

"It'd be expensive to get all of that in neon," said Calvino.

Patterson Roy came out a couple of minutes later carrying Calvino's Jack Daniel's and soda.

"I thought it'd be you ordering the Jack Daniel's," Patterson said. "You look like you could use a drink."

"What's up, Patterson?"

"You remember Nui?"

Calvino nodded. He'd bar-fined her twice.

"She's quit the bar."

"She's marrying the guy from Berlin," said Calvino.

"She told you?"

Patterson was upset at being excluded from the information loop, and humiliated that a customer knew more than he did about one of his girls.

"She asked my advice."

"Nui was my most popular bargirl."

"Did you expect her to stay until retirement?" asked McPhail.

Patterson stared at his drink, glanced up with a sigh and watched foot traffic passing on the street.

"It's a tough business," said Calvino, as the potential customers failed to give Mama, Don't Call a second look.

"Thank God for the 100 milligram little blue pills, or I'd be out of business," he said.

He faked a punch to Calvino's shoulder.

"You look like you're all tensed up. Relax. I've got a couple of new girls. When you want some company, I'll arrange it. They might not be up to Nui's quality, but they'll help you make it through the night."

Calvino removed the chits from McPhail's ribbed bamboo cup, which looked like a pencil holder, and handed the seven slips of paper along with two thousand baht to the waitress.

"Keep the change," he said.

Smiling, Patterson said, "And call your mama. Tell her you found the rent from a farang *jai dee*."

"Thanks, buddy," said McPhail. "Patterson's got some information on your boy, Akash."

Patterson slid onto the stool next to Calvino.

"What have you got for me, Patterson?"

"First, I heard he's not Indian."

"He's not Norwegian," said McPhail from the other side of Calvino.

"I never said that."

"Why would anyone fake being an Indian in Bangkok?" asked McPhail.

"McPhail, you are a fucking redneck," said Patterson.

"Thanks, buddy. I love you, too. So does Vinny."

Calvino eyed his Jack Daniel's and slowly raised it and drank.

"What have you heard, Patterson?"

"The guy who sells nuts on the soi is a Rohingya. He's from the same tribe as the ones the Burmese are slaughtering. He's probably a member of their top one percent. That's from selling a few bags of nuts each night."

"Get out of here," said McPhail.

"His papers say he's Indian," said Calvino.

Patterson laughed.

"His papers! His fucking papers are fake."

"What else have you heard?"

Patterson leaned in close and murmured into Calvino's ear. McPhail strained to listen on the other side, but the noise from the punters and girls on the soi made that impossible.

"He's involved in some kind of underground illegal migrant smuggling ring. Like those asshole Northern abolitionists in the US who helped escaped slaves cross the border into Canada."

"Akash has been smuggling Rohingya?"

"He's in competition with local fishing boats, factories and rubber plantations, who are in the business of increasing the profit margin by using unpaid labor. I hear he's found a way to get them out of the country. Malaysia, Indonesia, the places where Muslims are running things."

"Smuggling?" asked McPhail, hearing a fragment of what Patterson said.

Calvino thought the chances of a Soi Cowboy nut vendor from India or Burma running any kind of successful smuggling operation were about as likely as converting a steam engine into a 3-D printer.

"You sure about this?" asked Calvino.

"If you don't believe me, ask him," said Patterson. "Maybe he killed that girl because she was going to turn him in."

"Why would she do that?" asked Calvino.

"Mama might have called and said he had no choice but to do what Mama asked."

Calvino called the waitress over and ordered a Johnnie Walker Black for Patterson.

"What else have you got for me?"

"Calvino, has anyone told you that sometimes you sound like a bargirl?"

Calvino rattled the ice in his glass and then raised it to Patterson.

"Mainly to people who sound just like bar owners."

In the neon jungle what you want and what you get depends on opportunity, luck, timing, a good story and lots of cash. Another group of farang wildebeest were pulled inside the bar by determined hostesses. The three men watched them struggle like astronauts sucked through a ventilation hatch into the vacuum of deep space.

Patterson picked up his drink and drifted back into the bar, saying, "I've got to take care of these guys."

He let the curtain drop behind him as he followed the last customer inside.

McPhail lit a cigarette only to have a water gun turn it into a soggy mess.

"You got what you needed from Patterson?"

He stared at the transformation of his cigarette into a smudge of wet paper and clumps of wet tobacco. He threw it in the street, but it mostly stuck to his hand, which he wiped on the side of his jeans.

"He said Akash isn't who we think he is," Calvino said.

Judging how McPhail had handled the vandalism of his cigarette, Calvino judged that his friend was drunk. He'd been losing his humor the last half hour.

"Not who we think he is? Well, that makes him fit right into this place. What's your guy doing? Smuggling illegals? Is he selling dope? Children?"

"Patterson says he's involved with shipping Rohingya out of Thailand."

"Akash may sell nuts, but Patterson is fucking nuts. That skinny little Indian guy couldn't smuggle a soi dog off the street without getting caught."

McPhail was a good judge of character, but seven gin and tonics hadn't exactly put him at his best judging self. Calvino squeezed McPhail's shoulder.

"You know what's nuts? Someone firebombed a Burmese refugee camp in Mae Hong Son. Jane Doe came from that camp. She has a name, Ed: Ploy. She had a family. Except for a sister, they're dead as of yesterday."

McPhail beamed.

"At least you've got a name. You know where she's from."

"That's all I have."

"What you've got is a Rohingya who is a human smuggler for a client. If the dead girl is Burmese, man, they're going to throw the book at him. It starts to look like some kind of political shit."

"The cops have already done that."

"Then get ready for them to throw the rest of the library at him."

A customer staggered out of the bar with red paint dripping from his head and neck. At first it looked like blood. McPhail reached out and touched the wet red ooze and smelled it.

"Paint? What happened to you?" asked McPhail. "Are you some kind of painter who's been in an accident?"

"Ed, don't you recognize me?"

"Andy? What the fuck happened to your head?"

"I got caught in the cross fire of a couple of *katoeys* in the toilet. Then someone walked in with a bucket of paint. He threw it at one of the katoeys, who jumped out of the way. And as you can see, I didn't get out of the way."

"Do you mind if I take a photo?"

"Why?" asked Andy.

"I want to post it on Facebook."

He snapped several photos of Andy.

When McPhail turned back, Calvino had left. He looked down the street for him. First he scanned the foot traffic heading toward the Asoke end. No Calvino. He turned to look at the crowd throwing water at the Soi 23 end. Calvino had vanished. The street quickly became a battlefield again, the water gun combatants circling, jumping and running battles, and soon the battles got real personal. He looked through the photos of Andy. It had been a good night on the soi.

SEVENTEEN

CALVINO STOOD AT the Indian tailor's shop near the Nana end of Sukhumvit, realizing he'd walked past his destination. For many years the landmark for the Check Inn 99 Club had been a dwarf in a red vest. He'd vanished a few years ago. Calvino retraced his steps winding his way through a parade of women in burka pushing strollers behind men in white thawbs until he stopped at the long entryway. No dwarf. Just a sign that said "Check Inn 99." Entering the passage, he walked past the large, old-fashioned globes hanging from the ceiling and the walls. The muffled sound of a saxophone drifted in from the door ahead of him.

Calvino's impressions paralleled those of Darwin on the Galapagos Islands: "The black rocks heated by the rays of the vertical sun, like a stove, give to the air a close and sultry feeling. The plants also smell unpleasantly," and marine iguanas were "hideous-looking creatures, of a dirty black color, stupid and sluggish in their movements."

Instead of black rocks, the place had wicker chairs and tables and a stage, a couple of stools and speakers and sound equipment preserved from another age. It was mid-Sunday afternoon, and Colonel Pratt stood on the stage playing a mournful Dexter Gordon take on "Our Man in Paris," accompanied by a black guitar player named Billy Clarke, a grandfather who'd lived in Paris most of his life. (Later Calvino learned that Clarke had once played with Gordon there some thirty years before. During a break Gordon had told him that his grandfather on his mother's side had won the Medal of Honor for fighting in the Spanish-American War. He'd been proud of that, not that it had changed the life of a black man living in America.)

One iguana-like customer sat in the back, drinking double shots of rum, his red-rimmed eyes staring into empty space. There were no other customers. Calvino sat at a table near the stage, doubling the size of the audience. Colonel Pratt nodded toward him, and Billy reacted with a smile suggesting that things were looking up. "Hey, Vincent, welcome," said Billy from the stage, picking his guitar. "We've got one more Dexter Gordon tune, and then we're taking a break." Colonel Pratt never missed a beat, eyes half-closed as he worked the keys on the gold-plated saxophone, his cheeks puffed out, swaying his head, his lips on the mouthpiece.

After they finished, Calvino applauded. The iguana in the back sat quietly, lidless eyes staring ahead in the dim light. Billy Clarke and Colonel Pratt came to Calvino's table and sat down.

"The audience picks up later in the afternoon," said Billy.

"Glad you could make it," said Colonel Pratt.

At the same time he'd been surprised to see Calvino walk in. Stay away from jazz clubs, his doctor had recommended. Mya and Rob had been members of a jazz band called Monkey Nose. The idea was to break the associations with Mya. Live jazz joints ranked high on his list of hallucination inducers.

But Calvino felt nothing strange there. He saw nothing out of the ordinary. "You pinch the devil before he pinches you," his father had told him when he was a kid.

Playing to an empty club, Calvino knew, isn't a performer's worst nightmare. Not playing at all always retains the top spot on the nightmare list. For the Colonel, the absence of an audience was a reminder that since he'd had returned from his assignment in Burma, his career both at the police department and on the musical stage had plummeted into a void as deep as the Mariana Trench. He couldn't have stopped his colleagues from working over Calvino if he'd tried. They'd damaged Calvino partly just to show the Colonel that they could.

The fact was, Colonel Pratt couldn't draw an audience for a Sunday afternoon jazz session. His name wasn't big enough. Inside the professional zone where his name once carried weight, it no longer worked the old magic. The anonymous and the ostracized share the same fate—the loss of respect, authority and place. A wall of silence separated him from his colleagues and friends. The Check Inn 99 Club with Billy on Sunday afternoons was one of the few places that Colonel Pratt the musician had left.

"Maybe you two have some business," said Billy. "Besides, I need to take a piss."

Billy left them at the table.

"I need to talk with Akash again," Calvino said.

"That's difficult," said Colonel Pratt.

Calvino knew that when a Thai says "difficult," he usually means impossible.

"He's got a right to legal counsel."

"He does. But that right doesn't include a farang ex-lawyer."

Calvino saw that that line of reasoning was leading in the wrong direction and shifted his approach.

"What if I told you that Jane Doe has a name? Ploy. She's Burmese."

Colonel Pratt straightened up in his chair.

"Burmese? Are you sure about this information?"

Calvino smiled.

"Yeah, eighty percent."

"Why not a hundred percent?"

"Because that's not the world we live in."

At eighty percent, he'd passed along to Colonel Pratt information that would give him a lot of face inside the department. No one had a clue to Jane Doe's identity, and working Akash over hadn't produced any useful information. Either he was as tough as one of those Indians who walks over hot coals to lie on a bed of nails, or he didn't know her name.

"I can't give you my source," said Calvino. "Not yet. First, I need to talk to Akash. "

Wheels turned behind Colonel Pratt's eyes as he stared at Calvino.

"Ploy's not a Burmese name," he said. "You're saying the dead girl is Burmese and not Thai?"

Calvino leaned over the table.

"Pratt, I'm saying that all Akash has between him and a one-way ticket to death row is evidence that someone else was involved," replied Calvino. "He didn't kill her. Let me talk to him again."

"'Nature teaches beasts to know their friends,'" said Colonel Pratt, quoting *Coriolanus*. "Are human beings less teachable?"

The wheels turning inside the Colonel's head had turned up the Shakespeare quote he'd been searching for. It also left him with the existential question he'd been working out as he played the Dexter Gordon piece when Calvino had walked in.

"I don't know, Pratt. We have some unfinished karma to work through on the Burma connection. Why don't we get it done? So we can both move on."

EIGHTEEN

AN OVERHEAD FAN, its blades black with grime, slowly beat the air like the wings of an ancient flying reptile. The corridors stank of sweat, urine and shit. Men's voices reverberated at a low level, with the frequent spike of a cry, a shout, a cough or a threat registering above it. A mosquito with drone-like stealth landed on Calvino's cheek. He slapped it dead and removed his hand, now streaked with a crooked red jag of his own blood. Seated across from him was Akash, skinny, dark, with sharp features, his mustache glistening with a thin sheen of sweat. His eyes burned a fiery brown adrift in a red sea. The previous day Akash had heard the news of the death sentence handed down to four Indians convicted of raping and murdering an Indian woman. The message had sunk in that cultural currents were rapidly weaving a noose around his own neck.

"Who are you, Akash?"

Calvino looked straight at Akash, seated on a plastic stool on the other side of a mesh screen. He looked confused, dazed.

"But I don't understand, Mr. Calvino. You know me. I am Akash."

"Your name isn't Akash Saru."

A bead of sweat hung from the end of Akash's nose and dropped onto the back of his hand. The whole time Akash

144

worked his jaw, moving his head from side to side as if it were no longer attached to his spine.

"The girl you found dead was Burmese. I think you knew her. You'd arranged to meet her. Then what? You found her dead?"

Calvino let him absorb the implications of what he was saying. Akash twitched his nose, ran his hand across his mustache. He looked at the floor.

"Look at me, Akash. You're not Indian. You're from Burma. You're going to tell me the story of why you went to the Tobacco Monopoly Land to meet her. You weren't living there. That was a lie. No way you could pull that off. A dark-skinned Burmese, the Thais would spot you. Remember, if you want to get out of here, you need to help me. Start by telling me your real name. Then I want to hear why you went to meet Mi Swe. Or maybe you knew her by her Thai name, Ploy."

Akash looked like a sailor trapped in a submarine as depth charges above his head exploded ever closer. He sat back, arms crossed. Sweat rolled down his face, pooling on his chin before dripping on the floor. He rolled his head one way, then another, checking who was near him and behind him. A CCTV camera recorded the inmate's position from a perch on the far concrete wall. No attempt was made to disguise it. Inside prison the inmates understood they had utterly surrendered all rights to dignity, privacy or security. He was basically fucked, knowing that no position was comfortable; some were just less uncomfortable than others. And he had to choose one. Some tiny fragment of pride or fear held him in silence.

Calvino was on his feet.

"You don't want to talk. Fine. Whoever you are, you're on your own, and good luck."

He slipped the *Bangkok Post* across to him, with its front-page coverage of the four Indians sentenced to be hanged for rape and murder.

"Have a read, Akash. This will be your story if you don't tell me the truth."

"Deen Alam," he said. "That's my name."

Calvino sat back in the chair. The prisoner, who could not have been more than five-six when standing, strained himself not to fall apart. Calvino wondered how it was that he had not seen before that this man was a Rohingya, not an Indian. Probably it was for the same reason the cops had accepted the forged papers; no one looked beyond the surface appearance. Reality was a series of sideward glances. Selling counterfeit Indian documents wasn't hard for locals to make a reasonable living from, made easier by the fact that a large number of Indian documents were counterfeit to begin with. In skin tone, India had the full color chart from white to black. There was a caricature Indian, but people had long ago stopped confusing that with the range of Indians they saw on the streets in Bangkok.

"I am a Rohingya. I fled the attacks inside Rakhine State. It's in Myanmar. "

"I know where Rakhine State is, Deen."

Calling him by his real name for the first time changed a lot of things for Calvino. He was no longer the Indian, but a Muslim who'd survived a pogrom and escaped to Thailand. He'd been a lucky man. The odds of a Rohingya not getting caught and locked up in a refugee hellhole of a camp seemed about the same as the chances of landing a single-engine airplane on the moon.

"Are there others like you in Bangkok?" asked Calvino.

"You read the papers. Many have escaped from detention. Yes, there are others like me."

Rohingya like him migrated with phony identity papers and bribes. He watched his client's eyes dip to the floor in

146

time to see a large rat walk past—not run but walk, as if he owned the place.

"Ploy. The girl you were supposed to meet. Tell me about her."

Deen Alam started slowly.

"She was Karen. A Christian. I was told she wanted to leave Thailand and needed help."

"Who told you to help Ploy?"

The Rohingya shrugged.

"I don't have a name."

When he saw Calvino's expression, Deen Alam shifted on his chair.

"It was Lek, Nit or Noi. Something like that. I don't remember."

Calvino's suspicion increased. Deen Alam, or Akash—the pseudonym was the one that stuck in Calvino's mind—was evasive, his eyes giving him away each time he lied.

"You told this person that you could help Ploy? Isn't it strange that a Burmese Karen would ask a Rohingya for help? It sounds like a bullshit story."

He shrugged, nostrils twitching.

"Not so hard to believe, Mr. Calvino. She was a Karen and a human being. That's enough. I never had the pleasure to meet her, not when she was alive, and if I had, I would have said, 'It is my duty to see you safely out of Thailand.'"

Calvino didn't have the time to listen to speeches.

"You're making no sense. You went to meet a girl you never met or talked to. Was this a blind date?"

"That's it exactly. She'd came to me through my contact."

Calvino saw that his hook had lodged, and it was time to let the fish run before reeling him in. He let the questions about Deen Alam's contact ride.

"Ploy wasn't the first person you'd been asked to smuggle out of the country. You've done this before," said Calvino.

"Helping Rohingya get out of Thailand and the occasional Burmese—does that sum up your side business?"

Deen Alam smiled, puffed out his chest.

"It is not a business. It is my solemn duty to my people."

Patterson Roy's source had been accurate. The Soi Cowboy nut vendor was a cog in the clockwork of refugee smuggling. How he fit into the network was of less interest to Calvino than figuring out who had connected him to Ploy. Somewhere along that road was the person who was with her when she died.

"Ploy was Burmese, not Karen. Your contact lied, Deen. What was she to you?"

"Someone who needed help."

"You did it for the money."

His shoulders shook and he shuddered, more sweat rolling down his cheeks.

"I was paid. With the money, I could help rescue six of my people and get them into Malaysia."

"You're a humanitarian who doesn't care about the money?"

Calvino tapped his pen on the side of his notebook. He looked up at Deen Alam. A few minutes were left before the guard would come in and take him back to his cell.

"If she was loaded, she didn't need you. She goes to any travel agent, buys a ticket and gets on a plane."

"My friend said she had no travel documents."

"Did you know her family? Were you in contact with them?"

"No, I didn't personally know her. How could I know her family?"

"Did you know she was from a refugee camp?"

That question slowed him, twisted his expression so that his lower lip stuck out, touching the edge of his mustache.

148

One of those "tells" that Calvino imagined signaled the anxiety level was rising inside his skull.

"No," he said in a raspy voice just above a whisper.

"If you'd known, would it have made a difference?" asked Calvino, pushing him down the refugee camp road to see where it would end.

"It was a business deal. She wasn't Buddhist Burmese. Her people weren't the ones killing my people. Besides, she had money. People in refugee camps don't have that kind of money. Believe me, they have nothing. I think you are getting bad information."

"Give me the name of the contact between you and Ploy."

"I won't burn him. He's my friend."

"Burn him? From what pirated TV show did you pick up that phrase? Focus on the word 'friend' and ask yourself if this guy really is your friend? He's the reason you are sitting in jail, and he's free to walk the street. Your friend isn't facing the death penalty in Thailand. You are. Don't you think I should have a talk with him?"

Deen Alam sighed, a long, despairing expulsion of air. He hadn't thought of it that way until Calvino had made it starkly clear. Still, he refused to believe in the possibility that his friend would have betrayed him. The Prisoner's Dilemma only worked when both men were in separate rooms, both getting deals to turn on the other. Whoever the friend was, he was on the outside.

"He will stand by me when it comes to it. I have confidence."

Calvino spotted the sweet point in the Prisoner's Dilemma game—when one man declares his confidence in his partner. By merely raising the issue, he was questioning his belief.

"How's that confidence worked out so far?"

He started to weep, sobbing deeply.

"Are you going to tell the police my true name?"

"You gave it to me as your lawyer. So, no, I won't tell them. What you can do for me, Deen, is tell me the name of this broker who is your best friend," said Calvino.

Calvino leaned in with his nose touching the mesh screen.

"He doesn't have to know where I got the information."

"Please continue to call me Akash."

Calvino cocked his head to the side.

"Does it really matter?"

Two minutes later the guards came in and yanked Akash Saru off the stool and dragged him away. He looked back, holding the *Bangkok Post* with the story about the hanging sentence.

"Please come back soon," he managed to say.

He vanished with far less dignity than the rat that had earlier exited through the same door.

NINETEEN

ANAL KHAN FROM Uttar Pradesh, Akash Saru's friend, lived in a hotel on a small soi in the Pratunam district. Calvino found the run-down building, whose occupants sweated through drug-fueled dreams of snakes within striking distance and authorities knocking loudly on the door to demand papers. Buildings like Anal's were home to illegal migrants who silently streamed between cheap hotels, sweatshop factories and miserable, overcrowded prisons as if they had connecting doors. Calvino had seen an identical building in Bangladesh.

Anal—the name translated as fire—lived in a room on the fifth floor. Anal's name and the appearance of the hotel made Calvino wonder if the same blueprints had been used. He recalled the Bangladeshi factory that had recently caught on fire and collapsed, killing a thousand people. Dozens burnt to death in the Mae Hong Son refugee camp. Fire and flames, destruction and rubble were on his mind as he walked into the lobby.

In the lobby an old woman sat selling fried bananas. He looked around. No elevator. The old woman smiled and nodded at the staircase with scraps of food and paper leaving a trail. Calvino climbed the stairs. By the time he'd got to the third floor, he'd worked up a sweat. Reaching the fifth floor, he stopped to catch his breath, taking in the same smells of decay, rot, urine and curry that he'd experienced in the prison corridor.

A string of people whispering in twos or threes wound down the corridor. He looked at the first door number and made his way to room 512. Burmese, Indians, Nigerians and Bangladeshis in various stages of undress—some in shorts and no shirt, others with a towel wrapped around their waist, hairy with bony ankles and barefoot. There were no women. A couple of men smoking cigarettes and talking agitatedly pressed against the walls, blocking Calvino's way.

A wall of men between him and the door he was looking for parted as he pushed through. A habit they'd learnt from Orwell's time—make way for the sahib who has been summoned to bring order out of the chaos. The door of room 512 was open. Those standing nearest to the door held a cloth over their nose and mouth. That was never a good sign.

Calvino stepped inside to find two uniformed police officers standing next to a swollen, bloated body. The torso looked like someone had inflated it with helium and soon, lighter than air, it would float up to stick against the ceiling like a child's horror house balloon. The face was black. A rope was knotted around the throat. A large brown stain covered the carpet, soaking in—the discharge of a leaking corpse left in the heat.

"What was his name?" Calvino asked one of the police officers going through the dead man's wallet.

The cop pulled out an ID card and read it in Thai to his partner: "Anal Khan. Indian national. Born in Uttar Pradesh."

"Died in Bangkok," said Calvino.

First impressions matter in both love and death. Calvino's first impression of Anal Khan was it looked like he'd hanged himself. He checked himself, though, knowing that love and death both require more reflection. Death by strangulation could be made to look like suicide, though in a dump like this one, there was no incentive to overturn the first impression. He figured the police report would take the easy way out and conclude the deceased had hanged himself. Given the circumstances of the building, suicide was a common cause of death. And there was the cultural bias. The Indian disappearing-up-the-rope trick sometimes backfired and the rope took its revenge.

"Who are you?" the uniform asked Calvino as he sifted through the cash in the dead man's wallet.

Calvino caught sight of two reds and three greens. Sufficient cash to buy two bowls of noodles from a street vendor and a large Singha beer, or the old woman's fried bananas in the lobby.

"A visitor. I'm looking for a man named Deen Alam," said Calvino. "Is that Deen?"

"No, this is Anal Khan. Look at his ID."

A grinning Anal Khan, hair combed, young and handsome, caught in a moment of happiness or joy. The image bore no resemblance to the blackened face on the bed.

The other cop stepped away from the body and walked over to Calvino.

"We know from the neighbor that Deen Alam was this man's roommate. We'd like to talk to him."

"Why's that?"

"He's not been around since this man died. He hasn't come around, for what reason? He left Anal, for what reason? Did they have a fight? We don't know. We want to ask him some questions."

"If you find him, phone me," said Calvino, giving him his name card. "I'm a private investigator, and Deen Alam stole my client's money."

The two cops examined Calvino's card and exchanged a look of incomprehension.

"You, a farang, are looking for a thief?" one of them said.

The attitude of the cops indicated they didn't want to stick around any longer than necessary. The fact they'd been dispatched at all was evidence of a prior sin, and wiping the slate clean required them to deal with the Anals of their district until their bad karma was paid back.

"That's a Thai police job," said the other.

"You can punish him. My client only wants his money."

That explanation made perfect logic to the two cops. Who wouldn't want to get their money back? Getting money was police work, but giving it back to the owners, that was better subcontracted to private investigators. The cop fingered Calvino's name card, slipping it into his shirt pocket and taking out a mask.

"This man might have been a thief."

He slipped a white paper surgical mask over his mouth and nose, adjusting the elastic around the back of his head.

"*Men chip-haay*," he said, his muffled voice echoing the Thai words for "fucking stink."

His partner nodded, putting on his mask. They were right; the place had an overpowering smell of rotten flesh.

Calvino disappeared through the crowd of confused neighbors.

"What can you tell us?" asked a skinny-chested black man with a long, gray beard.

"From the state of the body, I'd guess Anal's been dead for a couple of days."

A gasp escaped from the man's throat.

"Terrible, terrible, to die alone. No one checks on you. Until there is a bad smell."

"You did the right thing calling the police. They're handling it. You can go back to your room now."

The old man's two bony hands clasped Calvino's right hand, shaking it. Calvino had figured this was the guy with the sensitive nose, the good citizen who had anonymously alerted the police, reporting a terrible odor from room 512. Given the competition from the general rat-shit smell of the place, it must have taken some time before the smell entered the consciousness of the building's other residents.

If Calvino was right about the state of decay, Anal had died around the same time as Ploy. The two deaths must be linked, and Calvino struggled to connect the dots. Anal had arranged for Akash to pick up Ploy. She had arrived dead or been murdered earlier and her body dumped, and not long afterwards Anal had hanged from the end of a rope. Why would a man kill himself after he'd enjoyed a good payday? Maybe he'd let someone into his room to pay the money owed, and that person had decided to cut out the middleman, keep the cash and get rid of a loose end. The killer had either wanted something from Anal or wanted to silence him or to close down a competitor. Maybe the killer had gone for one reason and then changed his mind and decided Anal was a liability.

Deen Alam had lost not just a friend but an alibi. Anal had been working in the human smuggling racket with him. They were engaged in a dangerous, violent business with potentially high rewards. One member of the smuggling team was alive. Was Calvino the only one who knew that Akash Saru and Deen Alam were the same man? The fact was that under duress he'd spit out his client's real name. And unless Deen had trained as a professional actor, he had no idea that he'd sent Calvino to discover Anal dead inside his hotel room. The Indian nut seller who called himself Akash Saru was a Rohingya involved in a human smuggling case that had gone sideways. Calvino had come with questions to ask Anal. That interview wasn't going to happen. But it didn't stop him from asking himself those questions and wondering where the answers might be found. Who gave you the job for Ploy? How long have you and Deen Alam been in the business of smuggling Rohingya out of the country? How many others have you worked with, and what are their names? Who are the uniforms you paid off to stay in business?

The last of Calvino's questions concerned the names of the others who weren't cops but were in the payment chain. Which of them had expertly tied a square knot in the rope around Anal's neck? It seemed that Akash Saru, locked up in prison, had a perfect alibi. Had Anal tied his own knot? That would be the police report conclusion. Any whisper that Anal might have had a little help in hanging himself from someone he thought was his friend remained inside the building.

TWENTY

CALVINO ARRIVED FIFTEEN minutes late for his therapy session. The doctor's receptionist frowned as he walked through the door. He'd stopped at a shopping mall to buy her a California roll. Calvino set it on her desk. She opened the plastic lid and looked inside.

"Dr. Apinya's waiting."

The doctor greeted him with the awkward smile of someone who is trying not to show annoyance.

"How was your week?" she asked, as he sat down opposite her desk.

"Same old, same old," he said.

Calvino watched her nose carefully to see if she picked up the smell of the decomposed body on his clothes.

"Are you still seeing bodies?"

"As a matter of fact, I am," he said.

No twitching of the nose.

Dr. Apinya pushed her reading glasses tight against the bridge of her nose and made notes.

"That's a setback, Vincent."

He shrugged his shoulders. It had been a bigger setback for Anal Khan. And compared with his client, Deen Alam—a.k.a. Akash Saru—whose prospects remained nearly hopeless, Calvino thought that in the land of setbacks, he'd had a relatively good week. Calvino also sensed that a comparison of his mental state with those of the dead and the imprisoned wasn't information Dr. Apinya wanted to hear. He nodded in agreement.

"You've been making good progress," she said, "until now."

"Have I?"

"Why don't you read your journal entries for me? Then we can both decide, progress or no progress."

She raised an eyebrow, waiting as Calvino shifted his weight in the chair.

"I fell a little behind this week. It's been busy. I know I promised. Sometimes life intervenes, and what you promise can't be delivered on time. Like late delivery of a pizza, you get a free one next time."

"I don't want a free pizza. What I want is for you to get better. But you have to make your getting better a priority. I feel you're not quite there yet. You're fighting getting better. Is that because you're happy with the way things are?"

He shook his head, thinking about the bargirl named Pizza and the boyfriend who had wanted her for free.

"I'll let you in on a little secret," he said. "I'm unhappy with the way things are working out. I have a plan to change that."

"I'm afraid you're still trying to change the world rather changing the way you live and feel about the world."

He shrugged, leaned forward for the water glass and took a sip.

"Tell you what, Dr. Apinya. When I leave your office, I'll go home and type up on my Remington—my visions, hallucinations, dreams, nightmares, obsessions, strange smells, music and sounds."

"You could make it easy on yourself and type your thoughts on your computer and email me the file."

She had raised his use of a typewriter before. Only now she was more insistent, more direct. If the intent had been to get a reaction out of Calvino, it worked.

"Right, I'll run along home and clean the crap out of the gutters clogging my mind, stuff it into words, store it in neat Word files, email it to you. Those who read our emails might find what I say interesting."

"Who do you think care enough to read your emails?"

"I'll type up a list of names. How does that sound?"

"It sounds hostile."

"You're sweating," she added.

"I'm hot."

"You're defensive and secretive."

"Check."

"You're at war inside your mind."

"Check."

"Wouldn't you like a ceasefire?"

"And you'll be my personal peacekeeper?" he asked.

"Tell me what happened in Rangoon."

"We've been through it."

Pressing the end of her pen against her lower lip as she looked down, she turned the pages of notes, read silently, turned another page.

"I have a feeling that something happened in Rangoon and you're bottling it up inside. Reach down where you've hidden the secret. It's tough. Bring it to the surface. You're finding it difficult to trust yourself or me with what you've hidden away. It's there. Waiting for you, Khun Vincent. Release what you experienced in Rangoon by talking about it. Tell me how you felt. How you feel now. What did you see or do that you can't allow yourself to talk or think about?"

"Two men tried to kill me. It didn't turn out that way. I saw my client's son, Rob, tied to a chair in my hotel room

159

with a bullet hole in his head. Isn't that enough violence to cause anyone's mental gears to slip and slide?"

Dr. Apinya's tongue touched the end of the pen.

"In your line of work, you've witnessed violent deaths before?"

Calvino sighed.

"It's inevitable."

"When is the last time you saw an actual dead body?"

Calvino rotated his shoulders, looked at his hands, glanced at his watch.

"About an hour ago."

The answer caught her off guard.

"That's why I was late for my appointment."

She tapped her polished nail on his folder.

"I see. Okay, as I was saying, in those other circumstances, you walked away each time without any issues."

He nodded.

"I am feeling pretty normal."

"You can't be normal if you are hallucinating. You have a mental health problem, and until you admit the problem, you will continue to see ghosts. You need to admit to yourself what happened and accept it. I feel you are holding back on something that happened to you in Rangoon. Something terrible is bottled inside. I want you to let it out."

"I'll try."

She smiled, put down her pen and removed her reading glasses.

"You're working again," she said.

She's talked to Pratt, he thought. It seemed to him that confidentiality in Thailand was as rare as freshwater dolphins swimming in the Chao Phraya River.

"I'm helping a guy who's in trouble work things out with the police."

"I hope you are getting more cooperation from him than I am from you."

Deen Alam was a hard case, he thought. For the first time Dr. Apinya had said something that actually reached him in the place where he lived with himself.

"All clients are difficult. That's why they come to me. To help them out of a jam they've put themselves in. They are convinced everyone else is confused why it happened the way it did. "

"We are in the same line of work," she said, leaning back in her chair.

"Everyone in this city is in trouble. The question is whether they know it and can do anything about it."

"I'm not convinced," she said. "But I do know you are troubled. Who's helping you?"

"You are, doctor."

TWENTY-ONE

INFORMATION WAS BECOMING ever more free—
if you were plugged into the grid, it would leak out. In
Calvino's world the problem for private eyes, who worked
on the margins society, was accessing information about
people who lived off that grid. Calvino opened up his own
channel and waited. The kind of information Calvino sought
came through on multiple frequencies. He'd been checking
his latest feed about the burnt-out refugee camp near Mae
Hong Son—scrolling through websites, Facebook, Twitter,
blogs and emails. All formats, like a row of cherries on a
slot machine, were lined up on his computer screen—each
with a name and address and the information supplied. As
he read the file, Calvino received a Skype call from Mae
Hong Son.

"Mon Hla has told me more, but maybe not everything,"
said Judy. "She doesn't know whom to trust. She's afraid,
and who can blame her?"

It made sense that she would relieve herself of whatever
burden she'd been carrying. Her family was dead; she'd lost
everything and everyone. She had been happy to see Judy,
a familiar face, and that had meant everything to her.

"Did she give you the name of the guy who bought her
sister?" asked Calvino.

"No, she either doesn't know or won't give it to me.
But I have the name of someone she trusts."

"Where is he?"

"In Bangkok."

"How does she know him?"

"She's never met him. But Ploy knew him well."

"How did you get her to cooperate?"

"I told her the truth. It is the only thing that works to convince a woman to violate an oath to keep a sister's secret."

"What truth was that?" asked Calvino.

"I told Mon Hla about you. If she wanted to know who was responsible for her sister's death, she should trust a guy named Vincent Calvino."

"Give me the name, Judy."

After a brief silence he watched as she leaned out of the camera frame and then reappeared.

"Yoshi Nagata. Ploy trusted him. I don't have specific details other than he's a teacher. He might be able to help, but I don't know that. Don't be upset if he can't."

"Judy, you're doing your best. How could I be upset?"

As soon as he asked the question, he started to count the ways that could happen.

A couple of hours later Calvino had tracked down Yoshi Nagata in Bangkok.

That word "trust" rang inside his skull—Ploy had trusted this Japanese man—as he stood in the elevator next to a security guard on his way up to Nagata's condominium on the twenty-second floor, with a brief stopover on the ninth. The neighborhood's bars, clubs, restaurants and shopping malls gave off the vibe of a young, wealthy person's patch of Bangkok, one staked out by the Japanese. Little Tokyo declared its stylish affluence like an artistic tattoo of a tsunami wave on the hip of the Bangkok night. Calvino had breezed past the front desk security guards, flashing a badge.

"I'm checking the condition of the common areas for Mr. Matsuda from Tokyo. He's the big boss. Mr. Matsuda hired me to report on the status of the swimming pool, exercise room and sauna before he buys five units."

The security detail in the lobby had given Calvino a blue visitor's badge, which he'd pinned to the lapel of his suit jacket, and then a second guard had buzzed him in. Calvino had thought of the old woman selling fried bananas in the lobby of Anal's walkup. She was friendlier. Much to Calvino's surprise, the second guard had followed him onto the elevator and pressed the ninth floor button. A little sign above the button bore the English words "Swimming Pool" with the Japanese script underneath. As the doors opened on the ninth floor, the security guard had walked out. Calvino called after him, "See you in a couple of minutes. I need to check the roof." He pushed the close button and the number 17 and the rest of the numbers above that, all the way to the penthouse.

The subterfuge turned out to be unnecessary. Yoshi Nagata had been expecting someone to contact him about Ploy.

After a long wait the door opened partway. Calvino had his first glimpse at the sparrow-like Japanese man in a blue and white kimono, who greeted him with wet hair and barefoot . He looked like someone's grandfather.

"Yoshi Nagata?"

"That is my name."

"I'd like to ask you a few questions about a young Burmese woman named Mi Swe. She also went by the Thai name Ploy."

The security latch clicked, and Yoshi Nagata opened the door and invited Calvino inside. As Calvino removed his shoes, a pure white light from a bank of windows washed over the white walls and marble floor of the foyer. He stepped around an Oriental carpet stretched in front of the door. Calvino positioned his shoes next to several pairs of sandals, perfectly lined up, and followed Nagata into a living room decorated with backlit shoji screens and finely woven bamboo mats and cushions on a floor of burnished-copper mahogany. Nagata sat on one of the mats, and Calvino eased himself down onto the floor nearby. The slender Japanese man sat in the lotus position, arms folded, saying nothing.

Yoshi Nagata observed Calvino for a long couple of minutes, until the moment arrived when the silence shouted for the companionship of words. He'd got the impression that Calvino had come to his door with good news—that he had located Ploy, who'd disappeared for more than a week.

"You've found Ploy?"

The more Nagata studied Calvino's expression as it darkened, the more he sensed the messenger of good news had arrived with a package wrapped in thin black rice paper—the wrapping in this case showing on Calvino's face. Ploy's whereabouts didn't include a living and breathing Ploy. He saw that now clearly.

"She's dead, Mr. Nagata. Her body's at the morgue awaiting positive identification from a relative. Only that's a problem. Except for her sister, her family are all dead. And her sister's stuck inside a burnt-out refugee camp. That leaves you to perform the duties."

Calvino watched as the old Japanese man sucked in his breath and stared down at the teacup on the table before him and to his left. On his right another table had a dozen small figures in rows: godlike figurines made from bronze, porcelain and gold. A grade way above what people put in a spirit house. One of them was Ganesh, the Hindu elephant god. Behind was another table with a guestbook and a pen, and a wooden stand that held half a dozen samurai swords.

"You want me..." his voice trailed back to the box of silence.

Nagata had picked up a two-headed figure, rubbing his thumb over the two faces.

"Not me personally. But the Thai police may ask you to identify her body. She's now listed as a Jane Doe."

Calvino watched for some sign that Yoshi Nagata wasn't in shock, that he already knew about Ploy's death and for his own reasons was disguising his knowledge.

"You didn't know?"

Nagata replaced the figure on the table. He shook his head, his eyes meeting Calvino's. He didn't blink.

"Poor Ploy. How did she die?"

"The police say that she was murdered."

Nagata smacked his lips twice and slowly shook his head.

"That is unfortunate. Terrible news. Poor girl."

Calvino saw the opportunity to make his play.

The sincerity of his "poor girl," "poor Ploy" responses had to be tested.

"Her sister in Mae Hong Son says you were the only man Ploy trusted here. And the sister could always contact you in case of an emergency. Sounds like you two were living together. Money changed hands. You bought her from the family. Paid cash. She got pregnant and the relationship went in the direction of Okinawa. She died. You disposed of the body."

"Mr. Calvino, I am Ploy's yoga teacher."

He paused to compose himself.

"I was her friend, not her boyfriend. I am gay. And I am not from Japan. I was born in Canada, Vancouver. If Canadians wish to express regret for a tragedy or something 'going south,' we say things are going in the direction of the United States."

Calvino looked at the old, thin Japanese man with long, white hair, a small white goatee and a broad, shiny forehead, dressed in ceremonial yoga whites. He had the serene smile of an ascetic who had climbed a mountain and witnessed an internal truth that existed at the beginning of the trail below.

"You were her teacher?"

Nagata nodded.

"For nearly a year she came to my studio for two-hour yoga sessions."

"In a group or on her own?"

"She asked for private lessons."

"Do you have an address for her? The name of her husband, boyfriend, associates?"

"She told me that she lived in the area. As for her personal life, she did talk about it in general terms. I knew that her family were in a refugee camp along the Burmese border, and her dream was to find a home for them outside Thailand."

Calvino leaned forward, trying to get comfortable on the mat.

"Why would she talk to you about the Mae Hong Son camp and not about her life in Bangkok?"

Nagata showed the faint hint of a smile.

"It was understood that her Bangkok life was off limits. She had her reasons."

"But she confided in you that she came from a refugee camp? That's admitting she was an illegal. Why would she trust you with that information and not tell you her boyfriend's name? It doesn't make sense, Mr. Nagata."

"She trusted me about the camp because I had personal experience of what a refugee camp does to a person. During the Second World War my parents were shipped from their home in Vancouver to a concentration camp in Alberta. Everything they'd worked for and owned—house, furniture and car—was lost in British Columbia. My father's life lost meaning. That's something I suspect you have never experienced. An absence of meaning destroys the reason for living, Mr. Calvino. Ploy's mother and father also had this experience. Ploy found that I understood what she'd experienced and what her parents had gone through. People who've not lived in these circumstances rarely do."

"The fact is, her family sold her to a buyer in Bangkok. I need the name of the man who bought her."

"I know nothing about him. But I understood how that family decision came about. You judge Ploy's family too harshly. That's understandable. For me, it was a perfectly natural decision for her father and mother to make. If your life no longer has any purpose or meaning, and you have lost any means to sustain your life, what is left to live for? You can kill yourself, and some do, or in order to survive, you do whatever is necessary. Selling your daughter is a terrible thing when your life is full of meaning and the money is used to buy a pickup or something to give face or comfort. That's evil. You can't judge Ploy's parents as evil. No, you must have experienced what it is to live with all hope and dreams stripped away, and then ask yourself, what would you do?"

"Ploy admitted that her parents sold her?"

Nagata blinked twice and nodded in a bow.

"She loved them."

"They're dead."

"That is sad news. We can never foresee another's destiny."

Resistance or acceptance, the fork in the road, and she had to go down one or the other lane. In the end it hadn't mattered. Nagata had a point—if she hadn't died in Bangkok, she likely would have died when the refugee camp went up in flames.

"She sent them money every month. Any idea how she worked that?"

Nagata quietly refilled his teacup.

"An NGO friend of mine helped."

"One of your clients?"

"Yes, but I wouldn't want to involve her."

"You might not have a choice. The person I want to meet is the man who bought her. Any idea at all where I can find him?"

"None."

Nagata's voice, cold as a winter chill, an echo against a mountain, turned one word into a library of Babel.

"You are looking for him?"

"I'll find him."

"I am confident that you will, Mr. Calvino."

"Could her buyer have introduced her to you?"

Nagata sipped his tea.

"No, Bow introduced her. Bow was Ploy's Thai teacher. She's a student from a respectable family and like Ploy has been one of my regular yoga students."

"They came to yoga together?"

"Only occasionally. Ploy had more flexible hours. And as I said, Ploy preferred private sessions."

"Any idea how Ploy and Bow met?"

"I never asked."

Calvino stared at the old man, who displayed no guile or evasion.

"You weren't curious?"

"It had no relevance to yoga. How people meet is mostly a matter of chance. To ask why is to ask why the wind blows from the south today and from the east tomorrow. Students come to me to practice an ancient art. Like most people, since the time they were children they saw all around them that they'd been born into a world where dreams died. Long before the physical death, we bury our dreams one after another. I teach my students how to mourn their dead dreams and to move on."

Nagata was in the same line of work as Dr. Apinya. Who hadn't watched innocence bleed out?

"Had Ploy moved on?"

"I can't speak for her. Her dream was to take her family to freedom."

"Ironic."

"Less a matter of irony than what desperate people do as they watch their dreams slip away."

Calvino rose to his knees and had a closer look at the collection of small gods.

"Is this part of the yoga class?"

"Spirituality is the essence of yoga practice. It is physical, very physical too, but inside a mental space that is difficult to achieve."

"Those figurines, except for one of them, don't look like Buddha."

"The Buddha might have replied that he saw no separation. Each one was his manifestation over time and space. A lesson. A guidepost on the path that leads to another path that otherwise is invisible."

"If you learn which of those paths might lead me to Ploy's boyfriend, you'll let me know?"

He rose to his feet and looked down at Yoshi Nagata.

The Japanese man looked up with a serene smile.

"You won't need me to tell you. Follow your own heart and observe what it reveals."

TWENTY-TWO

BOW'S EXCUSE FOR not meeting Calvino was straightforward.

"I'm graduating from university. I receive my diploma tomorrow. Very busy. No time. Next week, maybe."

"You're getting your diploma at Queen Sirikit Centre?" Calvino asked on the phone.

"How did you get my number?"

"Yoshi Nagata, your yoga teacher, gave it to me."

"Why would he do that?"

"I have a few questions about Ploy I'd like to ask you." *Click.*

She'd cut off the call. He auto-redialed the number and heard a busy tone. Nagata had given him Bow's full name, number, email and the name of her university. She was graduating with a BA in English literature.

TWENTY-THREE

COLONEL PRATT HAD waited fifteen minutes outside Calvino's apartment. He hadn't phoned ahead. It was a Thai inclination when in the area of a friend to unexpectedly arrive at the door. Calvino emerged from the elevator on his floor and saw the Colonel looking out the window at a vast stretch of slums—shanty houses, corrugated roofs, a uniform rusty brown like a huge interlocking nest.

"Pratt, I was about to phone you."

Calvino had loosened his necktie. Half-moon dark sweat stains were outlined under the armpits of his jacket.

"April's the hottest month," said Colonel Pratt. "No one wears a suit jacket in April except a masochist, a capitalist or someone carrying a gun."

"You came to check on my tailoring?"

Calvino opened the door to his unit, removed his shoes and stood to the side as the Colonel followed him in.

"I thought you'd want to know about Jane Doe's autopsy report."

Calvino led Colonel Pratt into the main living room, scooped up a remote and aimed it at the air conditioner.

"That was fast. The last I heard, the autopsy reports from May 2010 still hadn't been finished."

"That's political. Jane Does speed through the system. The decision to hang the four men in India gave them an incentive."

Ninety-two people had been killed in the streets of Bangkok in May 2010 in political disturbances. Finding the cause of death and those responsible in those cases had proved as challenging for the authorities as finding an elementary particle with a knife and fork.

Calvino took off his jacket and folded it over a chair. Colonel Pratt noticed the absence of a gun. Calvino grinned as he removed his shirt and tie. He walked into the bedroom and soon came back out wearing a polo shirt and a smile.

"You thought I was packing?"

"It crossed my mind."

Colonel Pratt stood in the sitting room, looking around at a display of photos related to the car bombing: the shell of the blown-up car, glass and debris and body parts on the street, publicity photos of Mya and Rob Osborne's band, Monkey Nose, elaborate pen-drawn diagrams of the scattered fragments, hand-written notes, faded newspaper clippings taped to the windows, enlarged photos of Mya standing in front of the Irrawaddy Bookstore, her family's business in Rangoon.

"Have you told Dr. Apinya about this?" Colonel Pratt asked.

"About what?"

Colonel Pratt gestured at the rat's nest lined with hundreds of clippings, printouts, documents, folders, photographs, models and bits of debris from the scene of the car bombing.

"You mean my research materials?"

"This isn't normal research, Vincent. And to call them materials is a stretch."

"If I told her, do you think she'd write me off as crazy?"

Calvino fought back a grin.

"It's not a joke."

Calvino sat on the couch, leaned over and grabbed a photograph of Rob Osborne and Mya.

"I told you that Rob saw things," said Calvino, looking at the photo.

"I remember at the time, you said he had strange hallucinations."

"At the time I thought it was crazy talk."

"Now you're not so sure," said Colonel Pratt.

He turned toward Calvino, his face showing the sadness of a friend staring at someone he recognized but no longer understood. The Colonel hadn't decided whether it was the shock of the bombing itself or Calvino's PTSD-driven obsession with understanding the tragedy that was the root cause for the hallucinations.

Colonel Pratt had not only known Mya and Yadanar but had played the saxophone in a Rangoon nightclub with their band. He'd been booked to go to New York to perform with them. He'd felt the loss as much as Calvino.

Calvino pulled out a poster of Mya on stage, singing into a microphone.

"As you opened the door, you said something about how you were about to phone me," said Colonel Pratt.

Calvino put the photo down on the pile of photographs.

"Ploy had a Burmese name, Mi Swe. You heard about the refugee camp in Mae Hong Son that was burned down?"

"It's been in the news."

"Mi Swe was a refugee in that camp. Her family were killed in the fire."

"It is very difficult for anyone to leave a refugee camp."

Calvino nodded.

"Not so difficult if the money is right."

"What's that supposed to mean, Vincent?"

"Her family sold her to a buyer in Bangkok."

Colonel Pratt sat on the sofa to Calvino's right side.

174

"Are you sure about this?"

"According to an NGO at the camp and Ploy's yoga teacher. The yoga guy is a sixty-something Canadian named Yoshi Nagata."

He opened his MacBook Pro and clicked on his favorite sidekick in investigations—Mr. Wikipedia.

"Nagata is some kind of mathematical genius. He was born in a Japanese-Canadian internment camp in Alberta in 1945. Taught at the University of British Columbia, MIT and Cambridge before he retired three years ago. It says here that he's won all kinds of prizes, awards and honorary degrees. Look at the list of publications. Nice Wiki photo. He looks younger with black hair."

"A professor," said Colonel Pratt, looking over Calvino's shoulder.

Calvino found that the Thais were inevitably impressed by anyone with a Ph.D. and an academic title.

"Will he come to the morgue and ID her?"

Calvino nodded.

"I told him to expect a call from the police. It seems that Professor Nagata was the only person in Bangkok that Ploy trusted. That's what her sister in Mae Hong Son told my NGO source."

He pulled up a photograph of Judy from Facebook. "That's Judy, the NGO at the camp." Colonel Pratt looked at the screen. "The autopsy report confirmed Ploy had been sexually violated," said Colonel Pratt. "It also confirmed that she was six weeks pregnant."

"Did they do a postmortem fetal DNA test for the father's DNA," said Calvino.

"Preliminary DNA says the father was Asian."

"That narrows things down to roughly a billion possible candidates. No chance of determining gender," said Calvino. The futility of information gaps and big numbers depressed him.

"No chance. She died too early in the pregnancy," said Colonel Pratt.

"That doesn't leave a lot to go on," said Calvino. He saw the colonel's signature smile, the one that met his search of his memory of the Bard had found a reply.

Colonel Pratt responded as held that faint smile, "'That function is smothered in surmise. And nothing is but what is not.' Macbeth. We might start by asking who is this person that Ploy trusted? Maybe he knows something that can narrow down who the father was."

Calvino switched back to the Wikipedia page for Professor Yoshi Nagata.

"You met him," the Colonel continued. "What doesn't that page tell me about Professor Nagata that I should know?"

"He's gay, Pratt. He never mentioned his Ph.D. or that he's thought of as some kind of genius in the world of six-dimensional geometry. And he collects samurai swords and little statues of gods."

"Gods?"

"Like Ganesh, the elephant god. He had about a dozen different ones. Some small enough for a spirit house, others the size for a prayer room shrine."

"Ganesh is the Hindu god of beginnings," said Colonel Pratt. "This professor left behind a brilliant academic career. Why?"

"Advice from the gods?"

"I am serious, Vincent. Why does a man like that walk away from everything to teach yoga in Bangkok? There's a line from *Richard III*: 'When clouds appear, wise men put on their cloaks; when great leaves fall, the winter is at hand; when the sun sets, who doth not look for night?' What cloud appeared that caused Professor Nagata to put on the cloak of a yoga teacher?"

"I don't know and don't care. All that matters is Yoshi Nagata isn't your guy. And no way my client killed her. Unless the pathologist found a DNA match to Akash when he examined the body."

"She'd been violated with an object. A sex toy is a possibility."

"Is that what the report concluded, that the murder weapon was a sex toy?"

"She'd been drugged. The *khaek* drugged her drink, violated her, and she died on him. I don't believe he intended her death. It was bad luck."

"My client's a peanut vendor in Soi Cowboy. Exactly how does he meet and drug Ploy? What drug did they find in her? Is there evidence she worked in a go-go bar? Or that she was a streetwalker with a movie star's face patrolling Sukhumvit Road in a designer tracksuit trolling for customers? And that she worked for peanuts?"

"He confessed," said Colonel Pratt.

Calvino shook his head and clenched his fists.

"How many phone books and broken ribs did that take?"

"Now that we know who she is and have the man responsible for her death, you can concentrate on getting better."

"I've never felt better."

"Good. Glad to hear that."

"I'd like to see a copy of the autopsy report."

Calvino waited in silence. Colonel Pratt had been sidelined in the department, his authority stripped, when during the course of the investigation into the car bombing, someone had revealed that he'd given a report on the bomb components to Calvino. His superior had wanted to know why and how he'd allowed a farang civilian to become involved in a highly sensitive investigation. Quoting

177

Shakespeare to his superior about the nature of friendship hadn't helped.

"I've already told you what's in it," said Colonel Pratt.

"And I've told you the name of a man who can make a positive ID of your Jane Doe. But you still need to talk to him, take him to the morgue, go through the formalities."

"I am a police officer."

"Pratt, arrange for me to get a copy of the report."

Colonel Pratt thought about a line from *Much Ado about Nothing* as he looked at Calvino: "Everyone can master a grief but he that has it." His friend Vincent Calvino had been in a deep state of grief for months, and he was using the dead woman's case to master a larger grief. He removed an envelope with the autopsy report and placed it on the glass coffee table.

"It's in Thai."

"Ratana will go through it with me," said Calvino.

"She gone through a lot with you, Vincent."

"Ain't that the truth."

TWENTY-FOUR

IN THE OLD days, to find someone missing in Bangkok, a private investigator relied on limited sources and on luck to pull the joker from the deck. There might be a chance of getting a photograph from an acquaintance or a friend, or a description of the person. The police had sketch artists. It was hit and mostly miss in those days as the details were too vague, mistaken or outdated. No need now for wasting shoe leather when a mouse working a cursor was faster.

Vincent Calvino sat in front of his computer, and within a couple of minutes he'd found Bow's page on Facebook. Bow's picture showed a reasonably presentable undergraduate, a young woman in university uniform—tight-fitting white blouse, top two buttons open to expose a bit of breast, and a short black skirt. He studied the picture Bow had chosen to tell the world something about her personality. Her message rang out: here is a confident, friendly, open, adjusted and feminine student. And, it might have added, available.

His goal was to befriend her. Like all good Bangkok private investigators, Calvino maintained a dozen Facebook pages under different identities. Three of his bogus pages had the right fit for Bow's Facebook profile. He asked himself which of the young Asian males living in Hong Kong, Singapore and Tokyo would work best.

He selected Takashi and added, under Books, "Professor Yoshi Nagata, *Six-Dimensional Geometry*." Then Calvino sent a request from Takashi asking Bow to accept him as a friend. Mr. Takashi, on Facebook, was a twenty-six-year-old engineer from Tokyo. The Nagata connection would give comfort, he thought.

Calvino had guessed her security level spot on the money. Bow accepted Takashi's friend request within thirty minutes. As a friend, Calvino could access her timeline and read her last two-dozen posts, including the ones about her upcoming graduation. Next he scrolled through ninety-five personal photos—Bow shopping at Siam Paragon, Bow at an RCA nightclub, Bow with her father, mother, sister, brothers, friends. Bow and more of Bow shot from every possible angle. There was a lifetime of information on her timeline—friends, food, fooling around at parties, clubs, the campus, cats, dogs, relatives and more food.

Calvino not only knew where she would be; he knew when she would be there, who she was going with and who was doing her hair, nails and makeup. He also knew exactly what she looked like. He searched for information about the graduation ceremony and found that about a thousand students would show up to receive their degrees on Saturday. Each graduate would arrive with an entourage of half a dozen or more relatives, family friends, neighbors, photographers, boyfriends and girlfriends.

"It looks like a scene out of the movie *Gandhi*, except with Thais instead of Indians as the extras," said McPhail as they walked through Queen Sirikit Center on the morning of graduation day.

Thousands of people milled around or squatted in corners, eating, talking, resting. Graduates in their black robes flocked like crows flitting from tree to tree, swarming down a hallway, blocking out everyone as they moved through the dense crowds. Their families followed behind like medieval court retainers.

"Have you spotted her?" asked Calvino.

"Vinny, all of these young women look like the Thai version of Stepford wives," said McPhail.

"What's with you, McPhail? Can you not see something without thinking of some movie? *Gandhi*, *The Stepford Wives*... where does it end?"

"That guy over there looks like the Thai version of the lead in *Breaking Bad*."

With the *Stepford Wives* remark, though, Calvino had to admit that McPhail had hit the bull's eye. The hundreds of young Thai women mobbing the place, underneath their makeup, must have had individual identities, but they had been erased with identically painted masks.

Calvino had Bow's Facebook profile photo saved on his Samsung. He looked at it and pushed his phone in front of McPhail's face.

"Man, I know what she looks like," said McPhail. "I've never seen so many women who looked like they'd been cloned from the same DNA."

"She's here somewhere," said Calvino, craning his neck to look over the crowd. "She might be outside."

He soon gave up. There were far too many people crammed into the confined space. He found that the claustrophobic feeling of the walls closing in struck farang much faster than Thais—if it struck the latter at all.

Streams of graduates, friends and family spilled out of the main hall and spiraled into the surrounding area. Hundreds of people in that pre-locust swarming mode filled the walkway around Lake Ratchada. The track boiled up countless young Thai women, all sweating and shaky in their high-heels, black robes and sashes with orange piping and red strips of ribbon. Their families, friends and neighbors hovered around the newly minted worker bees who'd soon be out in the field harvesting pollen with the rest of them. It was their big moment. A time for everyone to feel that the size of their face had inflated to blimp dimensions, casting shadows over the lake.

Calvino and McPhail split up at the lake. McPhail headed to the park and Calvino walked along the track. He followed a possible Bow who trooped behind a photographer. Platoons of photographers like seal trainers coached their subjects on where to walk or stand, when to smile and which tree or bush to stand before to make a good frame. Everywhere Calvino looked, he bumped against another hired hand for the day ordering his client into position below a planter of flowers or next to a small canal or a palm tree—all grayish shaft and green tube-like spurt, with faraway fronds that slowly moved in a light breeze.

As each black-robed woman passed, Calvino slowed down and searched her face before moving on. He checked Bow's photo again on his cell phone screen. He needed the refresher. Her face had blurred in his memory and blended into the endless painted faces crowding the public areas of the park and the track. Their hair had been sprayed until it acquired a lacquer-like quality as solid as African marble. Not only was their makeup identical, but adding to the sense of one person photocopied hundreds of times, they had the same hairstyle. In their black robes the women looked like cult members hatched from a honeycomb deep inside the Tobacco Monopoly grounds.

Calvino glanced at his wristwatch. It was 9:30 a.m. Not a single jogger could be found on the track. The graduates had invaded and held their ground. None of them were running. And none of them turned out to be Bow.

McPhail cut through the park and found Calvino on the track.

"She ain't in the park," he said. "I guarantee it."

182

"She's in plain sight right in front of us. Only we just haven't seen her."

"Let me have another look at the photo."

Calvino handed him his cell phone. McPhail, a cigarette in one hand, shaded the screen from the glare of the sun and scrolled through the Facebook pictures.

"I've seen this guy with the funny glasses and crooked smile."

McPhail looked up from a photograph of Bow with her father and mother.

"The old woman looks familiar too."

Sometimes McPhail showed signs of genius. If all the graduates looked alike, then look for their relatives and hope they hadn't gone through the same beautification process.

Calvino grabbed his phone from McPhail.

"Let's go find them."

The graduates and their entourages now milled around the park benches. McPhail headed back to the park, and Calvino followed after him.

"The guy in the photo was smoking a cigarette over there."

He pointed to a tree with a group of graduates and their families on both sides. Expats lived in confederations of autonomous individuals. They had trouble adjusting to tight-knit Thai families organized like military units, staking out territorial positions next to a park tree.

Everyone was smiling. Why wouldn't they be happy? The young women with flowers in their hair, their robes and short skirts underneath, the robe thrown back for the photographer to get the desired look of sexual abandon by a lake and under a palm tree. Photographed with their families, little sisters and brothers running around. Old grandmothers in their finest dresses stood under umbrellas, and mothers hovered around their beloved like mother hens, bewildered that it had all gone so fast. Where had the time gone?

Calvino spotted the Thai man in Bow's Facebook photo. The tag on her Facebook page identified the man as Bow's father.

Several children chasing each other cut in front of him. They were playing with helium-filled balloons with happy faces on them. Bow's mother—stocky, round-faced, her eyes behind glasses—clutched a bouquet of flowers. Fake flowers with millions of specs of glitter caught sunrays that reflected off the middle-aged woman's eyeglasses. Calvino noticed a young woman standing in high heels a couple of feet away, wearing a crown of fake flowers—pink, yellow, white and red. She was a princess for that day. The woman wasn't Bow, though as it turned out, she was talking to Bow. Only at that moment Calvino didn't know it.

Calvino closed in on the family surrounding another young graduate—a man. Medium height, wearing a dark suit and tie and a mortarboard. The square academic cap sat snuggly, properly squared at the right angle on the head; the tiny peak dipped to the unlined forehead, the tassel hanging on the right side. The young man's face smiled into the camera as he flashed the V-sign. His young face had the long, elegant chiseled features of a model, with full and sensual lips. His chin had a dimple in the center. The fingers on his hands were long, and the nails had a clear polish. The graduate's face had a hint of makeup.

"*Nueng, song, sam!*"

The photographer shouted "one, two, three" in Thai and then clicked off several shots. He wore a funny white cloth hat on the back of his head as shade against the sun. A young man next to the graduate, wearing a pair of large aviator sunglasses, leaned into the shot, flashing the victory sign. The photographer hadn't finished. He held up his index finger. Snap. He raised his thumb.

"*Dee. Dee, Dee.*"

Good. Snap. That was the end of his combo hand and verbal vocabulary.

The shoot appeared to have finished as the photographer started storing his camera gear. Calvino walked over to Bow's father, who had found a spot of shade with her mother.

"I am looking for Bow. A friend asked me to send her best wishes for her graduation," he said, showing him the photo on his cell phone. "Have you seen her?"

It was a small white lie—one that the father wouldn't question.

Bow's father nodded at the young man in a black robe.

"That's Bow," he said, smiling.

He looked happy, proud and nervous as he smoked a cigarette.

"What is the name of the friend?"

"Ploy," said Calvino.

The father smiled with recognition of the name.

"Bow taught her Thai. They are friends from yoga class."

"That's the one."

"Where is Ploy?" Bow's father asked. "I thought she'd come to Bow's graduation."

"She's gone away," said Calvino.

"That's too bad. Bow liked her very much. She will be disappointed."

McPhail tapped a cigarette out of a pack, lit it, and offered one to Bow's father, which he took. McPhail lit it for the father. They both blew smoke.

Turning to Calvino, he said under his breath, "Bow, huh? You could've fooled me. I thought she was a woman. That's a guy."

Bow's father called to her, gestured with his hand for her to join him. The person in the black robe walked over with the friend in aviator sunglasses trailing like a bodyguard.

"This farang wants to talk to you."

"My name is Vincent. I'd like to take a couple of minutes to ask you a couple of questions about your friend Ploy."

"Didn't we talk on the phone?" she asked. "And I said I was busy."

"I need information about Ploy," he said, offering no apology.

Bow raised her hand to her throat.

"Is she in some kind of trouble?"

She obviously had no idea what had happened.

"There is a problem. You might help solve it."

"How did you find me?"

"It wasn't easy. I was looking for this woman," Calvino said, showing her the Facebook photo.

As Bow glanced at her Facebook photo, the smile wiped away, and a serious, sad look replaced it.

"The most important day of my life, and they insist I dress as a man. It's terrible for me. I feel sorry for my poor parents, my family and my boyfriend. The university has this strict, stupid rule. If you are transgender, you have to wear the clothes of your gender at birth. No exceptions. Primitive thinking for a university, don't you agree?"

"Terrible," said Calvino. "Let's talk about Ploy."

"Not here," she said. "Over there is better."

After a brief exchange of words with her father, she led Calvino away.

McPhail kept staring at Bow. The transformation of the woman on Facebook into the young man walking alongside Calvino made his head hurt. His black and white world was dissolving in the heat. He trailed behind, trying to see if the way Bow walked was male or female.

They walked beside a small granite wall with palms planted in large rectangular stone containers, passing other students who smiled at the camera. Bow stopped, clutched the brown railing and stared down at the small canal. Other students lined the railing farther down, taking over a private space for their photo moment.

"Let's stop here," said Calvino.

He looked back at McPhail, who kept Bow's boyfriend in aviator sunglasses at a distance, talking about astrology, horse racing and massage parlors. The distraction gave Calvino the chance to talk with Bow without outside interference.

"When was the last time you saw Ploy?"

Bow thought, rolling her tongue against the inside of her cheek.

"Maybe two weeks. Something like that."

Calvino shrugged his shoulders.

"Before Songkran?"

"Definitely before."

"I saw her at yoga class twice a week. I helped her with her Thai. But I've been busy. She missed a couple of yoga classes. And some Thai lessons."

"Yoshi Nagata said you two were good friends."

The mention of the yoga teacher surprised her at first but soon gave her comfort that she was talking to someone who was part of her circle.

"We sometimes had lunch. She had a lot of free time. Often it was a last-moment thing. I phoned her and we'd meet at a restaurant. She always paid the bill."

"She was generous."

Bow nodded.

"Yes, *jai dee*." She had a good heart.

"She had a tattoo with a *jai*," said Calvino.

"It doesn't surprise me. Tattoos are in fashion."

"Did you teach her the *jai* phrases?"

"Ploy knew hundreds. She was a very good student with lots of time to study."

"Did she say who was supporting her?"

Bow smiled.

"A rich man. She never told me his name."

"That's strange. It never slipped out? James or John or Jason?"

"Not that I remember. She referred to him as *nai*. I don't think she'd call a farang *nai*," Bow said.

She sounded honest, looking him in the eye as she spoke. He couldn't identify a tell that betrayed her as a liar. "*Nai*" was Thai word Thais used to refer to a man of rank, power and influence, the master of a private realm, a person to be deferred to and respected. Farang mostly didn't fall into that category.

"Her *nai* was Thai?"

Bow stared at him.

"I don't know. I assumed he was. But I never thought much about it."

"Did you know Ploy escaped from a refugee camp?"

Bow closed her eyes and nodded.

"She told me about the camp. It was horrible. She never said anything about escaping. She sometimes talked about her family."

"They died recently in a fire. Except for her sister. Ploy's sister said a helicopter targeted the family house. Dropped a bomb on it. Any idea why someone would want to do that?"

"How would I know that?"

Bow's hands were shaking.

"When you last saw her, did she talk about her plans?"

"She had more plastic surgery scheduled."

"Plastic surgery?"

"That's why I didn't think too much about her being away. A labiaplasty puts you out of action for a week. I had mine done last year. I lost almost two weeks."

Calvino resisted showing surprise or ignorance about what was involved in a labiaplasty. He filed the medical term away for a later Google search. He wondered why a woman who was six weeks pregnant would undergo plastic surgery.

"Which hospital did she use?"

"She didn't go to a hospital. She went to my doctor, Dr. Nattapong. He has a private clinic. He's done a lot of work for my friends."

"You recommended the doctor?"

Bow nodded with pride.

"Dr. Nattapong is the best."

Calvino translated "the best" into a doctor who showed basic competence and paid kickback commissions for new patients referred by his old ones. The best plastic surgeon worked with his clippers and knives and scissors to create a large garden of trimmed, cut, pruned flowers.

"Where's his clinic?"

Bow turned slightly and pointed at a series of buildings across the road from the lake.

"His clinic is on the third floor of that one."

"You taught Ploy Thai. How was she doing?"

"Ploy's a very good student. My father said you told him Ploy has gone away."

"Actually, she's dead. I'm sorry to be the one to tell you."

Bow's face crumbled as the lips quivered. She shook her head.

"Ploy? You're joking!"

"*Khwam jing*"—it's true. "One more thing, Bow. Did you know Ploy was pregnant?"

She tried to say something but the words wouldn't come out. Instead Bow shook her head from side to side as if to shake off the impact of Calvino's words.

She'd just received her diploma, launching her into a scary world where even young people sometimes died, and two strangers came to her graduation to ask her questions without ever hinting that the death of a friend was the reason they'd appeared.

189

TWENTY-FIVE

CALVINO GOOGLED "LABIAPLASTY" as McPhail poured a two finger shot of late morning whiskey from a bottle of Johnnie Walker Black. He reached around and slipped the bottle back into the drawer of the office desk.

"It sounds like a French pastry," said McPhail.

"It's medical talk for surgery to redesign a woman's vagina," said Calvino, reading from the screen.

"Get out of here."

McPhail walked around to Calvino's side of the desk and read an article on the screen.

"What's 'clitoral unhooding'? It sounds like a street gang membership ritual."

"It's a simple procedure. Twenty minutes with a laser under general or local anesthetic and the hood comes off."

"Why would a pregnant teenager want her pussy redesigned?" asked McPhail.

"I don't know. But I intend to find out," said Calvino.

Calvino looked up to find Ratana standing frozen in the doorway.

"I made an appointment with Dr. Nattapong on Saturday at 3:00 p.m.," she finally said.

"Hey, Ratana, sorry," McPhail said, slamming back the rest of the whiskey. "Vinny, I'm moving on. You can handle things from here. Do you mind settling up? I'm a bit short of cash."

Calvino took out his wallet and removed two thousand baht. He handed the cash to McPhail, who folded the two notes and stuffed them in his shirt pocket.

"She *looked* like a man. That's why we kept walking past her. You think she was cut? Some ladyboys are, but some of them like to keep their weenie. Like switch hitters in baseball—left hand against that pitcher, right hand against another one."

After he left, Ratana returned to Calvino's office. She sat in the chair McPhail had vacated. It was still warm.

"Here's how we play it," he said. "You introduce me as your husband. Use the word '*fan*.' That leaves it ambiguous. The daughter of your friend, Khun Bow, recommended him."

"I already mentioned Bow. That's how I got a Saturday appointment."

Calvino saw the troubled expression that Ratana tried to conceal when she had a problem and expected him to detect what it was without being asked.

"You're worried," he said.

"If Ploy was in his office and something bad happened, he's not going to tell us. He'll throw us out. If we don't ask about Ploy, what is the point of talking to him?"

"We're going to leave a little present in his office."

Calvino showed her a small black shell that looked like a piece of rock candy. It was an electronic device that monitored conversations in the room. He had a second device that monitored keystrokes.

"While we wait in reception, I'll put this one in place. It will give us remote access to his receptionist's computer."

She looked uncertain.

"If Dr. Nattapong has something to hide," he said, "I'll know soon enough. If not, then I move on. It'll be okay, Ratana."

"What is he hiding?"

Calvino glanced at his screen, where Dr. Nattapong's face stared out.

"What are the odds he's doing abortions for the wealthy?"

TWENTY-SIX

From: Vincent Calvino
To: Dr. Apinya
Confidential: Patient/Doctor Privilege
Date/Time: 19 April, 23:37

To keep myself occupied and to reduce the chance of new visitations, I've been looking into the plastic surgery business in Bangkok. It's big business. Nose jobs, eye jobs, facelifts, breast implants, ass jobs -- all of these I've heard about. You can't take the BTS or MRT without seeing a wide selection of women who've had a nose job, Botox or an eye job. In my line of work, you learn something new most days. Labiaplasty, for instance, wasn't something I'd heard about. There's a debate about where to draw the line between necessity and aesthetic considerations. The face culture obviously extends below the waist, if what I've read about the huge increase of this procedure on Thai women is true.

Some women want to reshape overly large labia, other women want to fix damage caused by childbirth or by masturbation or from that drunken night when they thought it would be cool to have a piercing down there and a gold ring inserted. There is a long list of reasons. As with PTSD, the causes are multiple and depend on the patient's history.

How does an experienced private investigator with years in the field in Bangkok acquire PTSD? Why would a pregnant teenage girl from Burma want labiaplasty? Two mysteries don't make a library.

In the case of the Burmese girl, I doubt she wanted the operation because she found it uncomfortable riding a bicycle. I've been wondering if it might have had something to with her sexual partner. Could intercourse have caused her pain? Or maybe she or he didn't like the natural shape and look of her genitalia. Some women are embarrassed when they wear a bikini and large, protruding lips press against their bikini bottom. Or one of the lips is larger than the other, giving a lopsided appearance.

With a little study a man begins to learn that a woman's relationship with her sexual organs isn't all that different from a man's relationship with his. The comparison can be pushed too far. I've never heard of a man lining up to get the male equivalent of labiaplasty. Is there a surgery like this for me? Just asking. Because men don't talk about changing nature's shape. Why are women more open to such talk?

Plastic surgery is fed by strong emotions. The desire for control over one's body is as strong as one's desire for control over other people's lives and events. How we adjust to the lack of control determines how sane or crazy we end up.

I am starting to understand that superficial change doesn't really change anything. Data-mining the interior of my mind for clues about the images I see yields little more than low-grade ore. You say I've not been honestly mining the data. I've put large parts of the old minefields off limits. I'm afraid that if I dig in those spaces, I will find not gold but bones that I've buried in the middle of the night. It might not seem so, but I am getting closer to lifting that yellow crime scene tape and walking inside a room that's been sealed off. Investigations are about timing, observation, luck and knowing how to read the evidence, without getting distracted by the personality of the person who left it behind. I need to reach a point where the PI in me wants to look inside and understand why I needed to close that room off for so long.

TWENTY-SEVEN

THE DOCTOR'S CLINIC was a hole-in-the-wall operation. Like many Bangkok doctors, Dr. Nattapong was attached to one of the well-known private hospitals, big profit centers with large advertising budgets to bring in medical tourists for hip replacements, heart surgery and plastic surgery—the money spinners. Calvino and Ratana took the elevator to the third floor of the building. Walking down the corridor, they passed a Thai girl who emerged from Dr. Nattapong's office a few feet ahead. Her face heavily bandaged, she wore thick green sandals and carried her high heels like someone with false teeth rushing toward a buffet table and timing the insertion for the last moment.

Trailing behind her, as if on an invisible leash, a Thai man with more tics than a Kentucky hunting dog dragged a carry-on roller behind him like a ball and chain. Just as he passed Calvino, he froze and started to roll the carry-on back and forth, as if testing the wheels, his head tilted to the tiled floor, listening. He held out a half dozen shopping bags like a man with a divining rod searching for water. His cargo shorts exposed calves tattooed with fire-breathing dragons and colorful peacocks, tails fanned out in full display. Looking upset, he mumbled to himself, face twitching.

"Plastic surgery isn't for everyone," said Calvino, as Ratana looked back at the couple.

"He didn't look well."

Calvino grunted agreement.

"Both of them looked like walking wounded."

"It's not a joke," said Calvino.

"That's why it made me sad. "

Ratana had been briefed on her part as patient and wife. He'd play the supporting role of the caring husband who would foot the bill.

Ratana entered first into the reception area of Dr. Nattapong's private clinic. The doctor's receptionist wore a plastic photo name-tag with her name in English and Thai. Calvino trailed behind Ratana, keeping his head down. He'd noticed the woman's name and was thinking how it was a great name for a plastic surgeon's assistant—Sukanya translated as Perfect Woman. She wore a pair of large earrings, and her skin was a shade of copper that suggested she had some Indian blood. Seeing Ratana, she blinked her large brown eyes and asked for her name.

"My name is Ratana. I have an appointment."

"The doctor will be with you in a moment. Please take a seat."

"I'm with her," said Calvino. "Nice office."

The receptionist smiled.

"We like it," she said, exhaling a small amount of pride. "And we like it when a woman brings her husband too."

The corporate "We like it" from a doctor's receptionist was a short sentence that opened an encyclopedia of possibilities. He couldn't imagine Ratana using those three words.

Calvino sat on a sofa opposite the reception desk. Sukanya's cell phone rang. He watched her lean over and open a blue metal box with the Honda logo on top. She removed a cell phone. Why would she stash her iPhone inside a Honda box? Was it a weird personal habit? Or was the secrecy of the office such that it automatically spilled over into her personal life?

He waited until Sukanya's attention focused on her call. Then he opened his briefcase, removed an iPad and switched on the power.

"Do you have Wi-Fi?" he asked Sukanya.

She nodded.

"You'll need a password," she said.

She told him the password: "beauty101." A moment later, Calvino had his head down over the iPad. The receptionist glanced over and smiled, satisfied that Calvino was doing what most farang husbands did while their Thai wives waited. He reached inside his briefcase, palmed a listening device the size of a thumb—a video camera with a motion sensor and full audio—and as Sukanya returned her attention to the phone, he planted it beneath the table next to the sofa. Ratana held a copy of *Matichon*, turning the pages slowly and giving Calvino cover as he positioned the small camera with a color that matched the chrome tubing of the table. He turned on the camera and checked the view of the camera on his iPad screen—he was looking at a 140-degree arc of the room. Satisfied, he closed the window and opened the browser for the *Bangkok Post*.

Some serious cash had been pumped into the elegant, modern design and furnishings of the doctor's lobby area—Italian sofas, designer tables made from metal and glass, potted exotic plants and an aquarium with tropical fish in a backlit paradise. Polished floors clean enough to eat from were topped by a bank of windows overlooking the road toward Lake Ratchada. They weren't running a charity for orphans. It also didn't look like a backroom abortion clinic. Something didn't calculate. The money sunk into the office, the cost of plastic surgery... weighed against the risk of performing illegal abortions.

From a pair of hidden speakers the sound of soft, ambient music filtered through the reception area—the slightly ethereal, zen-tingling themes performed on a sitar, flute and harpsichord. Calvino discreetly watched Sukanya. She was an elegantly dressed Thai-Indian woman roaring out of the tunnel of her twenties and into the wall of her thirties. She worked without glancing up. Young, diligent and beautiful, Sukanya looked like an advertisement for the doctor's services.

Ratana nudged him.

"That's Bank," said Ratana.

She pointed at one of the photos among two rows of headshots of celebrities and hi-so clients, framed and hung on one wall. They seemed to be there to announce the doctor's importance, like trophies or award certificates.

"He plays a hero on a Channel 3 daytime show. And next to him is a singer named Benz. She's in a shampoo commercial on TV. And that one is Joey, a katoey who has won a game show. They are all very famous people. And there's—"

"I get it," said Calvino, "the doctor gives face to the stars."

The receptionist, who'd been listening in, laughed.

"We have many celebrity clients. Word of mouth brings in new business."

"You collect their autographs?"

"I have signed photos from all of them," Sukanya replied.

It was a little dig at Ratana to pay Sukanya absolute respect as someone connected with the stars.

Calvino considered what she'd said. Confident to the point where she head-butted with the wild beast of arrogance. He studied the photos. None of the faces meant anything to him. In his experience Thai celebrities rarely leaked through to the expat world. Celebrity, he thought, is like time in that it's relative to the position of the observer.

Just as a person's handwriting has an identifiable signature, a plastic surgeon has a signature too. Dr. Nattapong's signature was in evidence within the photo display and on the receptionist's nose, eyes, lips, breasts and chin. Sukanya's features had an unnatural balance and shape, as if she had emerged fully formed from the music. It was as if she'd popped out of a frame on the wall and had gone to work at the desk. Calvino could only guess about the breasts but would have bet some money that they would pretty much look like Ploy's.

Calvino saw two doors. The first led to the doctor's office. About the second, as he stared at it, the receptionist helpfully provided full information.

"That goes to the surgery room. Fully equipped. Everything you would find in the best hospital."

"Yeah?" asked Calvino. "All run by just the two of you? The doctor and you?"

Sukanya flashed a million-dollar smile, like someone who'd picked the right door and won the grand prize.

After a fifteen-minute wait they were shown into the doctor's office. Medical degree framed on the wall behind his desk. More celebrity photos with pursed lips, signed with hearts, framed and positioned on the credenza. The collection was a bit like a Chinese shrine, with all of the angels gathered around to watch the doctor's back.

"My wife wants surgery. Labiaplasty is what I think it's called."

The doctor nodded.

"That's the correct medical term."

"But she doesn't want to go to a hospital—do you, darling?"

"I really don't like hospitals," said Ratana.

"I've read that it's a straightforward operation. It takes under half an hour. Can you perform the operation at the office?"

"That's not a problem."

"Hey, that's good news, darling."

He squeezed Ratana's hand.

"She's been so nervous about the hospital."

"Just like Ploy said, Dr. Nattapong is the best..." said Ratana, smiling at the doctor.

Calvino cut her off.

"No, darling, it wasn't Ploy, it was Ploy's friend Bow who said that. Remember? Jesus, sometimes I wonder about your memory. You ever notice that about women? How they can get confused over who told them what and when? It happens with my wife all the time."

Dr. Nattapong's nose had twitched at the mention of Ploy's name. A flash of guilt crossed his eyes as he became conscious of Calvino's stare. The doctor tried to divert attention by turning around his computer screen.

"Here's a list of the charges for a labiaplasty."

Calvino removed his wallet.

"I can pay you now."

The doctor looked ill, his eyes glazed. The name Ploy had fired a couple of million neurons, simultaneously lighting up his brain like a Christmas tree. He recovered long enough to pull up his schedule on the computer screen.

"I can schedule you next Wednesday at 4:00 p.m. It is important that you don't eat anything twenty-four hours before the appointment."

"I don't want a local. I would hate being awake and knowing everything that was happening to me," said Ratana.

"Is it possible to use a general to put her out?" asked Calvino.

The doctor studied Calvino's face for a moment, looking for something. Or maybe thinking that he could use a nose job after being beat up in Rangoon.

"It is possible to arrange."

Calvino stood up, stretching out his hand.

"Good, then we have a deal. See you next Wednesday."

Ratana was on her feet, giving the doctor a deep *wai*.

"It won't hurt, will it, doctor?"

"No, it won't hurt. You may feel a bit of discomfort after, but I will prescribe pain pills."

"There we go," said Calvino. "Full service. That's why the stars come here. That's why we've come here—right, darling?"

He gently patted Ratana's hand.

After they left the office, Calvino stopped at the staircase at the end of the corridor. He opened the lid on his iPad. He still had a connection to the doctor's Wi-Fi server. He logged in and opened the app that gave him a live feed from the tiny camera in the reception area. Dr. Nattapong's office door opened and he emerged into reception. He looked visibly shaken, his face ashen, his hands trembling.

He was also angry.

"Why didn't you tell me that referral came from Ploy?"

"She never said anything about Ploy."

"What about Bow?"

Sukanya shrugged, the smile wiped off her face.

"Her name never came up."

"How did that woman and her husband find me?"

The receptionist pulled out the questionnaire that Ratana had completed. At the bottom, she had written, "Referred by Bow, your favorite katoey patient."

"Why did that woman use Ploy's name? Her husband corrected her and said it was Bow who recommended me. This isn't right."

"You worry too much. Bow and Ploy were friends. She got them mixed up," she said. "You've had farang and their girlfriends mixing up things before."

"This is different. You should've seen the way he looked at me. Like he knew exactly what had happened with Ploy.

He comes asking for the same operation for his wife. No, no. I am not crazy. He knows something."

"You're tired."

He ignored her, walking around her desk and typing on her keyboard.

"What are you doing?"

"I want to make sure Ploy's computer files are updated."

"You've checked them a hundred times."

"I want to check her file again."

He read the words written in Thai—"Failed to show for her scheduled appointment. Did not phone to cancel."

There were no holes or inconsistencies. There was nothing to connect Ploy to his office on the day she died except a canceled appointment. The maddening thing was someone had filled in the blanks anyway. Someone knew she had died suddenly in the surgery. It happened to the best of doctors: a random, unforeseeable death.

"What happened wasn't your fault. It was Ploy's fault. She ate an hour before the operation. You told her not to, but she didn't listen. *Som na nah*," Sukanya said—served her right.

"I should have called the police."

"The media would have ruined you. We did the right thing."

Calvino pulled up the doctor's email address and attached three digital photos of Ploy's dead body—a headshot, the tattoo on the breast and her full body on the morgue slab shot. He cc'd the general office email, figuring that one reached the receptionist, and pressed Send. He positioned the iPad to share the reaction with Ratana. The email was sent from a John Doe account using an anonymous proxy server. They watched as the receptionist opened the email and read, "Things didn't work out as planned. Ploy." Then she opened the attachments.

Both hands covered her mouth as she shook her head.

"No!"

"I told you something was wrong," said Dr. Nattapong. "You didn't believe me. Now we're being blackmailed. This wasn't supposed to happen. I paid three hundred thousand baht for the problem to disappear. You said Jaruk could do that. He was the one person who could guarantee no complications, no problem. Phone him. Tell him I want to meet him, now."

"In your office?"

"Of course not. Tell him Starbucks on the ground floor of the Exchange Tower. In thirty minutes. Tell him it's an emergency."

A person who scrubs a crime scene clean of all incriminating evidence is called a cleaner. The doctor had given Calvino his cleaner's name: Jaruk. Also the doctor had told him that Jaruk hadn't dropped out of the sky; Sukanya was his go-to person for contacting him. She had the cleaner's direct phone number. Cleaners, Calvino knew, are careful about giving out phone numbers. Either Sukanya slept with the guy or ran with the crowd whose line of work required the services of a professional cleaner to quickly handle the mess left behind in a killing. Men in this profession are systematic. Nothing is left behind after they finish with a job. After a cleaner closes the door, the location is no longer a crime scene—it is just another room.

In Calvino's experience, the best cleaners in Bangkok disposed of bodies in two ways. The first option was dumping it in the sea or an incinerator or a larger meat grinder; the second option was leaving the body in precisely the place they wanted the cops to find it. In the trade the second option is called the Magician's Solution, a kind of sleight of hand. To make the problem disappear in this way is to turn it into a new problem, one that belongs to someone else.

By the time they reached the ground floor of the doctor's building, Calvino had phoned McPhail and told him to go to the Starbucks in the Exchange Tower and follow a Thai named Jaruk.

"He's with the doctor and his office assistant, receptionist, nurse... whatever she is. The doctor is late thirties, slim, thick black hair, Chinese looking. He wears glasses. Black frames. His assistant isn't hard on the eyes. When you spot them, phone me. I'll be on the second floor."

"Give me a description of this guy, Jaruk. Fuck, that's a new name."

He applied a Scottish rolled R to the name.

"I don't know what he looks like."

"Then how am I supposed to follow him?"

"You'll see him at Starbucks. He's meeting the doctor and his receptionist there. She'll be wearing a name-tag that says Sukanya. Can you be there? It's important."

"One thing: what's with this Jaruk?"

"He's the cleaner who dumped Ploy's body at the Tobacco Monopoly."

"That's a good reason."

TWENTY-EIGHT

RATANA CHANGED OUT of the clothes she had worn at the doctor's office and slipped into a security guard's uniform with a hat. She wore a badge and a photo ID tag on a plastic cord around her neck. She stood next to the fruit juice counter on the ground floor of the Exchange Tower, talking with the vendor about the price of fruit. Around the corner from the fruit juice seller were the restrooms. The constant foot traffic there screened her from the main lobby. From her position she had a direct line of sight to the elevator leading to the parking floors.

Jaruk sat with Sukanya and Dr. Nattapong at Starbucks for twenty minutes before he stood up to leave. None of them smiled. Jaruk waied Dr. Nattapong, exchanged a few more words and then walked to the bank of elevators and waited.

Ratana moved forward a bit. When the elevator doors opened and Jaruk walked inside, she quickly slipped in with a couple of office workers. "B2" glowed red on the floor button panel. Jaruk stayed in the corner behind the chatting office workers until the doors opened on B2. He got out and Ratana followed. He pushed open the glass doors leading to the car park, turned right and disappeared around the corner. Ratana stood hunched over out of sight as Jaruk pulled out in a Lamborghini.

She phoned Calvino and described the car.

Jaruk swung a yellow Lamborghini Gallardo sports car out of the Exchange Tower parking lot and exited onto Sukhumvit Road. At the lights he moved into the left turn lane and headed onto Asoke. Calvino was waiting on a BMW 1200K racing motorcycle with McPhail seated on the back. Calvino had given the bike to McPhail. "If you were one of those kids with a rare, inoperative disease who could have anything," he had said, "what would it be?" And McPhail had said, "Easy, a BMW 1200K racing bike. Fully loaded."

Calvino tailed the sports car, staying two, three cars behind. Jaruk swerved in and out of the traffic, bullying any car in front of him, pushing the nose of the Lamborghini inches from the rear bumper of any car he wanted out of the way. He drove like a man possessed, a man with a grievance or a man who had a second double espresso from Starbucks racing through his blood.

McPhail shouted from behind, "The fucker's crazy!"

Calvino gunned the BMW bike, overtaking a white Honda Jazz as if it were driving underwater. At the Asoke and Rama IV intersection, the sports car was second from the red light. Just the fact that someone was ahead had Jaruk racing his engine.

"What's the deal?" asked McPhail, leaning forward. "No way that guy owns that car."

"Big odds it belongs to his boss. And that's where he's taking us."

The light changed. Jaruk moved to an outside lane and cut a sharp right turn onto Rama IV.

Whatever the cause, Jaruk used the imported car to demand that every vehicle in his path—car, van, bus or SUV—give way. Like putting on a Ring of Power, driving a Lamborghini in the streets of Bangkok was an addiction. It was a symbol of the driver's uncontested, naked supremacy. It was the driver's license to be exempt from laws. Other drivers surrendered without resistance. It proved one of Calvino's Laws—that the power of the engine and the make of the car determine whether the driver owns the road. A Lamborghini could own the streets of Bangkok.

The fact was, in Bangkok, Calvino hadn't ever seen anyone behind the wheel of a Lamborghini drive much differently. Why shouldn't Jaruk experience the sudden rush that came with perfectly matching the power of his machine, delivering the message to everyone watching, "Give way! I am untouchable."

The luxury car turned sharply into an entry ramp to park inside an office high-rise on Rama IV Road, a building with a bank on the ground floor. A couple of embassies occupied several of the upper floors, but mostly the tower was devoted to grade-A office space for companies that generated the income for expensive toys. Calvino still followed the Lamborghini, watching as it exited on the third floor. Calvino got off at the top of the ramp and gave the bike to McPhail, who rode it up to the fourth floor and parked in the area reserved for motorcycles. By the time McPhail had parked, cleared the stairs and entered the parking lot, the Lamborghini was empty. He found Calvino checking out the car.

McPhail lit a cigarette and shook his head.

Man, what's the mileage on this wagon?"

Calvino cupped his hands over his eyes and tried to read the dials through the heavy tint.

"Reads seven thousand kilometers."

"Man, that's new. It's only taken a few baby steps."

Calvino remembered a similar sports car parked in front of the 50th Street Bar in Rangoon. There had been other luxury cars parked alongside. He'd been with Colonel Pratt. Inside, Mya was singing the blues. The Colonel had played the sax.

"I said baby steps," repeated McPhail. "Something the matter with you? You look a million miles away. Like you've seen a ghost."

Calvino checked his watch.

"I've got a feeling our boy is going to be back."

He walked around to the front of the car with McPhail a step behind. McPhail dropped his cigarette and crunched it with his shoe.

"What do we have here?" asked McPhail.

Calvino knelt down and read the stenciled sign on the wall. Reserved: CEO Thanet, The Diamond Flagship Import and Export Ltd. Parked in the slot next to the Lamborghini was a new four-door silver Fortuner with the plate number 007. The sign for that parking spot read "Reserved for CFO Apichart, The Diamond Flagship Import and Export Ltd." Calvino took out his cell phone and snapped close-ups of the signs and the plates, and front and side shots of the Lamborghini. He crouched down behind the car, looked underneath. He laughed, "Ed, it looks like someone's already planted a GPS."

"He's gonna wonder about the parade following him," said McPhail. Calvino attached the GPS tracking device under the Lamborghini next to the one he found.

"What we have here is the name of our driver's boss," said Calvino.

McPhail walked over to have a look into the Fortuner parked next to the sports car. The Fortuner used a pickup chassis with an SUV body constructed on top. Calvino crouched down, removed a GPS tracking device from his jacket and attached it under the Fortuner. He put a second device under the rear fender.

"That should make babysitting easier," said Calvino, wiping his hands as he stood up.

"Look at that color," said Ed. "It belongs on a luxury car. Don't put silver on a Fortuner. It's like putting lipstick on a pig. If a car could get plastic surgery, here's where you'd start."

"We just want to follow it, Ed. Forget about the color. Stay on this floor, and when Jaruk comes back, phone me. I'll pick you up on the ramp."

"What if he doesn't come back?"

Calvino put a hand on McPhail's shoulder and squeezed it.

"In that case we've wasted a couple of hours. Life will go on."

McPhail lit another cigarette as he watched Calvino take the stairs to the fourth floor. Half an hour later Jaruk returned, got into the Fortuner and pulled out of the bay.

"Our boy just climbed into Frankenstein's car," McPhail said over the phone.

Calvino switched on the BMW motorcycle, revved the engine, counted three beats, then rode down the ramp just as the Fortuner cleared it. McPhail climbed onto the back and they tailed Jaruk through slow traffic. The Fortuner lacked the power to move mountain and man, and Jaruk was now stuck in a traffic jam. An hour after leaving the building where the Diamond Flagship Import and Export Ltd. had an office, Jaruk stopped in front of a mansion inside Soi 35 Ladprao Road. A metal automatic gate slowly opened. The driver had used a remote. Calvino and McPhail sat on the BMW behind a parked car and watched the Fortuner disappear inside the large compound. The gate closed behind, making a solid prison cell clang.

"We know where his boss works and lives," said Calvino.

"Thanet must be a filthy rich bastard," said Ed. "You sure you want to fuck with someone like this?"

"Maybe he doesn't know his driver has a sideline business as a cleaner."

"What if it isn't a sideline, and he was following orders?" said McPhail.

Calvino nodded.

"Cleaner for who? You're right, that is the question. Ed, don't think too much, it'll give you a headache," said Calvino.

McPhail recognized the old bargirl line for when a customer shifts from the *sabai, sanuk* state of mind to a serious, questioning mode. The fail-safe bargirl mind wants to float along a flat, effortless, problem-free road, and a foreigner comes along, maybe a customer paying for fun, who wants to shift the mindset to twisting, bumpy mountain roads with cutbacks that look down at an abyss.

"Who are you thinking of asking?"

"I think I'll start by asking the driver a few questions," said Calvino.

"That's not going to be easy. He lives in an armed fortress."

"After a little talk about his options, he might come to see this place isn't all that safe."

"And see his boss as the man in charge of death row."

Calvino nodded, observing the high stone wall with long spikes that protected the compound like the hide of an armadillo. He counted four CCTV cameras covering the street. Calvino photographed the cameras and the entrance gate. An hour later the gate opened and Jaruk walked out. He'd changed into a T-shirt screaming in large blue letters "I am Awesome," blue jeans and Nike track shoes. Jaruk pressed a cell phone to his ear.

Ten minutes later, the receptionist from Dr. Nattapong's office showed up in a red Honda Civic. Sukanya parked her car away from the compound's surveillance system. Jaruk opened the door on the passenger's side, got in and then leaned over and kissed her on the lips. The brake lights flashed, and the car pulled slowly away.

"Lovebirds," said McPhail.

"Even vultures show each other affection," replied Calvino.

Calvino slipped on his helmet, started the BMW 1200K and turned it in the direction of the Honda Civic. He followed the Honda to the Big C at Ladprao and watched Sukanya park it. They both got out and walked slowly, talking. McPhail tailed them inside to a pizza parlor on the ground floor. They sat at a table next to a window that looked out at the foot traffic in the mall. McPhail sat two tables away and ordered a Hawaiian pizza with extra pineapple and cheese and a Coke. After the waitress left, he plugged a wire into his cell phone and pushed an earbud into his right ear. Then he positioned the directional mike, adjusted the frequency until he captured their voices and cleaned out the ambient noise until their conversation was as clear as a bell ringing from the tower of a distant cathedral. It was like sitting in the confessional booth, and he was the priest listening to a couple of sinners spilling their guts. Neither one was asking for forgiveness, though they were singing from the same hymnbook. It was an ancient song about how to get away with murder and a suitcase of stolen money.

TWENTY-NINE

YOSHI NAGATA PAID for Judy and Mon Hla's airfares from Mae Hong Son via Chiang Mai. For Mon Hla it was a first experience of Thailand outside the camp. Bangkok's traffic, buildings, noise and speed confused and frightened her. The temple grounds were a refuge, but she still clung to Judy's side. At any other time she'd have been happy to visit the *wat*. There had been no funeral for her parents and brother. Her sister's funeral came at a time of great sadness for several reasons. When she met Nagata, her lower lip quivered and she hugged him, squeezing tears from her eyes. Judy handed her a tissue. Mon Hla blew her nose and wiped the tears from her face while Nagata spoke to her in his yoga voice, a decibel above a whisper.

Judy translated as Mon Hla nodded, fighting back more tears. Without the right Bangkok connections to smooth the way, she would never have received permission to leave the tent city built on the edge of the burnt-out refugee camp. Colonel Pratt had phoned one of his old classmates, and a couple of hours later a pass was signed, granting a forty-eight-hour travel permit on humanitarian grounds. She'd flown to Bangkok to attend the funeral of her sister and to cooperate with the police investigation into the rape and murder case.

McPhail, Ratana, Colonel Pratt, Bow and Bow's boyfriend made polite conversation at the sala. A handful of people had come to pay their final respects. Neither Dr. Nattapong nor Sukanya showed. Not that Calvino expected them to; they'd washed their hands of young Ploy. Nor did the man who had bought her from her family bother to show up. Why should he? What he'd paid for no longer served any purpose. Junk it. He was the kind of man who thought nothing of ordering his men to blow up a car. Such men were called psychopaths or sociopaths, and Bangkok was overpopulated with them.

McPhail couldn't stop himself from sneaking glances at Bow, who was all shapely legs, up and down.

Shaking his head, he said, "You look totally different."

She wore a short skirt and high heels. Her long black hair touched her shoulders, and her lipstick and eyeliner were transforming. Her accommodation for the funeral was a black armband. Otherwise, she could have just walked off the stage at Tiffany's with a crown.

"The university has a stupid rule," Bow said.

Her boyfriend looked bored, fighting back a yawn.

"You speak English?" McPhail asked him.

"A little."

"You take good care of Bow. She's a sweet, sweet girl."

"How do you know that?"

The boyfriend's face had a permanent smile, making it difficult to read the tone in his question.

"Calvino told me. How is it that all of Ploy's friends are good people? How does someone like that die? Calvino asked me that. But I think he was asking himself, and he wasn't just thinking about Ploy."

"You think Bow has a problem?"

For the first time the boyfriend showed an emotion. It could have passed as anxiety.

"Keep an eye on her," said McPhail.

McPhail had attended too many funerals with Calvino. He'd gone along with Calvino to Mya's funeral and watched the smoke rise from the crematory chimney. He'd watched as Calvino said goodbye the best he could. Again at Ploy's funeral, he witnessed Calvino drawn to a dead person he'd never known in life but who had the capacity to draw him to her burning. Fire on flesh, blood and bone signaled a sacred purity, a cleansing of form in preparation for the final journey into the eternal loop of nothingness. When Calvino talked about the scent of wet ashes, McPhail knew exactly what an existential loop smelled like.

Nagata said a few words before the crematory's metal door closed with the coffin inside and the flames ignited: "Her family named her Mi Swe. We knew her as Ploy. She lived in a refugee camp. She knew that world. I myself was born in a relocation camp my parents had been sent to. We understood each other in the way of people with no home in a land, who are mistrusted and despised by local people. If she were standing with us today, Ploy would say, do not weep or cry for me. I am free. Beyond pain, doubt, suffering and regret. When I spoke at my mother's funeral, I reminded her friends and family that death is release. It is not to be feared. It is natural. Death releases us from suffering. As Buddhists, we believe this is our highest achievement. Our lives are a path to the closing of the cycle of birth, death and rebirth in endless time. We gather here to pray for Ploy's release down that path. To be redeemed from redemption is not a contradiction. It is the key equation we must learn."

Nagata raised his arms slowly, making a perfect wai toward the coffin.

"Ploy, you will remain in our hearts and our memory. You touched our lives, graced them with kindness and love. We gather at this ceremony to witness your release to be as one with eternity."

After the cremation ceremony ended, they looked up at the sky to watch the last tails of the smoke, twisting, spinning as they coiled from the blackened mouth of the chimney. The heat from the crematorium and the sun left Bow and her boyfriend listless, their energy sapped. They waited for the right moment before making excuses. After they left, Colonel Pratt asked Judy if she and Mon Hla would join him for lunch.

Looking over at Calvino, Judy said, "Vincent, you join us too."

She relaxed and managed a smile. They stared at each other as two people who had misjudged one another only to come to the conclusion they'd been wrong. It was hard to admit. She reached out with her hand and Calvino grasped it.

"Yeah, I'll be there."

Two cars delivered the mourning group to a restaurant on a sub-soi deep inside Soi Thonglor, where they parked and entered the Cheesecake House. The staff recognized Colonel Pratt, who lived nearby. The owner asked him about his wife, Manee. Pleasantries accomplished, Colonel Pratt asked for a big table. The staff pushed two tables together and the group milled around, uncertain where to be seated. Colonel Pratt invited Yoshi Nagata to sit at the head of the table. It was the Colonel's way of acknowledging that Nagata was senior to him. With his speech at Ploy's funeral, he'd also established himself as a respected elder, making him both the keeper and messenger of the soul of the deceased.

Nagata accepted the honor with a slight nod and sat down. Calvino pulled out the chair between McPhail and Judy, who had Mon Hla at her other side. On the opposite side, Calvino faced Colonel Pratt and Ratana, who had opened their menus.

Colonel Pratt was hoping for a private talk with Mon Hla, but that would have to wait. As a Thai he understood that before serious business is discussed, the social side must be attended to. He was a patient man. A passage from *The Winter's Tale* came to mind: "What's gone and what's past help should be past grief." Shakespeare would in some ways always be a farang in Thailand. No Thai could conceive of letting go of the past, as grief never ended with the smoke up the chimney.

Judy ordered a banana shake and the salmon pasta for Mon Hla and an ice coffee and salad for herself. The post-funeral lunch was a quiet affair. Not so much awkward as washed out by a collective feeling of futility and exhaustion. Food arrived at the table, and only then did real conversation begin.

Turning to Judy, Calvino said, "Any more news on what caused the fire at the camp?"

"Mon Hla saw a helicopter drop fire from the sky. I talked with a couple of other witnesses who also saw it."

"Officials I've talked to say the fire was caused by an overturned cooking stove," said Colonel Pratt. "Other stories, of helicopters and bombs, bring more attention. I can understand the desire of refugees to want others to have sympathy for them."

Two versions of the fire had circulated through the media for days. The authorities had said there was no need for further investigation into the cause of the fire. No Thai person in the area had logged a flight plan for a helicopter, and no Thai person had witnessed a helicopter flying in the area on the day of the fire. In the battle of facts between the Burmese and the Thais, there was little doubt who would win. The standoff between the conflicting stories would soon disappear like smoke. Colonel Pratt was the kind of man who said the agenda was always open. "Show me the evidence" could have been his motto. But he couldn't consider conflicting evidence just now, as the people around the table had gone silent. Who would contradict a Thai police colonel?

After lunch was finished, Colonel Pratt saw his chance.

"Vincent said you saw a helicopter just before the fire started in the camp," he said.

Mon Hla nodded.

"I saw it drop a sparkling flare. It made a silver color against the sky. It hit the top of our house. My mother, father and brother were inside. They died."

Colonel Pratt sat silently, glancing at Calvino, then back at Mon Hla.

"Sometimes people think they see something, but it's not really there."

"I watched the helicopter," she replied firmly.

She was young and scared, but she held her ground.

The reality was that no one other than a couple of Burmese refugees had claimed to see the helicopter. What was Mon Hla's credibility? If she or the others had wanted the spotlight, then claiming they'd been attacked in a refugee camp guaranteed international press. An overturned cooking stove wasn't news on that scale, even if a lot of people had died. Colonel Pratt believed she had seen something.

With Judy by her side, Mon Hla seemed confident, more than she'd been when she had first arrived at the wat. The Colonel saw no point in further questions about the cause of the fire. For now he had only one more question for Mon Hla, but it was on another subject.

"Do you have any information about the man who paid money for Ploy to leave the camp and move to Bangkok?"

Mon Hla shook her head.

"I don't know his name. It was a secret. The day she left the camp, I was helping at the clinic. We never had a chance to say goodbye. My mother told me that Mi Swe had left with a man who'd found her work in Bangkok."

"Your parents never talked about who she was with or where she lived?"

"I don't think they were told."

People in refugee camps don't ask for information, the Colonel knew; they are given it. It's a one-way street, and people like Mon Hla and her family reside at the dead end of that street.

The others at the table sat in silence, listening to Colonel Pratt politely, gently asking his questions. Then Yoshi Nagata interrupted.

"Colonel, you must have many questions, such as who bought Ploy, and who sold her from a camp under Thai jurisdiction? How much money was paid and when, and to whom? Was it a one-off sale or part of a larger trafficking network? As you have gathered, Mon Hla is not someone who remotely knows the answers to these questions."

"She has to report back at the camp tonight or she has a big problem," said Calvino. "Unless someone extends her travel permit, Judy takes her back this afternoon."

Colonel Pratt assessed the situation as urgent. He knew that, as a rule of thumb, the more urgent the matter, the quicker time slips away. The future unfolded before him as he looked at Mon Hla, a young Burmese woman who had just attended the cremation of her sister's remains. She could be grilled for days and nothing more of value would emerge. Putting her in front of the press to recount her sighting of the helicopter would likely lead to reprisals. Nothing good would come of keeping her in Bangkok.

"You return to Mae Hong Son," Colonel Pratt said. "I am sorry about what happened to your family."

When they left the restaurant, McPhail lit a cigarette, turned and spoke to Colonel Pratt.

"Hey, I wanted to ask you if you need any Dexter Gordon. I've downloaded everything he ever recorded."

"On Sundays I jam with a guitar player who knew him. Billy Clarke once played as a sideman with Gordon in Paris."

"Life follows cycles, all loops and circles," said Yoshi Nagata. "Most of life is encrypted. We waste our lives searching for the wrong keys and forget where the right keys are kept. Life and death are matters of chance. A sideman for Dexter Gordon half a lifetime ago appears in your life in Bangkok. Perhaps this is a key to unlock a door for you."

Calvino waited until he had a moment with Colonel Pratt away from the others.

"Come back to my office. I have some videos I want to show you. And some audio that you will find interesting."

Ratana stood a few meters away, glancing in their direction. She wanted to join them but saw that Calvino and Colonel Pratt were in the middle of something. She could tell by Calvino's posture and expression that he was explaining about the plastic surgeon. The Colonel was hearing another story. Unlike the helicopter story, the plastic surgeon's botched operation had a recorded confession attached; it had arrived into the world with pictures and sound. Calvino figured that once Colonel Pratt saw the video and heard conversation between the doctor and his receptionist, he'd pick up the phone and send out the word that Akash Saru should be released from prison and the charge of murder dropped.

An outsider could be forgiven for assuming that release in such circumstances would be automatic, standard procedure, for it would now be clear that an innocent man was being wrongfully held. But in Thailand, as in a lot of other places, establishing a contradictory story about who committed a murder set the cat among the pigeons, mice and mad dogs, and each of these animals has its own way of dealing with cats.

THIRTY

AFTER COLONEL PRATT had watched the video for a second time and heard the conversation McPhail had taped at the pizza parlor, he got up from the chair, walked to the window and stared down at the sub-soi below Calvino's office. A patron rolled out of the No Hands message parlor, dancing on his heels and smiling. The customers who emerged from that place always seemed happy. A massage business was like a successful plastic surgery business—patients had a choice, and word spread. If a friend had "liked" a place, they expected to walk out feeling good about themselves, on top of the world. It didn't work out that way at all such businesses, though. Sometimes a customer made a mistake—wrong plastic surgeon or wrong massage girl—and never made it out the door alive.

Calvino waited as Colonel Pratt collected his thoughts—which galloped down a steep mountain pass.

Finally, Calvino said: "Looks like they set up the doctor. The receptionist works as the nurse and administers a double dose of anesthetic. The girl dies. The receptionist says it was an accident. If it's a botched abortion, he's ruined. No need to worry; she knows someone who can handle the problem. Make it go away. It will cost some money, but problems usually do. The doctor goes along with her idea. She calls her boyfriend, Jaruk. If you dig a little, I expect you'll find

222

he's not only a driver for CEO Thanet of the Diamond Flagship Import and Export Ltd. but also has a hidden talent. Jaruk is an experienced cleaner. You don't get that good without a lot of practice.

"I figure after he got the call from his girlfriend, he arrived in under an hour. I'd bet he borrowed the boss's white Fortuner with a couple of men he's worked with before. When they show up at the doctor's office, the doctor waves them into his surgery and they get down to business. Before touching anything, they suit up in surgical masks and surgery greens, shoes bagged and taped. Only then do they remove Ploy's body. They use the right chemicals to wipe the surgery clean. They dress the body in a designer tracksuit. By the time they leave with the body, there's not a trace of Ploy having ever being inside the surgery. The doctor has an overwhelming sense of relief.

"Jaruk and his girlfriend split the three hundred grand, giving a small percentage to the cleanup crew. Sukanya now has job security and sets her own annual bonus and pension plan, and basically makes herself a partner. The doctor is effectively married to her. She's put together a deal that puts her in the picture for the rest of his life."

"But it's not quite working out as planned," said Colonel Pratt.

Calvino leaned forward over the computer screen.

"There's been a hitch. Something they hadn't planned on."

"Now the cleaner and the receptionist are running scared," said Colonel Pratt.

Calvino nodded.

"But not of the doctor," Calvino said.

Colonel Pratt looked back from the window.

"No, he's in his receptionist's pocket. It's someone else."

Ratana walked into the office with a look of panic.

"Sukanya's office phoned me and said Dr. Nattapong wants to negotiate."

"Did he say about what?"

Ratana stared at the Colonel.

"She said that I knew very well what it was about."

"What did you say?"

"I told her I'd have to talk to my husband first."

"Don't worry," said Calvino. "The doctor's problem is Thanet's *luk nong*, Jaruk. Have I got that right, Pratt?"

"You have a theory about Khun Thanet, but where is the evidence?" asked Colonel Pratt.

The name rolled out with a mixture of regret and repulsion. Bold-faced names like black flies at picnic time, landings and quick escapes with a million years of evolutionary engineering.

Though still quite young, Thanet had assumed the top dog position of a powerful and rich Chinese-Thai family that owned land and rubber plantations in the South, along with a long-haul trucking firm to service it, and had expanded into shipping. The wives and daughters of the family regularly appeared in the Thai press—featured in pictures taken at hi-so parties, dinners, banquets and fundraisers. Members of the family were profiled as smart, foreign-educated and rich.

One of Thanet's brothers had held a series of important government posts. One nephew climbed the ranks in the army, while another was an officer in the navy who was tipped for promotion. Colonel Pratt had listened to Calvino's theory of how the murder had gone down. For the Colonel Calvino's theory left out an essential element— the psychological state of fear and the choice the doctor had made under duress of that emotion, not knowing the full price of what he'd bought. If Dr. Nattapong had known that he was about to connect his fate to Thanet's family, he might have decided that his chances were better coming clean, going to the police and taking the heat.

"Thanet's driver might have been hiding his moonlighting career as a cleaner," said Calvino.

Colonel Pratt sat back in the chair and crossed his legs.

"Was he moonlighting or acting on orders?" the Colonel asked. "We don't know. Remember the businessman who was killed by his driver and friends a couple of weeks ago?"

It had been widely reported that the gang had extorted millions of baht, strangled the boss and told a story that hadn't lasted through the first police interrogation.

"I read about it," said Calvino.

"What you don't read about in the newspapers is that a lot of important people in this country are having a second look at their drivers, maids and gardeners. Quietly running background checks, accessing their bank accounts, firing anyone with a question mark next to their name."

There was a long silence. Both men felt its weight pressing against them.

"The thing that bothers me most is the way Jaruk disposed of Ploy's body," said Calvino. "The body dump doesn't seem professional. Why not take it upcountry and bury it? Or transport the body to the Eastern Seaboard, load it on a boat, drop it into the sea? But he doesn't go for any of the obvious choices. Instead he goes to the trouble and risk of dumping the body on the Tobacco Monopoly Land. An Indian nut vendor goes to the same spot for an appointment to meet a girl, only he finds she's dead. The vendor is arrested. His go-between is murdered. Does that sound like something that makes sense if it were just Jaruk, his girlfriend and a small crew?" asked Calvino.

In Thailand premeditated murder tended to orbit around three parties: a mastermind, an executioner and a cutout. The last of these was the schlemiel whose role was to take the fall.

"Jaruk and Sukanya sure seemed nervous at the pizza place," said Calvino.

Clearly they had much to be nervous about. As the recording revealed, the little plot they'd hatched had begun unraveling, and their choices were narrowing. Jaruk had promised Sukanya he'd work things out. Meanwhile she should continue to go to the office as usual. After their pizza parlor meeting, she'd driven him to a couple of sois away from the Thanet family compound, and he'd taken a motorcycle taxi the rest of the way.

"I want to pay the doctor a visit," said Colonel Pratt.

"Why don't I come along, Pratt? I can introduce you. The doctor wants to open negotiations. Let's see what he has to offer. "

Colonel Pratt thought about the implications of Calvino accompanying him. Unexpected events happened when Calvino came along. Inviting the unexpected always sounded creative and good, but that was before anyone considered the downside. On the other hand, he told himself, without Calvino's help he'd have had no reason to go to the doctor's office. After watching the video in the doctor's office, he had no doubt Ploy hadn't been raped and killed by the Indian. She'd died in surgery with the "assistance" of the receptionist. Jaruk had been called in to dispose of the body. And as Calvino had said, there had to be a reason why the body was left where it was. He had a few questions for Sukanya.

"Vincent, it might be better if I went to the doctor's office on my own."

Calvino's wounded expression softened the Colonel.

"If I'm in the office, I can stand by the door so neither of them bolts," said Calvino. "He'll crack, and so will she. Watch their faces when they see me walk in."

"Looking for what?"

"That guilty as hell look," said Calvino.

THIRTY-ONE

CALVINO AND COLONEL Pratt turned up at the doctor's third-floor office and walked in. The reception area was empty. No one was behind the desk. On Sukanya's computer screen a pattern of marigolds exploded into a starburst. Calvino opened the door to the doctor's office. It was also empty.

Calvino nodded at the door to the surgery.

"That's where he operates."

No voices or music—only a deep silence.

"What do you think, Pratt?"

"Only one way to find out."

The Colonel swung the door open, looked inside and watched as Calvino walked in, shaking his head.

The silence of the surgery had become the silence of a morgue, with two bodies sprawled out.

Colonel Pratt knelt beside the body of the doctor.

"He hasn't been dead long."

The doctor lay on the floor face up, with a bullet wound between his lifeless eyes, which stared at the ceiling. A pool of blood created a red halo around his head.

Calvino stood over the operating table looking down at Sukanya. Dark red blooms like rosebuds with black holes covered the front of her white blouse. Calvino counted a bouquet of three small blooms sprouting from her chest. Liquid from her implants—which had taken a direct hit—bubbled through one of the flowers like a clown's boutonnière spraying water. Blood from her chest wounds dripped from the operating table into puddles on the floor below. A surgical mask covered her nose and mouth. Calvino leaned over and lifted the mask, pulling it back over her head. Sukanya's lips were bloodied and bruised, her teeth broken.

"Looks like the negotiations broke down," said Calvino.

Colonel Pratt rose to his feet, his knees creaking, and walked around the doctor's body on the floor, trying to locate where the shooter would have stood. He slowly shook his head.

"It is likely the gunman fired from this spot."

Colonel Pratt marked the spot a meter from the body. So much for a routine visit, with Calvino tagging along to guard the door in case of escape. The doctor and his receptionist were going nowhere.

"Where are you going?" asked Colonel Pratt, as he saw Calvino move to the door.

"To check out what my camera picked up."

He walked out of the surgery and back into reception. On Sukanya's desk he spotted the blue Honda box and opened it. Her iPhone was inside, overlooked by the killers. He slipped the phone into his pocket and put the lid back on the box. He walked over to the sofa, sat down and reached under the arm where he'd planted the camera. He played back footage from the past hour, fast-forwarding until he saw the two gunmen enter the office.

"Pratt, come and have a look at this."

Colonel Pratt walked around the blood and back into the reception area. Calvino had his iPad out and had logged into the app that hooked up to a feed from the camera. The Colonel watched the screen as the two men entered. They wore white Guy Fawkes masks and surgery green tops and

228

bottoms. One of the men pulled the doctor from his office. The other one ordered Sukanya to walk around from her desk. The doctor babbled, pleading for the men to leave, offering them money.

Sukanya seemed calm.

"Do what they ask," she said.

The absence of fear in her voice suggested she knew the men. The four then filed out of the lobby into the surgery. From off camera Colonel Pratt and Calvino could hear the trademark sound of a silencer masking a gunshot. Calvino played back the men herding Sukanya and Dr. Nattapong into the surgery. Then the unmistakable sound of muffled shots. That was all a silencer accomplished. It didn't silence the shot; it merely reduced the loudness of the slugs on their way out of the gun barrel. None of the people working in neighboring offices would have heard the shots.

The video footage captured two shadows dressed in surgery greens with their faces hidden behind identical masks. Not any mask, but a symbolic seventeenth-century face with a mustache, a goatee and black eyebrows—a face that for a brief moment had featured prominently in the ongoing political conflicts between the main factions in Thailand. One side had registered its protest by wearing Guy Fawkes masks to political demonstrations. The gunmen had found an alternative, more practical use for the masks. A mask that hundreds had worn in the streets of the city afforded professional killers a perfect disguise. They were indistinguishable from anyone who'd participated in the demonstrations. As with the street protests, the killers' appearance was an inspired piece of political theatre that deserved a larger audience.

THIRTY-TWO

IN THE FAR distance a large crow circled overhead, while another crow called out from the trees lining the access road separating Queen Sirikit Center and Benjakiti Park, which both ran along the Ratchadapisek edge of the Tobacco Monopoly grounds. Their cawing and its echoes sounded like the cries of wounded sentinels on a distant battlefield—shocked, angry, frightened and sad. Calvino and Colonel Pratt passed through the security gates behind Queen Sirikit Center and walked shoulder to shoulder down a narrow side road. Calvino then took the lead, cutting across a small canal and into a sprawl of tall grass, wildflowers and bamboo. Calvino stopped at the spot where he'd discovered Ploy's body. Colonel Pratt squatted beside him. The grass was still mashed down. He patted the ground.

"Someone chose this location for a reason. To make a point." Looking up at Calvino. he added, "A location is like a weapon. It leads to the man using it."

The Colonel understood that while weapons are easily switched or ditched, the physical place where a crime has been committed was unchangeable. The skill of an experienced cleaner can break the connection between the location and weapon, but the criminals usually leave behind some meaningful marker such as a fingerprint or DNA. Colonel Pratt had been trained to start with the location of the crime and work backwards so that the weapon, user and motive revealed themselves. He'd studied the body discovery scene before, looking for that piece of evidence that would point to the murderer's identity. The problems in the case had started when the police turned up a suspect, Akash Saru, and all their efforts shifted to finding evidence to prove his guilt.

"Akash Saru had been here before," said Calvino.

He hadn't come by chance. He'd come for a reason.

Colonel Pratt patted the grass again.

"Why did he lie about knowing about the girl?" he said.

"What other choice did he have? He denied raping and killing her," said Calvino. "He told you the truth. You saw the video with the doctor and his receptionist. Ploy died in their office. She died in surgery. What more do you want before you write on the file, 'Case open and shut'? Jaruk and his buddies loaded the body in the Fortuner, drove it here and set up the little shrine."

"Open, yes," replied Colonel Pratt. "Did Akash tell you his real name?"

At first Calvino didn't answer. He'd withheld that information. He found getting caught out in a lie the most difficult of human experiences.

"I found out about it from one of his friends."

"You didn't tell me."

"You didn't ask."

"Is that how it is?"

"It doesn't have to be this way, Pratt. If we can work together like before."

They both knew how that had turned out. Colonel Pratt had nearly lost his job protecting Calvino from an obstruction of justice charge in connection with the car bombing. Calvino's history of crazy visions had been enough to convince the Colonel's boss that Calvino needed psychiatric treatment. Dr. Apinya, with her foreign

231

medical degree and fluent English, had been chosen for him. Calvino hadn't had much choice—submit to therapy and rehabilitation or face criminal charges for tampering with crime scene evidence.

"As far as I can see, we are working together. What we saw in Dr. Nattapong's office gives me no other option. We've come back here because I want to show you something."

The Colonel reached into his pocket and held out a small object in the palm of his hand.

"One of these statuettes was found here. I thought it was unusual. I showed it to Manee and she recognized it immediately. It's a Hindu deity called Agni. See the two faces? He's the Vedic god of fire. Agni is the link between the gods and man, heaven and earth. Sacrifices are made in his name, and he takes the offerings to the world of the gods through his fire."

Calvino thought about Colonel Pratt's wife, Manee, drawing upon her knowledge of Buddhist, Hindu and Chinese deities. She'd recognized the icon. What she couldn't answer was what that particular deity was doing in a shrine next to a dead girl, apparently not a Hindu, in a remote part of the Tobacco Monopoly Land.

Colonel Pratt stood up, passing the figure of Agni to Calvino.

"Akash isn't a Hindu. He's a Muslim. So why would he bring a Hindu image to a shrine?"

"You didn't say anything about Agni before," said Calvino.

It felt heavier than it looked as he held it in the palm of his hand.

"Not everything is passed along. Like your being in the room where Akash's friend Anal Khan was found dead. I don't recall that conversation."

Calvino handed the icon back. He watched as the Colonel held the figure of Agni between his index finger and thumb, slowly rotating it, stopping a moment as each head appeared.

"I knew the cops on the scene would report and would pass it on to you," Calvino said. "No need to duplicate information."

Colonel Pratt shook his head.

"That's not the reason, and you know it. You didn't tell me because you knew that Akash hadn't accidentally stumbled upon the body. A friend had sent him to this place."

He looked at the ground where the body had been found.

"It would've been bad if I'd told you, Pratt. You've got orders to keep away from me. What's your boss gonna say when he finds out that we've kept a secret channel open? Rather than putting you in the position where you had to betray a friend or betray your boss, I kept quiet."

Colonel Pratt wiped his mouth with his free hand.

"Vincent, my friend, we Thais look for the middle path. Because we wish to avoid finding ourselves in an extreme position."

"I know a thing or two about that middle path. It's the one taken when you reach a dead end. There's no middle to it. You either climb over the wall or turn around, face the problem, take your chances, or you hightail it back to where you came and hope things blow over. The middle path is where we're standing. Do we keep going or retreat?"

The Colonel looked at the small Hindu god.

"What was this two-headed god of fire doing here?"

Calvino opened his briefcase, removed the tiny security camera and listening device and handed it to Colonel Pratt.

"Take it. It's evidence of the men who killed the doctor and receptionist. Why not call it in?" asked Calvino.

"No, I am not calling it in," said Colonel Pratt. "I'd like to talk to Jaruk."

"I suspect it's going to be hard to find him," said Calvino. "As Thanet's driver, he has unofficial immunity until video footage starts turning up. Then it starts to get interesting."

"The men wore masks. There is no proof that one of them was Jaruk."

"Exactly the point. Just enough doubt to let Jaruk slip away."

They'd had this discussion before they'd left the plastic surgery office. What should they do? Call the police, go after Jaruk or jump over the ring of fire that appeared on all sides? Colonel Pratt had decided to borrow some time, suggesting that they return to the place where Calvino had found the body. The Colonel had needed time to think over his options.

Before they'd left the doctor's office, Calvino and Colonel Pratt had wiped their fingerprints from the scene. The CCTV camera in front of the building couldn't be wiped. It would have recorded the time of their entry. The autopsy on the doctor and the receptionist would likely reveal the time of death to be close to the time of their arrival at the office. They'd left using the stairs at the back. "I'd be willing to bet those two guys came in and out this way," Calvino had said as they descended.

The men in the Guy Fawkes masks caught on Calvino's tiny spy camera had been professionals, Calvino was sure. Colonel Pratt didn't disagree. He wished that, like the killers, he and Calvino had used the back entrance without the CCTV camera, but it was too late for that. Besides, there'd been no reason when they'd arrived at the office building to suspect they'd be walking into a fresh murder scene.

Having been the first to arrive at the doctor's office, as a cop, Colonel Pratt knew the drill, the thinking and the kind of question that begged for an answer: how would he and Calvino explain their timing? If it had only been the timing, that could be a coincidence. But Calvino had previously been to the office using a phony identity. His secretary had pretended to be his wife.

"I've got the video, Pratt. The doctor and his receptionist spilling their guts about killing the girl. There is no ambiguity. And what's in the second video? There are two clowns in Guy Fawkes masks who strong-arm the doctor and his nurse into the surgery. We hear off camera the muffled sound of gunshots."

"The second video also shows us walking into the office."

"After the gunshots," said Calvino. "The sequence of events is clear."

"We have raw footage. A video can be edited."

The vulnerability to an accusation of video tampering wasn't the main thing bothering Colonel Pratt. He was far more worried about Thanet's connection: what Thanet knew, his involvement and his motives. If his driver had been caught freelancing and engaged in a criminal partnership with the receptionist, then greed and fear would have been two good reasons to have the doctor and the receptionist killed. The problem would have been eliminated. The receptionist and Jaruk had squeezed a chunk of change from the doctor to clean up the surgery, and Sukanya had earned herself a lifelong extortion threat over the doctor. The two of them were sitting pretty. Jaruk could hoist a mission-accomplished flag. That indicated to Colonel Pratt that either Jaruk was much smarter than a normal driver or he was working his relationship with the receptionist under orders from his boss.

Why would someone like Thanet have any interest in a Rohingya or Burmese refugee who had been sold from a camp? For a foreigner the evidence in the video was the deal closer; for a Thai the moving pictures were a mosquito in the room of an untouchable with a hide as tough as an elephant. The person possessing the video was the one doing the sweating. Does he sell it to Thanet? That would be suicide. Does he destroy it before anyone else sees it? Does he turn it into the department and possibly become marginalized or even forced into exile abroad with his family for their safety? The Colonel knew there were no good choices.

The fingerprints of Calvino, Ratana and Colonel Pratt had been all over the office. They'd wiped them down as best they could, but it would have been impossible not to miss a set of prints. The Colonel had acted against his boss's orders, helping his farang friend Calvino—the same foreigner who had embarrassed the department by questioning their report on the explosive device used to kill the two Burmese entertainers. Calvino had witnessed his first hallucinations in the days that had followed the bombing. When Colonel Pratt had convinced him that he needed therapy, Calvino had agreed not because he thought it would do any good but because it would help the Colonel out of a tough spot. The Colonel had been right. Once he'd started seeing the doctor, the cops had backed off, allowing Colonel Pratt's crazy farang friend to fade into the background—on the condition that the Colonel kept him away from the case or any other case. Calvino had been issued his retirement ticket, and Colonel Pratt had guaranteed that Bangkok would have one less private investigator sticking his long nose into police business.

"Has anyone looked into the possibility that Thanet has links to the smuggling and trafficking of illegals?" asked Calvino.

"Go home, Vincent."

"That's not answering my question," said Calvino.

"It's advice."

"And you? Where are you going?"

Colonel Pratt looked at the building in the distance where the plastic surgery clinic was located. Flashing red lights on police vehicles passed by and turned into the sub-soi leading to the building. "When sorrows come," he recalled, "they come not single spies, but in battalions." Shakespeare had voiced a number of universal truths, but none was more enduring than his insight into treachery and the dangers of secret lives and powerful people.

Calvino turned to leave.

"I'll hold onto the video camera and recorder," said Colonel Pratt.

Calvino stopped, turned around, briefcase in hand.

"They're yours."

"Stay out of the case, Vincent. You've cleared Akash. I'll see he's released. You've found out the identity of the murdered the girl. It's over for you. There's nothing more for you to do except get into deep trouble."

"That's what crazy people do," said Calvino. "Cause trouble for the sane."

They strolled through the Tobacco Monopoly grounds.

"See you later," said Colonel Pratt, before he disappeared down the MRT stairs.

Calvino didn't ask where he was going. He turned back until he came to the running track and walked around the perimeter of the lake. Joggers slowly huffed and puffed their way around him. Voices inside Calvino's head told him that it wasn't over. The same voices told him that Colonel Pratt would be surprised to learn that Calvino had followed his advice. He knew that Calvino was a different kind of bird. One that scratched in the dirt like a fighting cock, holding his ground in the pit, waiting for the chance to sink his spurs into the flesh of the champion cock who'd never lost a fight.

THIRTY-THREE

RATANA OPENED THE water tap, rinsing a plate in the kitchen sink and stacking it with the other plates, bowls and glasses in a drying rack. She'd used a spare key given to her by Calvino long ago along with the instruction that in the event of an emergency, she should let herself in. As Calvino lived in a constant state of emergency, she had a fair amount of latitude in using it, but this was the first time she'd done so.

She had worked for Calvino long enough to know the difference between a tough time and a life and death situation. His problem, in her mind, was he no longer saw the distinction. It had become all life and death situations without end, and that had burnt him out. Colonel Pratt had phoned her and said that he thought Calvino was in a bad way, and she might do well to check in on how he was living.

Assessing the condition of Calvino's condo, Ratana thought she'd seen this scene before. Anyone with experience of the living conditions following a typhoon, tornado, earthquake or flood would have wondered if a natural disaster had struck his condo unit. She'd cleaned the counters, changed the sheets on the bed, done loads of washing and ironing, cleaned the floors and windows. It was a difficult job as she carefully worked around his photographs, newspaper clippings, charts, diagrams and a miniature recreation of the car-bombing site on the coffee table.

The first thing that Calvino noticed as he walked into his condo was a pair of women's shoes neatly positioned near the door.

"Hello!" he shouted.

"In here!" came Ratana's familiar voice.

He removed his shoes and hurried through the kitchen, passing Ratana with a panicked expression.

"Well, hello, yourself," she said as he exited the kitchen area.

She found him standing in the sitting room, hands at his side, silently observing the cleaned room.

"I hope it is okay," she said.

Calvino nodded, as he glanced at his computer on the table. His Mac PowerBook had been moved slightly from where he'd left it.

"The place looks..."

"Something the matter?"

"Did you move the computer?"

She shook her head.

"I cleaned around it. I might have."

His eyes lit up as he contemplated the extent of the transformation. She'd restored his condo to a state of order so long removed that he had no longer remembered how it had once looked. The clutter, dust, mold and debris mirroring his state of his mind had disappeared. He checked the other rooms, hardly recognizing the space. In the sitting room, she had been careful to maintain his evidence of the car-bombing case. She'd done something that he'd no longer felt capable of doing; she'd restored order. Everything had been organized by a mind that saw how to lay out the documents without disturbing the nature of the underlying material objects. Inhaling the smells of soap, cleaning liquid and polish, he felt a glorious sense of renewal and rebirth.

"I'm glad you finally used the key," he said.

Ratana watched her boss pour himself a drink and sit down at the computer.

"It was the right time," she said. "I am surprised that even ghosts would come to your home as I found it."

Calvino looked up.

"They never stayed for long."

He glanced down at the Mac PowerBook, asking it, "What secrets do you hold about Agni?" It wasn't a question he could ask his Remington typewriter.

As Calvino began Googling, Ratana looked over his shoulder at Agni, the Hindu god of fire on his screen.

"Recognize him?" Calvino asked Ratana as he sipped from the glass.

She sat next to him and studied the image at the top of the Wikipedia page. Agni's profile read like some of the men she'd found on dating websites—ever-young, an immortal, a messenger and a go-between for the gods and mortals. She suppressed a giggle.

"Why don't you ask Colonel Pratt?"

"He's a little busy at the moment. What do you know about the Hindu deity named Agni?"

The flow of Hindu gods through the cultural back door meant Thais recognized many of the major ones.

"The god with two faces," Ratana said. "Manee is the expert in Hindu deities, of course. Actually, we were just talking about Shiva and Vishnu earlier today. Did I tell you that you that my mother bought an Agni amulet in India when I was twelve? Agni is a guardian between two worlds."

"Like the Romans. They had a two-headed god named Janus."

"You are always finding an Italian angle," she said, "just as we Thais find an Indian or a Chinese one."

Calvino smiled.

"Glad to hear you admit it."

"I thought you'd still be with Colonel Pratt."

"Something came up," he said, pulling up the Wikipedia page on Janus. "Janus was the god of beginnings, change, transitions. Among the Romans he cropped up as the god of choice in rituals for births, marriages and deaths. One of Janus's heads faced the past and the other faced the future. The Romans believed Janus occupied a middle ground between barbarism and civilization. The past was the time of the barbarian, and the future was the era of the civilized, refined Roman citizen. Janus had an eye on both sides of our human nature."

"Your mother taught you that about Janus?"

"My mother was Jewish. My Italian grandfather taught me about Janus."

"Janus and Agni are the same god under a different name. J and A."

"Yeah, that's good—J and A," he said.

"It's an easy way to remember things. Just memorize the first initials: J and A."

"Like JAI."

"I don't see any I in the picture," said Ratana.

"I'd like to ask Yoshi Nagata his opinion about the missing I."

"I don't understand."

"Ploy's tattoo. The JAI tattooed on her ankle. I thought it was her owner's initials. Or the Thai word for heart, transliterated, but when Pratt showed me a figure of Agni that they found near her body, he couldn't figure out what it was doing there. There's the Hindu and Roman mythology and the tattoo. Are they connected?"

"Are they?"

"I don't know."

"Why would Ajarn Yoshi know?"

"In his condo he's got a collection of bronze deities. One of them has two heads. I wondered where that god fits into

Buddhism, so I asked him. He said he'd devoted much time to looking for patterns in numbers, connections between objects and between this world and the next. He came across as what you'd expect from a yoga teacher. I thought it was just part of his sales pitch for students."

Ratana stood up from the sofa and walked over to the window overlooking the lake and the Tobacco Monopoly Land. She looked at the traffic below.

"At lunch Ajarn Yoshi seemed genuine, a sincere, good person. He paid for Ploy's funeral."

"There's something he isn't telling me," said Calvino. "Not yet."

"Like what?"

"I don't know. I'm thinking."

"Did Colonel Pratt talk about Ajarn Yoshi?"

Naturally Ratana wanted to know if the Colonel shared her high esteem for Ploy's yoga instructor.

"Pratt agrees with you. But I saw an Agni statue on his bookshelf, and another turned up near Ploy's body. It's not like everyone in Bangkok is running around with an Agni icon in their pocket."

"Would you like me to go with you to see Ajarn Yoshi?"

Calvino stood up and joined her at the window.

"It's not necessary," he said.

"Did I do a good job at Dr. Nattapong's clinic?"

The doctor's name drifted like a bird looking for a place to land. She waited for him to say something, but for a moment he remained silent, staring into the distance.

"You did good. I couldn't have planted the security cameras without you."

She looked happy.

"Thanks. What did Dr. Nattapong say to Colonel Pratt?"

"He said nothing."

"He was scared?"

"He wasn't cooperative."

Calvino had hoped to avoid telling her about the carnage they'd found when they'd stumbled into the surgery. But he knew it was only a matter of time before she found out. She had been busy cleaning and washing, but news of the double murder would soon reach her through the social networks and local newsfeeds.

"That surprises me," she said, looking back from the view.

"The doctor's dead. The receptionist too. Both of them shot at close range in the surgery. The surveillance camera captured two men in Guy Fawkes masks in the reception area. It also recorded Pratt and me coming in a few minutes later. The bodies were still warm. We'd just missed the hit."

The color drained from Ratana's face, her knees buckled and she started to collapse. Calvino caught her before she hit the floor. He carried her over to the sofa, gently laid her down and went into the kitchen to pour a glass of water. Her eyes were open when he returned. He sat next to her. She raised her head, drank some water.

"Who would do such a thing?"

"Who they were and why they killed them are the big questions. We didn't stick around after finding the bodies. We walked to the park and stopped at the location where I'd found the first body. Pratt showed me the Agni icon forensics found at the scene. We talked about Agni and how to handle what we found in the clinic. Everything was happening so fast it made my head hurt. When we heard the police sirens arriving at the clinic, Pratt headed back there. He said I should go home. I didn't expect to find you here."

"Playing the part of your wife at the clinic..." she said. "It wasn't hard to do."

"You were convincing," he said.

"I hope you don't mind that I used the key to let myself in."

"What you did was a good thing, Ratana. What comes next won't be easy. The police will know that we went to the clinic. They will want to know why you had an appointment with Dr. Nattapong, and why I used 'Jack Smith' rather than my own name. Tell them it was my idea. I was investigating a wrongful death, and the victim had been a patient of the doctor. That's all you know. That's all you have to say."

She nodded, sipped from the glass of water and slowly rose up to a sitting position.

"I am not afraid," she said.

She drank more water.

"That's good," he said, smiling. "Because I am. So is Pratt. He's on the outside of something looking in and seeing something much bigger coming at him, you and me. It terrifies him."

"Khun Vinny," she said, "what can I do to help? Tell me what you want. I trust you and want you to know that you can trust me."

She'd been thinking of the doctor and his receptionist. The doctor had trusted her. She had likely said words to the same effect. He had believed in those words, shallow, empty and hollow as an unmarked grave.

"I know. And that makes all the difference," he said.

He wasn't thinking of the doctor or his receptionist. Instead Calvino was thinking that there had been no one there for Ploy. Or if there had been, something had gone wrong.

"Dr. Nattapong had a wife," Ratana said.

Calvino nodded.

"Yeah, he did. Think she knew about him and the receptionist?"

From the sofa Ratana gazed out the window at a group of young men, shirtless and in shorts, playing football on the large open dirt patch beside the MRT station. They looked so young, carefree and happy, as if they lived in a totally different world.

"Well, do you?" asked Calvino.

"Maybe," she said, nodding. "She might even have warned him about the sword tree," she said.

"What's the sword tree?" he asked, waiting for her to explain.

Instead of explaining, she said, "You'd never heard of Agni and a million other things either."

She suddenly sounded upset, frustrated as she got up from the sofa, found her handbag and walked across the room.

"Don't you want to have dinner?"

"Sorry, I have plans."

He found her in the hallway, slipping on her shoes at the entrance with the door open.

"Take care of yourself, Khun Vinny," she said.

Without a further word she left. He had no idea what he'd said or done. Or if her sudden change of mood had even been about him. Her attitude had shifted after she'd mentioned the sword tree, and something about it seemed to upset her.

After Ratana left, Calvino raised his hands over his computer keyboard. He was about to Google "sword tree Thailand" when he caught a glimpse of a regular visitor. A phantom image, moving like a wild animal, like a large black cat, darted across the wall as if climbing out of one of the newspaper clippings taped there. The presence wasn't stable enough to disclose its form. The presence had entered the room and that was all that mattered. He felt her, smelled her and tasted her—Mya, the Black Cat—circling the room.

His hands shook as he typed a journal entry. He would describe exactly what he saw in front of him. Dr. Apinya

245

would be asking him for his diary again, and he'd have something for her this time. His fingers struck the keys on the old Remington. He watched the shadows moving across his room. When he paused, Calvino thought of how he'd been shuttling between doctors' offices like a permanent patient—one doctor to cure the insane and the other to enhance the bodies of the vain. One was alive, one dead.

Ratana had brought him order. The place was clean. Why did he feel a dead spot in his heart, and that it was decaying and soon his entire heart would be dead? He tried to pull himself together. He ripped the paper out of the Remington, balled it up and tossed it across the room. With a fresh sheet into the typewriter, Calvino started again, slowly typing as if pushing a boulder up the mountain, hoping to find answers.

THIRTY-FOUR

DR. APINYA REMOVED her glasses, lazily cleaned the lens with a tissue and slowly peered up from Calvino's typed journal pages. Sixteen days had passed since Calvino had found Ploy's body.

She had put down her pen.

The doctor leaned back, her head against the headrest on her chair, her long immobile fingers touching. She studied him, thinking about what he'd written. For a moment she was silent, as if digesting something, seeing in him a stranger who'd revealed an inner core. It was the first time. She knew that when patients choose to write honestly about their fears, that is progress. It means there is genuine hope. But in Calvino's case Dr. Apinya wasn't so sure. With this patient there was no clear line between his fears and the scent of fear that he'd extracted from others and made his own.

"How frequent were your hallucinations this week?"

"Four times," he said, watching her pick up her pen and write down his answer.

She looked up from her notebook.

"How long did the longest hallucination last?"

"They all last about the same. Forty-five minutes to an hour."

"Were you in the same place each time?"

She waited for his answer. He rotated his shoulders, moved his head.

"Once in my office, but the other three times in my condo."

"Do your office and condo have a similar layout?"

"I use the same organization of working papers and evidence of the car bombing in both."

"Do the hallucinations emerge out of the papers and evidence?"

Calvino nodded.

"They burst out," he said, his tone sharp and firm.

She asked, "Do you feel a sense of violence?"

"More like extreme urgency. The visitors arrive in a worked-up state. Upset, threatening and worried," he said.

"How do they make you feel?"

"Frustrated, angry."

"Do you know why you feel these emotions?"

"This time they cried for payback. Revenge. They howled for Thanet's blood. Told me how I'd broken my promise to nail him. How I'd failed, failed. Why had I allowed this murderer to live free with their blood on his hands?"

"Have you ever tried to make the hallucinations disappear?"

He laughed.

"It doesn't work that way. If it did, I wouldn't be in your office."

"So you feel that they are powerful and you can't control them?"

"No more than I can control storm clouds, fire and rain."

"Like an act of nature."

"They're outside nature."

"You know they aren't real?" she asked.

"They are washed out, faded, indistinct, but I know each of them by their form and shape. Like an old black and white TV show with lots of atmospheric static blowing through. Is what you see on TV real? If you can't turn it off, what does that mean?"

She saw him rubbing his hands.

"They make you anxious."

"They are both real and unreal. I can't explain it any other way. You can know it's someone even though the image is clouded, vague—you know, shifting in and out of focus."

"What triggers the hallucinations? Is it the same each time?"

"I'm still working through the bombing case. I'm tired. I get lost in the details. It makes me feel sad, irritated. It's night. I'm doing this for them. I've had a couple of drinks. I close my eyes, open them, and the visitors appear."

"Why do you call them the visitors? Don't they have names, or are these strangers?"

"They are the worst kind of visitors. They invite themselves. They stay as long as they want. They demand that I help them. Names? Yeah, they have names. Rob, Mya and Yadanar. They scream and rage at each other. They shout obscenities. They talk about hate. They make threats. They insult each other. Sometimes they play musical instruments and sing. The lyrics are filled with blood and revenge."

"Are you afraid when you see and hear them?"

"I tell myself they aren't real. They're coming from inside my own head."

"Do you believe that?"

"I'm not sure anymore. I believe a lot of things. One of them is that unless you've experienced what I'm talking about, you haven't got a clue how it feels."

249

He glanced at his watch. Time had slowed down. He closed his eyes, wishing it would speed up, wishing the visitors would appear and she could see what he saw.

"I thought we agreed the first time we met that you'd be honest with me. That without honesty, therapy wouldn't work."

"I'm being honest."

She shook her head.

"You're hiding facts, important events."

"Like?"

"Anal Khan. Why didn't you write about what you saw when you found his body?"

"He lived in a shoebox room half the size of your office. The room was in an area of Bangkok you wouldn't have ever seen. Mainly Africans and low-life types from the Middle East, black, dark, bearded, slender and hungry. All of them barely surviving, running some scam, planning a heist. Desperate and dirt poor, living no better than rats. You walk into their lives and you see close up what it means to live hand to mouth, and when one of them dies inside one of those rooms, you see how it all ends. Anal had been dead a couple of days. No air-conditioner, no fan. The bacteria in his gut multiplied. He'd been dead long enough for the smell to drift down the hallway and into his neighbors' rooms. Someone called the police. By the time I arrived, the police were inside the room standing next to Anal's bloated body. His face had gone black as coal. It no longer looked like a human face. More like one of those too-real Halloween masks that scare kids. That's what I saw."

Dr. Apinya poked her lower lip with the end of her reading glass frames. She tried to hold her composure, not blink or show any reaction, but it wasn't easy.

"How did you feel inside that room?" she finally asked.

Calvino shrugged.

"Disappointed. I'd wanted to ask him some questions. One of his friends is in big trouble with the law. Instead I had to spend my time answering questions from the police about what I was doing there."

"What did you tell the police?"

"Just what I said. I didn't know him. A farang in the building wasn't what they'd expected. We all have our expectations about what and who belongs in a place, isn't that right, Dr. Apinya? And when something happens to surprise us, we react with anger, fear or frustration."

"Why do you think that, Khun Vincent?"

"It's our wiring. We have this need for everything to be certain, precise and predictable. The unexpected makes our head hurt because we have to ask lots of questions to try to make sense of it, and when we can't make any sense of it, we suffer."

"You've suffered for some time," she said. "Hallucinations are a way some people try to find answers to difficult questions."

Calvino thought about the body and the cops. That had been real enough.

"Dr. Apinya, Let me ask you a question."

"Please ask," she said.

"How did you know I found Anal Khan dead in his room? I mentioned last time that I'd found a body, but I didn't give you a name."

Her white Chinese face blushed, turning her cheeks a bright red. She softly pushed the wing of her eyeglasses against the inside of her lower lip, as she picked up her pen and wrote in her notebook.

"You'd missed an appointment. I phoned Colonel Pratt because I was worried. I'd not heard from you. I thought something might have happened."

"You could have called my office."

Dr. Apinya struggled for a reply, her eye movement rapid as she searched his face.

"I wanted to know how honest you are in this office."

"You discussed my case with Colonel Pratt. Is that the deal you made?"

"No, nothing like that. What you say is confidential. It always stays inside my office."

"There's a smell, Dr. Apinya," he said, twitching his nose, "like something has died. That stink is beyond what's coming from a dead body. The smell of trust gone cold and dead is one you can't get out of your mind."

"I want you to get better."

He rose from his chair and stood in front of her desk. She looked up to meet his eyes.

"Did the Colonel mention a Dr. Nattapong or a woman named Sukanya?" he asked.

Her perplexed expression suggested he hadn't told her. That's something, he thought. He'd given her selective information.

"No. Should he have?"

"No reason I can think of," he said.

By evening she'd remember this precise moment as she watched the news. She'd remember his words, "No reason I can think of."

He turned to leave the office as she called out his name. Calvino didn't break his stride. He opened the door and left without turning to say goodbye. He walked past the receptionist without a glance. All he wanted was to be outside, on the street, to fill his lungs with the polluted air of Bangkok to cleanse his nose of the smell.

Only then could he begin to find an answer to the question he'd wanted to ask Dr. Apinya: why is death stalking me, and why can't I shake it? On the way to her office he'd felt that she might help him find an answer. But back on the street again, he was now certain she had no more idea than he had.

As he walked to his car, the scorching heat wrapped its arms around his neck and throat like a determined strangler. He slowed his pace. Maybe there were some people that death chose to accompany him on his rounds, companions to witness the places of the dying or soon-to-be dead. A missing person case in Rangoon had kick-started Calvino's apprenticeship as death's assistant. Maybe the daily visitations from the dead were not his plague; maybe they were his reward, the key to the door, and all he had to do was open it.

THIRTY-FIVE

YOSHI NAGATA ANSWERED the door in a loose-fitting white shirt and trousers. He stood barefoot by the door as Calvino walked in and took off his shoes. At five after ten in the evening, he'd been meditating. His last students had left at eight and he had eaten alone, a light dinner washed down with green tea. He'd been expecting Calvino. To quiet his mind, he'd meditated. When the doorbell had rung, his mind had cleared. He smiled up at Calvino, who stood a head taller than him.

Nagata bowed and gestured for Calvino to follow him.

"I have prepared tea."

"You heard about Ploy's doctor and his assistant?"

It was clear from Nagata's expression that he'd been sealed away from the outside world.

"They were murdered," said Calvino, waiting for a reaction.

"That's unfortunate."

"That's one way of looking at it."

Nagata hadn't expected Calvino's response anymore than Calvino had expected his. He saw the error of his first reaction.

"Do the police know who committed this terrible act?"

Calvino followed him to a lacquered teak table at one end of the room. Nagata gracefully eased himself down on a floor mat, tucking his legs into a lotus position as Calvino examined a set of glass shelves built into a mirrored niche in the wall.

"No, they don't know who killed them or why," he said.

As Nagata poured tea, Calvino picked up one of the two-faced figurines and turned it around in his hand. Putting it back on the shelf, he removed a second, bronze one, of Janus.

"Janus and Agni," Calvino said, glancing at Nagata. "I've been reading about them."

Nagata matched his smile.

"I wouldn't have thought you possessed such an exotic interest, Mr. Calvino."

"The gods of beginnings and passages. One head looks at the past, the other at the future. Two heads are better than one. Now I know the inspiration for that old saying."

Calvino placed the Janus icon back on the shelf to the left of Agni. To the right of Janus stood another icon, a golden Buddha-like figure that was a bit taller than the other two. Calvino picked it up and admired it.

"It's a Buddha," Calvino said.

Nagata slowly shook his head like a patient teacher with a benevolent smile.

"It's not Buddha. It's a Hindu god called Ishvara. The god who created all there is and entered his creation. He became the negative and the positive, right and wrong, good and the bad, light and dark, false and true. He is the god of contradiction. Ishvara is in motion and still as he infinitely contradicts and confirms his existence and non-existence."

Calvino put the Ishvara icon back on the shelf and positioned the three figurines together in a row.

Stepping back, he pointed at each one and said, "That's J. Here's A. And finally, I."

Nagata applauded softly.

"Excellent. But what possible meaning are you hinting at?"

"I'd like you to explain why Ploy would have had 'JAI' tattooed on her ankle?"

"Mr. Calvino, you look surprised and disappointed at the same time. The look reminds me of my father many years ago when he discovered that I was gay. He said the knowledge of my sexual orientation was more painful than the four years he spent in a relocation camp in Alberta. Inside the camp what kept him going was the knowledge that the war would end sooner or later and we'd go back home. But with a gay son, that war would never come to an end. Despite his reaction, over time he came to accept me as his son. He encouraged me to study and learn from the Hindu gods and the Buddha, whom he saw as an extension of the Hindu tradition. The first step was to acquire vast knowledge, understand it and then seek release from meaning. To be redeemed from redemption was my father's wish."

An athletic-looking *mem-farang* appeared at the opposite end of the room. Medium height, thick blonde hair, in her late thirties or early forties. White silk blouse, dark pants, barefoot.

"There you are, Marley," said Nagata. "Come in. I'd like you to meet Mr. Calvino. We were speaking of you earlier, Mr. Calvino."

Marley approached like a dancer striding into an audition room. She held out her hand for Calvino to shake. He tried to stop his jaw from falling and banging against the hard wooden floor. She had the sort of face that men dreamt of, coveted, fought for, died for and killed for. The line of her cheek, the shape of her nose, her long neck and full lips created the perfect symmetry. Her clear blue eyes never blinked as she stared at him.

"I've been hearing a lot about you," said Marley.

Calvino gripped her hand. The skin was soft like an unused tissue. She had the hands of someone who sat before a computer all day.

"That's strange. I've heard nothing about you."

"We couldn't tell you until we were sure, Mr. Calvino. I hope that you understand. It was nothing personal."

Calvino met Marley's eyes and was the first to break free of the gaze, as if he knew that to look too long into them would end in his being lost. He turned to Nagata with a harder, more troubled look.

"Sure about what?"

Calvino still felt the power of her blue eyes. He closed his own, asking himself if this was another of his spontaneous hallucinations. When he opened his eyes again, he slowly pivoted a quarter turn. She hadn't vanished into the shadows or passed through furniture, windows or walls. She watched him with her easy, confident smile, the expression of a woman who'd never known a fear that she couldn't coax into a cage and lock the door on.

Marley and Nagata exchanged a look.

"It's okay," said Nagata.

She turned to Calvino and said, "I needed to be sure we could trust you. We needed to know whether you were part of their network. They are quite powerful and have people in many walks of life."

"A network we are quite sure we could never close down," said Nagata. "But if we're careful, we can use it to help people like Ploy."

"That didn't quite work out for Ploy, did it?" Turning back to Marley, he added, "I didn't see you at the funeral."

She bagged the winning smile as she glanced at Nagata.

"I was in the South."

"Right. Something to do with that network you're talking about?"

"A number of Rohingya escaped from cages on Koh Tarutao. Let's say I gave them a ride. I wasn't in Bangkok then. I regret missing Ploy's funeral, but it was unavoidable."

He looked at Nagata and then Marley again.

"You're involved with illegal migrants?" asked Calvino.

"Yes, we provide assistance. I asked Professor Nagata if he was clear about your loyalties," Marley said.

Calvino looked at Nagata.

"And you've cleared me?"

Yoshi Nagata smiled and gave a slight tilt of his head as a gesture of confirmation.

Marley pressed her tongue into the side of cheek.

"You know the problem," she said. "Let's start with the smuggling of Rohingya to work on rubber plantations, on fishing boats in the South or in locked door brothels. That's running illegals. There is a loose but well-connected network that coordinates every stage of the sale, and after the sale, the servicing."

"Their after-sale servicing is the network's selling point," said Nagata.

Calvino laughed.

"They sound like a car manufacturer. I don't know who these guys are, and I suspect you don't either, but I'd appreciate it if you'd enlighten me about your own little network. Who are you and why it is your business to worry about trafficking in Thailand?"

"You are right. We are a little, insignificant group that works off the grid," said Marley. "We keep our heads down. And we wish to stay invisible."

Nagata raised his hand and said, "I think we'd better sit down. We have a lot to discuss."

He filled a third cup of tea for Marley.

"Dr. Marley Solberg was my most talented post-doc student at UBC. I was her thesis adviser, though I think I learnt as much from her as she did from me. She wrote a thesis entitled Multi-Dimensional Forms for Constructing a Quantum Nanotube Communication Network Human Interface.

Marley saw that Calvino was lost.

"You're wondering what that means?" she said.

"It's not pulp fiction. I'm an American. I don't know enough mathematics to keep my office petty cash balanced. I have trouble in three dimensions, but four? That's where I fall asleep. I'm only good at finding people who've gone missing. Or at least I used to be, until too many dead people began turning up in my life."

"Dead people. You mean ghosts?" asked Marley.

"I don't know what to call them. All of them were murdered. I've asked myself, what are the chances of that happening to one individual?"

Her smiled widened. She paused for a moment and drank tea.

"Missing people is why I'm in Bangkok. It's an interest that I share with Professor Nagata," she said. "My professor tells the story much better than I can."

Nagata explained that Marley's work combined an instinct that few software developers could match with a rare math wizardry, conjuring algorithmic magic like rabbits out of a magician's hat.

"Marley's family name, Solberg, is Norwegian. It means sun and mountain. Women weren't supposed to be capable of working at the highest levels in our field. I predicted that one day Dr. Marley Solberg would plant her flag on top of the mathematical Everest."

A quarter of a billion dollars later, she had cashed out. Marley had sold a dozen patents to a company that specialized in lock-and-key, staying one step ahead of information-gathering systems, with self-learning mega-data-mining protocols, running her 2Work, 4Geo analysis matrix. Why had Yoshi Nagata left teaching? He'd become weary of training the greatest math minds to work for the military and intelligence communities, which were spread across thousands of agencies and private companies. When she'd been his post-doc student, he'd thought he'd spotted a star, one who would escape the pull of the money. Several years before, Dr. Solberg had made her fortune from selling her patents to a company controlled by nominees of the NSA. In an email from Nagata, she learnt that the professor happened to be holidaying in Vancouver. She chartered a private plane to fly her there. Over dinner she offered to write him a check for two million dollars.

"Atonement money," said Marley. "But he refused."

"We talked until three in the morning. She can be very persuasive," said Nagata. "At last she conceded defeat. She asked what she could do if not give me money. I told her I had been living in Bangkok for five years. To pass the time, I'd started a small group of yoga students. I taught them the basics. We discussed the brutality of the refugee camps and the terrible problems faced by the Rohingya fleeing for their lives from Burma. She asked what she could do to help."

At the time of their meeting Nagata had made a summer trip back to Vancouver to visit a colleague and some neighbors who had known his parents, and to walk along English Bay in the early morning.

"Professor Nagata was born in a Canadian-Japanese relocation camp," said Marley.

"He told me about it," said Calvino. "My mother's side of the family lost a dozen relatives in Nazi concentration camps."

"Then you've experienced the loss, but not the direct suffering," she said. "From the moment of his birth he was a prisoner because of his name and ethnic background."

Nagata poured more tea into the cups.

"Those were old-world camps and are now gone," he said. "The underlying thinking has changed. Race, ethnicity, religious belief are still the raw calculus, the formula the authorities everywhere use to determine the probability of a person's loyalty, their rights and destiny. But we've gone from barbed wire to surveillance cameras, and now to Dr. Marley's nanotechnology tracking system."

"I was naïve, idealistic," said Marley. "I'd lived in a world of pure mathematics, and my friends were all mathematicians. Nothing had quite prepared me for the non-mathematical world outside the university and its twisted way of thinking, and how these people used our equations in ways we had never imagined. I developed a system to help parents and the authorities find missing children. Millions go missing every year. With my technology, every parent could know at any moment of the day the location, heart rate, hormonal levels and rate of movement of their child. They would know whether they were walking, running, cycling or riding a car, bus or motorcycle. It was very advanced. Of course, it was never used for that purpose. It was sold to the government and classified as top secret. I had three separate visits from members of the intelligence community. Each of them, in their own way, told me that I should never discuss my work with others. If I talked about my work to anyone, I would endanger lives and national security. I was asked to sign documents. I refused. They said that was a mistake. I said, how so?"

Her face clouded, lips tightened. Yoshi Nagata reached over and patted her hand. The Norwegian face of a goddess hadn't worked on the people who'd been sent around to convince her to sign a new round of confidentiality agreements.

"The agreements I'd signed for the transfer of the patents hadn't given sufficient protection, they said."

"You came to Bangkok to get away from them?"

Nagata intervened.

"No, that's not why she came. I invited her to come."

"I invited myself, Professor Nagata."

Nagata replied with his signature little bow of the head.

"I said that if you wanted to do something positive for children who went missing, you could come to Thailand. I asked you to help with some creative ideas to deal with those locked up for years in the refugee camps."

Turning his attention back to Calvino, he added, "I showed her the evidence of how the Rohingya were being exploited, trafficked and sold. Men, women and children. No one who could be sold was left out."

"Frankly, I was appalled by what I learned," said Marley. "I saw a chance to use one of my software programs for the purpose I'd intended. I arrived in Thailand two years ago."

"Marley understood the basic idea that if we accept the existence of long-term detention camps for refugees and their children, we are returning to a time of great darkness. We like to tell ourselves that because the authorities don't gas refugees these days, they and we are more civilized and humane than our parents and grandparents."

When Nagata had told her that he wanted something other than money, he'd told her he wanted only one thing— to liberate refugees, especially the children, from slavery and trafficking.

"Not long after I met Ploy," Nagata continued, "she asked if I could help her family. I introduced her to Marley. Ploy idolized Marley. She had plastic surgery to make herself look like Marley. She wanted to be Marley, free and beautiful and talented, admired, rich, and happy."

Marley flinched as Nagata used the term "idolized." Clearly it was true, though she'd done all she could to prevent it from happening.

Marley picked up the story: "Ploy couldn't shed the pain she felt for her family. The way they suffered. She regularly sent them money and they lived better than the other refugees. That didn't matter to her. Ploy couldn't stop thinking about how to get them out of the camp."

"You told her you could help," said Calvino.

She paused to drink her tea.

"Yes, but also that she would have to be patient."

"Whose idea was it for the tattoo? The JAI on her ankle?" asked Calvino.

"JAI was Professor Nagata's idea," said Marley. "The Thai word '*jai*' means heart. But JAI wasn't just heart. It was East meets West—the frontier where Agni joins Janus. Professor Nagata taught that they meet in Ishvara—the world creator—the place of boundaries and no boundaries, matter and anti-matter, the wave that is a particle, and the particle that is a wave."

"Make it simple for me. Why a tattoo?" asked Calvino.

"So that we could use the tattoo, something we see so often that we don't notice them anymore, to embed a new technology in plain sight," said Marley. "I used nanotechnology to create a tracking device inserted as part of an ordinary tattoo. Who would ever think of a tattoo as a telecommunication channel plugged into the World Wide Web, accessible on hundreds of monitors?"

Professor and former student exchanged a glance, a smile that signaled a solemn pact they'd made—to set free the illegals from the brothels, fishing boats, factories and mines.

"Who else knows about this device?" asked Calvino.

"Professor Nagata and now you."

"How about Ploy and her family? Were they in on the operation?"

"There was no need for them to know."

"Because Ploy looked up to you, she went along," said Calvino.

"We were helping her," Marley said. "But Ploy felt I was taking too long. She couldn't bear having her family in the camp another day. So she made her own arrangements."

"She ran without telling you."

Marley nodded.

"We had an underground network for the Rohingya but not for illegal Burmese," said Nagata, refilling Marley's cup with tea.

"Time was needed to test the new technology," said Marley.

"We have Rohingya waiting to help them. They escaped from a detention center in the South," said Nagata.

"It's messy," said Marley.

"Using tattoos to track people gives me a bad feeling," said Calvino. "It might be okay if you and Nagata are running the world. But you're not. Think about the implications of what you're doing."

It was after midnight and they'd been talking for a couple of hours. Despite his age, Nagata showed no sign of tiredness.

"We have," said Nagata. "Tattoos are a different cultural artifact in Burma and Thailand. They are common. No one imposes them on people. But the Rohingya are Muslim and tattoos are forbidden. It wasn't easy to ask them to go against their religion. Marley solved the problem by making the tattoo invisible and calling it a vaccination. With what little free choice the refugees have in life, getting a vaccination was hardly one that raised an official eyebrow."

The influence of being born in a camp had structured Nagata's thinking about values, choices and karma. The tattoos would function as part of an official record-keeping system. The focus wasn't on the person but on the person's number and the details sketched alongside it. Nagata was right that the Thai and Burmese poor often displayed tattoos anyway. But he couldn't help feel there was something reminiscent of Nazi Germany in the idea of tattoos to ID refugees in detention. On Calvino's mother's side, his relatives had been tattooed and murdered in concentration camps. What Yoshi Nagata explained about these new tattoos suggested that, once equipped with long-range transmitting capability, the software could monitor location, emotional state and bio data as well as recording name, age, gender, DOB, place of birth, if known, and name of camp or detention center.

"If you were tracking her, then you knew she was dead."

"I had disabled the tracker three days earlier," Marley said. "I found a hacker who might or might not have been in Russia trying to break into the system. I coded the program in a high-level encryption. They were trolling for exotic encrypted data and flagged it. It told the hacker there was something worth stealing. NSA, outlaws, a kid in his bedroom with the door closed—it could have been any of them. I work in a bad neighborhood. Digital muggers prowl my turf, waiting for the moment when I blink. Whoever it was, they were good. I shut down the tracking because I didn't want them to locate Ploy. I told Ploy the system would be offline for a few days. And if any strangers tried to contact her, she should phone me immediately. I played cat and mouse with the hacker. Once he, she or they gave chase, I faded away. The project will come back in another place, with a new look, and the cycle will start again. If you look into the past, you get a glimpse of the future."

"We are a small rescue unit. A very discreet one," said Nagata.

"Why are you telling me this now?"

"We need your help," Marley said.

"Two geniuses from Canada need my help? Wait till I write my relatives in New York. They'll say, what's the punch line? And I'll say, I have no idea. Is there a punch line?"

"We've checked your background," said Marley.

Calvino raised an eyebrow.

"I bet you have. And you've found I'm an ex–New York lawyer who has a marginal private investigation business."

"Which is a surprise given that a few years ago you became independently wealthy," said Nagata.

"Nothing on the order of Marley. And you too, Professor Nagata," said Calvino.

Nagata replied with a smile.

Marley jumped back in with a story that struck Calvino as based on highly competent investigative work: "But you continued to accept new cases. Not for the money, but because you felt it was the right thing to help someone who needed it. You've been looking for Ploy's killer even though you've been pressured to let it go. Your Thai police colonel friend is an honest man too. You've worked together before."

Marley Solberg's voice, soft and confident, carried a deep sense of conviction.

Calvino looked at her and at the professor, trying to understand what he could bring to them that in any way would justify the risk of exposing their little rescue operation to a stranger.

"I'm no boy scout," he said.

"We're not asking you to escort us across a busy street," said Marley.

"I'd like to hear more about what I'd be getting involved in. And after you level with me, I can't promise I can or will help. But I'll think about it. It's up to you."

"That's a very Thai phrase, Mr. Calvino," said Nagata.

He sat erect, motionless, as he had done for a couple of hours.

The discipline to stay in a fixed position had a positive affect. Calvino thought anyone who had some mastery over his own body had a good shot at approaching every other aspect of his life with the same iron determination.

"We've been very careful to limit our exposure," said Marley. "I have refined, expanded and improved my original equations. What we've come up with is more powerful, more secure and accurate than the previous generation of algorithms."

She stopped and stared at Yoshi Nagata. He nodded his approval.

"Not all those who are inside the one percent turn a blind eye to what is going on around them," Marley said. "Please wait a moment."

She disappeared into another part of the condo and then reappeared with a laptop. Nagata cleared a space for it on the table. She folded her legs underneath her as she sat down on a bamboo matt. Opening an application, she typed in a password and clicked on an icon in the shape of a star. A map of Thailand appeared, and on the map three red dots flashed. The designations avoided names and instead used numbers—1, 2 and 3—for three camps.

"We targeted the detention centers with the worst records of abuse," said Nagata. "Those centers were paradise compared to illegal camps in the South are under the control of the local mafia. They own the authorities and make their own rules. They are dangerous and heavily armed and connected. Rohingya who've washed up on the shore—the ones not pushed back to sea in boats with no motors or supplies—have been sent to these camps.

"We found detention centers and illegal camps scattered across the South. Some are versions of hell. More than one trafficking network is feeding off the human misery inside. We had credible information from inside Camp 1 that young Rohingya women are routinely abducted. Men in uniform, carrying weapons, arrive at dawn in pickups and load the women into the back. The others in the camp are helpless to do anything to stop what's going on. Any NGO who complains is threatened. Several Rohingya men who protested have since disappeared. The women are taken to a remote location and raped. Afterwards, they are sold to brothels in Malaysia.

"Camp 2 was nicknamed the Body Shop. The Rohingya men are sold to sweatshops, canning factories and fishing boats, where they work in virtual slavery. Each fresh supply of refugees find themselves transported to employers who have bought them. Camp 3 was Marley's idea. It wasn't a Rohingya camp. Camp 3 housed Burmese refugees. We knew a girl from Camp 3. And Ploy told Marley about a number of young women who'd been sold to brothels in Chiang Mai."

"Ploy feared her sister was next. It was only a matter of time before she'd be sold," said Marley. "You saw her at the funeral. It was a reasonable fear."

"In phase one we isolated a group of five or six women and men in each camp," said Nagata. "We employed a Canadian nurse from East Vancouver whose hobby was tattoo art. She used the ink prepared by Dr. Solberg. It was injected into their skin."

"A tattoo artist? How would you get such a person into the camp?" asked Calvino.

"Our lawyers processed her credentials," said Nagata. "It wasn't a problem. Our nurse had paid her way through nursing school working as a tattoo artist. We had a nurse and tattoo artist in one person. Without her, we wouldn't have had the opportunity to go ahead with phase two."

Marley clicked onto the Camp 3 red dot and photographs of the Mae Hong Son camp—before the firebombing—appeared. She moved the cursor over one of the old photos and pictures of five refugees popped up—Ploy looked younger in the shot as did her sister Mon Hla and the group included three young men.

"We tracked each person, storing full bio records," said Marley. "We knew each brothel, sweatshop or fishing boat location. We knew exactly where they'd been taken. We had read-outs of their mental condition, how often they were fed, the length of time they worked and the amount of sleep they had. You look at the records and you see a true picture of slavery in human terms.

"Phase two was our rescue plan," said Nagata. "We could have anonymously given this information to the UN or local authorities. But we knew that local officials would deny involvement, and nothing but committee meetings and reports would result. That's when having a lot of money makes a difference. We recruited three five-man teams to rescue refugees. A rescue in three different places of refugees would make enough noise internationally that no one could ignore what was happening. We would shame governments into action. The overwhelming evidence we'd accumulated would make denials impossible."

"The rescue screwed up," said Calvino.

Silence descended as Marley opened more files.

"We were betrayed by someone on the inside, someone we recruited," said Nagata, "or we were hacked from the outside despite all our precautions. The point is, someone closed down my system. The screen went blank the day before the rescue was scheduled to launch. We lost track of all fifteen people who'd been tattooed with the nano implants. We had no choice but to call off the rescue.

"I saw an opportunity. With the tracking system down, no one could follow the refugees, and that included Ploy. She was already in Bangkok. The Rohingya underground had already been paid to pick her up. We weren't certain if they'd been compromised. We tried to contact Ploy, but she hadn't turned on her cell phone. She'd used the excuse of having some minor surgery to leave her condo. Whoever killed her had knowledge of the spot where the smugglers would meet her and escort her to the boat. The killers might have told her that her family was waiting for her. The refugee camp went into lockdown mode once our tracking system had been discovered. I think you know the rest."

"I still have gaps in what I know," said Calvino. "Why does a pregnant woman go for plastic surgery the day she's fleeing the country? If she's on the run, why is she stopping to have plastic surgery? It makes no sense."

Nagata nodded.

"Women often have reasons that men can't understand. When they are young, they still think things always work out for the best. The fallacy of best-case scenarios isn't limited by age."

The professor hadn't answered his question.

"Don't you think it's strange that she had a doctor's appointment that day? It has the look not of plastic surgery but of an abortion. She didn't want to be on the run and pregnant."

"She would never have thought of an abortion," said Marley.

Nagata said, "Frankly, we will never know."

"We want to identify the person who killed her and her child," said Marley. "He will be the same man who tried to frame our two local men who helped us arrange safe passage for smuggled refugees out of the country."

"You knew she was pregnant?" Calvino asked, looking at both of them.

"We suffer for what has happened to Ploy, her baby and her family," said Nagata.

"You're about to tell me about phase three," said Calvino, "and I have a strange feeling that you've run out of equations. When a mathematician runs out of numbers, he figures there's nothing to lose in bringing in someone who knows how things work on the street."

"You can help us find out who did this," said Nagata.

Calvino searched Marley Solberg's cold blue eyes, which remained focused on the computer.

"You're hiring me to work with you and Dr. Solberg?"

"We will pay your usual fee and expenses," she said.

Marley turned back to the screen, which now displayed dozens of photographs of himself, his clients and newspaper clippings. She clicked on one photograph, enlarging it to fill the entire screen—the blasted, torn shell of the Benz that Mya and Yadanar had been riding in when a roadside bomb exploded.

"What if it turns out that we're looking for the same killer?" she said.

"You'll be paid either way," Nagata said.

"That's it? It's just about the money?"

Marley's blue eyes fixed on Calvino as if she could see straight through him. She seemed to find a connection there that brought a smile to her lips.

It was Calvino's turn to go quiet, asking himself how much she thought she knew and how much she might be bluffing. In between was the reality of how much she actually knew.

"It's about much more than the money, Mr. Calvino," she said.

"Will you take our case?" asked Nagata.

"I'll think about it," Calvino replied.

In the world Calvino had been living in lately, stability and coherence no longer dictated reality. All pattern recognition depended on those two elements functioning together. He'd been through the evidence of the car bombing hundreds of times and had visualized multiple realities until he could no longer fix on just one. His experience had been more like that of a glass blower than a private investigator—someone with the basic skill to create objects, each a unique vision, each feeding on the heat generated by the flame of evidence— and he'd shaped the silicate tubing each time until the object emerged. And each time there had been a tiny flaw in the pattern, and he'd destroyed the glass.

THIRTY-SIX

CALVINO HAD A hunch that Marley Solberg wanted more from him than he could deliver. In his experience that was the problem with women—they either wanted too much or not enough, and a man could never quite figure out which end of the "want barometer" he was reading. She had wanted him to arrange a meeting with Colonel Pratt. His first reaction had been that whatever Marley and Nagata had been working on was something the Colonel should know about. Trust over a couple of decades rested on sharing information. But this case felt different. On reflection, as he looked at her in the hallway outside Nagata's condo, he thought about what options Colonel Pratt would have. Sometimes knowledge doesn't set a man free; it chains him to a limited number of choices. In this case the choices stretched along the road ahead as traps, ambushes and heavier chains.

"Do you like jazz?" Calvino asked Marley.

They were on the elevator as she escorted him to the lobby.

Looking puzzled, she said, "I'm not very good at small talk."

"Have you heard of Dexter Gordon? He's a jazz legend. He even starred in a movie about a sax player."

"*Round Midnight*," she said.

Calvino smiled, tilted his head.

"On Sunday, how'd you like to meet a man who played with Dexter Gordon in Paris? He's a friend of Colonel Pratt."

"Your colonel made a good impression a few years ago at the Java Jazz Festival," said Marley.

"Is there any information you haven't found out about me or Pratt?"

"Get used to it. This is only the tip of the information pile that others have access to."

"Then you know I'm in therapy for hallucinations?"

The realization that a stranger—or anyone—might have compiled his complete personal information caused him to squirm. He felt a shiver. It was like stepping into an elevator full of nuns with a bargirl in cutoff jeans hugging him and calling him *tilac*, or his weekly humiliation of writing down a full account of his personal thoughts and fears for Dr. Apinya to dissect for signs of madness.

"I've found life makes the thoughtful a little crazy," she said.

"That's it? The new normal is a little crazy?"

"No, the new normal scales to a different level of insanity."

A light drizzle fell as they walked through the Sunday afternoon crowds of desert people at the lower-numbered end of Sukhumvit. Arabs in traditional white robes, veiled women pushing prams through a throng of other nationalities—three-day bearded, hard-looking men in shorts, sandals and T-shirts, smoking cigarettes, no umbrellas to shelter them, talking as they elbowed their way forward. Not a white-toothed smile to be found among the desert faces.

Calvino and Marley followed behind the ragtag army of foreigners who descended on the stalls selling compasses, knives, brass knuckles, shirts, underwear, porno DVDs, perfume and knock-off Viagra. Now and then a man would break formation and disappear into a massage parlor, a restaurant or a luggage shop. The sound of the street was colored by a dozen languages as potential customers negotiated with sidewalk vendors, streetwalkers, pimps and door girls. On the street side of the pavement, transactions were forged with calculators in hand to punch out final offers.

They slipped into the entrance of the Check Inn 99. Marley folded her umbrella. Calvino was a step behind her.

"For years a dwarf worked out front as the doorman."

"What happened to him?"

"No one knows. He disappeared. No one had any reason to go looking for him. You're only missing if someone notices and wants you found. Some people stay lost because no one cares enough to worry about them. No one hires a private investigator to look for someone they don't care about. "

Bird's composition "Visa" drifted from the stage to the entrance. Calvino recognized Colonel Pratt's tenor sax and smiled. It was a popular jazz melody for long-term expats who had their own blues story to tell about visa runs.

"That's a Charlie Parker piece called 'Visa,'" he said to Marley. "Sad case, Parker. Don't know if you know, but he died in New York at thirty-four. When they opened him up for the autopsy, the doctor thought this old man's time had expired. His liver was gone. His heart had exploded like a supernova. But in those few years, he made music no one would ever forget. It's like John Coltrane at forty in New York—his liver gave out. If Henry Miller had died at thirty-four or forty, no one would ever have read his books because they'd never have been written. Henry had an indestructible liver. The history of musicians and writers is a study of the durability of the liver."

The sound of guitarist Billy Clarke blended and shaped the sax like a fine single malt whiskey kissing the throat of a sad, lonely man whose parched life had turned to sand.

The interior of the room was as dark as a half-moon night. One of the ancient waiters stepped from the shadows and showed Calvino and Marley to a table near the stage. A scattering of people sat at the bar and a few more patrons sat on stools, slouching against a wall. Marley ordered white wine and Calvino a Johnnie Walker Black on ice and a glass of water on the side. Colonel Pratt worked the buttons on his sax, leaned forward and dipped the horn at their table. Billy Clarke flashed an electric smile at Marley Solberg. He had a Parisian's eye for a beautiful woman, and even in the near darkness, peering out from the stage, Billy saw a vision of heaven who'd floated in on a rainy Sunday afternoon. Her attention was elsewhere. To the left of their table was a grotto with Christmas tree lights and two large plastic flamingos standing on stick legs in a fake grotto, the backlit in a soft porn like electric blue.

"In Vancouver, Stanley Park is filled with flamingos," she said, seeing Calvino watching her.

"In Bangkok flamingos are plastic. They do better in the pollution."

The fake flamingos stood amid a garden of fake flowers and ferns.

"The ones I remember as a child were real. When I was four years old, my mother would wait until I counted them. Each Sunday we'd return to Stanley Park and I'd count flamingos at the same place. I'd announce to my mother if any were missing or new ones had joined the flock."

"In New York we'd count the number of junkies, homeless, dropouts and losers. There was always someone missing, and some new ones to take the place of those who'd flown away."

"You're making fun of me," she said.

Calvino took the Johnnie Walker Black from the waiter and threw back a long drink.

"Not really. Your counting flamingos led to a brilliant career. My counting drunks and junkies prepared me for finding the birds that flew away to Bangkok."

Colonel Pratt was halfway through his set. They listened as Billy Clarke introduced the next song.

"This song by Dexter Gordon, "Our Man in Paris," is for our friend Vincent Calvino and his friend, whoever she might be."

Billy Clarke led in with the guitar and Colonel Pratt, wetting the mouthpiece on the sax, looking out at Calvino's table, eased into the melody. No matter how often Calvino heard his friend play, he still found something strange about the way Colonel Pratt embraced the saxophone. No other musical instrument looked so much like a machine with the skin stripped away and internal workings on display. It was as if the backbone of an ancient creature that had hit an evolutionary dead end had given the blueprint—a latticework of tubes, struts, buttons, bends and twists that moved in synchronized fashion to produce a signature sound, free and pure, climbing through the scales of sadness and despair to joy and the sublime.

As they played on stage, a camera fixed to the ceiling projected their images onto a screen on the near side of the grotto. From the moment Calvino saw the images of both men projected on the screen, he froze; he stopped breathing. Neither man looked like a man. Billy was black, and the Colonel brown, but their projected images were a ghostly, faded splash of white. The saxophone and guitar blurred against their bodies. He turned back to the stage. Both men appeared normal, defined in shape and color, but the screen images were the same ones he saw inside his condo. Only those people were dead. He recognized the forms as the indistinct figures of Mya, Yadanar, Rob and

Kati. It didn't matter that most of the detail was absent. The remaining twenty percent was enough to identify each one amid the vague, surreal fog stripped clean of all identifiable face, neck, trunk, arms and legs—all one moving sheet of white in constant motion.

After the set ended, Colonel Pratt joined their table.

"You look like you've seen a ghost."

"Not yet, but the day isn't over," said Calvino.

He made the introductions between Marley and the Colonel. Billy Clarke came over too and started to sit down, but one of his fans who'd been at the bar walked over to drag him away for a drink. Torn between wanting to sit next to Marley and drinking with a fan, he had the decision made for him.

"Billy, go have a drink and come back," Colonel Pratt said.

"I told Marley you played with Dexter in Paris," said Calvino.

"I'd like to hear that story, Billy," she said.

"I won't be long," Clarke said, as if he meant it.

After Clarke had left, Colonel Pratt and Calvino exchanged some small talk, the equivalent of dog paddling until someone decided which end of the pool they were swimming to—the shallow end or the deep end, where fools and plastic flamingos were found face-down and motionless. A silence started out like a crack, then widened to a yawning gulf.

"Colonel Pratt, what happened to Ploy isn't unique. It happens many times every day in Thailand."

Marley's opening was a little abrupt. Calvino thought she might be nervous. But in any event, no one got anywhere with a Thai police officer starting with a lecture.

Colonel Pratt's smile turned into a strained expression.

"I accept that her case isn't the only one. We have people inside my country who, when they think of the illegal

Burmese, would agree with Shakespeare: 'Having nothing, nothing can she lose.' Not even her life."

"Sorry, Colonel, if I've crossed a line."

The smile returned to Colonel Pratt's lips.

"Yes, the ever-shifting line that, when we retrace it, walking back and forth, following where it has gone, makes us look like we are staggering drunks."

It was an awkward way for the Colonel to prepare them for his shame. Calvino had only seen that look of defeat on his friend's face a couple of times. Colonel Pratt had the resilience and strength to endure the trouble he brought down on himself by being a good, honest cop. He expected a rough ride and gave as good as he got.

"Dr. Marley is a world class mathematician," said Calvino.

"The last time we sat down with a world class mathematician named Andrei we almost didn't get up," said Pratt, exchanging a glance with Calvino. He remembered how the scaffolding of their friendship and luck had been enough to keep them alive.

Calvino turned to Marley "We were working a case a few years ago in New York, and Andrei was involved."

Calvino and Pratt shared a history of head on collisions with ambitious people in the business of international criminal activity. They spoke in a shorthand code used by old friends to outline a common space in the past where a double coffin had been prepared for them. The full name of Andrei, the mathematician in New York, came into Marley's mind.

"Not Andrei Smirnov?"

"You know the Russian?" asked Pratt.

"Only by reputation and that he disappeared. No one has heard from him."

"He had some good reasons to disappear," said Pratt.

"What's up?" Calvino asked him in Thai. He could see that Pratt was agitated. "*Mee arai rue plow?*"

"I'm about to disappoint your friend. She came to talk with a police officer, only to find an officer who has been suspended," he said in English.

"It's bullshit. Appeal it," said Calvino.

"I've been assigned to an inactive position pending an investigation into the circumstances of my possessing a video from a murdered doctor's office. Men in white masks made it a political case. That makes any investigation toxic. Everyone is running away from it, except for me. I ran straight into it. Appeal? There is no one to appeal to, Vincent."

The Colonel hadn't told his inquisitors that the video had come from Calvino, though they weren't buying his story of an anonymous source either. Colonel Pratt had protected him. Any link between Calvino and the video, and he'd be back in lockup. It shouldn't have mattered who made the video; the video spoke for itself—the images of the two Thai men walking in and the sound of the handgun from the room next door. Bodies falling. But none of that was important to them, only who had made the video. Whose side were they on? Who was their paymaster and what was his position?

"I am very sorry, Colonel," said Marley.

"'Sorry' is what I've been getting since I was given the news. When you hear that word, you know one thing for certain," Colonel Pratt said.

He waited a moment, looking at Calvino before focusing on Marley.

"You know what that thing is?"

She shrugged, fingering her wine glass.

"No, sir, I don't."

"And I believe that's an honest reply, what you just said. You've never experienced failure. I've failed as a cop, failed as a musician, failed as a man. My failure makes a lot of people feel sorry."

"Pratt, you've never failed as a friend," said Calvino.

Billy Clarke was back on stage strumming his guitar.

"Back to work," said Colonel Pratt, as he rose from the table.

Calvino reached out and grabbed Colonel Pratt's arm.

"We'll make this right," he said. "The fight's not over. This is only round two."

They could hear Colonel Pratt's sax playing a Coltrane blues piece as they left the Check Inn 99. The drizzle had turned to rain. The street vendors in the narrow walkway clogged the foot traffic like grit in a fat man's arteries. But luck was with Calvino, who managed to flag a taxi. Marley climbed into the back and Calvino followed, closing the door. The taxi had passed several other potential passengers. A farang with a mem-farang was blood in the water for a taxi shark. With some well-chosen Thai words Calvino made it clear to the driver, who was fingering half a dozen amulets hanging from the rearview mirror, that this wasn't his lucky day and that he should turn on the meter.

Marley leaned against the door. She remained silent as the taxi inched forward in the traffic, slowed by the rain.

"Where are we going?" she asked.

"I want your opinion about a complex puzzle I've been working on. I'm stuck. I can't fit the pieces together. Could you have a look?"

"Where is this puzzle?"

"It's at my condo."

"That's one of the worse pickup lines ever."

"I'll settle for a ranking in the top ten. But the puzzle I'm talking about is real."

The fact that ghosts periodically jumped out of the puzzle was, he felt, better left unsaid until she got to know him better. First she should have a chance to look at his collection of puzzle pieces and how they fit together to tell what he thought of as the car-bombing story.

They sat in the back of the Bangkok taxi, a huge space between them, each looking out their own window. People are a puzzle, he thought, even as she asked herself, would puzzles continue to exist if there were no people? Had her wealth changed her, he wondered, and would it have changed him? She asked herself what his reaction had been to finding out who she was, and whether, if he'd known before, that would have changed anything.

In the digital information age, the gradual discovery of a new person, and the element of mystery that entails, had long since dissolved into the analog past. People never had a chance anymore to learn information over the first days and weeks and months of an acquaintance. Marley's life had been revealed in full on Calvino's screen.

He'd Googled her name and found enough information to fill every warehouse inside one of those small industrial estates on the Eastern Seaboard. The details of her life were public knowledge; she'd been profiled in magazines and newspapers in Seattle, Vancouver, New York, London, Berlin and Paris. Dr. Marley Solberg had already been a celebrity in the cyber world when she walked away with a cool $250 million in cash and shares. She'd sold a series of data mining programs. She was called the Queen of Quantum Algorithms.

"You have to understand something about Pratt," he said. "When you have enough wealth to move a mountain, what you don't take into account are the limitations the rest of us face moving in the real world. There are lots of people like Pratt and me living a few hours' hike up that mountain doing the best we can. We're hanging in, thinking we might still climb a little higher, when really we should be grateful we've got as far up that mountain as we have."

"When you reach the top of the mountain, do you know what you think as you look out at the view?"

Calvino shook his head.

"Nothing has fundamentally changed for me. I make certain I'm still anchored to planet earth. No one escapes gravity."

She stopped just short of recommending Professor Nagata's yoga practice as her pair of gravity boots.

"Pratt was shoved off his mountain," said Calvino. "When you're in free fall, you see the ground coming up fast, and there's nothing to break your fall. When you live on top, you forget what it's like for someone who's been thrown off the top. You saw Pratt. He's not in good shape because he's still falling."

The last time Calvino had talked with Colonel Pratt, he had still been in the job. The reassignment must have come down on Friday. That figured about right. The senior brass could disappear for the weekend. Leave Colonel Pratt a dangling man.

"I liked him," said Marley.

"People love him. Pratt was a hit at the Java Jazz Festival. But that was a few years ago. I thought, he thought—we all did—that he was going to make it big-time with the saxophone. It was his dream to leave the police force and tour at music festivals, getting bigger and bigger gigs. He waited and waited for a breakthrough. When he was in Rangoon, he played with a band that drew crowds. The owners of the 50th Street Bar loved Pratt. The band had a great vocalist, too. She was a young Burmese singer named Mya. Her nickname was the Black Cat. Pratt was riding high on that dream boat, seeing himself in the middle of the ocean when he was still in the harbor. The band's piano player had big plans too. Yadanar—that was his name— not only played the piano, but he came from big Rangoon money and had high-level connections in the government and the military. Yadanar signed a contract with the Blue Note in New York. My cousin helped set up the gig. Pratt saw himself meeting up with the two of them in New York.

He'd play the saxophone at the Blue Note. They'd draw the crowds just like they'd done in Rangoon."

"What happened?"

Calvino looked at her as they arrived at his condo. He took out his wallet and paid the driver.

"The Black Cat and Yadanar were killed when the car they were in blew up in Bangkok. The case is in the unsolved file. It's a puzzle.

"That's the puzzle you were talking about," she said.

He nodded.

"Yeah, that's the puzzle. But there's another one. Pratt's a decade older than Coltrane when he died. Does he still have time?"

THIRTY-SEVEN

CALVINO OPENED A bottle of red wine and carried two glasses from the kitchen into his sitting room. Marley stood in front of the artifacts of the car bombing he'd reconstructed across the walls. It looked like a modern art collage—images, glass, metal and paper. A4 color printouts, photographs and zippered plastic bags segregated by content—glass, nails, metal, upholstery and clothing. All the pieces had been hand-gathered from the scene of the blast. He came up behind her quietly as she leaned over the Remington typewriter about to advance the carriage return and read what had been typed on the paper.

"I haven't seen one of these for a long time," she said, having a quick look at the heading on the paper.

```
From: Vincent Calvino
To: Dr. Apinya
Confidential: Patient/Doctor Privilege
```

He slipped the paper out from the paten, wadded it up and threw it in a pile of crumpled papers. "It's gone. With a computer the words are never gone."

"True," she said. "But revision is a nightmare."

"If you write for only one person and from the heart, there's no need for revision."

"The medium is the message," she said. "I don't know if I agree with it, but I like the sentiment."

He stepped away from her and the typewriter and stood beside a map. "The location of the bomb was there," Calvino said, holding the two wine glasses, pointing at the map suspended from the ceiling.

"When you came in just now, you scared me," she said, her hand touching her throat.

He poured wine into the glasses and handed her one. Her hand was shaking.

"I sometimes get scared in this room too. I've been known to get the shakes standing here."

He gestured toward a photograph of a crater in the middle of the street.

"The bomb was detonated by cell phone. Someone waited for the car to pass. There had to have been more than one person involved. The bomber needed to know that Yadanar's Benz would pass over that precise stretch of road and to be ready to target it during a narrow window of time."

"That wouldn't be difficult. It's a simple logistical problem. Why haven't the police arrested someone?" said Marley.

The tone of her voice—deliberate, emotionless—had the feel of a careful mathematical formula. Calvino wondered if she had ever used the coy dance of a beautiful woman as a shortcut, a way to break through the defenses of men to harvest information she wanted. He seriously doubted it. She had discovered resources powerful enough to run circles around any man. Feminine charms, in comparison, were crude tools.

"The failure of the police investigation is a very long story," said Calvino.

"If you want me to help with the puzzle, I need to understand something about these pieces."

Calvino nodded, sipping the wine.

285

"You're right."

He leaned forward, reaching for a newspaper story with a half-page color photograph. In the picture a dozen forensic and bomb disposal experts squatted and bagged evidence within a ten-meter radius fanning out from the point of the explosion. There had been a lot of twisted shards, burnt debris and smashed and broken things scattered along the road and sidewalk. The men in the picture were dressed in green single-piece jumpsuits, peaked black caps and white surgical gloves.

"That's what the road looked like the next morning."

She studied the photograph.

"You've reconstructed pieces of a puzzle from the crime scene. So what's missing? What piece are you still looking for?"

"I don't know. But it's here somewhere, staring at me. Mocking me. I just can't see it."

"Because you see what they want you to see. You're focused on what's in front of your eyes. What if what you're looking for is not in this evidence?"

She sat on the sofa and opened her handbag, removing a thumb drive.

Nodding at his computer, she said, "I'd like to show you something."

She inserted the thumb drive, and an icon appeared on the right side of the screen. She clicked on it and opened a menu, scrolled down and opened a file.

After two or three minutes of searching, she said, "The police identified the time of the bombing. A cell phone was used to detonate it. I've triangulated the cell phone traffic, text messages and other calls half an hour before and after the explosion."

Marley scrolled through a spreadsheet file with pages of columns containing codes, dates and times, locations of senders and receivers, cell phone numbers and IDs.

"How did you get this information?" asked Calvino.

She looked up from the screen.

"The Israelis have an effective piece of technology called a GSM interceptor. It intercepts text messages, and if you want to be very clever, you can change the message. Write a false flag message or an incriminating one. It's great for monitoring calls. But if you want to gain access to the call logs, that's another device. I simply modified the two devices so they worked together, gathering call information from a central database."

"And what have you found?"

"From that location and at the time of the explosion, there were one hundred and twenty-eight separate text messages and calls. One of the text messages was sent to an encrypted phone. The message said in Thai, '*Set laew, mot panha.*'"

"It's done, no further problem," said Calvino.

He stared at the screen, reading the details of the message. Marley had enlarged the font size to make it stand out.

"The location of the caller was fifty meters from the blast site."

"He had a line of sight to the car."

"It was sent two minutes and thirty-four seconds after the bomb went off," she said.

Calvino sipped his wine, shaking his head.

"If the receiver was using encryption, that sounds like someone with connections to military intel or the government."

"Private companies are big consumers of encryption these days, for their cell phones and computers. They actually believe the sales hype that it keeps their communications secure."

"You know who received the text message?" Calvino asked.

She thought for a moment.

"I can tell you who is the registered, listed person for the phone. In this case it's a company. The Diamond Flagship Import and Export Ltd.," she said.

"Twenty-third floor, Abdulrahim Place, Rama IV Road."

"That's the one."

She sat back from the screen, watching Calvino, his eyes half closed, shaking his head. For months he'd been studying the evidence before him, and he could have kept on studying for years and never found a link to the bomber and his employer.

"Wait a minute," he said, disappearing into the master bedroom.

He came back holding Sukanya's iPhone. He handed it to Marley.

"It belonged to Sukanya, the receptionist at the plastic surgeon's office. I nicked it. She and Jaruk set Ploy up. Maybe you can find something."

He thought of Jaruk, whom he had tailed, and suspected that the phone he'd used to call Sukanya was the same one that had been used to set off the bomb.

"I'll check it. There's more," she said. "When I sifted through the database at the time that the Mae Hong Son refugee camp was firebombed from the air, a text message from that location was sent to the same encrypted number. And the same message: '*Set laew, mot panha.*'"

She ejected her thumb drive from the computer and slipped it back into her handbag. The iPhone also disappeared into her bag.

"The Burmese woman who died in the car bombing... If I'm not mistaken, you cared very much for her," Marley said.

A heavy sadness hit him like a punch on his blind side. When that happened, the visitations always followed. He waited for the washed out figures to float through the wall of evidence.

"Her name was Mya. The Black Cat was her professional name. She was a jazz singer. I'd gone to Rangoon to find her boyfriend, a young musician named Rob Osborne, who'd run off to be with her."

He stopped, picked up his glass and sloshed the wine in the bottom against the sides.

"She's not in there," said Marley.

Calvino grinned.

"No, she's not. It's complicated."

"So is encryption. But no matter how secure something is, there's always someone who can find a back door and get inside. But you have to need something inside to make it worth the effort."

"I don't know," he said.

"Don't know what, Mr. Calvino?"

He filled her wine glass, buying time. Thinking, afraid and waiting, feeling a presence that pressed against his chest. Then he felt something inside shift, a blockage cleared, and he could breathe.

"I slept with her only once. Her family owned a bookshop in Rangoon, the Irrawaddy Bookstore on 42nd Street between Maha Bandoola Road and Merchant. Orwell had bought books there in the distant past. The night I slept with her was the same night Rob was killed in Rangoon. I should have stayed at the hotel and watched over him. But I didn't. I never told Pratt or anyone what happened that night. Or the night when we showed up at Yadanar's birthday party. The party was in a mansion with many rooms and what seemed like hundreds of guests. On the walls were paintings of dreams from his parents and relatives, going back several generations. We were separated at the party and someone pulled me into a room. Mya was inside along with Yadanar and a couple of other people. Against the wall I saw three people tied up with hoods over their heads, two men and a woman. The hoods came off. The woman was a Thai named Kati. I knew her.

"Kati's Thai elegance and beauty, two assets that had given her an edge as a 'pretty' in the circuit of auto shows and perfume and watches, had been punched until it was hard to imagine the face had ever sold anything. Kati hadn't been smart enough to see the warning signs ahead and had got involved with some dangerous people. She'd shot Rob in my hotel room when I'd been with Mya. I'd been brought to the upstairs room in Yadanar's house for a specific reason. Yadanar handed Mya a gun. The hood covering her head was pulled off and I saw the damage done to her. Her face was puffy, bruised, her lip cut. You could see the terror in her eyes. Mya stood in front of her, and slowly she glanced over her shoulder at me with the same look I'd seen when we made love. I felt the swell of words rising in me: 'Don't kill her.' Each of the words failed to escape; they stayed in my throat, black, empty sounds with no place to go. She held that expression, an intimacy that had passed between us in a room. Yadanar saw what had passed between us and must have guessed what it meant. She held the gun in both hands and shot Kati in the head. After the body fell over, Mya smiled and found my eyes watching her. 'That's for Rob,' she said. 'And it was for you, Vinny.' In truth it was for Mya. Her guilt about what happened to Rob vanished at that moment."

"But you felt guilt."

"I felt nothing. I could see what she was doing, why she was doing it, but I did nothing to stop her. I watched her pull the trigger. Killing Kati solved nothing. It just made things that much worse."

Marley reached over and pressed her hand against his.

"I think you're going to be all right, Mr. Calvino."

He was on his feet, pulling down the bank of photos taped to the wall, the zippered plastic bags, the clippings.

"I should have told Pratt what happened that night. But I didn't. I locked it away. Why did I do that? Do you have an equation to explain why I've told you something I've told no one else?" he asked, wadding up the paper and tossing it on the floor. "Do you have any idea how I've tried to forget what happened that night at the bookshop with Mya or at Yadanar's house? I kept the sex and the murder—my personal involvement in what happened—as a private thing. I kept it so secret that I lied to those close to me. At first I kept it inside, and one day it tumbled out into this room. I had a problem. I couldn't wipe my memory clean of what happened in Rangoon, or what happened to them here. I'm worn down by the living and the dead."

"But you kept on going because you couldn't stop," she said. "You had no choice but to find out who killed Mya. But you hit a dead end. You discovered Ploy's body, and unconsciously you found a second chance to redeem yourself."

"You sound like Yoshi Nagata," said Calvino.

"I was his student."

She watched him standing with wads of paper scattered around.

"Are you finished with your puzzle?"

"I'm ready to get back to work," he said. "I'll take your and the Professor's case."

Marley gathered up her handbag and rose from the sofa.

"That's good news. How much money do you want me to advance?"

Calvino stretched out his hand, made a zero with his thumb and forefinger.

"I want you to stay."

She searched his eyes and found tears. Dr. Marley Solberg had no algorithms to process his tears. This was Yoshi's

291

world, the one where Janus and Agni stood guard, looking to the past and the future at the same moment. She faced a man in the present whose past had opened a vein and spilled out of his heart.

She reached for his hand.

"I promise not to forget you," he said.

"That's a good start, Mr. Calvino," Marley said.

"My name is Vincent. Vinny."

"Vinny, then."

And so it was to be. That balmy late April night in Calvino's condo she helped him transform his sitting room. They cleaned out every scrap of the debris. What he'd so dearly clung to for months fit into two large plastic garbage bags.

At dawn the next morning, when they returned to the sitting room, Calvino felt free for the first time he could remember. He stood by the bank of windows overlooking the Tobacco Monopoly Land and didn't feel sadness welling up. He felt like his old self, a person he'd forgotten existed. He smiled at Marley, who sat at his side, her arm wrapped around his waist.

"What's so funny?" she asked.

"The visitors didn't appear last night when I sat in the sitting room," he said.

Calvino had emerged from a room of darkness. He wanted to hold that moment and this woman in a way that would stop time. But the river of time couldn't be dammed.

"I'd given up thinking that was possible," Calvino said.

He'd slept the entire night for the first time in months. With Marley next to him, he told himself that he'd woken up. That she was real. Still, some small part of him thought his visions had only temporarily vanished and would return.

"You are real, aren't you?" he asked, running a hand gently down her skin from her neck to her belly.

She smiled.

"Do I feel real?"

He kissed her as the warm light of early morning revealed Marley Solberg, eyes open, staring at him.

"I'm glad that you didn't die at thirty-four," she said.

"Thirty-four?"

"Charlie Parker died at thirty-four in New York," she said. "John Coltrane at forty."

He smiled, wondering if this woman remembered every number she'd ever heard, each attached to a name. Charlie Parker, thirty-four. John Coltrane, forty.

"That would have been a shame. We'd never have met," he said.

Her breath on his neck, soft and regular, signaled a quality of intimacy.

"The probabilities are very much greater that we would not have met."

"We were lucky," he said. "How do you explain luck?"

"Patterns repeat themselves, and if you can filter out all the noise, you can find them like hidden jewels. Luck is what we call it when we find hidden treasure that enriches our lives. Some people who die young still manage to find it in music, poetry or numbers, while some with long lives never get beyond building sandcastles. Living is the quest to understand the reality of life. You need to go deep into the information and not just scratch the surface. The point is not to get sidetracked. That's hard because the distractions are infinite," Marley said, her blue eyes filled with kindness, the numbers all drained out.

"You're sounding like Yoshi again."

Being naked next to her gave him the license to use the Professor's first name. She lay still against his body.

"It is something he said."

"You want to stop the human trafficking with a formula or an equation?"

Marley raised her eyes and found his eyes.

"How would you stop it?"

Calvino grinned.

"I'd exile the traffickers into the world I just left. I'd beach them on an island from which there was no escape. Let them live among the angry ghosts of the people they've murdered."

THIRTY-EIGHT

HIGH-RISE CONDOS THREW long, thick-bellied shadows over Colonel Pratt's family compound. In the past his neighbor had raised orchids, but the neighbor and the orchids had long since gone. The Colonel had planted trees to screen what was left of his garden's privacy. The canopy of trees blocked some of the lower condo balconies from sight, but higher up the building, eyes watched him and his wife through the branches.

Colonel Pratt and Calvino sat in the teak sala at the far end of the garden. The Colonel had his saxophone strapped around his neck. His garden shears and gloves lay on a small wooden bench his father had once used. Calvino watched as Manee, the Colonel's wife, walked down the stone path into the garden with a tray. She smiled at him. Manee, who was middle-aged, wore her years like a cloak lightly thrown over the shoulders of a younger woman. Colonel Pratt reached down and opened the small gate to the sala.

As Manee set the tray down, she nodded toward the south wall.

"Vincent, do you remember Khun Somchai's orchids that used to grow along the top of that wall?"

Colonel Pratt watched as his wife poured tea.

"Khun Somchai's family moved to Pak Nam a few years ago. They bought a three-rai plot on the beach. He still grows orchids, and they have a pond and banana, mango and papaya trees. Each day they watch sunsets and sunrises looking over the sea. They have money in the bank. No worries in the world. They don't miss Bangkok."

"But they miss their friends in Bangkok," said Calvino.

"We will visit them next week," she said. "Maybe we will stay."

She looked over at Colonel Pratt, who smiled.

Manee had always fought for her husband, stood by his side. She wanted him to retreat away from the city, return to another time and place, one she had locked in her memory—smaller, more intimate, slower and connected with nature. That her husband had been sidelined in the police department had broken something in her life in Bangkok. She wanted out. She wanted Colonel Pratt to turn away from the political infighting within the department.

"You could come and stay with us," she said.

Calvino raised the teacup.

"I remember the orchids," he said.

"Khun Somchai is very proud of his orchids. A man needs to have pride in what he does."

She took the empty tray and walked down the three steps of the sala to the lawn.

"I'll leave you two."

Colonel Pratt drank his tea slowly, watching his wife walk back to the house. Calvino sat on one of the cushions, arms stretched out, admiring a large frangipani tree, smelling the intoxicating scent, part jasmine and part coconut. It reminded him of Marley's scent. He smiled as he looked at the star-shaped flowers with a deep yellow fanning outward from the center.

"Manee is campaigning to sell the house and move out of Bangkok," said Colonel Pratt. "She's had agents around."

"You're ready to pack it in? Leave your job?" asked Calvino.

"My job has left me. I've been transferred to an inactive position. That's where the department sends the living dead."

Calvino recalled that the scent of frangipani was sometimes associated with vampires.

"It's temporary, Pratt. You've come through worse," said Calvino. "You'll bounce back. It's part of being a cop in Thailand. Sooner or later you're sent to the inactive position doghouse, and then they let you back in."

"Maybe, maybe not," said Colonel Pratt. "Manee's right about how things have changed. Our neighbors left a long time ago. What's left to hold us here?"

Until ten years ago they had sat in the garden of Colonel Pratt's Sukhumvit family compound and watched the sunset. But that view had vanished a long time ago. It lived only as a memory of another time and place. The modern world had closed in, and high-rises like weeds had overtaken the garden. The real estate agents that Manee had showed around the property had told her that it would easily sell to developers. With the money they could move on from the land of his inactive post, become independent and live in a place where they could once again watch the sun set and admire orchids. The value placed on the family compound land came in at a cat's whisker under four million dollars.

"You're going to sit on a beach and play your saxophone all day and night?"

Colonel Pratt tilted his head as he set down his cup.

"'We know what we are, but not what we may be.'"

Hamlet was the right play for Colonel Pratt to seek refuge in. Especially when it came to making a decision about selling the family land and moving out of Bangkok.

"You know what we've become, Pratt?"

"Tell me, Vincent. What are we?"

"Two troubled men drinking tea in a sala and trying not to give in to despair," said Calvino. "When you get older, it becomes a full-time job."

"When you got big money, you didn't run. That's what I tell Manee," said Colonel Pratt. "And you know what she says?"

Calvino shook his head, inhaling the scent of frangipani.

"'Vincent sees ghosts seven days a week and a shrink once a week. Maybe he should have run.' The system breaks people who challenge it. That's never changed."

Calvino let the silence stretch for a minute.

"In Rangoon there were things that happened that I haven't told you about."

Colonel Pratt's attention shifted from the biscuits and tea.

"A secret?"

"Exactly right. A secret. The night Rob was killed, Mya and I... we... we made love. It happened at her family bookshop. The place where Orwell bought books in Rangoon."

Colonel Pratt grinned.

"Given the way you looked at each other, that's no surprise. Hardly a secret."

"There's more."

Colonel Pratt fingered the mouthpiece on his sax. A strong feeling passed through him that he was about to hear something he'd rather avoid, but he knew he couldn't. Like waiting for a punch when you know you can't raise your hands to block it.

"The night of Yadanar's birthday party, you and I were separated."

"I remember. You were there, and I looked around and you were gone."

"I went upstairs. Kati was in the room with Yadanar, Mya and a couple of Yadanar's men. Kati and a couple of Thai men had been tied up, hooded. When the hoods came off, I saw they'd been beaten up. They'd worked Kati over real good. Her face was a mess. I saw her eyes staring at me. Pleading, begging, desperate. Mya had a gun. She walked over to Kati. She squeezed off one round. A head shot. Bang. Kati fell over dead. It was for Rob, Mya said. She'd killed Kati for me, she meant. If I'd gone back to the guesthouse where Rob was hiding out, he might have lived. He was my responsibility. I should have protected him. I should have known. And I should have told you. I don't know why I didn't. But I couldn't for some reason, and I can't figure out what that reason was. Another thing..."

They exchanged the look of two old friends.

"Mya appears with my visitors. She always says the same thing. I owe her. In a way she's right. I do. There was a real connection."

Colonel Pratt stared at his saxophone, raised it as if to play, stopped and shook his head.

"Kati came to my room. I don't know how it started, her dress, the light on her face, the perfume, but we made love. She asked about you. I told her that you weren't at the hotel. She remembered seeing you at the Savoy Hotel Bar. I told her you weren't staying at the Savoy but nearby."

"Mya must've known. The way she was beaten, Kati would have told Yadanar's men everything," said Calvino.

Colonel Pratt shrugged.

"Someone texted Manee that I slept with Kati in Rangoon. They attached a picture of the two of us. I was going to tell you. But what was the point? You were going through your own hell."

Calvino closed his eyes, shaking his head.

"You should have told me, Pratt. I know I should have told you about that night. So what do we do now?"

"Selling the place and moving away is her way of dealing with it."

"Do you have any idea who texted Manee?"

"Someone who wanted to cause me maximum harm," said Colonel Pratt. "There were people who didn't like that we were shutting down the cold pill smuggling business. Or going too deep into the car bombing. There's a long list of possibilities."

Before falling asleep each night, the Colonel had tried to trim the long list to a short one. The people who gathered around his end of the water cooler were the people who he talked and listened to. But in the policing game the water cooler crowd included strangers, informants, commanders and support personnel. He'd reviewed the parade of acquaintances stretching from Bangkok to Rangoon. There were also too many anonymous faces. People from his sessions at the 50th Street Bar where he'd sat in as the sax player, for instance. They'd seen him in the distance with Kati at his table. Strangers like those peering from their high-rise windows above his compound. He'd catch a glimpse of their movement, but he didn't know them, and they'd disappear from sight. How could he isolate the person on his list who had sent the message to Manee? The reality was he couldn't.

"You're tougher than me, Pratt."

Colonel Pratt shook his head.

"I don't think so. And even if it were true, what does toughness matter? Most of the time, being tough doesn't help. It gets in the way."

Calvino wondered if that was the first time a cop anywhere had ever said something like that. He watched as Colonel Pratt wetted the mouthpiece on the saxophone and played the opening of Sonny Rollins's "The Freedom Suite." He lowered the sax and smiled.

"We both had our Rangoon secrets," the Colonel said. "What do we have to show for them now? Only that they messed with our minds and lives. There's a lesson."

"The lesson is that what happened in Rangoon isn't going to leave you or me alone," said Calvino. "They know we'll find a way sooner or later to get them. That's the lesson. Don't imagine that the Rangoon business stopped when we left. It hasn't stopped. And won't stop. There are people who want you to take the money and retire to the beach. They have me boxed in with the crazies. We're making it easy for them, Pratt."

"What do we have? We have a couple of videos. We watch an anxious doctor and his receptionist talking about the cover-up of a death caused by a surgical mistake. We have a couple of men in masks and gunshots. That's not much to connect someone powerful to a murder."

"Thanet's companies are a conglomerate that earn out from secret dealings—cold pill smuggling—China, Burma, Thailand. Human trafficking—Burma, Thailand, Malaysia. Weapons sales—Thailand, Russia and America. Have I left anything out?"

"If we suspect this is true, where is the evidence? It's not in the videos, Vincent."

"What if I told you someone had the data on all three—cold pills, Rohingya trafficking and arms sales? And she can give you the evidence. Emails, text messages, phone logs, memos, videos. All the evidence leads to Thanet's office as the operational center."

"It's public knowledge that one of his companies is a middleman for the sale of attack helicopters to the government," said Colonel Pratt. "He's a clever man. He is protected, Vincent. That's no secret."

"You asked me for evidence," said Calvino. "Simple. You can look through the evidence and ask yourself how many serious crimes you count."

It was never that simple, they both knew. Everyone broke a law a couple of times every day. Things stayed easy so long as the small money squeezed out of people remained small. In the big cases, things were different. In a big-shot family evidence is only one factor in determining whether someone has broken the law.

"You know how the system works," said Colonel Pratt. "Depending on who you are and what you've done, you are exiled, disappeared, killed or arrested. There's a VIP gray area where an important person is invited to come to talk to us with his lawyers. He holds a press conference with his supporters and important people. The public loses interest. No charges are filed. Finally there's a special category. Not all VIPs are equal. There exists a place ten kilometers above the surface elites. That's the place where men like Thanet operate. Men like him can't be touched. They are the gods. We know one when we see one, just as you know pornography when you see it. You don't need a definition. It's stares straight through you without fear."

"You're saying that Thanet is in the god category?"

"A celestial being protected by forces way beyond our resources. To take down a god, you don't need evidence, you need another god to give the nod."

Colonel Pratt guided Calvino down the shore of Thai culture and into its shallow waters. He could only take his friend so far. But Calvino accepted his limitations, like a man wading knee-deep into the sea admitting the experience doesn't make him an oceanographer.

"On Sunday you talked about being a failure," said Calvino. "I've been thinking about what it means. You know, what it means to fail."

"What does it mean, Vincent? You realize the gods are untouchable. Whatever you do to challenge them will never be enough."

"Despair is the one drug that should be outlawed. I won't give up. I won't give in."

"Your video of the men in the white masks disappeared."

"I have a backup."

Colonel Pratt shrugged.

"You don't understand. It doesn't exist. Back the video up to eternity and it will remain lost."

"There is always a way, Pratt."

"I admire the American attitude in so many ways. But it makes you ill-suited to stay alive in the Thai world of Bangkok lowlifes."

"Leaving behind some kind of mark of hope isn't American. It's human."

"That was a different age, Vincent."

"Every age is different and the same. Why can't it be enough to have had an ordinary life? Why has that become a failure?"

"We expect too much. We don't want to accept what is. That makes us troublemakers."

"When I left New York, I was washed up. I had nothing," said Calvino. "If that isn't the definition of failure, then what is? I didn't give up."

Colonel Pratt looked back at the main house. Manee stood near the door looking at the sala and the grounds, her arms folded. She had a still, faraway look as if she were already on a distant beach watching the tide wash over the sand or waiting for a boat to appear on the horizon.

"That's true, Vincent. You never gave up or asked for pity. You've been a very good, loyal friend. Let go of what happened in Rangoon. Let go of the car bombing. And the dead girl you found on the Tobacco Monopoly Land. Let it all go."

Manee went back into the house.

"Manee has let it all go," he said. "Pay attention to the present. Live in the now."

"Shakespeare?"

"The Buddha."

Calvino leaned forward, thinking of the two-headed statue of Janus. Did one face eventually surrender, or were the two in eternal conflict, fighting for the present to pay attention to the past or to the future?

"You're right," said Calvino. "As long as we have life, we've won the best thing. Take a guy like Thanet. How's he different from you or me? He's yoked to the same twenty-four-hour day. He sleeps and eats like us. But he needs something the rest of us don't. He lives for the recognition that he's special. That he's entitled to swim in a sea of awe and respect."

"Gods rarely are found with the fishes in the bottom of the sea. That's why they're gods, Vincent."

Calvino nodded. He got the message—the law had little traction when it came to dragging the powerful to justice. Was it so different anywhere else? The earth had long ago been colonized by local gods. Therein lay Colonel Pratt's despair.

"The gods have their weaknesses," said Calvino.

"Where will you find his Achilles' heel?"

"The hind legs of the elephant," said Calvino.

Marley's work decoding Sukanya's iPhone had disclosed a herd of elephants standing on their hind legs.

"Elephants never forget an enemy," said the Colonel. "An enraged elephant charges without mercy."

"As happened with the firebombing of the refugee camp in Mae Hong Son."

The Colonel looked at his watch.

"I'm off to the office. I need to sign some papers," he said. "Despite what people think, an inactive position has as much paperwork as any other position. Be careful, Vincent."

He reached over and gave Calvino a bear hug. That was uncharacteristic for a Thai, Calvino knew, even one educated in the West.

"And thanks for telling me what happened that night in Rangoon."

"I think the ghosts are gone, Pratt."

"That's why you're feeling hopeful."

Calvino grinned.

"That's a good space to be in, Pratt. It's large enough for more than one."

THIRTY-NINE

AKASH SARU RODE a bus from the prison to Pratunam. His intention was to temporarily blend back into the great throng of poor immigrants and wait for the final arrangements to get him out of Thailand. He told himself that Wednesday had always been his lucky day. May Day, the day set aside for workers, was the day of his release. Akash Saru should have been transferred to immigration jail, held in a small cell with forty other detainees and deported to India. But a sudden turf battle between immigration and the police had temporarily closed down the administrative processing that connected the two.

Akash walked out of the prison not believing his luck. Then, halfway from the bus stop to his apartment building in Pratunam, he ran into a Burmese friend who told him about Anal Khan. The smile vanished from Akash's face. His lucky day suddenly filled with dark, threatening clouds.

Akash Saru, the Rohingya smuggler whose real name was Deen Alam, should have felt on top of the world, but he was sweating hard. Fear galloped through him like wild horses. He phoned two people, both farang—the white-skinned, privileged clan that the police and gangsters mostly left undisturbed.

As Calvino ordered lunch, he took a call from Akash. McPhail was on his second gin and tonic, smoking a cigarette and flirting with the waitress who'd come to tell him he had to put it out.

"When did you get out?"

Calvino looked warily at McPhail.

"An hour ago."

"Where are you now?" asked Calvino.

Akash told him.

"Who are you with?"

"I wait for my friend."

"Who's the friend?"

"Sarah from Wisconsin."

He said it as if he were pronouncing the first, middle and last name of a person.

"Who does Sarah from Wisconsin work for?"

"Sarah's a missionary."

Calvino repeated for McPhail's benefit.

"A missionary from Wisconsin."

"Praise be the lord," said McPhail, crossing himself. "Ask him if she makes cheese."

Akash gave him the building number and, as another call came in, said, "It's Sarah. I have to go. But please come to see me this afternoon. I have something to give to you, and I won't have another chance to repay you for all you've done for me."

Calvino set out for Akash's room in Pratunam in the early afternoon. McPhail came along as backup. After all, Anal Khan had been found dead on the floor below in the same building. On the way there Calvino stopped by his condo and found Marley waiting for him. Calvino pulled out his shoulder holster and checked his .38 Police Special. Colonel Pratt made a judgment to return the handgun. He didn't need to say anything. The unspoken condition was— don't make me regret this decision. Without trembling, Calvino held the gun at arm's length, the barrel pointed at the head of a woman in a painting. His arm and hand were dead steady. He holstered the .38 and, checking his face in the mirror, told himself it was time for his face to turn from the past and look into the future. He'd gone several days without any hallucinations. The past was another head, another space and time. He'd never felt better.

Marley had been watching him, leaning against the wall. He turned to face her. The way she looked at him, he sensed she was seeing something that she'd missed before. With a half-smile she concealed whatever emotions had arisen from crunching the data inside her head.

"Are you okay?" he asked her.

She nodded.

"I'm not used to seeing someone with a gun."

She left it at that.

"I won't be long."

Marley moved away from the wall.

"I'd like to come along," she said.

Calvino thought for a moment.

"Where I'm going isn't the best part of Bangkok."

"I'll have a bodyguard," she said. "You are armed."

Calvino wasn't so certain it was a good idea. She stood a few inches away—the distance only sanctioned by a certain level of intimacy.

"Sure, come along. But stay close. I don't want you disappearing into a harem in the Middle East."

They were out the door and down to the parking floor, where McPhail waited next to the car. At last he'd found a place where he could smoke.

"Marley's coming along."

"She can shop for clothes while we have a talk with your boy."

"I have all the clothes I need," said Marley.

"My name's Ed," McPhail said. "You know, you could do a lot better than this guy."

"Get in the car, Ed," said Calvino.

McPhail climbed into the back seat of the car.

"He told you on the phone he had something for you," said McPhail, lighting a cigarette. "Any idea what that might be?"

Calvino glanced in the rearview mirror.

"No idea, Ed. What were you thinking? A pound of hash?"

"That would be nice."

"He's joking," Calvino said, looking over at Marley. "There are parts of Pratunam crawling with junkies and drug dealers. It's not a place for the average tourist."

"It's a third world dump," said McPhail. "Bums, beggars and blow. Expect the unexpected."

She lowered her window. The heat of the day sucked out the cool air-conditioned air like a giant straw, pulling McPhail's stale cigarette smoke from where it hung frozen in the chilled air. Calvino drove through heavy traffic and finally gave up, parking his car at a nearby shopping mall. They walked the last three hundred meters until they entered Akash Saru's building—an eight-story concrete box with grills covering windows glazed with dirt, laundry still as death hanging on balcony clotheslines and the sound of a baby bawling barely audible above punk rock music blaring from an upper room. At the elevator a sign had been taped to the door saying "Out of Order." It was an old sign.

The woman who sold fried bananas on the ground floor recognized him and waied. She had a good memory. A couple of weeks had passed since she'd seen Calvino in the lobby. On that day the police had come and removed a body on a stretcher. Calvino figured the authorities had probably returned twice since then to collect other dead bodies.

"Good to see you, son," the old woman said in Thai.

"Is there anyone you don't know?" asked McPhail.

"*Mae*, have you eaten yet?" Calvino asked her in Thai, addressing her respectfully as "mother."

Her red–rimmed–teeth smile hinted at the wad of betel nut tucked into the pocket of her cheek.

"Not yet," she said.

Calvino bought fried bananas and handed them to McPhail and Marley.

"An energy boost before we climb the stairs."

He pulled up a photo of Akash on his iPad screen and showed it to her.

"Have you seen this man?"

She nodded as she stuffed the twenty baht notes into her bra.

"He came back several hours ago."

"Was he alone?"

"I didn't see anyone with him," she said.

Calvino gave her another two hundred baht. She looked confused.

"For your dinner," he said in Thai.

Akash's room was on the sixth floor. They walked up the fire escape stairs, passing migrants camped out on the landings.

"Nice joint," said McPhail, looking back at Marley.

"Compared with life in a refugee camp, this is luxury," said Marley.

Finally reaching the sixth floor, they walked through the open fire door. The empty corridor, dirty and smelling of hash, vibrated with the deep bass of heavy metal from one of the rooms. Doors of the dingy, tiny rooms stood open to the hallway. Inside, brown-skinned people sat in their underwear in front of fans. Only a few children ran up and down the hall, shouting and playing.

McPhail wiped the sweat from his face.

"I've been in cooler saunas," he said.

Marley didn't complain. She stood behind McPhail, just listening.

"We're on the right floor," said Calvino, checking a door number.

"Give me a minute. I'm winded," said McPhail, leaning against the wall.

A four-year-old ran past him with a water gun, laughing. He aimed the water gun at McPhail's head and squeezed off a blast of water.

"Man, why is it, whenever you ask me to go somewhere, I'm the one who gets ambushed?"

"He's just a child," said Marley.

"An apprentice gunman is what he is."

The boy disappeared into one of the rooms.

The illegal migrant diaspora collected in buildings like this one like overflowing gutters after a torrent. They lived in neighborhoods populated by violent, scared or dangerous people like a pack of hungry dogs showing their fangs over every bone. Calvino, as a private investigator, retained his comparative advantage in such streets and slums. No mathematician or brain surgeon could calculate the life inside such places. Even if they did, they wouldn't know what or whom they should pay attention to. As an ex-New Yorker, Calvino understood before there were computers that most of the murders, assaults and robberies in the slums are committed by slum dwellers killing, mugging and robbing each other.

As they continued down the corridor, Calvino waited for Marley to stop beside him.

"Here's how it works," Calvino said. "You stay on that side of the door."

He pointed to a spot.

"Wait until it's clear that nothing funny is going on, and then you can follow us in. But wait until I tell you it's okay.

If it's not okay for any reason, you go back the way we came. Only go much faster."

"If you're trying to scare me, I want you to know I am not scared," she said.

She worked the probabilities by the numbers. He worked out things using a different calculator—his gut feeling.

Looking at McPhail, he said, "Let's say hello to Akash."

Both of them stood to the side of the door. Calvino moved forward and knocked three times. The door opened and Akash stuck out his head. Calvino pulled him out into the hallway. Akash nearly fell down. Recovering his balance, he leaned over, grabbing his knees and catching his breath.

"Anyone else inside?"

Akash gestured to the door.

"My friend, Sarah from Wisconsin."

Sarah stood in the doorway holding a bible with a thick black leather binding. On the front cover was an embossed gold cross. Sarah appeared to be in her early sixties.

"Marley?" she said. "I had no idea you were coming."

Calvino looked at the two women hugging.

"You know each other," he said, realizing why she'd not been frightened in the corridor. "Why am I not surprised?"

"Without Dr. Solberg's sponsorship, I wouldn't be here."

Turning to Marley and trying not to show his anger, he said, "What is it with you and secrets?"

"I wouldn't have come along if I wanted to keep my friendship with Sarah a secret. And don't forget, you're working for me."

"So that's how it is," he said. "It's always good to clear the air with a new client."

She had insisted on coming along because she knew Sarah would be there. Her way of revealing information, piece by piece, on a need-to-know basis, had become a pattern in their relationship. They walked into Akash's squalid little room, taking in at a single glance the unmade bed, the crumpled, dirty sheets, the pillowcase gone grayish and the smell of a room that hadn't been aired for months.

Akash closed the door and turned on a small floor fan.

"How long have you been working with Akash?" Calvino asked Marley.

"About a year ago we set up an underground railroad to move Rohingya women and kids out of the country," said Marley. "Akash and Anal Khan helped us make arrangements in some cases for refugees hiding in Bangkok."

Calvino, his mood swinging to the black end of the spectrum, looked upset as he paced back and forth in the room, his jacket armpits wet with sweat. He had a gun under the jacket. He left it on. He had no reason to show it.

"You said you had something for me, Akash. Is this what you meant?" he asked, looking at Marley and Sarah from Wisconsin.

"Boss, I wanted you to know I didn't hurt that girl," Akash said. "I was trying to do good. Like Miss Marley said, I help people. Akash always wishes to do nothing but to help my people."

"That didn't quite work out for Ploy," said Calvino.

"I did nothing wrong, boss," Akash said.

"I'm not your boss," he said and turned to look at Marley. "She's your boss."

Marley came to his defense.

"When Akash found Ploy, she was already dead. He walked into a trap. He'd been set up. This wasn't an accident or chance. It was planned."

Calvino believed those words were true—they had walked into an ambush without realizing that sooner or later it was inevitable. The trap wasn't a black swan of bad luck that blindsided them. An amateur operation run by outsiders would be living on borrowed time, existing only until the

Thais noticed it was cutting into their own business interests and shut it down.

"You don't know who set up Ploy?" said Calvino. "Or why he wanted her dead?"

Their silence offered no hint of an answer.

"The probability is it was Thanet," said Marley, breaking eye contact with Sarah.

"He bought her?"

Marley nodded.

"He owned her."

The buying and selling of illegals was done through a hidden backdoor into the refugee system, creating a form of modern slavery silently absorbed into the economy. It was a difficult system to escape. Those who tried and failed to escape paid a high price as did their families. For anyone wanting to stop it, the problem was finding evidence incriminating a buyer. Powerful men like Thanet were unlikely to have any direct connection with an individual human trafficking case. Like the top boss running an illegal drug operation, he was bound to have a group of walk-around men to keep him in the clear. There were no average customers among the buyers. Average men didn't have employees like Jaruk on the payroll to help them buy and sell migrants like any other commodity. Ploy had become damaged goods. What does a man do with such goods?

"You've got evidence to connect Thanet and Ploy?" asked Calvino.

"He was obsessed by her," said Marley.

"That's not evidence," said Calvino. "That's an opinion."

Marley closed her eyes, shaking her head.

"I met with Thanet, several times. I offered him a blank check for Ploy. He refused."

"Did he say why?" asked Calvino.

"He told me he was in love with her," said Marley. "He wouldn't let her go. This love didn't stop him from hitting on me."

McPhail flapped his arms.

"That's crazy. Not only that he hit on you. But that he would kill her if he loved her."

"She didn't love him," said Marley. "He did everything he could think of to keep her."

"The autopsy said Ploy was six weeks pregnant," said Calvino. "What are the chances it was Thanet's? DNA tests would establish if he was the father. Would he have killed her if he'd known she was carrying his child?"

Marley shook her head.

"She's dead. That's your answer."

"I feel responsible," said Sarah. "I should have seen this coming."

"It wasn't my fault. I was very careful," said Akash.

They all looked at him, wondering if he'd misunderstood what they'd been discussing.

"No matter how careful you think you are, sometimes the condom breaks," said McPhail, who had kept quiet.

The two women looked at him with revulsion.

"They break sometimes. That's a fact," he said.

"Ed's got a larger point," said Calvino. "Everyone was being careful. But it wasn't enough."

In the underworld of illegals the amount of chaos and noise made "careful" an exotic concept.

"We were betrayed," said Akash.

"Who betrayed you?" asked Calvino.

"Anal," he said.

His partner had been found dead nearby.

"What was his motive? And why was he killed?" asked Calvino.

Akash shrugged.

"Anal was very unlucky," he said.

"Right," said McPhail, rolling his eyes.

The default when no one could explain why someone had been killed was always the same. It came down to bad luck.

"Someone has been watching us," said Marley, glancing at Sarah and Akash, who looked away. "Killing Ploy was Thanet's way of sending us a message. Keep out of our territory. Stay away from the illegals. And he was saying something else quite specific: 'If I can't have her, no one can.'"

"Thanet's men saw something. Spotted a couple of Rohingya getting into an SUV or getting out of one. Or saw one climbing onto a boat. It could have happened a dozen different ways," said Calvino. "Or Thanet found out by ordering you followed and your telephone tapped."

"That would have been difficult," Marley said.

Calvino believed that to be true. She was, after all, a security and surveillance expert who could have set up a string of blind alleys and dead ends. But she wasn't a Bangkok expert, and Thanet had a wealth of other resources to draw on. Human traffickers, Calvino knew, create networks staffed with the eyes and ears of many people, from the camps to the halls of power to the streets where mules are recruited.

Calvino looked at the two women. Both of them were outsiders who lived in a bubble of illegal immigrants. Marley and Sarah likely had no idea that sooner or later someone connected to the network would hear a whisper about a refugee who got out of Thailand for free. Farang. Sticking their long noses into Thai business. Farang. That word would have been said with a long hiss. They'd talk about the rumor for days. Like a communicable disease it would spread. People up the chain would start to hear of this farang virus infecting a perfectly healthy, well-oiled distribution system. Ears and eyes, switched from passive to alert status, would have a good look around, ask questions, watch and report back. More talk, gossip and rumors would bubble just under the surface—Thais talking to Thais with eyes adjusted to the dark of night.

Someone had heard a rumor about a non-Thai group helping refugees. Akash had been soliciting money on Soi Cowboy from punters. If the word had spread from Soi Cowboy that an Indian nut vendor was collecting money for refugee assistance, it would have been passed down the line. Marley had seen the non-Thainess of her small group as their strength, as if what they were doing were encrypted in a code the locals could never beak. But as Calvino knew well, that kind of encryption came with a built-in weakness—foreign secrecy could never work because the secret keepers still have to function inside Thai society, and no one can ever keep a secret in Thailand. People always talk, even if in a roundabout way. Akash had been talking without knowing his words were being heard, remembered and passed along via the bamboo telegraph.

Thais break down the codes of others in the old-fashioned way, through the brute force of social interactions. Observing each gesture, move, relationship and snippet of small talk, Thanet and his circle would not have been working in total isolation. Girls on Soi Cowboy had brothers and husbands who drank with men who knew men in the network. Marley and her group had no choice but to move among the Thais. Keeping numbers encrypted was a universe away from concealing a people smuggling operation. She had believed that she could camouflage a society of amateurs, not understanding that whatever they did, said and planned was in plain sight. Not to notice an operation of that kind would have meant they had gone blind and deaf.

There is competition in every business, but in an illegal business there are other ways of discouraging competition, especially an operation that gives away a valuable commodity and service for free.

"How did you work out pickup and delivery?" asked Calvino.

Dr. Marley Solberg shot a long look at her two colleagues.

"We had a formula that worked for over a year," she said.

"I am trusting that it will work one more time," said Akash.

"McPhail, take my car back to the condo."

Calvino tossed him the remote for his Honda.

"You can show me how it's done," said Calvino, looking at Marley and Sarah.

FORTY

THE TWO WOMEN sat in the front of Marley's SUV. Calvino sat in the back with Akash. The eighty-percent tint on the windows stopped anyone from looking inside. The front fender sported a logo from the Royal Sports Club, the windscreen a logo of the NGO and a small Canadian flag. The plates showed Thai letters for vehicles registered in Bangkok. Sarah had been careful to never transport more than three refugees at a time. She entered the elevated expressway at the Port of Klong Toey. They were on their way to the Eastern Seaboard.

Sarah headed an NGO—Women Helping Women— with its head office in South Pattaya. She occasionally disappeared in the SUV and drove to pick up Rohingya refugees delivered by Akash and Anal. The other staff, by design, were kept in the dark about the sideline operation.

Five staff members provided counseling and advice for sexually abused women and children, HIV/AIDS awareness programs and a women's shelter. Marley paid the bills and salaries. No one on staff suspected the organization had a sideline of smuggling Rohingya refugees out of shelters, camps and detention centers; they had started small and remained under the radar by staying that way. Marley funded two more NGOs in Indonesia and had set up a camp for Rohingya refugees on the island of Java. Fifty or sixty refugees bunkered down while Marley used her connections to negotiate with UNHCR for the outside chance it might find other countries to accept them. But it had been a tough, slow battle.

In the huge ocean of Rohingya refugees flooded out of western Burma, the number of refugees Women Helping Women had helped to escape was no more than a rounding-off error. Marley Solberg said that would all change once the tracking tattoos came online. She had a working database with locations and personal details already in place. The information was stored in a safe box in the cloud.

Her plan was to collect irrefutable evidence of the official lies about trafficked refugees and go public like a good whistleblower to expose the space colonized by corruption, greed and brutality along with the names of those involved. As he rode in the SUV, Calvino thought about what Colonel Pratt had said about the gods being untouchable. But he kept his thoughts to himself. The Colonel's assessment, based on a lifetime of experience, was no doubt right, but being right required finding a way through the wall that protected the gods.

As the SUV entered Bang Lamung district, Marley was saying, "The Rohingya need camps with proper medical equipment, medicines, nurses, schools, clean water, shelter and food."

"That's what they need," Calvino said, "but how will it work out once those have been provided? Once the word spreads that Thai camps are better than their hellholes at home, anyone with an education or money will take their chances. Smugglers will then ask for more money to deliver them to these well-equipped camps."

"So we should just turn our backs on them?" she asked.

"All life flowed through channels of cruelty and violence. It's as common as the air around us. We no longer think about it except in a remote way when we read about someone who was washed away."

"Whose side are you on?" Marley asked.

"In Rangoon I had a similar discussion with a singer about taking sides. She said there's a war raging inside everyone. On one side you have George Orwell, and Henry Miller on the other. Those who refuse to accept injustice and violence and inequality quote Orwell's work. Miller accepted that the murderers would continue to roam free, making the rules to their own advantage, and for the free man, escape was losing oneself in the world of song, dance, wine and sex. Miller didn't believe that any principle could protect you against those with real power. He thought that nothing can blunt the exercise of power over the exploited. Miller's idea was simple: stay off the predator class's grid. When someone puts their life in the hands of a human smuggler, they ignore the fact that it's his job to deliver them to their new masters. It doesn't matter that you pray for a savior who thinks like Orwell because you'll never have a chance to live the free life of a Henry Miller."

"The fact that you can't eliminate all the pain and suffering isn't an excuse to retreat as much as you can," said Marley, who had turned in her seat to look at Calvino.

He said nothing in reply. He appeared lost in thought as he stared out the window at the fields, factories, shops and houses. They drove on in silence.

She hadn't expected him to disagree with her, but she knew that abstractions at this level are like the water cooler in the desert that everyone claims as their own. Calvino realized that Marley's beautiful mind, decorated by a thousand elegant equations with a glossy coat of Yoshi Nagata's spirituality—like a penthouse on top of Akash's slum building—was at odds with the real world run by men who ran smuggling operations under Thanet's big tent. She was rich beyond the imagination of most people, but one woman's wealth wouldn't prevent a couple of hundred thousand refugees from being cut adrift and sold off like livestock. Most people who spent a lifetime riding a high moral horse failed to experience what it was like to spend a lifetime walking behind the horse and knowing they could never escape what came after horse's tail lifted.

The SUV turned in to a soi that served as an entrance to a Buddhist temple. Monks' quarters, salas and large grounds lined both sides of the narrow road. Tourist buses were parked in front of one sala.

"They sell amulets to the Chinese tourists," said Marley. "They come in huge buses by the hundreds every day."

The soi narrowed as they drove past the temple buildings and gardens and finally into the local rural community. Ramshackle structures, weathered by the seawater, stood isolated amid the lush overgrown green of an encroaching jungle. The road turned into a single-lane dirt path, inclining to a fork. At the juncture stood an ancient *bodhi* tree with sprawling branches brushing against the ground.

Sarah braked, slowing the SUV to a stop as Calvino looked out the window. Marley powered her window down. Calvino looked out at the gnarled trunk of the bodhi tree, wrapped with dozens of traditional Thai costumes, shiny sequins reflecting the light from copper, red, green, yellow and blue dresses, all fixed to the tree.

"Shopping at the local clothes market?" asked Calvino.

Marley's laughter echoed through the SUV.

"It's not a market. It's a sacred place. The bodhi tree has been converted into a marriage tree," said Marley. "The belief is that young women who die before marriage should have a husband in the next world. Their relatives bring a wedding dress and monks to this tree and perform a wedding ceremony. The spirit of the dead woman is married to a famous singer, poet or magician who died many years ago. The families believe that he'll be a good husband and will look after each wife as if she were the only one. He'll lavish riches and sublime wisdom, wash their feet at night with his hair and serve them fruit and tea at bedtime. He'll entertain them with illusions. Cards, coins, dice, rabbits, colored balls that he juggles for hours. He'll be forever in their presence, never leaving their side or turning away."

"In other words, he's the perfect husband," said Calvino.

Akash looked on silently. His eyes were wide open and fearful.

"I am not liking ghosts," he said.

"The spirits of the young women are at rest," said Marley, "if you believe the legend."

"I am believing that spirits never rest. That is their misfortune. They have no choice but to roam endlessly and never to arrive. It is our belief."

It wasn't difficult to understand how a Rohingya had come to adopt such a view of the fate of those in the afterworld, a place that mirrored their world on earth.

"You'll be safe, Akash," Marley said, glancing back at him.

He didn't look comforted. His wet black eyes blinked as he stared at the tree.

"I would feel safer if we continued."

Marley powered the window up, and Sarah turned right at the fork and drove ahead, pulling into a large secluded mansion on the beach. A small dark man in his early twenties stood at the gate, smiling. Spindly legs, thick with black hair, stuck out of his red longyi; he wore his long raven black hair to his shoulders. A second Burmese servant, older by a decade, who appeared wearing a green longyi, helped close and lock the heavy iron gate. A couple of soi dogs, tails wagging, circled the servants. Calvino noticed the CCTV cameras on the gate and what appeared to be sensors along the driveway that curved around the garden. The SUV pulled in close to the house, and Sarah switched off the engine. A third man, wearing a baseball cap, appeared dressed in jeans and a T-shirt. He opened the door for Marley and bowed to her as she climbed out.

"This is my crew," she said, checking her watch. "We still have a little time before Akash must leave us."

Sarah gestured for Akash to follow her. At first he ignored her, his mouth wide open, staring at the house.

"Come inside. We have a case with clothes and necessities for your trip."

He stumbled forward as if in a dream.

"Where's he going?" asked Calvino.

"Norway, of course."

"Why 'of course'?"

Calvino followed her as she walked down the flagstone pavement surrounding the house and emerged through a gate into the back garden.

"We have a history of helping people escape. You should read our history sometime."

The two-story mansion was set back thirty meters from a white sandy beach. A concrete pier extended out another twenty meters, and midway down the pier Calvino spotted the dock lines anchoring a power launch and used-tire fenders cushioning the boat from the concrete pier. The tide was coming in. The launch had an enclosed cabin and a radar dish rotating on the roof. A small Norwegian flag flew on one side, a Canadian flag on the other.

"He's going to Norway in that boat?"

"No, that would be impossible. The launch will take him out to meet a Norwegian ship, and the captain will make sure that Akash arrives in Norway. Smuggling people is like any equation. Each sequence must have its own beauty and lead to the next."

"Your place?" asked Calvino, looking back at the mansion.

She nodded.

Sarah and Marley's crew worked together to smuggle Rohingya refugees out of Thailand and on to Norway, Indonesia and Malaysia. Akash had received a warning from stone-faced men to restrict his business on Soi Cowboy to selling nuts. Akash and Anal had brought dozens of refugees to rendezvous points in Bangkok, where they had all climbed into the SUV so that Sarah could drive them to Marley's compound. Neither Akash nor Anal had any idea where the refugees ended up. If they had known, the weight of too much truth might have broken their will, and they'd have wanted out too. The deal had always been that they'd be looked after. Marley had been true to her word.

Inside the house Akash stood in the window, looking at the launch and the sea.

"It is so beautiful," he said, repeating the phrase.

He'd helped Rohingya to get out of the country before. The only difference this time was he was the one going. He could see the endgame, and for the first time since he'd been beat up in prison, he smiled.

Marley saw him in the window and waved. He looked resigned to his fate, like a man auditioning for a police crime reenactment.

"With Akash safely delivered to Norway, you'll be out of business?" said Calvino.

"That's what we want Thanet and his friends to believe. But we've just changed our business model."

"With all the money in the world, this is what you choose to do?"

"How do you spend your time?"

She paused.

"What you do," she said, "helping people find lost ones, is not that different."

Finding the missing, he thought. Reuniting them with those who care for them. He accepted individual cases, one at a time. One person who'd disappeared. But Marley's client was a large group of people who'd gone missing. She operated on a different scale, which expanded the scope of risks.

The Rohingya fled with the clothes on their backs and with memories of villages burnt, women raped, men killed as their wives and children looked on. They carried with them images of monks in robes at the front of a mob, inciting violence, as if the lid of decency had blown off the pot of humanity. Marley was a small-time player on the fringe of the big-time Thai operators, the men with the network whose eyes and ears were plugged into the ranks of the military, the navy, the police and the immigration authorities. At every intersection someone had their hand out, taking a cut, to pass the refugees through the long intestine of a hungry dragon. It was nothing personal. It was the nature of business and clans; it was the way the hands moved on a clock face—one second, one minute, one hour at a time, relentlessly, as time and business never rest or stop.

One day Marley had woken up. Yoshi Nagata had helped her open her eyes. She'd crawled out of bed with the sheets wound around her neck, shutting off the oxygen flow to her brain, and once she'd cleared the air passage, she breathed in the truth of where all those numbers led her—to individual lives retreating from violence, hatred, brutality and death. It was too late to return to bed and the sanctuary of sleep. She was awake. Eyes wide open, what had she found? That despite all her knowledge, education, connection and wealth, she could carry no more than a candle as she stepped into a dark, deep forest.

FORTY-ONE

THE NEXT MORNING Marley's SUV stopped in front of the marriage tree shrine, and she and Calvino got out and walked over to it.

"That's a new dress," she said, gesturing to a traditional Thai silk dress—long, sleek, the shoulders lightly padded.

An old woman came out of a nearby house with a small bowl of rice, candles and flowers on a tray. She carried them to a table next to the tree.

"Grandmother, who left this dress?" asked Calvino in Thai.

The old woman flicked a cigarette lighter and touched the flame to a candle.

"They never said their name. I heard their pickup last night and saw them out the window. A couple. Old or not, I can't say. It was dark. I went out to the road and asked them to come back in the morning."

"They said it was already done," she continued, lighting another candle. "They left me money to look after Joom's spirit."

She pulled a five hundred baht note from inside her blouse and showed it.

"They said Joom was killed in a motorcycle accident in South Pattaya. It has happened before."

She walked a couple of more steps and touched another of the dresses.

"This one, Tim, died on a motorbike in Rayong. This is her dress. They are young and never think it can happen to them. That is the meaning of being young."

At the bottom of a tray was a picture of a young, smiling girl. The old woman lifted it and showed it to Marley and Calvino.

"The dress is for Joom for her marriage in the next life."

The old woman stepped closer to the tree and waied, her head half-bowed. She was silent for a couple of minutes, ending her meditation by running her fingers through her long, graying hair. She looked at Marley as she pointed at another wedding dress on the tree to the immediate right of Joom's.

"That's Pook. She died of AIDS. Wouldn't take her medicine."

Her finger moved to the next dress on the tree.

"Kaeo died of a drug overdose, Nee was a suicide, Pui was found murdered and Toy drowned."

She paused like a good curator, getting a good grip on her audience.

"Each was young, unmarried, with a life ahead of her."

Marley took a thousand baht note from her handbag and held it out for the old woman.

"You live in the big house over there," said the old woman, nodding at the right fork in the road. "I've seen you many times."

"I've seen you too," said Marley in Thai.

She held the old woman's hands in her own.

"I hope that I'll see you again," Marley said.

The old woman smiled with a slight upward curl of the lip, an expression of the old who have come to terms with lies that belong to the future, and they are unlikely to travel to that destination.

They drove half an hour toward Bangkok in silence, listening to Glenn Gould playing Bach's *Goldberg Variations*.

Lowering the volume, Marley broke the silence.

"Last night you said Thanet was beyond the law."

"Law is just one tree in the Thai garden," said Calvino. "It's pruned down, so it's hard to see among the forest of tall, important men."

"That is profound coming from a lawyer."

Calvino shook his head, watching a black pickup cut in front of Marley as she braked to avoid hitting it. He saw nothing abnormal in the behavior of the pickup driver. Marley caught her breath, held it and then slowly let it out.

"Nothing profound in avoiding a collision," he said. "When you work for years in the garden, your hands are used to turning over dirt. The law of what survives and what dies rests with nature and not in human documents. You think the law is your friend. It can also be your adversary's weapon."

"I won't be defeated," she said.

"This is beginning to sound very personal."

"It is. No way am I letting that bastard get away with murder. That would be surrender."

He glanced over at her.

"Who's talking about surrender?"

"Isn't that what you've been saying? Let nature take its course?"

"Human nature is the nature I'm talking about. Colonel Pratt said only the gods can bring down another god. I'm thinking about how to plant a 'god' killer app inside Thanet's garden."

Ratana's story about the sword tree and the old woman's stories about the marriage tree had him thinking about the forces that would lead an army of angry gods to Thanet's door, forces that would deliver the magic key to opening it and the strength to pull him down from his pedestal.

She looked over at him.

"Nothing would please me more."

"Can you pull up all of Thanet's cell phone records? Sukanya's iPhone had Jaruk's number."

"Numbers," she said. "He used more than one."

"Trace them. Then grab all of his emails," he said.

She nodded, serving up her reply with a knowing smile: "Can."

"That's very Thai—can, cannot."

"What else?"

"He uses a secure phone. How difficult is it to get the locations and times? Text messages?"

"Depends. How many phones does he use? How good is his encryption?"

"You need someone who works on the inside."

She smiled.

"Of course, that would make it much easier. Who do you have in mind?"

"An employee," said Calvino.

"That's how all the best stuff is found. A disgruntled employee."

"Only this one isn't disgruntled."

"Then why would he help you?"

"You flip someone for one of two reasons. He's afraid you've got something that will discredit him with his boss, or he's greedy. One is shame and humiliation and the other is cold cash."

"How much cash to flip the employee?"

"Around ten million baht would do it."

She looked at the road.

"Okay, ten million baht. And for that we get the phones registered in other names but used by Thanet?"

"That's the idea."

"When do you need the cash?"

Calvino shrugged as he glanced at her.

"I know that's a lot of money. And there is a possibility of a double cross."

"What are the probabilities?"

"Sixty, seventy percent we get the information."

"That's an honest assessment."

"I put up half," he said, smiling. "Never trust a man who doesn't have skin in the game. To be on the safe side, I'm also thinking you might be able to find out a few things if we can get Thanet's credit card numbers and bank accounts."

"I like the way you think, Vincent Calvino."

"That means I no longer work for you. We're partners."

"I'll have the cash tomorrow, partner," said Marley.

"It'll take a day or two to set it up," said Calvino. "I'll need Sukanya's iPhone, if you're finished doing what you need to do with it," said Calvino.

"I'm finished with it."

Marley never asked for the name of the employee. She only cared what the employee might deliver for the money. They both knew that "employee" was a broad term, covering different personalities, capabilities and risks. Some serious unpacking would be required before the money could be handed to Jaruk.

FORTY-TWO

CALVINO DEBATED HOW to handle Jaruk. He had one chance to get it right. Jaruk's number was stored in Sukanya's iPhone. Ratana could phone him and request a meeting. Or Calvino could return to Thanet's office on Rama IV and stake out the parking lot. After Jaruk dropped the boss at the office, Calvino could corner him. The first option had some problems. Giving Jaruk time to think and plan and organize a response meant losing the element of surprise. There was the risk that Jaruk might see no good choice and take off, disappearing into the woodwork.

The second option, surprising Jaruk, also had some downside. Likely he'd be armed, and as he was in the killing business, his instinct would be to use his weapon to get out of a corner. Timing the ambush would depend on predicting Thanet's schedule. He travelled around the city to meet up with his minor wives, he played golf, and he attended business appointments. He was one busy criminal. Determining when he might be at his office would be like forecasting the weather.

McPhail sat in Calvino's office, slouched back in the chair, a cigarette in one hand and a gin and tonic in the other. Calvino turned away from the window. The small sub-soi below was empty except for an old woman who slowly walked to the end with her offerings for the spirit house.

"If we hang out in the parking lot a couple of days, we'll get picked up by the security cameras," said McPhail. "No good."

With a couple of gin and tonics in him at ten in the morning, McPhail was fueled with insight.

"We could get lucky," Calvino added.

"We go back to the Ladprao house and wait until he comes out."

"And if he stays inside?" asked Calvino.

"The smart money says Jaruk is a creature of habit. My guess is that he goes back to the same restaurant as before and orders the same bowl of noodles."

"If he helps us, he knows that he can't live in Thailand anymore. That gives him a strong incentive to fuck with us."

"Vinny, for ten million baht he won't care about living in Thailand."

The bet depended on calculating the scale of Jaruk's greed against his loyalty to Thanet. Would that amount of money turn him? Jaruk had scammed a doctor for a half share of three hundred thousand baht. Calvino suspected that Jaruk had also grabbed another two hundred grand from Ploy's handbag. That would have been the amount for the illegal abortion. Jaruk had helped set up Ploy's death. It had been a lot of risk for what translated as a fifteen thousand dollar crime. It hadn't taken much money to turn him then, and he'd shown that if cornered, he eliminated the problem— doctor, nurse, Anal—and cleaned up his own mess before walking away. His prior record shouted his willingness to engage in a cool-hearted betrayal if the price was right.

"When is the last time a guy like Jaruk had dinner alone?" said Calvino. "He'll be meeting with half a dozen friends," said Calvino.

"We grab him on the soi."

"No need," said Calvino.

He pulled out the receptionist's cell phone.

"I'll give him a call from a familiar number. One that will get his heart pounding."

McPhail nudged Calvino when the compound gate on Ladprao opened and Jaruk rolled out on his motorcycle. When Jaruk was twenty meters along the road, Calvino phoned his number on Sukanya's iPhone. They saw the motorcycle brake light flash as Jaruk pushed his phone under his black helmet. A moment later he pulled his motorcycle off to the side, removed his helmet and looked over his shoulder.

"Hey, Jaruk. Sukanya said to say hello. She didn't recognize you in the white mask."

Jaruk's hand reached into his jacket. Before his hand emerged, he looked down the barrel of Calvino's .38 Police Special at him.

"Easy now. There's no reason to make a problem. Don't give me a reason to shoot you. I have a problem. And I need your help."

"Why I help farang?"

"Because I've got a business proposition that's going to make you rich," said Calvino, keeping the .38 Police Special trained on him.

"Farang speak bullshit."

His eyes wild with fear, he looked over his shoulder and around the street to see if he was being observed.

"Yeah? You've been talking to the wrong farang. This farang has some truth and a lot of cash. You'll agree that's a good combination. Get inside and we can talk over your future, come to an understanding. Everyone will be happy. No one gets hurt or has a problem. Or I could send the videotape of you and your friend in Guy Fawkes masks killing the doctor and his receptionist. You think your boss might recognize you behind the mask? It's up to you."

McPhail, who was in the back, opened the rear door. Calvino had parked on an isolated stretch of the soi, pulling to the curb beyond which rose a high stone wall overgrown with vines that twisted through the iron spikes on top. Branches from old mango trees from the other side swayed lightly. Opposite the wall, another mansion and another family with tentacle-like vines on the wall weaving into the grid of power. There were no street vendors, shops or foot traffic.

The streetlight pooled around Calvino's car. Outside the cone of light it was pitch dark. Jaruk stared at Calvino's .38 and nodded.

"Make me rich," he said, sliding into the back next to McPhail.

His face in the back of the car, still lit by the streetlight, had the look of a man who had woken up to find a sheet tightly knotted around his neck, cutting into his oxygen supply, gasping, and with no chance to pull himself free.

"I want a list of Thanet's friends. Names, phone numbers, rank or position. I'll make it easy. The top twenty-five big guys your boss pals around with, has dinner with and plays golf with. The ones he does business with. His *giks*, girlfriends and wives too. What I don't want are names and phone numbers of drivers or *luk nongs*. I want the *nai*, the bosses, his women."

Calvino stopped and let the request soak in for a minute.

"You understand what I'm asking?"

Jaruk grunted, and it could have meant anything. McPhail took away Jaruk's gun and gave him a hard elbow in the ribs.

"You didn't answer the question," said McPhail.

"Okay, understand," he said, looking at his own gun pointed at his chest.

"What do you know about explosives? Can you make a car bomb?" asked Calvino.

Jaruk's jaw firmed and he looked ahead in the darkness outside the window.

"He asked if you know how to blow shit up?" asked McPhail.

"I was in the army. In bomb disposal unit," said Jaruk, slumped back against the seat, smarting from the elbow in the ribs.

"Remember almost a year ago, when a car bomb killed two Burmese in a Benz? A cell phone was used to remotely set off the device. I want that cell phone. Can you get it for me?"

"Don't fuck with us, Jaruk," said McPhail, both hands on the gun. "I'll fucking blow out your brains even if I have to clean up the car later."

"Okay, okay."

"You have the phone? Yes or no?"

He nodded.

"Yes."

"Good. I want it. You are going to get it and give it to me. Understand?"

Jaruk understood that he had no choice but to agree.

"*Khowjai*," he said—I understand.

"I'm not finished. I need information. The numbers of Thanet's bank, financial statements and credit card receipts. You've seen his bank statements and credit card slips lying around his office. Get me the bank and credit card names and account numbers. The ones in his name and his wives' names. Here's how you get paid. Email me the information. After you've delivered, I wire four million to your bank account, which you will send me in the email. We meet and you hand over the phone used in the bombing, and I give you five million cash."

Calvino reached over and opened a briefcase on the passenger side.

"There's a million baht upfront. Goodwill money. You have forty-eight hours."

Calvino glanced at his watch.

"From now."

Calvino passed the briefcase to the backseat.

"If I don't hear from you, your boss will hear from me. A few weeks ago in Bangkok a driver and a couple of his friends killed a big boss. Someone who was rich and famous lost his life because he got careless in trusting his people. That has made a number of bosses nervous. Thanet is looking at his people and thinking, could someone like Jaruk tie a rope around my neck and strangle me? It doesn't take much for a boss to think, better to get rid of a *luk nong* than to be sorry. That's how bosses think. He'd listen to what I have to tell him. What do you think he would do?"

Jaruk had no more fight left.

"Ten million baht?"

"You're getting out of this much better than anyone should, Jaruk. You have some luck on your side. But don't push it. Luck comes unstuck when pushed. And there's usually a mess to clean up."

"Are you listening?" asked McPhail, slamming the briefcase hard into Jaruk's chest.

A huff of air released from his lungs and he muffled a groan.

"Yes, yes. I hear you, okay?" said Jaruk.

Calvino turned in his seat and stared hard at him.

"Inside the case is a piece of paper with an email address. Send the information to that address."

McPhail opened the door and Jaruk climbed out, clutching the briefcase. Calvino wasn't finished with him. He powered down the window, stuck his head out.

"Remember something, Jaruk. Thanet can squeeze your balls until you pass out, and squeeze them again until you die. There's only one way this can go. Don't think your problem will disappear. You missed removing Sukanya's phone from the office. That should tell you something. You didn't know her as well as you thought. You aren't as good as you think. I'm giving you a chance. One that Ploy, Sukanya and Nattapong never had. You won't get a second chance. I'll be waiting."

He drove off, leaving Jaruk standing next to his motorcycle, still clutching the briefcase.

FORTY-THREE

RATANA GLANCED UP from her computer screen as Calvino closed the entrance door behind him. He walked into the reception area with a wide grin on his face. Behind his back he hid a bouquet of orchids he'd bought at Villa Market.

"At Pratt's house Manee mentioned how their next-door neighbor used to grow orchids. Then he sold his family compound and moved everyone to the beach."

He held out the flowers.

"These are for you."

She took the flowers, pressed her nose against an orchid, a slow smile crossing her lips.

"They're beautiful."

She'd matured from the early days, when she had come to the office in tight-fitting skirts and gold chains. Even her self-consciousness over a scar left from a childhood dog attack receded to another story among many. She'd come to terms with how her life had turned out, accepted herself and her situation. It helped that her mother no longer lobbied for her to leave her job and marry a rich Chinese banker. Her family had resigned themselves to the choices she'd made.

Ratana racked her memory for the last time, in all the years she'd worked for Calvino, that he'd brought her flowers. She decided that the previous instance had been seven years before. Calvino had arrived at her hospital room with flowers the day that her son, John John, had been born. From her hospital bed she had opened her eyes to find him standing next to her like a proud father. John John wasn't his kid, but that hadn't mattered to him. He shared her happiness.

She judged her boss as the kind of man who gives a woman flowers to mark a special occasion. Flower giving without a holiday obligation behind it seemed to her to mark the gap between heterosexual and homosexual men. He showed no indication of becoming gay, so she suspected that the flowers meant that something special had happened. She looked at her calendar. It was the Tuesday after Mother's Day.

"Thanks for cleaning up my place. Another week and my condo would have been jungle vines and spiders and snakes. But you saved the day with your dusting, washing and cleaning. Doing your thing."

"Doing my thing?"

She removed a vase from a shelf, untied the string around the orchids and put them in the vase, carefully arranging them until each flower had a precise place. She could see from the way he was standing that he had something on his mind.

"I like the way you handled yourself at the plastic surgeon's office. You pulled it off like a pro."

"You mean, pretending that we were a married couple?"

He raised an eyebrow.

"Yeah, that."

There had been a silent agreement about the use of the M word. Marriage was a subject they avoided. Like a katoey showing up with his draft notice for a medical examination, the outcome was certain but nonetheless embarrassing for

340

everyone involved. She was widowed with a child, and he was single with a recent history of hallucinations.

"It wasn't that difficult," she said.

"Of course not," he said a little too quickly. "Like married people, we know a little too much about each other's faults. It's like we are family members. Tied together for life, but no one would call the tie a marriage."

"What would they call it?"

Calvino shifted weight from one foot to the other, the tips of his fingers balanced on the edge of her desk. He pretended to smell the flowers. She wasn't making this easy.

"Family," he said, looking up from the flowers. "That's what they'd call it. Family. When two people come to terms with each other's strengths and weaknesses and accept what they find. A bond of intimacy binds them. When people work together for years it happens."

"We rely on each other," she said.

His face brightened.

"That's what I've been trying to say."

"I'm not certain I understand," she said.

"It's like this. I can share my full range of moods, failures and craziness with you. People who are married have too much at stake, so they share a lot less information. They agree to share an illusion of each other's best self; they pretend they're on the perfect, eternal date, sealed with sex, that promises to never end. No married couple could ever know all the stuff that you know and I know about each other. We know too much. To stay married, you need a fair amount of ignorance. Selective forgetting is what makes close proximity possible. It's what we forget about someone that lets us find some peace, some happiness."

"Thank you for the flowers, Khun Vinny," she said, turning back to her computer screen.

Calvino continued to stand in front of her desk. She glanced up.

"There's something else?"

"Pratt told me what happened in Rangoon and how Manee found out."

"Is that why you brought me flowers?"

His first reaction was to deny, but he knew that wouldn't work.

"I brought you the flowers because I thought you liked orchids, and I wanted to say thank you. And yeah, I wanted to know how Manee is dealing with this."

"You once told me that the real reason always comes last."

"There is one more reason, Ratana. I'm seeing someone. A new client. She's a Canadian-Norwegian named Dr. Marley Solberg. I don't know where it's going or if it's going anywhere. But there is a possibility. I didn't want you to find out from anyone else. Or think I was hiding the fact I'm seeing someone."

"A doctor?"

"Not a real doctor. A Ph.D."

"Anything else?"

Calvino shook his head.

"There's someone waiting for you in your office."

Ratana smiled and nodded toward the closed door.

"Who?"

Her smile widened as she turned away and focused on the keyboard, her fingers flying as if *affettuoso*—passion and feeling—had inspired her. Calvino took her non-response as an invitation to discover for himself the person waiting in his office. McPhail, he guessed, would have pulled his office bottle out of the desk drawer and helped himself. When he opened the door, it wasn't McPhail who looked up. Dr. Marley Solberg sat in a chair, her Mac Power Pro open on a table, with his papers and books pushed into neat piles behind it.

"Did you hear my conversation with Ratana?"

Marley looked up.

"It is a small office, Vincent."

He stood in the door, Ratana behind him, Marley in front of him—in a straight line between the two women—and he felt balanced on a rope walking high above the street.

"Every word?"

"Yes," she said. "Why? Does speaking from the heart embarrass you?"

"I wasn't expecting you."

"That's pretty obvious."

"The thing about being a doctor..."

She cut him off.

"I have good news. I can save the ten million baht for Thanet's cell phone information."

"You tracked down Sukanya's phone directory?" asked Calvino, walking around to his desk and sitting down.

"I'll spare you the technical details. We ran an intercept on Jaruk's phone. So we had several of Thanet's numbers. He had secure phones and used them to phone an unsecure phone. He was lazy or stupid. I met Thanet's receptionist when I went to his office. I gave the name to Ratana, who found a mutual friend. Thanet's private secretary has worked for him for fifteen years. She knows everything. Once we had that name, we traced three more cell phones registered in her name. Ratana is translating the names and details of the people we traced. We have locations, times and duration of all of his incoming and outgoing calls. We know everyone he's talked to in the last year. And there are patterns in his phone call data. Certain calls at certain times with the same people."

Calvino sat back in his chair, shaking his head.

"How many minor wives?"

"Three minor wives, a couple of *giks*. Thanet's been a very careless and naughty boy," said Marley. "He mixed up his phones. Once that happens, everything is easily revealed. You need special ops training to run secure phones. Play acting only works in the movies."

"When can I see what you've found?" said Calvino, staring across the room.

The image of Ploy's body lying in the grass flashed through his mind. The bodies of the doctor and the receptionist then merged into Mya's face next to his and Yadanar's on his birthday. It was different from the visitations. He wasn't seeing ghosts going through walls. He was experiencing the memories of the people he had known whom Thanet had dispatched to the other side.

"It won't be long. I also have information about his friends, including generals, monks, civil servants, politicians and businessmen and telephone data about their wives and minor wives," said Marley.

Calvino felt a shudder that comes when a possibility is so disruptive that all stability is lost. Once gone, it can never be established. When a ship sinks, everything on board goes down with it.

"We can take it any number of ways," he said.

Marley agreed, nodding and listening to the sound of Ratana, typing again at her keyboard in the next room.

"It's time to put Thanet's minor wives in contact with each other. The sisterhood needs the ability to compare notes on monthly payments, cars, condos and extras. Let's see what they do with it. If that doesn't work, we go and find his associates' minor wives. We tip over the whole hive of wives. Hornets would weep with envy at the sting of a colony hit with that stick."

"I don't know if that's a good idea," said Calvino.

"Why not? It will work."

"So will chemical weapons of mass destruction, but we still ban them."

"Okay, Mr. Henry Miller. It was your suggestion to get the information."

"I know, I know. Using it is another thing. Colonel Pratt's convinced that the law doesn't apply to the gods, that only the gods can dispose of another god."

"The wives of gods are god killers," she said. "Welcome to a brave new world for gods, where they can no longer keep their secrets."

"How are you going to contact his wives?"

"They're all on Facebook and Twitter. They've uploaded photographs. At the beach, their food, their dogs, with their friends," said Marley, "but never with Thanet."

Ratana walked into Calvino's office with a printout.

"I told Marley the legend of the sword tree," said Ratana.

The two women exchanged a smile. Ratana handed her the printout.

"That's the English translation of their latest Facebook updates," Ratana explained to Calvino.

"There's one more thing," said Calvino.

Both women waited for him to continue.

"I want the cell phone used to set off the bomb that killed Mya and Yadanar. I offered Jaruk five million baht for it."

Marley shook her head.

"He'll have thrown away the SIM card. Having the phone is not going to prove anything."

Calvino removed his jacket. He wore a shoulder holster and his .38 Police Special over an Oxford blue shirt.

"You don't understand how the mind of someone like Jaruk works."

"Enlighten me," said Marley.

"The SIM card is an insurance policy for down the road. I don't need to tap into a vast database or run algorithms or come up with equations. People in the killing business don't throw away their Get Out of Jail Free cards. There's only one way to find out if I'm right. Get the phone and check the SIM. Only then will I know for sure if I've found the man who killed them."

"And what will you do then?" Marley asked.

"What would you do?"

He stared at her until she looked away.

"The rich never dirty their hands. They hire shadow men like Jaruk to do what they can't stomach doing themselves. I don't subcontract revenge. Neither do I enjoy it. Making things right means doing what's right."

"Sometimes you sound like George Orwell," she said, smiling.

Ratana nodded at Calvino. She understood what was inside his heart and soul. As he'd reminded her a few minutes earlier, she understood the places where he stored his hopes, dreams, disappointments and failures, and saw that he needed to close the case with Mya if he was ever to move on.

FORTY-FOUR

JARUK WAS NO one's fool and neither was his boss. Ploy had first double-crossed Thanet. She had second thoughts. She knew what he was capable to doing. She changed her mind reasoning that double-crossing the Norwegian woman had less risk. Marley would be angry and disappointed. But Thanet would kill her family. Could outsiders like Marley and Yoshi could protect her and her family? It wasn't, at the end, a hard choice for Ploy to make. She started to doubt whether outsiders like Marley and Yoshi could protect her. She'd told Thanet that she'd agree to an abortion. By this time Thanet had made up his mind to get rid of her and assigned Jaruk the job. She thought Jaruk was taking her for an abortion. The thought made him smile. Stupid girl, he'd thought. She'd made it so easy.

He'd made a quick half a million baht setting up an abortion and a hit, and now he'd already pocketed another million from the farang. It wasn't enough to achieve self-sufficiency at the level to which he'd become accustomed. Five million would make all the difference in the world, he thought. In the back of his mind he had no doubt that Calvino and his friend would expose to his boss that he'd been double dipping by making a side deal with Sukanya. The farang was also right that Thanet, like most of Thanet's friends, had been joking nervously about whose driver would be next to murder one of them for three million baht.

They laughed like it was a joke, but Jaruk smelled genuine fear when he overheard them talking. He had decided to take a precaution. Thanet had been extra-attentive about his driver's private life, asking about Jaruk's family and friends.

Jaruk sat down in an Internet café in Khao San Road. Backpackers wearing headphones chatted on Skype to their parents or girlfriends or boyfriends. He pulled out the piece of paper with Calvino's name written on it and put it next to the keyboard. He'd managed to get the name by running a trace on the license place of his car. He smiled when the name came back. It wasn't Jack Smith, the name he'd used at Sukanya's office. He thought how stupid she had been to have believed the farang was who he said he was.

The tourists left him alone to conduct a search. He found that Vincent Calvino, a private investigator, an American from New York, was also an ex-lawyer. What interested him most was Calvino's connection with the people killed in the Bangkok car bombing. Calvino had a personal connection to the man and woman, a couple of entertainers from Rangoon, who'd died in the bombing. After the blast Calvino had become personally involved in the case. Now Jaruk knew why Calvino wanted the cell phone.

Calvino had gone too far in his investigation. Some cops discovered the farang had taken evidence from the bombing site. A Thai police colonel, Calvino's friend, had been removed from working on the case. The case was personal for Calvino. And that element meant the farang wasn't going to go away. Jaruk didn't have a lot of good options. Once he had emailed Calvino with the information about Thanet's cell phones and banking and credit cards, meeting the farang to hand over the phone would involve a high risk of violence.

Jaruk spent hours thinking about where and how to execute the handover, traveling on the BTS and MRT to the farang places in Bangkok, public places where he'd feel safe. The more time he spent, the more Jaruk decided there was only one way to deal with the farang. He'd lure him to his own turf. He'd ambush him, kill him, snatch the money and take off. With five million baht he'd set up in Cambodia, where old army buddies had gone into hiding after a drug bust. They'd been bailed in Thailand and skipped over the border to a safe house where he could stay.

"Hello," Jaruk said into the phone.

He paused.

"I have it."

Calvino heard him breathing on the other end.

"You have the phone?"

"Have. You meet me second floor parking lot, MRT Ladprao."

"I avoid meeting in parking lots," said Calvino.

"No one will see us."

"I want people to see us."

"Why?"

"It makes shooting me riskier for you," said Calvino. "That's a pretty good reason, wouldn't you agree?"

"Where you want to meet?"

"Siam Paragon. Kinokuniya. You come alone. Don't send someone else to pick up the money. I want you to hand me the phone personally. Got that?"

Jaruk cleared his throat, clenched his jaw. His line of work, like any other business in Thailand, had more uncovered manholes than an unlit street in Islamabad. It made him very careful where he walked.

"What is Kinokuniya?"

"It's a bookstore. You know, a place where they sell books. Those bound paper objects you read in school. Ring a bell? It's on the third floor. There's a corner near a window. I'll be sitting on the bench. I'll be there with your money."

"Five million baht."

"Four million. Remember, I gave you one million already. And I transfer another five million when you give me Thanet's cell phone numbers, bank and credit card details. That was our deal."

"Ladprao is better."

Calvino laughed.

"Not a chance. I like bookstores. You can learn something. Parking lots make me nervous."

Calvino waited for Jaruk to say something.

After a couple of seconds, Calvino added, "If you want to call it off, no problem. Your boss can handle you in his own way."

"Bring the money in thousand baht notes. In two hours we meet," said Jaruk.

Typical, thought Calvino. The Thais are either two years late or two hours early in business deals, depending on whether they're paying or getting paid.

"The original SIM card has to be in the phone. If it's gone, no money."

"Okay, okay, whatever."

Jaruk ended the call. He hadn't waited for Calvino to negotiate the time. It was his little victory. Setting the deadline. Confirmation and questions made him restless and angry.

Calvino put his cell phone down on the coffee table. Marley sat on the sofa across from him.

"That was Jaruk. He has the phone I want."

He checked his watch and got up. She reached across and took his hand.

"Vincent, let it go."

He smiled.

"My therapist said the same thing to me."

"What did you say to her?"

"I need to finish this. Afterwards I can let it go."

"I'll go with you," she said.

He shook his head, taking her hand in his, raising it to his lips and kissing it.

"You need to understand who I am. What I need to do."

"You're going to kill him," she said.

Her eyes froze with an arctic fear. Viking women must have had a sudden realization of what their men were about to do as they left for their waiting ships.

"Killing someone in a busy bookstore would be a lousy idea."

"Promise me you won't."

He stood holding her hand, noticing a coldness in her eyes and wondering what numbers she used to measure the value of a promise.

"I don't make that kind of promise. But I want you to understand this much—Jaruk is a small wheel inside the clockwork. What he did wasn't out of hate or malice or revenge. It was a job, an assignment from his boss. The mission is to take Thanet down. I'm betting that when I give you the SIM card, you'll find that he phoned his boss on that phone after detonating the bomb. That's a little present I want to give Colonel Pratt. Not that it will make any difference. Thanet is a god, after all. But I want Pratt to know I'm not crazy."

"He knows you're not," she said.

He raised an eyebrow, smiled.

"When you live in Bangkok long enough, you start to believe ghosts might be real after all. You become crazy in a different way."

Calvino spun the combination lock on his wall safe, opened it and removed stacks of thousand baht notes, stuffing each wrapped packet into a backpack. The notes weighed about four kilos and fit inside easily. Marley watched from the doorway as he counted the money and arranged it.

"Corruption is a mixture of greed, opportunity and secrecy," said Calvino. "If you watch your boss cheat and lie, always putting himself first, his conduct becomes your role model. In Jaruk's mind, he's not doing anything different from what his boss taught him. He knows that if he sticks around, he's dead. He's less afraid of me than Thanet, or he wouldn't have phoned."

"When you get the phone, call me. I'll put the number through the database right away to see if there's a match to any of Thanet's cell phones."

"I am looking for a series of outgoing calls to Thanet at the time the bomb exploded," said Calvino.

"Maybe Jaruk didn't phone his boss or he used another phone," said Marley.

"Phone me back either way," said Calvino. "I want to know if there's a match at the time and place of the bombing."

From the safe Calvino pulled out a device the size of a thumb drive. He opened another pouch of the backpack and then a hidden pocket within it, where he slipped the device inside. He zipped up the backpack.

"That's a tracking device. We'll want to know where Jaruk is going next."

FORTY-FIVE

CALVINO ARRIVED AT the Siam Paragon branch of Kinokuniya fifteen minutes early. He walked in wearing the backpack over a blue polo shirt, dark gray trousers and black loafers. He looked like a middle-aged tourist shopping for a paperback as he wandered around the fiction section, picking up books, reading the blurbs and asking himself why the fictional world of criminals never quite exposed the real one. The boredom, the sparks that almost ignite an act violence but fizzle out, the daily life of gangsters, mostly filled with utter, useless stupidity, old recycled jokes, expensive clubs. Or their confusion, half-baked ideas, schemes and plans, and their laziness and sense of entitlement. Or how good cops in a corrupt system, cops like Colonel Pratt, struggled to believe they could make a difference despite being compromised, sidelined and stripped of their dignity. If someone wrote a book that real, no one would buy it, he thought.

Images of Mya in her family bookstore in Rangoon floated through his mind. How many Burmese women had read Henry Miller? She'd mainlined Miller like he was a drug that opened a new landscape of consciousness. In the non-fiction section Calvino found a shelf with a collection of George Orwell's writings. He took a few of the volumes and sat on a bench near the window, facing the view. While in Rangoon he'd grown to like Orwell's take on the dangerous hairpin corners of life, judging that not much had changed since the author's time. People crashed at the same points and for the same stupid reasons—greed, envy, arrogance and desire. Orwell had spent a short life writing out a system of road signs. But most people were ignorant of them or ignored them. Reality was discouraging.

A few minutes later Jaruk appeared, dressed in jeans and a nylon workout shirt. Muscled and young, tough looking, he stood looking out the window near Calvino. He didn't look like someone who belonged in a bookstore. Calvino sat reading Orwell's *Burmese Days*, a story about an outsider joining a private club and the obstacles in the way. It occurred to Calvino that the world is filled with Jaruks, excluded from club membership.

Calvino saw a reflection in the glass window. A young Thai man in black—black jacket, black T-shirt and black jeans—slipped in like a cat stalking a mouse.

"You might like this book," said Calvino.

Jaruk turned from the window. His eyes said he didn't think so.

Calvino gestured for him to sit on the bench.

As Jaruk sat down, Calvino said, "You told your boss that you threw away the cell phone."

Jaruk looked at him.

"In a *klong*," said Jaruk.

"You lied to him. How do I know you're not lying to me, that the phone you're giving me is the one that you used?"

"Check it here."

"I will," said Calvino, as Jaruk slipped the phone onto the seat next to Calvino.

Calvino picked up the phone and called Marley.

"Check this number," he said. "Phone me back with what you find."

They sat side by side, staring out the window. A couple of Japanese housewives walked past, stopping at the shelf of Japanese books.

"Give me two, three more days to get the other information," said Jaruk. "The boss will be out of town. I can get it when he's gone."

Calvino opened another book, a collection of Orwell's essays. He'd bookmarked "Shooting an Elephant."

"Two days, no more time after that. Do you understand?" asked Calvino.

Marley's SMS intercepts indicated Thanet was planning a trip to Hong Kong in two days.

Jaruk nodded, and Calvino saw one of the Japanese housewives leave with books. He returned to Orwell's account of a colonial official who'd been pressured into shooting an elephant. The creature had destroyed a market and killed a man, but its musk-fed rage had ended by the time the official caught up with it, and the elephant grazed calmly in an open field. The field was ringed with thousands of villagers waiting for the big boss, the man with the gun and the authority, to show the use of both.

Calvino figured that men like Thanet were like that colonial official who must restore order after someone has committed an act of outrage against his authority. Not shooting the elephant was never an option. For that reason Jaruk had always understood that one day he might need a means of escape, some insurance against the eventuality of his boss needing to make an example of him. That day had arrived. Calvino's own cell phone rang.

"It's the real deal," said Marley.

"You're sure?"

"Time, location match the bombing. He phoned one of Thanet's cell phones moments after he set off the bomb."

Calvino moved the black backpack with his foot in front of Jaruk. He lowered his cell phone from his ear.

"The cash is in the bag."

"All four million? How can I trust you?"

"Because I need your cooperation to pass along Thanet's cell phone and financial information."

Jaruk slipped one arm and then the other through the straps on the backpack and smiled.

"Good thinking. You cheat me, and I don't what give you want."

"The backpack matches with your outfit," said Calvino.

"Don't try and follow me."

"One thing before you go," said Calvino, pulling Jaruk back down on the bench. "You set the bomb and detonated it?"

Jaruk pulled a face, shook his head.

"It was long time ago. Why you ask?"

"The Burmese girl that your girlfriend killed and that you dumped at the Tobacco Monopoly Land was pregnant."

Jaruk still wore the same "Why you ask?" expression. What in his childhood had stripped the guilt of killing from his conscience? Calvino couldn't begin to formulate an answer. He doubted Jaruk could either.

"Thanet was the father?" said Calvino.

"No, that was the problem."

Calvino stared at him hard. This wasn't the kind of man that looked back. He only looked forward. He had blown up two people and helped plan the murder of a pregnant girl, but the memories had flown away like a caged bird. Calvino could see from the look in Jaruk's eyes that Mya's and Ploy's deaths were just two on a long list.

"There is a video of you and a friend in white masks murdering the doctor and Sukanya. With the mask it's difficult to identify you. But I think you wouldn't want anyone to try."

"You have the phone. That's our deal."

He rose back to his feet, and this time Calvino made no effort to stop him. What was the point? Jaruk didn't kill out of passion; it was the way he made his living—killing and cleaning up the mess of death. A cleaner restored order. Jaruk worked those ropes, tied those knots, like a sailor who understood how to stay afloat on the open sea, and never had any reason to dive below the surface where the bodies fell.

As Jaruk disappeared out of the bookstore, Calvino phoned Marley.

"Light up the sword tree," he said. "Introduce Thanet's wives to each other."

FORTY-SIX

WHEN CALVINO GOT back to his office, he stood in front of Ratana's unoccupied desk and listened to voices coming from his inner office. He opened the office door and found Ratana and Marley sitting together, perched in front of two separate computer screens. They were scanning the two screens simultaneously as Ratana translated the Thai into English. At the other end of the desk, fresh flowers from Villa Market lay inside their paper wrapper. Next to the flowers was a white china plate with pieces of sliced pineapple assembled in three neat rows and two dessert forks positioned like fortress cannons flanking the ends. The sweet scent of the pineapple and flowers filled his room. The handgrip from his .38 Police Special protruded from his leather holster, which hung on a coat stand.

"Jaruk looked, acted like a tough guy until the very end," said Calvino, "when I noticed he sounded nervous. He couldn't wait to get away. I wonder, was it me? Or being surrounded by all of those books?"

He looked over Marley's shoulder at one of the computer screens.

"How many of Thanet's sword trees are you growing?"

"A forest. All the saplings are getting to know one another," she said with a smile, turning to look up at him.

They exchanged the unmistakable look of two people trying to clearly communicate shared feelings.

Calvino stepped back from Marley's side and moved closer to Ratana, who sat forward in his chair.

"Where's he going with my money?" he asked.

Ratana pointed at the screen.

"Ladprao. After he left Siam Paragon, he changed taxis twice."

She zoomed in on two spots on the map where the switches were made.

"He wants us to think he's using classic avoidance techniques to shake a tail," said Calvino. "He's seen too many car chase movies."

"Khun Vinny, what if he finds the tracking device?" asked Ratana.

"He will assume I planted one. This guy is smart and capable. That's why Thanet hired him. Jaruk's counting on the theory that farang are stupid and will have underestimated him. By changing taxis, he's confirming that he thinks we're physically following him. That should shake us, he's thinking, and he doesn't have a clue. He's bought into the decoy as the only tracking device he has to worry about. Hightailing it back to Ladprao is what we expected him to do. He's a cleaner. He knows what people look for, and how to hide or dispose of evidence that makes people ask embarrassing questions."

"He's stopped at a Big C," Ratana said, pointing at the screen. "It's not far from the MRT station. Have a look."

Calvino saw the flashing red dot as Ratana enlarged the image on the map.

"All that money, and he can't wait to going shopping," said Calvino.

Marley had set up the two sets of tracking software the day before. A Google map of Bangkok's streets with a flashing red pinpoint identified Jaruk's exact location. On the other computer Ratana was helping Marley understand the stream of Thai data flowing in and out of Thanet's cell phones.

Four women were the targets of the surveillance. Three of them were Thanet's minor wives—Nuu, Toy and Kaeo. A JPEG photo of each woman was positioned above the stream of data from her cell phone, Facebook and Twitter accounts. The fourth target, Nee, was Thanet's major wife. For the Chinese four is an unlucky number, Ratana told Marley as she scrolled through the data, translating what popped up on the screen from the SMS feeds.

"Looks like Thanet's sword tree seedling is growing into a redwood tree in record time," said Calvino.

Activity onscreen with the wives suddenly jumped like the New York Stock Exchange during a buying frenzy. The stats pump had been primed, and masses of real-time telephone data appeared: calls back and forth, and then a stream of calls exchanged between the numbers, showing the phone users were contacting one another. The rate of new Facebook postings and tweets shot up like a rock star caught with his pants down in a cowshed. Their accounts caught fire once Marley had emailed a package of data, the text translated into Thai, to each of the four women—photos of each minor wife, age, name, weight, education, ID card number, place of birth, Bangkok address, make of car and registration number, and bank account balances. A second round of information followed fifteen minutes later that included intimate text messages exchanged between each of the women and Thanet. Fifty, sixty percent of it was simple cut and paste, the same message sent to each woman.

"He's moving again," said Ratana.

"Fast shopper," said Calvino.

The three of them watched the red dot move down Ladprao Road and stop at the entrance to Soi 35.

"What's he doing?" asked Marley.

"Getting a bowl of noodles," said Calvino. "Or conducting business—there's an Internet shop near the top of the soi. Or maybe he's thinking over what his next step should be."

Using one of the forks, he speared a slice of pineapple. He chewed the fruit and speared a second slice, offering it to Marley. She hadn't been spoon-fed for some time.

Ratana smacked her lips.

"Oh, my God!" she said, reading one of the feeds.

"What do you have?"

"These two are actually talking to each other: Kaeo and Nee."

That was a mia noi, minor wife number three, and the *mia luang*, the major wife. And Toy and Nuu had also been sending Thanet SMS messages. Toy sent a message to Thanet saying she'd slept with Jaruk. She must have also sent it to Kaeo, who said she'd also slept with Jaruk."

"Jaruk's homecoming might not be what he expects."

"Kaeo and Toy both sent SMS messages to Jaruk, begging him to take them away from Bangkok."

Marley said, "Forward those messages to Thanet."

Calvino and Ratana exchanged a look. He thought about the cold look in Jaruk's eyes when he'd asked him about the car bombing.

"Send it along," said Calvino.

Ten minutes later, the red dot moved down Soi 35. A second red dot, tracking the wireless radio-frequency ID strips in the stacks of thousand baht notes appeared on the screen. It was going in a different direction.

"He's switched the money into another bag," said Calvino. "Bought it at the Big C is my guess."

They watched as the red dot from the RFID strips moved at considerable speed away from Ladprao. Jaruk was in a hurry to get out of the area. Calvino had figured Kaeo or Toy would have shared not only a husband but also the same gigolo. Jaruk was exposed as Exhibit A in the debate about the need to employ eunuchs to run a well-managed harem.

The red dot stopped moving. The screen showed a program error.

"Try rebooting," said Calvino.

Marley's effort to reboot failed to bring the program back online.

"The server's down."

"They don't have a backup?" asked Calvino, shaking his head.

Marley worked to find one as Calvino and Ratana watched her quickly going from one page to the next without success.

"I'm not waiting," said Calvino.

He pushed away from his desk and reached for his leather holster.

"Where are you going?" asked Ratana.

"To get my money before Thanet finds him."

"Be careful, Vincent," said Marley.

Calvino leaned over and kissed her on the forehead.

"Track his SMS," he said. "He might text where he's heading."

He checked his .38.

"My grandfather taught me never to take the easy way out," said Calvino. "He was a painter. There are lots of ways to save on paint and canvas. You can hire someone to do the painting, and your name might be on it, but it will never be yours."

Ratana continued to track the SMS traffic between the wives and Thanet, as well as the messages sent to Jaruk, to which there had so far been no reply. Like a hive brain, the collective consciousness had come to the conclusion that Jaruk was on the run. In the great unravelling, the yarn never spools back into the perfect pyramid in which it was sold; it spirals into knots, tangles and braided loops, forming a jumble of potential couplings. When Ratana looked up, both Calvino and Marley had disappeared. She thought it funny that Marley had called him Vincent and not Vinny. And that Marley hadn't spoken what had passed through Ratana's brain: "Vinny, don't go after him." But that was wives' talk, and Ratana understood that kind of talk was not their shared language. The irony being that Calvino would love Ratana for that.

When she went downstairs, she looked out on the sub-soi. She saw no sign of them.

Jaruk was slouched in the back of the taxi when he took the call from his boss.

"What the fuck is going on? I'm getting messages and calls about you and Toy, and now about you and Kaeo. What is this? How do they know to talk to each other? How do they know?"

He'd lost face, but Jaruk didn't need a visual to see that. It echoed in his voice, all that hurt and rage boiling over inside. Just a bit more and he'd lose control. Jaruk had seen his boss reach that point with others who'd crossed him. Men Jaruk never saw again.

Jaruk screamed for his taxi to stop. The driver eyed him in the rearview mirror and decided it was a good idea to pull into a parking place in front of a row of shops.

"You'd better come to the office."

Jaruk heard the tremble in his boss's order. He got out of the taxi, paid the driver and walked into an Internet café.

He didn't like his boss's attitude.

"I've got an appointment, boss. Can Lek handle it?"

"I said come to the office. Now."

The bluster made the voice gravelly.

"Sure thing. I'll be right there," Jaruk said, ending the call.

FORTY-SEVEN

THE NEXT MORNING Marley phoned Calvino just after 8:00 a.m.

"I found where Jaruk's hiding. I just emailed you the location. I suggested to Ratana that she let Colonel Pratt know."

"He's no longer on the police force," Calvino said, sitting up in bed.

"He's your friend," she said. "He's involved. I thought he might want to know."

"You're right. It's five after eight. Jaruk's either sleeping or he's halfway to Cambodia. But there's only one way to find out."

"He didn't make any calls from his phone," she said.

"Good, it means he's sleeping."

Calvino got out of bed, showered and dressed. He looked out the window at the traffic flow toward Klong Toey and decided driving a car in that neighborhood was a good idea. His motorbike would get snatched in ten minutes.

Before Calvino was out of the shower, Colonel Pratt was on the road after Ratana's phone call. Cop or not, he had to check out the information. When she told him what district Jaruk had fled to, he remembered the place from the old days. He'd known the location as a boy and had no trouble finding it again. Marley had picked up the signal, a strong, steady frequency.

Calvino pulled up to the curb, looked at his cell phone screen and got out of his car. He paced up and down the street until he found himself standing in front of Colonel Pratt, who wore a white shirt and dark slacks. They were outside the building where Jaruk or at least his money was resting. Colonel Pratt held a black gym bag with "Manchester United" in red on the side.

"Got something for you," said Colonel Pratt and tossed Calvino the bag like a football.

The bag sailed through the air and Calvino caught it with both hands. He judged the weight to be around five kilos' worth of thousand baht notes.

"What's inside, Pratt? Mangoes?"

"It's Jaruk's bag."

"Where is he?"

"He's inside. But you don't want to look."

Calvino moved forward.

"He's been disemboweled," said Colonel Pratt.

That was enough to stop Calvino.

"You're sure it's him?"

"Same guy."

Colonel Pratt held up Jaruk's Thai ID card.

Calvino felt a wave of relief. It had been a loose end that needed to be put right.

"Jaruk's the asshole who set off the bomb," said Calvino. "He gave me the phone that he used that night. It was an old eight hundred baht Nokia. Not even a maid would be caught dead with one. But it's perfect for a bomb disposal guy like him. I've got it at my office. It's yours. The same SIM card he used that night is still in it. He hadn't changed it, which tells you something. Leverage against the boss."

"The phone has to connect him to Thanet," said Colonel Pratt.

"Marley found out that Jaruk phoned Thanet only a couple of minutes after the blast."

He looked at the west end of the building, which was near the canal.

"He got what he deserved, and then some," said Calvino.

He wondered if the building flooded in the monsoon season.

"Karma," said Colonel Pratt, watching Calvino turn and walk toward the building.

"Room 103," said the Colonel.

Calvino walked along the footpath in front.

Colonel Pratt called after him.

"He cost me my chance at the Blue Note when he blew up Yadanar's car. I know you lost someone you loved, but I lost something of value that night as well. It changed the course of my life. We both lost something we can't get back."

Calvino didn't look back and was out of earshot after hearing "my chance at the Blue Note." It didn't matter that Colonel Pratt's voice trailed off in the distance. Calvino could fill in the blanks. He knew the pain in the Colonel's heart and the words it would use to express itself.

Calvino walked inside and down the corridor, stopping in front of a wooden door with "103" painted in green. He tried the door. It wasn't locked. Slowly he pushed the door open and stepped inside, closing it shut behind him. The curtains were closed, and the place stank. Calvino took out a handkerchief and put it over his mouth and nose, but it didn't stop the fetid smell of a slaughterhouse from invading his nose and mouth. He opened the door of a cheap plywood closet with mirrors on both panels. Calvino pushed the hangers with a few shirts and trousers down the rail.

He'd already, out of the corner of his eye, seen the form of a man on the bed. He wanted to take his time, save the inspection of the corpse for last. He wanted to know something about how the man who'd killed Mya lived. He looked at a shelf and the other walls. Not a single book in the room. A microwave oven, a guesthouse room-sized fridge, a small sink, an oval mirror—the guy had enough mirrors to replicate a short-time hotel—a table and three chairs. There were some photographs of Jaruk in uniform a decade younger. More photographs of him with a woman in Pattaya—the location's giveaway was in a sign on the side of a hill at the end of the bay. In one of the photos Jaruk looked nine or ten years old, holding a fishing pole and standing next to a man showing off a string of fish. The man was in his thirties. The boy squinted against the sun, smiling into the camera. A river and fields spread out behind them. Jaruk's father was a good bet for the identity of the older man. How had the smiling boy who'd gone fishing with his dad become a man named Jaruk with a heart so chilled that no feelings leaked out when he killed? Nothing in the pictures gave a clue.

After he'd seen enough, Calvino walked to the back, where the bed stood under a window. He pulled up a wooden chair and sat next to the bed. He sat there in silence for a couple of minutes, staring at the corpse. It wasn't a hallucination. He was in a room with someone who was not only dead, but someone whom Calvino had wished dead. Seeing the body butchered like that of an animal, the dead man's face bloodied and with eyes wide open, staring at the ceiling. The bladework had carved a deep gorge from the chest downward through the stomach cavity, exiting at the groin. Calvino had expected to find peace once he'd seen the body of the man who'd killed Mya. He felt nothing close to that release. He only wanted to vomit. Before he'd been murdered, Jaruk had experienced genuine suffering and pain. The death scene pointed to a killer who was high either on drugs or hate. Professionals were violent and efficient and had no reason to leave behind a message. It was simple—do the job and leave the scene immediately. A Guy Fawkes mask was angled against the pillow so that it appeared to be staring at the body with its empty eyeholes and wide grin.

A message intended for someone, but for whom?

Was this the state of a man's body climbing the sword tree for eternity?

By the time Calvino emerged from the building, Colonel Pratt had walked down to the canal and squatted down, watching the barges.

"When I was a kid," said the Colonel, "my father sometimes brought me down to the river to watch boats. He said the barges and ships brought us our food and coal and sugar and rice. That without the river the lifeblood of Bangkok would be destroyed. Our ancestors came to these banks to make offerings to the goddess of the river. A few of the old ones still do the rituals. But look at it now. I no longer see the holy place I remember as a child."

Colonel Pratt glanced over at Calvino.

"What do you think about what you saw inside?" he asked.

"Good luck finding who killed him," said Calvino. "The police will take one long look at him, the Guy Fawkes mask and who he worked for, and will tell the press, 'It was either a personal or a business conflict. Investigation to continue.'"

In Jaruk's case there was much to investigate: his boss, the way he was killed, the manner of displaying his body next to a mask used at political rallies and also captured on video in the office of Dr. Nattapong, before he and his receptionist were shot. A cop like Colonel Pratt would know this world and find it alien and unknowable at the same time. For Calvino there had been a missing dimension of meaning inside the room, one he'd looked to reveal itself.

Someone had left a coded message and all he had to was break the code.

"Someone who knew his deepest secrets," said the Colonel.

"Who does a Thai man tell his secrets to, Pratt?" asked Calvino.

"His woman."

"In Jaruk's case make that plural."

"When you go plural in the secrets business, you're shortly out of that business," said Colonel Pratt.

FORTY-EIGHT

DR. MARLEY SOLBERG sat on the floor in the lotus position, her eyes closed, her hands upturned, thumbs touching index fingers. She had calmly held the position on a bamboo mat for fifteen minutes. When Nagata had gone to answer the door, her mind had relaxed, been transported to another place and time—inside a place she didn't recognize, a time outside memory. Beautiful mathematical equations with limitless possibilities appeared against a sky saturated with a granularity of blues she'd never seen. She felt her breath disappear into the sea with each heartbeat. The sound of ocean waves, chimes and a flute flowed from speakers. Nagata returned to find that Marley still hadn't moved. Calvino crept into the room and stood, waiting.

Marley appeared unaware of his presence. Nagata lit three incense sticks, placing them one by one in a narrow-necked bronze vase. He waied the vase and lowered himself onto a bamboo mat gently so as not to disturb Marley's meditation. Gray smoke gathered in braids above the low-slung table. A large assortment of statuettes made of porcelain, bronze and gold was organized in a large half-circle—a gathering of the gods of many different religions. Calvino recognized the two faces of Janus, Buddha in the lotus position, right hand raised palm out, Shiva dancing inside a circle, Sisyphus slumped forward with a large round boulder on his shoulders,

Zeus, the Greek god of law, order and fate, and Ganesh with a crown of gold, trunk decorated with ancient writing. A dozen other gods he couldn't assign a name to.

In a soft voice Nagata spoke: "To believe or not to believe is a false choice. Our beliefs and actions ripple through the lives of others. Most of the time we filter out what we see and hear. We don't pay attention. Our ancestors looked to myths, faith and beliefs to explain the nature of the ripples they noticed. Our grandparents found meaning and understanding with these tools. Do you know what is the best part of mathematics?"

Calvino watched Marley as she answered the question.

"It organizes your attention. Like the right music, it deepens your understanding of what you attend to."

Nagata smiled.

"A perfect answer. It doesn't filter. Mathematics predicts the movement and outcome of all natural forces. We are a part of nature. All of our thoughts and actions are forces organized mathematically inside nature. Sometimes we forget that we are part of nature. We are prone to seeking equations as if we were gods existing outside the world, looking to bring order out of chaos. But we fall short. We always will as our nature shows how capable and quick we are to act with brutality and cruelty, out of love and compassion, out of deception and lies, and out of a love of truth and justice. The seeds of all choices are within each of us. None of us can ever resolve our conflicting nature. If we did so, we'd no longer be human."

Marley's eyes opened and she shifted on the mat.

"Just now I saw Ploy. She is happy, content. She has no pain, bitterness or regret. She is with the baby she carried. Mother and daughter bound together. Each with the radiant smile of someone at peace."

Nagata smiled, his white robes hanging loose. Seen from one angle, he might have been a hundred years old; from another angle he looked like a young man. Nagata glanced at Marley.

"She has been waiting for you, Vincent."

Calvino removed his jacket, folded it and laid it on the wooden floor. He loosened his tie. Leaving behind his holster and handgun, he had changed into a white long-sleeve shirt and pressed gray trousers—his official face-making outfit—worn out of respect for Yoshi Nagata. He rolled up his sleeves.

"I've been waiting for her," he said. "For her to return my call."

"I've been meditating," she said.

"Jaruk is dead," said Calvino.

Marley tilted her head.

"You located him?"

Calvino nodded.

"What was left of him."

Calvino eased himself down on the floor opposite Marley.

"Pratt saw the body too."

The new age music swallowed up the silence as they looked at each other.

"You've been difficult to contact," said Calvino. "I guess you wanted it that way."

"I needed to speak with Professor Nagata."

"I thought you might be here. Your phone has been off for the last twelve hours."

She looked down at the floor. He sounded annoyed, upset. She didn't want to enter that space. Not yet.

"I asked her to turn off her phone," said Nagata.

"I came here to talk about what we've been doing for the Rohingya," said Marley. "I had no idea something like this could happen. I was feeling lost. And If I don't know what to do, what do I say to those I've asked to help me?

I've found a way forward, but before I made a decision I wanted Professor Nagata's opinion," she said.

"What kind of decision are you talking about?"

"I want to expose not just Thanet but his friends and associates. I want their wives to know their husbands are buying and using women like Ploy."

"You don't know the details. It might be true or it might not be," said Calvino.

"You're defending them?"

"It's an observation," said Calvino.

"Marley wishes to reinvent the world," said Nagata.

He was protective of her and at the same time saw that what was passing between Calvino and Marley was more than an intellectual conflict. A deeper meaning contained in their words suggested an emotional high tide was rolling in, breaking onto the shore.

"Wisdom is accepting the world as it is," said Nagata, "but the knowledge of my limitations doesn't stop me from helping to free those in slavery. However, I can't change the world to one that is slavery-free."

"We have the technology to change the world," said Marley. "I have the data for all of them. It could be a game changer. If you had a chance to stop the Rwanda genocide by exposing a few high-level people's infidelity, would you say, 'Don't do it'? Would you allow the slaughter to go on and on?"

"I have my doubts that your interventions would make any difference," said Nagata. "It is one thing to target a person you know to be a human rights violator, and another to target everyone around him. That's not targeting; that's saturation bombing. You take out a whole neighborhood or city because of your personal assessment of someone's friends? Put all Canadian Japanese in a concentration camp because we don't have to go to the trouble of finding whether any one of them is a traitor? We've come a long way with the new technology to collect information, analyze it and track people, but it hasn't made us gods."

"Professor Nagata, please understand. This is a rational, practical and effective extension of our technology," said Marley. "It's what we should do."

"There is no higher moral value, any more than there is a highest mathematical truth," he said.

"What value is higher than truth, Yoshi?"

"Trust."

"But if trust is based on lies and deception, it is meaningless," Marley replied.

"Truth works only if it is consensual. It is never absolute. Destroy trust and truth breaks down. You want to expose Thanet's lies and hypocrisy. You also believe his friends are guilty. What happened to the presumption of innocence?"

"A relic of the past. Disrupted by technology. Horse and buggy thinking. All of these come to mind," said Marley. "The old rules are broken. They're gone."

Calvino found his opening.

"The problem's not Thanet's friends. The problem is you, the person who appoints herself to exercise the power to destroy. That's a hard problem. Professor Nagata is right; you want to play god and make your own rules."

Nagata picked up the statue of Sisyphus and handed it to her.

"Sisyphus wished to cheat death for immortality. You wish to expose all cheaters in the name of eternal harmony and happiness. The punishment of Sisyphus fell on the shoulders of one person. Without trust, each day we'd push the boulder up the side of the mountain only to find that the gravity of mistrust sent it crashing back to the ground. Do you wish for a world where you can trust no one with personal information; where all channels to send personal, private information are open source for all?

Trust no neighbor, associate or official—assume they will, in time, betray your confidences? Assume all large political systems are collecting, storing and analyzing your private communications and will use information to violate your person and life? Assume that anything you say can and will be used against you at any time?"

The incense sticks had burnt to thin, ghostly ash, crooked and gray, ready to fall on the heads of the gods around the bronze vase. Calvino rose to his feet.

"I'm a small picture guy. I've never understood the big picture. But I know this much—there's no statute of limitations that protects you against predators who believe that you have a dangerous idea or plan. Once that happens, and they can lock down your life and decide your future, you're on your own. Maybe that's the way it's always been, and our idea that we have privacy and rights is just a shared illusion. But that way of thinking is above my pay grade. I've helped find some justice for many people who were murdered. Little people with a small lives, people who got involved in situations without appreciating they were in something over their heads. They were found dead or had gone missing. Their families or friends asked me to help. That's the size of the picture that's good enough for me."

FORTY-NINE

LATER THAT FRIDAY evening, having returned to Calvino's condo, they lay together in bed, shoulders touching. The lights of Bangkok shone beyond the lake. Colonel Pratt's CD from the Java Jazz Festival played in the bedroom. Marley asked him for his thoughts.

"I was thinking of the Crusades," he said, "and how our ability to control what people do or think isn't much different from a thousand years ago. "

She touched his face with the back of her hand.

"I'm letting it go, Vinny," she said.

In the half-darkness she saw him smile.

"How's it feel to let go?" he said.

"Different than I thought. Not like falling. More like being at peace."

"That's what Pratt said when I asked him about leaving the police department."

"What about Ratana? Do you think she's at peace?" asked Marley.

"Yeah, she's in that space too."

"As we were leaving tonight, Yoshi gave his blessing, and you looked at peace tonight too. It showed," she said.

"I haven't told you about Jaruk's body. I'm not certain I should."

"Tell me."

"He'd been killed with a knife or a sword. The killer had slit him open from chest to groin. What does that tell you?"

"Fear, anger, hatred," she said.

"Atrocities are hard to understand. Mutilating a body isn't something a professional killer does. Fanatics and crazies cross that boundary. During the time of the Crusades people slaughtered others like animals. That's why I was thinking about the Crusaders. How strong convictions distort everything they touch. The person who killed Jaruk can never turn back and return home. His bridges are burnt. The soles of his feet are sticky with blood. Wherever he goes, you won't need a computer to track his footsteps."

They fell into silence, listening to Colonel Pratt's saxophone. Calvino saw his medieval warriors with their shields and swords, mounted on horses in long columns. Their Crusades had been launched in the belief that naked force and faith in a god had the capacity to change the world of men. But to win battles was never sufficient to secure the victory of the Crusade, and that is what doomed the winners as much as the losers. Through strength and endurance a warrior might survive in battle, but nothing would allow them to survive once the hearts and minds of man changed against them.

Calvino broke the silence as the saxophone played.

"Like I said at Yoshi's, I have a simple outlook. I search for missing people. Someone is willing to pay me to find that person. That matters because many people go missing and no one cares. Caring about someone is as rare as an orchid in a Brooklyn flowerpot. I don't try to save the world or to find everyone who is lost. I take a case from someone who cares enough to find one person."

"You nurture people who care," she said. "Not many people do that."

He rolled onto his side and tried to find her eyes in the refracted light from the sky above the city.

"I don't put much trust in the world of ideas."

"Why are you against ideas?"

"I'm not against them. I'm afraid they'll make decisions about who we are, how we should live and how we control our emotions. They are too abstract. When you make a decision based on an abstraction, you are a step away from turning a human being into something abstract, and when you do that, the results look like what I found in Jaruk's room."

One thing Calvino had learned over the years was that every woman wants to know about other women in a man's life, and Marley was no exception. Calvino had mentioned the Burmese singer to Yoshi Nagata. Marley had been surprised to hear of Mya and wanted to know more about this Burmese woman who had a hold on Calvino.

"Mya. What was it about her that attracted you?"

"We thought alike," said Calvino.

"You processed patterns in the same way," said Marley.

He looked at Marley, smiling.

"That's the point. We shared the same language about things and life, and it never occurred to her that she was processing patterns. She thought, she performed, she acted, she desired. She thought of Henry Miller as a kind of role model. I understood her. I'm an ordinary guy like Henry Miller. We came from the same background, same kind of upbringing, which never prepared us for life in the world beyond New York. We were taught to avoid big ideas. Because living for big ideas means you stop thinking, seeing and caring about the people closest to you, understanding their world and finding your place inside their world. I prefer to find those who are lost and bring them back to their world."

"You've made a career of finding the lost souls," she said.

"Finding the lost person is a task that is near and small. Inside that dimension I can handle life."

"I was lost and you found me," said Marley.

Calvino raised his head from the pillow. She saw him smiling.

"You've always known where you were, who you are, that you would come out on top no matter what. That's good. I'm happy for you. But inside my world people know they can never come out on top without a fight. It's that world that sends those in the square world running to hide. What are they hiding from? You live in the other world, the place that launches crusades. I'm a go-between. People in your world hire me to go inside, find someone and bring them out, if they want out. But to convert them to your way of thinking, I never try to do that."

"I want a better world," she said. "People shouldn't have to drop out and disappear."

"I don't know how to make it better. But most of the time I can find someone who is lost and restore that person to someone who has missed them. I have no idea if that makes it a better world. So it doesn't matter.

He saw a vision of Mya. This time she came not as a hallucination but as a vivid memory of that last night in Bangkok before she died.

"Mya got lost inside Henry Miller's dream—the one Miller preached that he used to invent his own reality. Mya connected her reality with music, and the audiences loved her because they could feel that she had made herself whole and real and had overcome doubt and fear. She took from Miller that we are guided by flesh and blood, by our instincts, which flow through us like an electrical current. They light us up like a skyline. What an artist like Mya does is dig deep and learn to channel that flow. Think about it too much and it disappears. Whatever you are, no matter how old you are, how educated or screwed up, you find answers by living among the gangsters, whores, pimps, crazies, discontents and artists. These people have a weird kind of freedom that is lost to others."

"I want freedom for the Rohingya who are living in slavery."

"Funny thing is, you can't give someone freedom. They have to learn to take it. This I know. I am one of the last of the free men. And when you are next to me, like tonight, I forget that equations can turn into vampires sucking the freedom out of life. It won't be new ideas that change the world; it will be the same old ideas but with powerful numbers behind them. The opportunity to live free is diminishing. The belief in its place in our lives will soon end."

Marley touched his cheek with the back of her hand.

"I like that you are free."

"Are you?"

"Free?"

He nodded as her hand travelled below the sheet, her fingertips riding the slope down his belly and exploring the region below.

"If you went missing, I'd hire someone to find you. Because I care."

She had his number. Once she had that, it was simply a matter of speed dialing, and it wouldn't take long before he answered. He felt a strange mixture of feelings. He knew that there was no shortage of women who would take care of him for a price, but that price never included the deep caring that cost them something.

FIFTY

ON SUNDAY MORNING the uniformed security guard relaxed, listening to music with earbuds as he made his rounds through the levels of the parking garage. There were never many cars there on a Sunday. His routine was to check registration plates to see whether someone had parked his car in a place authorized for another car. Nothing caused more conflict in a Bangkok building than a tenant discovering a strange car parked in his reserved parking slot. The building management pressured the security company to pressure the guards—and the buck stopped with a guy making four hundred dollars a month, who had to deal with people who couldn't read, or refused to read, the signs that prohibited unauthorized parking.

Every couple of weeks a security guard on weekend duty interrupted a couple using a car as a short-time hotel. Most of the time it wasn't unauthorized parking, but nude bodies still caught a guard's attention on a Saturday or Sunday. A gentle tap on the window would register a jolt inside the car, the flurry of hands and arms in motion, reaching for clothes, the covering of faces. It was one of the rare opportunities for a security guard to receive a large tip—the size that sometimes matched the guard's share of all tips distributed at New Year's.

It was this guard's occasional good fortune to find a goldmine rocking the chassis of a luxury car. Once he'd received a five hundred baht tip from a SUV owner. On this particular morning, as he walked past a familiar yellow car, he saw a man inside. The guard pulled out the earbuds. Only a circus acrobat could make love in a yellow Lamborghini Gallardo sports car without causing a hernia. The security guard cupped his hands against the window and peered at the man seated behind the wheel. He wasn't moving, or if he was, it was at such a slow rate that a happy ending might take some time. The security guard scratched his chin, circled the car and tried to look through the window on the passenger's side. From the angle of the man's head on the steering wheel, the security guard could see a hole with dried blood around the ragged edges. He tried the door. It was unlocked. He thought for a moment about whether to open it. Finally he got up the courage, opened the door and stuck his head inside.

He pulled himself out of the car. Walked a couple of feet away. He wanted some distance between him and the car with the body in it. His hands shaking, he raised his walkie-talkie and called his boss.

"Phone the police. We have a dead man on the third floor. Yellow Lamborghini. Khun Thanet's parking spot."

The security guard walked around to the front of the car and noted the license plate number. Within twenty minutes several police cars had arrived and parked near the Lamborghini. A police van disgorged a forensic team. Wearing white surgical gloves and one-piece jumpsuits, they took pictures of the car and the dead man at the wheel. They asked the security guard if he'd touched the body, and he said he hadn't. They took his name, copied down his ID and snapped his photograph. After the police finished questioning and photographing the guard, he rushed downstairs and bought a lottery ticket with the car's license number.

The police waited for the arrival of another car, a gray BMW carrying senior police officers. An important man had been found dead. The officers who reached the scene first briefed the brass that a security guard had discovered the body while making his routine rounds. He'd found Thanet's body slumped over the wheel of his luxury sports car, a bullet wound in his left temple. A 9mm handgun had been found on the floor on the passenger's seat along with three amulets on a gold chain. The brass listened as the head of the forensic team told them that his team hadn't found any sign of a struggle. No bruises on the face. An autopsy would confirm if the body had cuts, wounds or abrasions elsewhere. Nothing appeared to have been stolen from the car. Thanet's wallet, cash, credit cards and the amulets hadn't been stolen. No cell phone was found on the body or in the car, however. That was a mystery. Who would have killed him for a cell phone and left everything else? The police had already ruled out robbery. His office had quickly confirmed that Thanet had returned two days earlier from a business trip to Hong Kong.

He'd been under a lot of pressure at work. His secretary had told the police that her boss had been depressed by marital problems. For this understatement the secretary deserved an award for discretion beyond the call of duty. On Friday they had launched an investigation into the murder of Thanet's long-time driver. Jaruk's murder had caused them a serious headache. Now, on Sunday, his boss had shot himself in the head. The police at the scene wanted Thanet to have been the one to pull the trigger. A verdict of suicide cleaned the gutters of suspected killers, and in a high-profile case, especially one involving an influential figure, the gutters were clogged with a multitude of personalities, some obscure, some connected, most with reasons to see him dead.

Colonel Pratt arrived on the scene in the back of a police car. The car had been dispatched to his house, which was filled with shipping boxes. Officially, the Colonel had retired from the force. For the Colonel, leaving the police force brought to mind the old saying about bargirls—you could take the girl out of the bar, but it was much harder to take the bar out of the girl.

His old boss had informally asked the ex-colonel for a favor. Come to the scene before Thanet's body is removed. Colonel Pratt couldn't formally participate in the investigation, but his commander had a reason. Thanet's name had been raised during the police investigation into a car bombing. When Colonel Pratt showed up, the senior brass asked him for an unofficial assessment. As long as it remained unofficial, no rules would be breached.

The 9mm from the car had been bagged and tagged. One of the forensic cops handed it to the Colonel's old boss.

"That's the gun the guard found inside."

"Whose name is it registered in?"

The senior cop frowned.

"I sent in a request, and it came back registered to Jaruk, his driver, the guy who was murdered near the river."

"Doesn't mean much. Influential people have guns registered in the names of their drivers, maids, minor wives and secretaries," said Colonel Pratt. He'd deliberately slipped minor wives into the laundry list.

"Someone murdered his driver. But they didn't use a gun. They used a knife," said the Colonel's old boss. "Could the same person who killed Jaruk have stolen his gun and used it to kill Thanet? What do you think?"

"I'd want to know if Thanet was right-handed. If so, would someone who is right-handed use their left hand to shoot themselves?"

His old boss scratched his stubble of a beard on his cheek. He was going to miss Colonel Pratt. Smart, honest cops had their value, but rarely did they last to retirement.

Colonel Pratt leaned forward with his head in the car, looking at the body.

"If he was killed, he knew or at least trusted his killer enough to let his guard down. You say there was no sign of a fight. It looks like suicide. But you can make a murder look like a suicide."

"His secretary said he was having trouble with his wife."

Colonel Pratt thought about what he should say next.

"People kill themselves for personal or business reasons. The same set of reasons they'd murder another person for. I'd say, wait until the autopsy. Tell the press it appears to be a suicide at this stage. But until there is a pathology report, the final decision has to wait."

"I don't know. Men like Thanet rarely kill themselves."

Colonel Pratt nodded.

"Rare things happen."

He watched as the forensic team took fingerprints from the interior of the car. His old boss looked on as police officers climbed inside.

"You think he paid import taxes on this car?"

Colonel Pratt grinned.

"One more thing to check out. Not that it much matters now. I doubt if he killed himself over tax fraud."

"His business meeting in Hong Kong was connected with the Triad."

"But if the Triad was behind the hit, how do you explain his driver's gun was found at the crime scene?" asked Colonel Pratt.

"I can't. Not yet."

"Good luck."

Now that Colonel Pratt had retired, he could engage in some light irony, even though it sailed over the general's head. In his freshly starched uniform the general leaned in close to the Colonel.

"Let's keep in touch."

They exchanged wais. The general walked back to his men, and Colonel Pratt stood apart from the others. For the first time he wasn't one of them. Like other civilians, he was on the other side of the fence.

As Colonel Pratt walked out to Rama IV Road, searching for a taxi to take him home, he wondered if the suicide theory would hold. Only in books and movies, he knew, is it easy to fake a suicide. In real life one small telling detail, like an acorn found growing in the Arctic, can blow a hole in a hundred theories. But only an experienced investigator looks for that detail, the one in plain sight that everyone sees and ignores, while the brass want to keep the freezing winds circulating, blowing freely across the landscape. Colonel Pratt's gut told him that if Thanet had been whacked, it might have been for something unconnected with the money, the bombing or the trafficking racket. The list of suspects had a lot of names.

Once Thanet had discovered that Jaruk had been sleeping with two of his minor wives, he wasted no time in dispatching someone to kill him in a way that would make a statement—a cleaner could be cleaned, gutted and defiled. He thought about what he'd recently told Calvino, about how in Thailand bringing a god to justice was no easy matter, and how only another god could do that. What he'd neglected to tell his friend was that gods like Thanet had multiple wives and complicated secret lives, and the main or minor wife of a minor god, once betrayed, sometimes learnt that she had the cool heart of an executioner.

Calvino had been right—Thanet had likely ordered Yadanar killed because he had shut down the Burmese cold pill smuggling racket. That had caused a big financial loss, and Colonel Pratt had learnt that the Hong Kong people had a part of that business. Yadanar was murdered for business reasons—for revenge. In the underworld the rule of law applied capital punishment to a range of activities, and betrayal was a capital offense. Yadanar must have known in the back of his mind that he might be marked for a hit. He had made enemies. No one could touch him in Burma. But being young convinced him that he was immortal, made him forget to watch himself once he left home.

Yadanar had been wrong about a couple of things, one of which was judging his Thai partner's character. Udom, the gangster who had given him flowers after he performed on the saxophone at the Living Room, must have known the flowers weren't for his performance but for his funeral. Udom carried out his part well. Colonel Pratt suspected Udom had been instructed to phone Jaruk when Yadanar and Mya left the stage. Udom didn't have to give him Yadanar's destination. That part had been prearranged. Yadanar had the address where he'd pick up fifty grand US in cash, money that Udom owed him from their last deal. The girl had been collateral damage. No one had anything against her. She was in the wrong place at the wrong time.

Ratana had put the Colonel wise to the back-and-forth among Thanet's wives. From their first frantic calls, it must have crossed Thanet's mind that some people, and not just his wives, might want him dead. But he'd no doubt told himself, "I am a god, and gods can't be easily killed." He had three famous amulets that were advertised to make the wearer bulletproof. A superstitious man thinking he was a god was never going to turn out well.

Colonel Pratt had a heavy feeling of the inevitability of Thanet's fate as he sat in the back of a taxi. As a police officer, he'd been blind to what had been in front of him for years. Now he felt that his eyes had finally opened. He stared out the window at people on the street. He breathed in a deep lungful of Bangkok air and coughed. Bad air didn't matter, though; he was about to escape to freedom. At the new house he'd breathe freely, draw in the breeze from the sea, walk along a sandy beach, water his mango trees and cut wild orchids for Manee.

Still ringing in his ears were the last words of his old boss: "Keep in touch."

Colonel Pratt had said nothing. There had been nothing to say. He didn't want to lie and tell him that he would. But he thought they both knew that he wouldn't.

He was leaving behind an old life, one that had worn out. Soon enough it would be nothing but a patchy collection of memories belonging to another time.

FIFTY-ONE

THE HORIZON DISSOLVED to black as a squall quickly swept ashore from the sea. A hard monsoon rain pounded the coconut and banana trees and left branches scattered on the road. By the time the rain passed, they had arrived. Calvino had started over twice counting the number of monks sitting on mats around the bodhi tree. The branches still dipped toward the ground, heavy with rain. Umbrellas obscured some of the monks' faces; others were half-hidden by the enormous gnarled trunk of the ancient tree. The monks, with their shaved heads, saffron robes, similar stocky bodies and cloudy eyes, looked like one person at different stages of life. Their sameness made concentration more difficult. Calvino's first count was twenty-four monks, but on his second count there were suddenly thirty-three. The inflation continued on the third count with thirty-seven monks, as novices appeared and disappeared like the phantoms of his old hallucinations.

Marley had asked her house staff to arrange for nine monks to perform a blessing on her launch. Somewhere among the throng of monks were her nine, but there was no way to tell which ones they were.

Colonel Pratt and Manee were in the back of Marley's car.

"Any idea what's going on?" asked Calvino.

The Colonel leaned forward.

"It's a *tamboon* ceremony," he said. "I've never quite seen one like this before."

"Your new neighborhood is filled with surprises," said Calvino.

"It's a blessing ceremony," said Manee, opening her door and getting out.

"It's a good number, thirty-seven," Marley said.

"It's a large number," said Colonel Pratt.

The Colonel considered ceremonies with nine monks lavish enough. This "blessing," to use his wife's English word, was beyond the means of ordinary country people. He stepped out of the car, and from what he could see, all the people present fell into the ordinary category.

The sky toward the seaside had cleared. The rain had blown through, and appearing between the breaking clouds were brilliant patches of blue. Marley switched off the car engine and got out and joined the others. Calvino walked ahead to where the tables had been lined up end to end and were covered with pots of green curry, rice, chicken, pork, *somtam*, fried fish and fruit. Manee and the Colonel, hands raised in respectful wais toward the monks, stood in the back of fifty or sixty villagers who had gathered around the bodhi tree, seated on mats, hands folded into wais as the monks chanted. The villagers chanted along with the monks. An old woman with missing teeth and deep wrinkles shooed flies away from the food table with a bamboo fan.

What caught Calvino's eye wasn't the food but a large stupa—the Thais called the structure a *chedi*—that had been built from sand not far from the bodhi tree. Colonel Pratt walked up beside Calvino and examined the chedi.

"You ever see a chedi made of sand?" Calvino asked him.

"I like the idea," said the Colonel. "A sand chedi reminds us of the impermanence of all things, and that message is the essence of Buddhism."

"I thought a chedi was a place used to keep Buddha relics," said Calvino.

"Only in some temples. But mostly ashes are placed inside. Usually a monk's ashes," said Colonel Pratt.

He watched his wife guide Marley over to the head monk. A middle-aged man wore silver-rimmed glasses that made him look owlish. He had a line of sweat on his upper lip, which quivered slightly as he chanted. Also he looked at Marley as if he recognized her. Apparently, the monk spoke some English.

"Ashes of a monk and sand a chedi. I can't think of a better definition of impermanence," said Calvino.

"A chedi is sometimes built as a tree of life. But that is more a Tibetan tradition. The belief is that you make a powerful wish," said Colonel Pratt. "A chedi is also a place of meditation."

"It might be a sign of good luck," said Calvino.

"I could use some of that," said the Colonel.

Calvino paced around the sandcastle chedi, stopped and squatted down, tracing a finger along the intricately sculpted furrow that ringed the chedi with terraces reaching to the top of the spiral structure. Set against the terraces the walls were hundreds of small, brightly colored stones and pieces of glass and ribbons. A large red umbrella had been placed over the chedi to protect it against the rain. Patches of sunlight caught the colored glass, creating a rainbow that arced toward the bodhi tree.

The music started softly and gradually increased in volume. A popular Thai song from sixty years ago was sung in a style that belonged to another time.

A young Thai girl sat behind a small table adjusting the sound system—speakers, old-fashioned turntable, vinyl records and a framed picture of a Thai singer who wore his hair in a style like someone who walked out of a 1950s Thai movie. The monks' chanting drifted until it reached a finale. Two monks' assistants removed the umbrella over the chedi. The DJ lowered the arm of the record player onto an old LP. The wailing of a male voice singing of love, longing and broken hearts filtered through the air. The ceremony entered a second phase. Several of the villagers served food to the monks and offered them robes, followed by a second offering of yellow plastic buckets filled with instant noodles, soap, toothpaste, candles and incense sticks. After the merit making, the villagers left the monks to eat and lined up at the food table, talking over the music.

Manee asked a small group of village women about the ceremony. They were happy to talk about the rich mem-farang who had paid for all of the monks, the building of the sand chedi, the food and the DJ to play the music. The villagers waied Marley as she walked to the bodhi tree, tracing her finger over the dresses hanging from the vast gnarly trunk. One of the dresses was nearly swallowed up by the others. The size was small enough to fit a child's doll. Manee and her group watched her bow her head and appear to say a prayer. When she opened her eyes, she saw Manee and three or four village women beside her.

"They are grateful for your generosity," said Manee, translating for her.

The ceremony had ended. The head monk had promised the villagers that the mem-farang would come for the ceremony, and she had. Marley stood next to the bodhi tree. She continued to run her fingers over the belt on the wedding dress fixed to the tree, spun with gold sequins, the silk dyed aqua and copper. All eyes were on her. The village women behind the food table stopped serving to watch. The villagers who carried the plates to the monks stopped to watch. Even the monks looked up from their plates.

One of the women gave a plate of food to Colonel Pratt, and another woman handed Calvino a plate piled with rice, chicken, fish and green beans. Marley waved away the plate offered to her. She had no appetite. The villager looked disappointed. She listened to the music, staying close to the bodhi tree and watching the monks.

Manee finished eating and found herself talking to a middle-aged Thai couple. The woman cried, and the man put his arm around her for comfort. They had lost a daughter, and her wedding dress hung from the tree. After the monks finished eating, Marley approached the senior monk to request that he send nine monks to her house down the road. No further directions were necessary; they knew where the mem-farang's house was.

"Ten minutes," the senior monk said, removing his glasses and cleaning the lens on the sleeve of his robe. "I will come myself."

Marley walked back to her car with the others following. There wasn't much to say. They sat quietly, lost in thought, as she drove the short distance to her house.

Manee broke the silence.

"A fifteen-year-old girl died in a motorcycle accident. Her father is a government official. He had no money to pay for the food and the monks and the wedding dress. He said Khun Marley paid for everything. I saw him with his wife in the front row. They looked happy that their daughter was now married in heaven to a famous Thai singer."

"Her ashes were inside the sand chedi," said Marley, using the rearview mirror to look at Manee.

A new, deeper silence fell over those in the car. A rainbow had arced from the colored stones strung like rows of Christmas tree lights around the sand chedi. What had muted Colonel Pratt and Manee wasn't the rainbow but the mystery of how this foreigner had gone to the trouble and expense of the ceremony. The way she'd touched the wedding dresses and talked to the monks, and the way the villagers had accepted her without knowing her or why she had arranged the ceremony. Calvino wondered how

Marley, a mathematician, could believe what the villagers believed. She was a foreigner, and foreigners could only play the game of pretending to believe. Foreigners were among the last to understand the local faith, let alone share in it. Calvino tried to understand Marley's connection to the ceremony. If it wasn't merit she was after, that left the acquisition of inside information, data of the kind that would not be found on the Internet. Calvino wondered what bits of hidden information the locals possessed that they'd shared with her.

Marley, the brilliant and rich mathematician who lived in a mansion by the sea, down an isolated road not far from an ancient bodhi tree, had surprised him before. When he'd watched her caressing the tiny dress among the others, all intended for the marriage of the dead girls to the dead singer, he saw the pearl of a tear roll down her cheek. He remembered the first time they'd passed the shrine dedicated to the memory of unmarried women who'd died young. Once she'd driven past it, she'd sped up as if in a hurry to put the tree behind her.

FIFTY-TWO

YOSHI NAGATA EMERGED from the mansion and walked to the main gate. Marley waited until he'd opened it, and then her car slipped inside as quietly as an iguana under cover of night. Calvino glanced back at the familiar figure. His image of Nagata had up to then been of the ascetic dressed in white yoga clothes. "That looks like Professor Nagata," he said, not quite believing his eyes. The yoga mystic wore gumboots, jeans and a long-sleeved workingman's shirt, the sleeves rolled up to the elbows. His faded blue collar was damp around his neck. He flicked away a fly with the back of his hand.

Marley powered down her window.

"No problem getting the gas at the marina?" she asked.

Nagata shook his head as two stray soi dogs stuck their noses through the open gate.

"None. I filled up the tanks, paid cash. We won't run out of fuel."

Marley smiled.

"Professor Nagata arrived last night to make preparations for the journey," she said.

Nagata saw a look of disbelief on Calvino's face.

"My father taught me how to sail in English Bay when I was six years old," he said.

"You bought the provisions?" she asked.

"Everything is ready. When do you want to go out?" he asked.

She had asked him to take charge of organizing the memorial service.

"As soon as the monks arrive," she said.

Manee looked through the back window.

"They are here."

The color of saffron filled the space between the bars in the gate. Nine monks stood outside, waiting to be summoned in. The morning had started at a bodhi tree. They'd performed a ceremony to celebrate the marriage of a dead unmarried Thai girl with a dead singer. The sea memorial ceremony, their second act, allowing a blessing of the spirit of an unmarried Burmese girl who'd died with child.

Colonel Pratt climbed out of the back of the car, walked to the gate and invited the monks inside. He watched the nine monks silently file into the compound. A couple of feet away his wife stood, head slightly bowed, her tapered fingers forming a perfect wai as they continued around the back of the mansion. After they had passed, Calvino saw husband and wife exchange a look. He tried to understand what it meant—understanding, peace, love, respect, whatever name it had, the effect communicated the strength of their connection, illuminated a spiritual space they shared.

A novice would have asked the senior monk why the rich mem-farang had paid so much money to honor a dead Burmese. The Thais had little love for the Burmese, and it would not be in their memory for a Thai to have done this. Why would she do something so strange? Even the senior monk would have no idea how to explain such behavior except that foreigners think in a different way. There had been sightings of Rohingya in her compound. People gossiped. The monks listened to what people said. They also believed what the government told them—the authorities were doing everything they could to help the Rohingya. Villagers and monks alike believed what they were told to believe. That story excluded the part about the Rohingya boat people who'd died off the shores of Thailand or those who'd been forced into slavery. They knew almost nothing of the Rohingya escaping a pogrom in Burma. The authorities told them the Rohingya were faking, lying Muslims who could cause problem in Thailand.

With the monks inside her compound, Marley wanted to tell them the true story. But this wasn't the right day, or the right time, after a rain, a rainbow over a sand chedi and a full belly while sitting in the shade of the bodhi tree. Normal monks lived a simple existence. They didn't know of matters in the outside world. It wasn't important for them to know, perhaps. What mattered wasn't their knowledge of how those they blessed came to die. What they brought were their chanting and presence at sea, as they believed that the lost ones at sea would hear their names called in those chants and rise to the heavens. Psychoanalysis, thought Calvino, was for the living and not the dead.

Lost at sea was a type of missing person case that he'd never had walk into his office. Finding people who'd gone missing on land was difficult enough.

Nagata approached Marley, greeting her with a smile. She stood beside the car, instructing two servants to take the monks to the boat.

"The marriage tree ceremony ran longer than expected," she told him.

"We were halfway from the marina in Jomtien when the squall rolled in," Nagata said.

Marley stood beside Calvino, who had gone around to her side of the car. She introduced Colonel Pratt's wife. Manee hadn't taken her eyes off the mansion, with its Doric columns, circular driveway and manicured hedges and gardens off to the side.

"It's beautiful," she said.

"The rain was beautiful," said Nagata.

He spoke with the awe of a child. His tone touched Colonel Pratt.

"Rain and mercy are companions," said Colonel Pratt, guiding Manee along a footpath around the side of the mansion.

Marley turned around.

"I like that," she said.

"So did Shakespeare: 'The quality of mercy is not strain'd. It droppeth as the gentle rain from heaven upon the place beneath. It is twice blest. It blesseth him that gives and him that takes,'" said the Colonel, quoting *The Merchant of Venice*.

"To be once blessed is more than enough," said Yoshi Nagata.

"Later, when we return from the boat, we'll have tea in the house," said Marley. "I'll take you to your the rooms."

Manee pondered what marvels awaited inside the house.

"I'd like that very much," she said.

Calvino sought to come to terms with the idea of Yoshi Nagata as a sailor. Nagata easily bounced from one identity to another—mathematics professor to yoga teacher to mystic to doorman to sailor—like a sure-footed child landing each foot dead center on a flagstone path.

The grounds of the mansion facing the sea had walls on both sides sloping down to the beach about fifty meters away. A private pier had squid boats lined along one side of it. On the opposite side of the pier, the nine monks sat at the bow of a fifty-seven-foot yacht. As they approached the boat, Calvino saw several familiar faces standing at the stern. He saw Judy from the Mae Hong Son refugee camp. And there was Sarah from Wisconsin. And there, between them, dressed in white slacks, a hat and sunglasses, was his secretary.

Ratana removed her sunglasses and waved as she caught sight of Calvino. She looked happy to see him, breaking away from her companions to greet him in person.

"Khun Vinny, you are finally here," she said.

He shot her a crooked smile.

"Working overtime, are we?"

"Working all the time," she said, slipping alongside him as he walked to where the others waited.

Marley had kept the women's appearance a surprise, thought Calvino. Ratana disappeared below deck. By the time Calvino had settled onto the boat, she had reappeared in a traditional Thai raw silk dress. Flowers were pinned in her hair. She exchanged wais with Colonel Pratt and Manee, who had gone to the salon.

"I arrived last night with Ajarn Yoshi," Ratana said. "There was so much to do. The boat, the monks, the ceremony... Too much for one person."

"You volunteered?" said Calvino.

"We all volunteered," she said, glancing over at Judy and Sarah.

Calvino saw how Marley organized everything—by the numbers. Marley took his hand in her own and gave it a squeeze.

"I wanted the people who touched Ploy's life to come today," she said. "It wouldn't be right otherwise."

Calvino followed Marley to the bridge and she sat in the captain's chair.

"You've been in that chair before. Did your father teach you how to sail?" asked Calvino, as she checked the gauges and flipped the controls for the twin engines.

"I am Norwegian and a Canadian west-coaster. The sea and boats are in our blood. It's like teaching a bird to fly."

"I grew up in New York right next to the sea, but I never learned to sail. I navigated the streets and that's in my blood. The only birds I remember were pigeons shitting on drunks sleeping on doorsteps."

Nagata untied the bowline from the cleats, and then the aft and forward spring lines, before hopping over the hull as Marley powered up the engines. He jumped on the stern and they were under way. Below deck Ratana and Manee admired the wreaths laid out on a table. Sarah and Judy huddled in the salon, their voices lowered to a whisper. Colonel Pratt left the women in the salon, continued to the galley and checked out the three cabins and two bathrooms. He estimated a couple of dozen people could squeeze into the quarters. All this space for six people, he thought. In most of Asia six people would have fit into one of the cabins.

As Colonel Pratt returned to the salon, Nagata wielded a calligraphy pen, writing names on pieces of rice paper that the women then attached to the wreaths. Nagata finished with a calligraphic flourish to write Ploy's name. A second wreath next to Ploy's had a name that the Colonel didn't recognize. It wasn't a Thai name, or at least one he'd ever come across. It didn't look Burmese or Muslim. The name was Skuld. Yoshi placed the banner with "Skuld" on a wreath of red roses, carnations and chrysanthemums. It was otherwise stripped of any identity and that made it stand out against' Ploy's wreath which had her photograph and two other photos—of her mother, father and brother—had been pinned.

Nagata saw Calvino staring at Skuld's wreath, made with orange gerberas and white chrysanthemums.

"That one's for Ploy's unborn," he said.

"The unborn child had a name?" asked Calvino.

"'Skuld' comes from a Norse legend. It means destiny or the future."

"The name came from Marley?"

Nagata returned a smile, tilting his head as he attended to finishing his work on the wreaths.

"It's a beautiful name, don't you think?"

Calvino was going to ask about the doll's dress on the bodhi tree when Colonel Pratt asked Nagata about the third wreath, which featured white orchids.

Nagata was happy to explain: "The wreath is for the Burmese who were killed at the Mae Hong Son refugee camp."

More than thirty refugees had died in the fire. The wreath might be the only commemoration for their loss of life, thought Colonel Pratt. It had been left to foreigners to make the arrangements. The Colonel felt sad, even depressed, touching the flowers. More disturbing was that he knew no one back home who had any sympathy for the Rohingya—a dark-skinned people with cruel mouths and large black eyes. Being at sea with monks and foreigners honoring the death of illegal migrants was the Colonel's introduction to civilian life. He allowed himself thoughts he'd screened out as a man in uniform. Only now he couldn't stop such thoughts from flooding his mind.

Why had people like him shoved dark-skinned men adrift at sea with no motor, no water or rice? Put them in cages and sold them like livestock? But if your house is broken into and overrun by strangers from another land demanding food and shelter, what do you do? He went back and forth on the problem, unable to find a satisfactory answer. At that moment he didn't think of Shakespeare. He thought about his father.

What Colonel Pratt's father had taught him wasn't about boats; it was about fate. His father had said that fate neither loves nor hates. Instead, like the monsoon floods, a person's fate or the fate of a group depends on karma. Fate washes over all lives. Some will inevitably drown; others will survive. Why one lives and another dies is something only

Buddha knows. Letting go of attachments is the first lesson toward finding the strength to swim against the riptide that is life.

People had always been like that, Colonel Pratt thought, never questioning or seeing that what they thought or believed was wrong, or that it could be based on fear or ignorance. The Colonel had no doubt that he would have to answer for his role either in this life or the next. He felt good to be clear of the department, the petty politics, the jealous rivalries, the need to look away so often that his neck shot with pain. But no physical pain ever matched the suffering of the human heart.

Colonel Pratt touched one of the orchids on the third wreath, the one for the dead in the refugee camp bombing.

"Beautiful orchids," said Manee, touching the top of his hand.

"We'll grow orchids at the new house," he said.

"Yes, we will," she said, squeezing his hand, telling him in her way that she'd forgiven him.

Ratana glanced sideways at Nagata, who smiled radiantly as she admired his finely crafted calligraphy on the three wreaths. They'd gone nearly a kilometer from the shore when Marley cut the engines and the propellers stopped. Nagata lowered the anchor. The swell of the sea softly swayed the boat.

Calvino stuck his head into the salon, saying, "Marley says the monks are ready."

The sound of their chanting filtered from the top deck throughout the boat. Calvino returned to the main deck where Marley, barefoot and chin lowered, now sat in the lotus position on the bow. The nine monks sat in front of her. Nagata, Ratana and Manee each brought up a wreath. Judy and Sarah crept forward and sat alongside Marley. Both women hugged her. Soon Marley rose to her feet and walked erect with her shoulders back. Towering above

Ratana, who knelt on the deck, Marley leaned down to accept the wreath Ratana held out. It was for Ploy. Marley turned and held it out before the monks before moving silently to the railing and dropping it over the side.

Ratana bowed her head and waied the monks.

Nagata handed her the wreath for the unborn child, Skuld. Marley stared at the wreath, a shudder emanating from her lungs and emerging as a short, sharp cry. Finally she swung around with the wreath, facing the monks. She stood as if she were made of stone. The chanting continued. With tears streaming down her face, she then went to the railing and gently released the wreath as if it were a bird she was setting free.

She was spent and collapsed beside the railing. Calvino went to her side.

"Are you okay?"

"I'll be fine. Give me a minute," she said.

The final wreath was for the Rohingya, those who had died at sea and those who had recently died by fire. Yoshi Nagata stepped forward, taking it from Ratana. Nagata then spoke to those on deck.

"Not long ago, our TV screens filled with images of the Pope throwing a wreath into the Mediterranean Sea to honor the illegals who'd drowned there trying to make it from Africa to Europe. No one placed a wreath in the Gulf of Siam for the Rohingya dead. The sea had swallowed the Rohingya as surely as it had the Africans the Pope wished to remember. In the memory of the Rohingya who died striving for safety and freedom, we wish that you find eternal harmony and peace, a place free of conflict and pain."

Nagata then gave a short benediction for the Karen-Burmese who had died in the fire at the Mae Hong Son refugee camp. Nagata's words merged with the chanting, the slapping of waves against the side of the boat and the sound of one of the monks, green-faced, vomiting with seasickness. No one knew who these people were—their names, ages, how they looked, whether they had fathers, mothers, sisters, brothers, wives, husbands or sweethearts, or what their plans were for a life free of violence. Mourning in the abstract was an intellectual exercise and satisfied the mind, yet with the heart disengaged it was also empty and shallow.

Nagata didn't say a word as he offered the wreath for a blessing. When the senior monk nodded, Nagata went to the railing and sent the third wreath on its way. As the pace of chanting accelerated, Marley leaned forward, watching the wreaths over the gunwale.

The others came to the railing then, holding hands, staring at the wreaths floating on the water. The red roses rocked back and forth gently in the small waves that slapped against the yacht. The chanting had stopped for a couple of minutes. The the void was filled with silence, one broken by the soft slapping of the sea against the yacht.

Colonel Pratt opened his leather case and removed his saxophone. He played Dexter Gordon, one of the down-tempo melodies that reminded him of being lost on a dark street at three in the morning in a strange city. It was the Colonel's vision of death.

As Colonel Pratt played, he looked at the faces in front of him, people touched by his music but with their real emotions unable to ignite a flame of anger from the cold numbness they felt for the deaths of these faceless refugees they didn't know. Why were sorrow and grief so far out of reach when it came to the death of a stranger? Calvino looked for the answer encoded in Dexter Gordon's music.

The group watched the three wreaths become more distant until they disappeared. The other women followed Marley to her captain's chair. And Calvino, Pratt and Nagata sat in the salon.

"Some were thrown overboard," said Nagata, settling himself on a sofa. "Others were left without food or water by authorities who towed them out to sea and cut them adrift."

"It's hard to accept this diamond-hard cruelty, but these aren't isolated events. Cruelty is deep inside man's nature," said Calvino.

Nagata smiled.

"Do you know what haunts us? It's our potential for savage cruelty. The possibility of cruelty forces us to feel loneliness, fear and mistrust. No one is immune."

Colonel Pratt packed up his saxophone.

"Hamlet says, 'Conscience doth make cowards of us all.' Don't you think that our conscience stops the worst behavior? It takes a kind of brutal courage to be cruel."

"Shakespeare was right, of course ," said Nagata. "Except not everyone has a conscience, Colonel. You must know that from your police work."

"I am no longer a colonel."

"Colonel or not, you are right about the nature of evil. Vincent told me of your interest in Shakespeare. Quite unusual for a Thai police colonel to quote the Bard."

"Ex-colonel," said Calvino. "As with 'expat,' you have to understand the 'patriate' part before the 'ex' makes any sense."

Nagata's eyes brightened.

"Yes, that explains the 'ex,'" Nagata said. "Shakespeare also wrote, 'Good without evil is like light without darkness which in turn is like righteousness without hope.' It is like the sky to the sea, at times a seamless whole that taunts us to find the horizon. It isn't possible to defeat evil any more than we can banish the sky. But we can understand its nature, prepare ourselves and give shelter to those who flee the darkness."

"How many Rohingya have you and Marley smuggled out of Thailand?" asked Calvino.

Nagata smiled, slowly nodding his head.

"One hundred and forty-eight. If a man is on his knees, you have two choices. Finish him off or give him your hand to pull him up. That is the choice between darkness and light."

"Why did Marley give the unborn child a name from the Norse gods?"

"That's a question you'll have to ask her."

FIFTY-THREE

AFTER THE CEREMONY the yacht returned to Marley's estate. Inside the mansion the group settled around a large dining table. After they'd finished dinner, they found it natural to break into smaller groups sharing their feelings of the day. It wasn't a night for the mind; it was a night for matters of the heart.

Ratana started talking about trust—how men trust women and women trust men in different ways. It was a brilliant way to clear the trivial from their isolated conversations, giving the atmosphere of gossip traction and respectability. Earlier Judy and Sarah had told Ratana it looked like they'd have to close down their rescue mission. After what had happened, they wondered who they could possibly trust to work for the refugees. Sarah talked of giving up her job and returning to Wisconsin.

"It's real culture, the one at street level, that defines a culture of trust," said Sarah, whose storefront was around the corner from Walking Street.

"Or distrust. Along with culture, I'd take a look at geography, and figure out how much you need the cooperation of others to get anything done, and whether those people are taught to cooperate," said Judy, thinking of lives of the Burmese in the camps along the border.

Colonel Pratt quoted Shakespeare: "'He's mad that trusts in the tameness of a wolf, a horse's health, a boy's love or a whore's oath.'"

"*King Lear*," said Nagata.

Colonel Pratt arched an eyebrow in surprise.

"Yes, Act III."

Just as the conversation appeared to flicker like the end flame of a candle, it came back to life, as if a flare had been shot into the night sky.

"Who can you trust not to be cruel?" asked Manee, turning her head, taking a glancing look at her husband and then looking back at Calvino.

"That is never an easy question," said Nagata. "It's very messy. But that doesn't mean we shouldn't place trust in others. It means don't be indiscriminate, and don't think trusting is ever an easy decision. Shakespeare understood that madness is trusting without first carefully weighing the possibility of betrayal or compromise. The worst crime isn't the violation of trust but the failure to recognize that human nature means there are some people you should never trust. And it's up to you to find that out."

"We live in a world where no one can keep their secrets safe," said Marley. "That is tragedy beyond the hardships found in Shakespeare's world."

"Opacity is the stepchild of tyrants. But it has also been the godchild of those who wage battle against tyrants. It is both a sword and a shield," said Nagata.

Colonel Pratt wondered if Nagata might have been Thai in his last life. He possessed a natural ability to see how the prism shifted the light waves depending on the angle at which it was held to catch the light.

"What happens with the underground Rohingya network?" asked Calvino. "Who can you trust now?"

"We will need time to rebuild," said Nagata, looking over at Marley.

Marley nodded her agreement.

"On the boat this afternoon, with the monks chanting, I asked myself Vincent's question. What happens now? Do we stop? Do we move on? Like Janus, do we focus on the past, or on the future, or do we work to rescue these despised people in the present?"

Ratana, who'd sat quietly listening to this part of the conversation, said, "I will help."

Manee reached across the table and squeezed Marley's hand, "And so will I."

Marley saw Judy and Sarah had stayed quiet. She asked them how they felt.

Sarah said, "I feel burnt out."

"I can't decide," said Judy. "I mean it's hard knowing that no matter what you do, it doesn't make much of a difference."

"Think about it. You don't have to decide tonight," said Marley, who put her arm around Sarah's waist. Judy stood up and the three women hugged. It was a language working on a different frequency, penetrating to places beyond the reach of words.

"I'll stay, if you'll have me," said Sarah, sniffling and wiping her eyes. "I'm sorry I'm so emotional."

Twenty minutes later they'd switched to talking about the differences between the morality of Jane Austen novels and that of the TV series *Breaking Bad*. Judy and Sarah slowly drifted upstairs to one of their rooms. A door opened and closed, silencing their voices.

Colonel Pratt and Manee disappeared with the expertise of two professional magicians who'd worked together for a long time. They sat in their room overlooking the sea, the jetty and Marley's yacht, tied there. Lights beamed from the radar unit, like lasers programmed to produce a smooth, clean line in a regular rhythm. In a half-trance Colonel Pratt felt his mind circle back to the bodhi tree. He remembered the singer from his boyhood. He'd never thought of him as being a saint. He doubted the singer was anywhere but a mist of molecules fanning through space, leaving such a small trace that no sentient being could ever discover it. But there he was. He'd become the spirit of a bodhi tree, with the spirits of young women sent to his side to marry and entertain. The more he thought about the singer, the more he thought about whether the dead heartthrob was the Thai version of Sisyphus.

Ratana returned to her room, sat on the edge of the bed and phoned her son, who'd stayed at her mother's, and learned they'd been fighting over the completion of his homework.

Nagata gave Calvino and Marley a small bow as he left for the meditation room. His parting look at Calvino lingered almost a minute as if he were studying an object he hadn't seen before.

"Is there something?" asked Calvino.

"No, nothing of any importance," Nagata said.

"If it's not so important, then it should be okay to ask what's bothering you," said Calvino.

"I was thinking how earlier today, when I saw you pet those two stray dogs, you seemed to see a chance for a connection. As one outsider to another, I saw myself through your eyes, and I saw the dogs for the first time."

Nagata turned and left, leaving behind a sense that nothing much escaped his notice.

The day had been filled with events—tiring, confusing, surprising, boring and exciting in turn. There'd been too much to absorb in the span of a day: the monsoon rain, the bodhi tree marriage ceremony, the arrival at Marley's mansion, boarding her yacht, the chanting monks, the wreaths thrown into the sea and a dinner conversation touching on trust, betrayal and the nature of compassion.

Nagata had been the one to suggest a third ceremony—an unwinding of the day's images and words and thoughts, letting them go into the mist of silence.

In their room alone with her husband, Manee gently massaged her forehead. She felt a throbbing behind her eyes. She was exhausted.

"My head is hammering," she said.

Colonel Pratt gently pressed two fingers to her forehead.

"It will pass," he said.

Smiling, she leaned toward him.

"It always does."

FIFTY-FOUR

OUTSIDE THE WINDOW a flash of lightning warned of more rain. Marley and Calvino sat alone downstairs in the living room surrounded by empty glasses and wine bottles. With the room to themselves, it was their first chance for the private discussion they needed. More lightning outside caught Marley's attention.

"Welcome to my world," she said. "Thunder and lightning reminds me of home. Thor and his hammer."

Calvino looked around the large sitting room, with its paintings, books, vases with flowers and a large statue of a bearded man.

"Is that a god?"

"That's Henri Poincaré. If you're a mathematician, he's a god. He believed that intuition was the lifeblood of mathematics. He conceived chaos theory and relativity from his intuitive imagination. Add those to his more exotic theories, like hyperbolic geometry, number theory and the three-body problem and yes, you have the mind of a god."

"I'll stick with Henry Miller," said Calvino. "He found the mind of God among the ordinary people on the street— the hustlers, whores, racketeers, gamblers, drug addicts, drinkers and whoremongers. All of them outliers who survived by gut instinct."

"You speak of them as if you're one of them," she said.

"I know them, and they know me. We don't judge each other or invent theories about the meaning of life. We get by day to day, celebrating that we didn't get eaten by a bigger fish," said Calvino, pouring wine into her glass and his own.

Marley lifted her glass in salute to the statue.

"To you, Henri."

She turned and clicked Calvino's glass.

"And to you, Vincent, another intuitive man who finds the missing person someone cares enough about to look for."

He raised his own glass.

"To Henry Miller, who went missing in Paris for seven years," he said, smiling.

He drank from the glass.

"When Miller found who he was, he went home," said Calvino.

"And when will you go home?" she asked.

He grinned.

"I am home."

Most of the people Calvino knew who lived inside the zone accepted his presence, even though he wasn't the kind of man who had always been one of them. Most of them had no such choice. Their membership had come attached at their birth. Calvino had been born into the world of normal people who got up every morning and went to normal jobs and returned home at night to normal lives. When that life and world had vanished from his life, Calvino had made a living as a go-between, slipping into the zone, learning from the inside the meaning of their abnormal lives, appetites, loyalties and violence.

"Why do you think so many foreigners go missing in Thailand?" she asked.

Calvino rotated the wine in his glass, pondering how to answer a question that had no intuitive answer.

"Why do ordinary people drop off the grid? For a number of them, they've found a new world that's alive and without delusions, and it makes their normal world seem as dull, gray and dead as last week's dream."

"Escape," she said.

"One person's escape is another's liberation."

He was an honorary member of both tribes—and that gave him safe passage to find and pull out those missing from the normal world.

She set her glass down.

"I want to go and walk in the rain. Do you feel like joining me?"

The storm had moved in from the sea, bringing a light rain that pelted against the windows. It seemed a strange request, but she was already pulling out two large umbrellas.

"Let's go," she said, as she stepped outside and opened her umbrella. "I can think better in the rain."

"I think better with a whiskey and Coke," he said, raising his umbrella.

He followed her down to the beach. The first quarter moon, passing through the sign of Virgo, was invisible behind the storm clouds. They walked barefoot in the rain. The lights on the pier exposed the hulls of wooden squid boats dragged onto the beach, anchors lying sideways, dug into the sand. Feeling the warm, wet sand under his feet and between his toes, he wondered how long it would be until the rain destroyed the sand chedi, leaving just a smear of wet gray ash under the bodhi tree. Calvino inhaled the smell deep into his lungs. Illusions like the sand chedi are as fragile as cut flowers, he thought, and wedding dresses, monks, rain and whiskey can't stop the inevitable withering and dying process at the heart of each day. The impossible idea of death seemed exposed like the squid boat hulls. Maybe, he thought, death is nature's way of establishing the boundary line between truth and lies, existence and non-existence, and the limits of what can be thought and known.

He folded his umbrella and felt the rain on his upturned face. She watched him, his eyes closed, feeling the water. Calvino had been troubled for days. He'd tried over and over to work out the facts of the case, assembling the chain of deaths, examining each one as part of a larger chronology and always arriving at the same conclusion.

"Ploy belonged to Thanet," he said, opening his eyes. "He owned her. She was an off-the-books sex slave. She was his private property. But he fell in love with her. She pumped him for money to pay for the plastic surgery needed to reinvent the new Ploy. Maybe she thought that by creating a new self, she could be free. But then she found out she was pregnant and panicked. She asked you to help her and her family. You did your best. It just didn't work out the way you wanted. All the talk around the table tonight about trust and betrayal made me think that something more than the Rohingya was behind it. It was about Ploy and you, wasn't it? Something went sideways between you two. Maybe you want to tell me what happened."

Marley had been walking along the water's edge, the tips of the waves splashing against her ankles. She stopped and slowly turned toward him.

"What makes you think something happened between us?"

"You and I went from employer and employee, to partner and partner, to lover and lover, but what's missing from this transition is your connection with Ploy. I know it was about more than getting her and her family out of Thailand. I asked Nagata."

"What did Professor Nagata say?" she asked.

"He said to ask Marley. So I'm asking."

They continued walking along the beach. She walked a couple of steps ahead. Then she waited until he caught up.

"Yoshi knows everything," she said.

Calvino leaned down to pick up a small stone and pitched it at the moonlight pooling on the sea.

"I figured he did," he said. "But I don't know what secrets you've shared. Don't you think it's time you told me?"

Marley stopped, leaned down to pick up a stone and threw it in the sea. The sound of the splash seemed fragile, distant and inconsequential.

"It no longer matters," she said.

"What goes missing does matter. Whether it's a person or the truth, finding them matters."

She brushed back her hair, wet with rain. She stared out at the black sea, raising her umbrella again.

"Ploy and I had an arrangement."

"Yeah, what kind of deal?"

"She agreed to act as a surrogate mother. I am thirty-eight years old. I couldn't get pregnant. I saw the best doctors in New York, London and Singapore. None of them could help. One suggested a surrogate. One of my eggs and a donor's sperm was the only way I could become a mother."

"And who was the donor, the father?"

"I asked Professor Nagata if he'd consent. He agreed but not without a week to think it over. It was a big decision for him to go to a fertility clinic."

It was Calvino's turn to find a stone in the wet sand and throw it into the sea.

"How did Thanet find out she was pregnant?" he asked.

He was guessing that was what had happened.

"It came out in a routine medical check. Thanet had all of his women checked every month by a doctor. When he found out, he was happy. He thought it was his. Ploy

416

could have played along, but she told him it was someone else's child. He told her to get an abortion. She refused. He insisted. They fought."

"Ploy didn't tell you about the monthly medical checkups, when she agreed to carry the baby?" asked Calvino, kneeling on the beach, touching the sand with one hand, letting it fall between his fingers.

Marley knelt beside him, watching him pour sand onto a small mound.

"She never told me."

"Strange she wouldn't. She must have known he would find out."

Marley sighed and stood up, brushed her hands on her jeans.

"I guess she avoided thinking about it. She knew I planned to fly her to Vancouver. Another few days for the visa and she would have been on a plane. All she had to do was wait."

"You were her hero, and she thought you'd come to her rescue," said Calvino.

"I was so close to getting her out," she said. "I told her to hang on a couple more days and I'd put her in a safe house. But Jaruk tricked her into going in for plastic surgery. He told her that the doctor, who'd already done work on her, had promised a big discount. It was a crude way to achieve what his boss had ordered, which was to handle the problem—get rid of her. Jaruk had a way with Thanet's women. He lured her out from the place I told her to stay, a place where she would have been safe. It was so stupid of her."

In the night rain she could no longer conceal her feelings of alternating helplessness and bitterness, and regret and rage.

"And also it was so stupid of me to trust that she'd do what I asked," she said.

"Something's been bothering me. How could you know Ploy's baby was a girl?"

Marley watched the sea as if searching for an answer. "I had a very strong feeling it was. A baby girl came to me twice in a dream. My baby was reaching out to me."

The rain had stopped as they walked back and then along the pier, passing the pools of light, until they reached the yacht.

"Thanet couldn't have killed Jaruk," said Calvino. "He didn't have enough time. Someone was waiting for Jaruk when he walked into his room. Someone who knew that he'd left Siam Paragon. You were tracking his location. You had seen the SMS traffic and knew his secret hideaway. When he walked in the door, you were waiting with the sword. Was he surprised?"

"Is his kind of evil ever capable of surprise?" she asked.

"You didn't answer my question. Was it you who killed him?"

She sat silently, one leg folded under her like a schoolgirl. He could sense that she was thinking over whether to tell him and hadn't decided.

"What do you think? You're the private investigator."

Calvino sighed and looked at the moonlight on the water.

When he turned back and she was still silent, he said, "You found a 9mm in his room and slipped it into your handbag. It would take a mathematician to calculate the odds of a dead man's gun being used in a later homicide. It's a perfect murder weapon, one traceable to a dead man. I think you'd need to be very smart. What did that French genius Henri Poincaré call it—intuitive, the bubbling up of a creative idea from the unconscious mind?"

Her answer was silence.

"And Thanet?" Calvino asked.

On this subject she didn't need to say anything. Her answer was in the tilt of her head, the total control and calmness that came with the truth tumbling through the body—the eyes, the mouth, the hands, the posture.

"Thanet ordered the bombing that killed your friend from Rangoon."

"I know that. So does Pratt, but we could never prove it."

"If you'd had the evidence to prove his guilt to the police, would it have mattered? He would never have been charged. You had to live with that fact. Not the lack of evidence, but that he was untouchable. You told me that the very wealthy never bother going to the police. They handle matters in their own way. They see no need to wait for the cops or anyone else because they know a shortcut in the equation. I would have done it, again and again. No matter how many times he was reborn, I would have shot him. I planned to. We had an appointment. But it turned out that someone else got to him first. Thanet was already dead in his car. The car door was unlocked. I climbed into the passenger's side. I put the gun in his cold hand where it had fallen on the passenger's seat. And I left," she said, her voice breaking as she spoke.

Her arms trembled at her side. Her heart was clearly broken as she stood on the deck of her yacht, the soft moonlight falling on her shoulders, face and hair. She looked an unlikely avenger as she stepped closer to Calvino, wrapping her arms around his waist. Her body stiffened against him and she dropped her arms.

"Now what?" she asked, looking up to read the expression on his face.

"I don't know, Marley. I don't know 'what' and I don't know 'now.' But it looks like someone was trying to set you up for his murder."

"That's what Yoshi thought too. He said that in Buddhism those whose lives are filled with evil become hungry ghosts when they die. They will be reborn in days, weeks or months. I pray that Jaruk and Thanet return as Rohingya escaping for their lives, sold into slavery, begging for rescue."

"And if they come to you for help, then what?" said Calvino.

"I would help them," she said.

Calvino wanted to believe that what she said was true. She continued to tremble. Folding her arms over her chest, she walked across the deck to the salon, and Calvino found her curled up on a sofa.

"When you live in the normal world," he said, "you believe sociopath's death ends the misery and suffering he's created. But it only brings a change of faces. Nothing else changes in the world he leaves behind. The next in line steps forward to take over the leadership. Otherwise, everything stays pretty much the same."

"That night at your condo you summed me up as a woman of abstract ideas, while you said you're a man of the street, of instinct, intuition, blood, smoke and ash. You said we come from completely different worlds, one bounded by feelings, sensation, pleasure and action, and the other a closed world of ideas, theories, equations and pure thought. You told me how Mya experienced the reality of life through her music. How she seized life with both hands. She imagined herself as a woman for whom all things were possible and limits were only failures of imagination. In Rangoon you watched her kill a Thai woman named Kati. She was avenging the death of the young man you planned to return to his father in Bangkok. But she wasn't acting out of instinct; she'd planned the execution in great detail as a performance for you. It wasn't for her. She killed Kati as an offering for you, Vincent. She knew it was the only thing she could give you. The rest of Mya was going in a different direction, on her way to another place and time. You wouldn't be there, but you would remember that performance forever. Was it your karma that she fulfilled? Or was it something else?"

She grabbed his hand.

"I didn't kill him, Vincent. And I regret that I didn't have the chance."

The slight motion of the sea turned the boat into a gently rocking cradle. She reached over and switched on a light, and the moon outside the port window disappeared. Flowers left over from the wreaths lay on the table—roses, orchids and carnations, scattered like children's toys.

She rested her head against Calvino's shoulder and told him that she trusted him with the truth. Marley had been both avenging an unborn child's death and competing with Mya. The problem with her confession was it implicated him as well. He felt a twinge of a dark, dense feeling of sadness. He tried to remember the words he'd used to describe what had happened in Rangoon. Whatever they had been, Marley had remembered. He regretted speaking of the events of that night.

Calvino snapped his fingers. As a gesture, it lacked the magical power to turn time back and trade those disclosures for the hallucinations of before. When did murder become a sign of commitment, loyalty and affection? Or was there always a part of humanity that adopted that side?

"How did you find Jaruk's hideaway?" he said, feeling the wine and the movement of the sea.

In Calvino's world finding people and hideouts required skill, experience and luck. Any inside information she might have to improve his future luck had potential value.

Marley understood his motivation. It seemed natural. She smiled as if she'd stumbled across an underground tattoo parlor in Riyadh. If access to knowledge and information are reflections of power, he thought, then she must be one of the most powerful people in the world.

"I collected information about Jaruk from earlier intercepts. It wasn't that difficult to track his movements and location," she said. "As with most people, his actions were predictable—in the routes he took, the people he met, the time of day and location. He set the whole thing up with the receptionist. He took Sukanya to his secret room in an old building near the river. But she wasn't that special; it was also where he took Thanet's mia nois in the afternoons."

Jaruk's secret sex life expanded far beyond anything D.H. Lawrence imagined in *Lady Chatterley's Lover*. Lawrence's English gardener wasn't a cleaner or a hit man, and Lady Chatterley's life was uncluttered by the actions of her husband's mia nois. Multiple minor wives were Jaruk's specialty. Inside his small room Jaruk had spun them stories of grand dreams and grander adventures, mapped out plans, told lies, made pledges, talked about their lives together, and how Thanet had loved only Ploy.

"It wasn't you who killed Jaruk," he said.

When she didn't reply, Calvino pressed her.

"Who was it? You either paid someone or sent someone you trusted. Given the timing, I'm guessing it was someone you trusted."

She whispered the name.

"Yoshi. He agreed that I could tell you."

Calvino's deadpan expression signaled the he wasn't entirely surprised. Dressed like a monk or a laborer, Nagata would have gone unnoticed in Jaruk's neighborhood. Yoshi, the man of peace.

"You have no right to condemn him."

"His earlier talk about cruelty is starting to make sense."

Marley had monitored in real time Jaruk's location after he left the bookstore in Siam Paragon and saw that he'd headed back to Soi 35 Ladprao. She'd timed the release of information to Thanet's wives to coincide with Jaruk's departure from the bookstore. Then, after the call from Thanet, he'd swung back from Ladprao and headed toward the river. She knew it had worked. Nagata had arrived at the back of his building earlier that morning by boat. He'd had lots of time to gain entrance to Jaruk's room and wait for him to come through the door. They had planned it together.

"And that takes us back to Thanet," said Calvino. "He decided that Jaruk should get rid of his problem. Jaruk was just a tool. You personally wanted Thanet dead. Only someone else saved you from shooting him. You rarely find someone like Thanet alone."

"Unless you're a woman and he wants to have sex with you. We arranged to meet in his office. When I went to his office, it was closed. I tried to phone him. I knew where he parked his car. I went down to the parking level and found him. Just as you found Ploy, already dead."

All of the alarm bells had rung at the same time for Marley.

"I had no idea if the killer was still nearby. I knew from reading SMS messages that one of his minor wives had texted another that Thanet hadn't paid the tax on the Lamborghini. The police have been cracking down on the rich who import expensive cars without paying the tax. His driver had been killed. He had revolt in his harem. His friends refused to talk to him. I found out that the people in Hong Kong had threatened him. I wasn't the only one who was reading his emails and text messages. Someone knew I was meeting him. They had the place and the time."

"Someone tried to set you up," said Calvino.

"I should have been more careful. He had a lot of enemies suddenly wanting him eliminated. One of them got to him before the others. I believe there was a very long queue."

The police at the scene had agreed that it was better to write down the word "suicide" as the word "ghost" was not something the police were permitted to use officially.

Having finished her story, Marley waited for Calvino to react. Had she not known Thanet's security had been breached and others had hacked into his communications? She was supposedly a genius. How could she not know?

"It was a professional hit?" asked Calvino. "You designed a reality that he could imagine. Only someone got there before you."

Marley wore her melancholy like an old heavily disguised bruise. A flicker of a smile illuminated this hidden sadness and like a flare it quickly died.

"Basically, yes."

She came from a world of numbers and equations. Mya had come from a world of music and lyrics. The two had reached a common solution using different languages. Calvino leaned in close to examine Marley's features, just as he had Mya's that night in the bookstore in Rangoon. He understood that some people are natural programmers cradled inside the Big Sleep, and that the sleepers drift along under the illusion that they are fully awake and that the optimal path was theirs alone to take. Dangerous dreams were something Calvino knew something about. It was a major reason why people he'd been hired to find had gone missing in the first place. As he sat in the yacht in the presence of a beautiful woman who had helped to kill one man and conspired to kill a second, he wished, for her sake, that it had turned out differently.

What he believed, though, was that it is never an option to return to the original state of not knowing. Oblivion is the only place where that could occur. He wasn't ready for that place yet. His failure to accept what had happened had brought him the hallucinations to witness the performance of his mind at war with itself. Now that they'd gone, he wouldn't miss those performances. Nor did he regret having lost a part of himself when Mya died.

"I want to sleep on the boat tonight," she said.

"Okay," said Calvino.

He picked up his wet clothes from the floor and moved toward the master bedroom.

"Alone, in the moonlight," she said, eyes sparkling. "Second floor, third bedroom on the right is yours."

"Are you going to be all right?"

She smiled.

"Good night, Vincent."

Calvino returned to the mansion and on one of Marley's computers drafted a message to Dr. Apinya. In it he explained why he wouldn't be going back.

The next morning when he came down for breakfast, he found the others sitting and eating in the kitchen. No one had seen Marley. Sarah told him she'd seen Nagata go outside. Calvino found him at the end of the pier, seated in the lotus position, his thinning white hair brushed back. In his rough cotton blue shirt, he might have passed as one of the local rice farmers whose faces, like sculptures made from wood, had been sandpapered down with the years, leaving deep furrows, hollowed-out cheeks and a faint memory of the rough bark of youth. Calvino saw reflected in Nagata's face a mirror image of himself down the road—a semi-old man sitting on a pier, silently gazing at the horizon with a sense of loss and longing. One of the soi dogs from the day before stretched out beside him, its muzzle resting on its paws. Nagata's hand stroked the dog's neck. Calvino walked out onto the empty pier.

Marley and the yacht were gone.

"Did she say where she was going?" asked Calvino, kneeling next to Nagata.

Nagata shook his head.

"She wrote me a note," said Nagata.

"What did it say?"

"I've gone missing."

"Did she say anything else?"

Again Yoshi shook his head.

"Nothing much."

"Any idea why she'd write something like that?"

Nagata looked out at the sea again.

"Don't you know?"

A wise man like Yoshi Nagata had the ability to write a book that started with those three words. Calvino waited for his first chapter, the one in which Nagata told his version of what had happened. Instead Nagata said nothing.

"Know what?" Calvino asked.

Nagata scratched his chin as he reached into a pocket with his free hand and pulled out a piece of paper.

"She wrote it out for you to read. She said you'd understand."

The note had been hand written. Calvino did understand—hadn't Marley once quoted Marshall McLuhan that the medium was the message?

Calvino also understood that most people who go missing want to be found—after they've found themselves. Some never do find themselves. Others, who do, are never found. The messiness of finding and being found was as good a place for Yoshi Nagata to begin his Chapter 1, a new equation to explain time and space, thought Calvino.

When Calvino turned back to the mansion, he saw Ratana standing on the balcony outside her room.

She waved at him, smiling. Calvino waved back.

FIFTY-FIVE

New Message   —   X

From   Vincent Calvino

To   Dr. Apinya

Subject   *Plueay Jai* เปลือยใจ

Date/Time: 20 May, 22:37

Recovering from a nightmare and returning to the present has been my mission. I've let go of Washington Square, the Lonesome Hawk, George, Max, Gator, Bill, Dennis, Kurt and others. The Square is demolished. I'm left standing. I've let go of Mya. The Rangoon missing person case is now in a closed file. My life feels different and the same. I've discovered the secret door with the voices on the other side clamoring to get out, and I've looked inside. It is an empty locker; the images lost in torrents and undertows. I carry the memory around like a turtle carries its shell. I've even curled up inside and felt the silence.

I've heard many times the story about the bargirl who, when asked whether she believed in ghosts, said she didn't. But when asked if she was afraid of ghosts, she said yes, she was afraid of them. The story cracked people up. It was one of those funny expat stories that punters love to retell. I don't laugh anymore. I understand what she meant. You can be afraid without fully believing in whatever makes you fearful. You can accept that when that state of fear accelerates, we lose our connection with reality. Fear is what makes us human. Too much or too little fear, and we are less than human. Machines may do many things, but they don't experience the power of fear; it's an alien concept to them.

It wasn't the guilt but the fear that pushed me over the edge. I can now carry the load of both without breaking down. I don't know where the fear has gone, but I'm not going to beat the bushes to find its hiding place. If our humanity is lost, so is everything that humanity values—our sense of amazement and wonder, and our possibility for courage, kindness, generosity and empathy. That's who we are. That's what machines can never be. But we are also selfish, biased, suspicious, hateful and aggressive, and we retain a possibility for violence, meanness, indifference and treachery. I walk a narrow path between the two sides, looking for those who go missing on the dark side of the track.

All the trains end up at the same terminal. On the journey I look out the window. The window's purpose isn't to provide my own reflection. The journey isn't about me. It's to understand what is outside and not be afraid of what we find.

I look around a train filled with many others. We share a common fate on the journey. Some will go missing. Some of the missing will be found, others will be lost and beyond rescue. Having found myself, I have a better idea of how to search for others who go missing inside themselves. The fear won't ever go away, but the ghosts, for now, have disappeared. And I can feel they've let go of me. I feel that I've already let go of them. I feel that words are recovering their color and meaning. I can start to trust them again.

I am back.

Send

ACKNOWLEDGMENTS

Three friends of the Vincent Calvino series offered to read and to make constructive comments on an earlier draft. Thank you Charlie McHugh, Michaela Striewski and William Hoey for your time and effort. Your comments allowed me to make this a better book.

Martin Townsend, my long time copy editor, worked his usual magic and saved me from the usual author's errors of commission and omissions.

Two people assisted in proof reading the final text. Chad Evans in Australia who has an uncanny ability to find my mistakes. Also, my wife Busakorn Suriyasarn proof read the final layout, catching a number of annoying mistakes. Whatever errors remain are the result of my own success in making them invisible until after publication in order to give a reader that extra pleasure of discovering a piece of loose debris. That belongs to me alone. No excuse. Mine only.

Thanks to Dr. Penguin who lives nearby a 'marriage tree' for guiding me through the rituals that locals perform at that location.

SPIRIT HOUSE
First in the series
Heaven Lake Press (2004) ISBN 974-92389-3-1

The Bangkok police already have a confession by a nineteen-year-old drug addict who has admitted to the murder of a British computer wizard, Ben Hoadly. From the bruises on his face shown at the press conference, it is clear that the young suspect had some help from the police in the making of his confession. The case is wrapped up. Only there are some loose ends that the police and just about everyone else are happy to overlook.

The search for the killer of Ben Hoadley plunges Calvino into the dark side of Bangkok, where professional hit men have orders to stop him. From the world of thinner addicts, dope dealers, fortunetellers, and high-class call girls, Calvino peels away the mystery surrounding the death of the English ex-public schoolboy who had a lot of dubious friends.

"Well-written, tough and bloody."
—Bernard Knight, *Tangled Web* (UK)

"A thinking man's Philip Marlowe, Calvino is a cynic on the surface but a romantic at heart. Calvino ... found himself in Bangkok—the end of the world—for a whole host of bizarre foreigners unwilling, unable, or uninterested in going home."—*The Daily Yomiuri*

"Good, that there are still real crime writers. Christopher G. Moore's [*Spirit House*] is colorful and crafty."
—*Hessischer Rundfunk* (Germany)

ASIA HAND
Second in the series
Heaven Lake Press (2000) ISBN 974-87171-2-7
Winner of 2011 Shamus Award
for Best Original Paperback

Bangkok—the Year of the Monkey. Calvino's Chinese New Year celebration is interrupted by a call to Lumpini Park Lake, where Thai cops have just fished the body of a farang cameraman. CNN is running dramatic footage of several Burmese soldiers on the Thai border executing students.

Calvino follows the trail of the dead man to a feature film crew where he hits the wall of silence. On the other side of that wall, Calvino and Colonel Pratt discover and elite film unit of old Asia Hands with connections to influential people in Southeast Asia. They find themselves matched against a set of farangs conditioned for urban survival and willing to go for a knock-out punch.

"Highly recommended to readers of hard-boiled detective fiction"—*Booklist*

"Asia Hand is the kind of novel that grabs you and never lets go."—*The Times of India*

"Moore's stylish second Bangkok thriller ... explores the dark side of both Bangkok and the human heart. Felicitous prose speeds the action along."—*Publishers Weekly*

"Fast moving and hypnotic, this was a great read."
—*Crime Spree Magazine*

ZERO HOUR IN PHNOM PENH
Third in the series
Heaven Lake Press (2005) ISBN 974-93035-9-8
Winner of 2004 German Critics Award for Crime Fiction (Deutscher Krimi Preis) for best international crime fiction and 2007 Premier Special Director's Award Semana Negra (Spain)

In the early 1990s, at the end of the devastating civil war UN peacekeeping forces try to keep the lid on the violence. Gunfire can still be heard nightly in Phnom Penh, where Vietnamese prostitutes try to hook UN peacekeepers from the balcony of the Lido Bar.

Calvino traces leads on a missing farang from Bangkok to war-torn Cambodia, through the Russian market, hospitals, nightclubs, news briefings, and UNTAC headquarters. Calvino's buddy, Colonel Pratt, knows something that Calvino does not: the missing man is connected with the jewels stolen from the Saudi royal family. Calvino quickly finds out that he is not the only one looking for the missing farang.

"Political, courageous and perhaps Moore's most important work."—*CrimiCouch.de*

"An excellent whodunnit hardboiled, a noir novel with a solitary, disillusioned but tempting detective, an interesting historical and social context (of post-Pol Pot Cambodia), and a very thorough psychology of the characters."
—*La culture se partage*

"A bursting, high adventure ... Extremely gripping ... A morality portrait with no illusion."
—Ulrich Noller, *Westdeutscher Rundfunk*

COMFORT ZONE
Fourth in the series
Heaven Lake Press (2001) ISBN 974-87754-9-6

Twenty years after the end of the Vietnam War, Vietnam is opening to the outside world. There is a smell of fast money in the air and poverty in the streets. Business is booming and in austere Ho Chi Minh City a new generation of foreigners have arrived to make money and not war. Against the backdrop of Vietnam's economic miracle, *Comfort Zone* reveals a taut, compelling story of a divided people still not reconciled with their past and unsure of their future.

Calvino is hired by an ex-special forces veteran, whose younger brother uncovers corruption and fraud in the emerging business world in which his clients are dealing. But before Calvino even leaves Bangkok, there have already been two murders, one in Saigon and one in Bangkok.

"Calvino digs, discovering layers of intrigue. He's stalked by hired killers and falls in love with a Hanoi girl. Can he trust her? The reader is hooked."
—*NTUC Lifestyle* (Singapore)

"Moore hits home with more of everything in *Comfort Zone*. There is a balanced mix of story-line, narrative, wisdom, knowledge as well as love, sex, and murder."
—*Thailand Times*

"Like a Japanese gardener who captures the land and the sky and recreates it in the backyard, Moore's genius is in portraying the Southeast Asian heartscape behind the tourist industry hotel gloss."—*The Daily Yomiuri*

THE BIG WEIRD
Fifth in the series
Heaven Lake Press (2008) ISBN 978-974-8418-42-1

A beautiful American blond is found dead with a large bullet hole in her head in the house of her ex-boyfriend. A famous Hollywood screenwriter hires Calvino to investigate her death. Everyone except Calvino's client believes Samantha McNeal has committed suicide.

In the early days of the Internet, Sam ran with a young and wild expat crowd in Bangkok: a Net-savvy pornographer, a Thai hooker plotting to hit it big in cyberspace, an angry feminist with an agenda, a starving writer-cum-scam artist, a Hollywoord legend with a severe case of The Sickness. As Calvino slides into a world where people are dead serious about sex, money and fame, he unearths a hedonistic community where the ritual of death is the ultimate high.

"An excellent read, charming, amusing, insightful, complex, localized yet startlingly universal in its themes."
—*Guide of Bangkok*

"Highly entertaining."—*Bangkok Post*

"A good read, fast-paced and laced with so many of the locales so familiar to the expat denizens of Bangkok."
—*Art of Living* (Thailand)

"Like a noisy, late-night Thai restaurant, Moore serves up tongue-burning spices that swallow up the literature of Generation X and cyberpsace as if they were merely sticky rice."—*The Daily Yomiuri*

COLD HIT
Sixth in the series
Heaven Lake Press (2004) ISBN 974-920104-1-7

Five foreigners have died in Bangkok. Were they drug overdose victims or victims of a serial killer? Calvino believes the evidence points to a serial killer who stalks tourists in Bangkok. The Thai police, including Calvino's best friend and buddy Colonel Pratt, don't buy his theory.

Calvino teams up with an LAPD officer on a bodyguard assignment. Hidden forces pull them through swank shopping malls, rundown hotels, Klong Toey slum, and the Bangkok bars as they try to keep their man and themselves alive. As Calvino learns more about the bodies being shipped back to America, the secret of the serial killer is revealed.

"The story is plausible and riveting to the end."
—*The Japan Times*

"Tight, intricate plotting, wickedly astute ... *Cold Hit* will have you variously gasping, chuckling, nodding, tut-tutting, ohyesing, and grinding your teeth throughout its 330 pages."—*Guide of Bangkok*

"The plot is equally tricky, brilliantly devised, and clear. One of the best crime fiction in the first half of the year."
—*Ultimo Biedlefeld* (Germany)

"Moore depicts the city from below. He shows its dirt, its inner conflicts, its cruelty, its devotion. Hard, cruel, comical and good."—*Readme.de*

MINOR WIFE
Seventh in the series
Heaven Lake Press (2004) ISBN 974-92126-5-7

A contemporary murder set in Bangkok—a neighbor and friend, a young ex-hooker turned artist, is found dead by an American millionaire's minor wife. Her rich expat husband hires Calvino to investigate. While searching for the killer in exclusive clubs and not-so-exclusive bars of Bangkok, Calvino discovers that a minor wife—mia noi—has everything to do with a woman's status. From illegal cock fighting matches to elite Bangkok golf clubs, Calvino finds himself caught in the crossfire as he closes in on the murderer.

"The thriller moves in those convoluted circles within which Thai life and society takes place. Moore's knowledge of these gives insights into many aspects of the cultural mores ... unknown to the expat population. Great writing, great story and a great read."—*Pattaya Mail*

"What distinguishes Christopher G. Moore from other foreign authors setting their stories in the Land of Smiles is how much more he understands its mystique, the psyche of its populace and the futility of its round residents trying to fit into its square holes."—*Bangkok Post*

"Moore pursues in even greater detail in *Minor Wife* the changing social roles of Thai women (changing, but not always quickly or for the better) and their relations among themselves and across class lines and other barriers."
—*Vancouver Sun*

PATTAYA 24/7
Eighth in the series
Heaven Lake Press (2008) ISBN 978-974-8418-41-4

Inside a secluded, lush estate located on the edge of Pattaya, an eccentric Englishman's gardener is found hanged. Calvino has been hired to investigate. He finds himself pulled deep into the shadows of the war against drugs, into the empire of a local warlord with the trail leading to a terrorist who has caused Code Orange alerts to flash across the screen of American intelligence.

In a story packed with twists and turns, Calvino traces the links from the gardener's past to the door of men with power and influence who have everything to lose if the mystery of the gardener's death is solved.

"Original, provocative, and rich with details and insights into the underworld of Thai police, provincial gangsters, hit squads, and terrorists."
—Pieke Bierman, award-wining author of *Violetta*

"Intelligent and articulate, Moore offers a rich, passionate and original take on the private-eye game, fans of the genre should definitely investigate, and fans of foreign intrigue will definitely enjoy."—Kevin Burton Smith, *January Magazine*

"A cast of memorably eccentric figures in an exotic Southeast Asian backdrop."—*The Japan Times*

"The best in the Calvino series ...The story is compelling."
—*Bangkok Post*

THE RISK OF INFIDELITY INDEX
Ninth in the series
Heaven Lake Press (2007) ISBN 974-88168-7-6

Major political demonstrations are rocking Bangkok. Chaos and fear sweep through the Thai and expatriate communities. Calvino steps into the political firestorm as he investigates a drug piracy operation. The piracy is traced to a powerful business interest protected by important political connections.

A nineteen-year-old Thai woman and a middle-age lawyer end up dead on the same evening. Both are connected to Calvino's investigation. The dead lawyer's law firm denies any knowledge of the case. Calvino is left in the cold. Approached by a group of expat housewives—rattled by *The Risk of Infidelity Index* that ranks Bangkok number one for available sexual temptations—to investigate their husbands, Calvino discovers the alliance of forces blocking his effort to disclose the secret pirate drug investigation.

"A hard-boiled, street-smart, often hilarious pursuit of a double murderer."—*San Francisco Chronicle*

"There's plenty of violent action ... Memorable low-life characters ...The real star of the book is Bangkok."
—*Telegraph* (London)

"Taut, spooky, intelligent, and beautifully written."
—T. Jefferson Parker

"A complex, intelligent novel."—*Publishers' Weekly*

"The darkly raffish Bangkok milieu is a treat."
—*Kirkus Review*

PAYING BACK JACK
Tenth in the series
Heaven Lake Press (2009) ISBN 978-974-312-920-9

In *Paying Back Jack*, Calvino agrees to follow the 'minor wife' of a Thai politician and report on her movements. His client is Rick Casey, a shady American whose life has been darkened by the unsolved murder of his idealistic son. It seems to be a simple surveillance job, but soon Calvino is entangled in a dangerous web of political allegiance and a reckless quest for revenge.

And, unknown to our man in Bangkok, in an anonymous tower in the center of the city, a two-man sniper team awaits its shot, a shot that will change everything. *Paying Back Jack* is classic Christopher G. Moore: densely-woven, eye-opening, and riveting.

"Crisp, atmospheric ... Calvino's cynical humour oils the wheels nicely, while the cubist plotting keeps us guessing."
—*The Guardian*

"The best Calvino yet ... There are many wheels within wheels turning in this excellent thriller."
—*The Globe and Mail*

"[*Paying Back Jack*] might be Moore's finest novel yet. A gripping tale of human trafficking, mercenaries, missing interrogation videos, international conspiracies, and revenge, all set against the lovely and sordid backstreets of Bangkok that Moore knows better than anyone."
—Barry Eisler, author of *Fault Line*

"Moore clearly has no fear that his gloriously corrupt Bangkok will ever run dry."—*Kirkus Review*

THE CORRUPTIONIST
Eleventh in the series
Heaven Lake Press (2010) ISBN 978-616-90393-3-4

Set during the recent turbulent times in Thailand, the 11th novel in the Calvino series centers around the street demonstrations and occupations of Government House in Bangkok. Hired by an American businessman, Calvino finds himself caught in the middle of a family conflict over a Chinese corporate takeover. This is no ordinary deal. Calvino and his client are up against powerful forces set to seize much more than a family business.

As the bodies accumulate while he navigates Thailand's business-political landmines, Calvino becomes increasingly entangled in a secret deal made by men who will stop at nothing—and no one—standing in their way but Calvino refuses to step aside. *The Corruptionist* captures with precision the undercurrents enveloping Bangkok, revealing multiple layers of betrayal and deception.

"Politics has a role in the series, more so now than earlier ... Thought-provoking columnists don't do it better."
—*Bangkok Post*

"Moore's understanding of the dynamics of Thai society has always impressed, but considering current events, the timing of his latest [*The Corruptionist*] is absolutely amazing."
—*The Japan Times*

"Entertaining and devilishly informative."
—Tom Plate, *Pacific Perspective*

"Very believable ... A brave book."—*Pattaya Mail*

9 GOLD BULLETS
Twelfth in the series
Heaven Lake Press (2011) ISBN 978-616-90393-7-2

A priceless collection of 9 gold bullet coins issued during the Reign of Rama V has gone missing along with a Thai coin collector. Local police find a link between the missing Thai coins and Calvino's childhood friend, Josh Stein, who happens to be in Bangkok on an errand for his new Russian client. This old friend and his personal and business entanglements with the Russian underworld take Calvino back to New York, along with Pratt.

The gritty, dark vision of *9 Gold Bullets* is tracked through the eyes of a Thai cop operating on a foreign turf, and a private eye expatriated long enough to find himself a stranger in his hometown. As the intrigue behind the missing coins moves between New York and Bangkok, and the levels of deception increase, Calvino discovers the true nature of friendship and where he belongs.

"Moore consistently manages to entertain without having to resort to melodramatics. The most compelling feature of his ongoing Calvino saga, in my view, is the symbiotic relationship between the American protagonist and his Thai friends, who have evolved with the series. The friendships are sometimes strained along cultural stress lines, but they endure, and the Thai characters' supporting roles are very effective in helping keep the narratives interesting and plausible."—*The Japan Times*

"Moore is a master at leading the reader on to what 'should' be the finale, but then you find it isn't...Worth waiting for... However, do not start reading until you have a few hours to spare."—*Pattaya Mail*

MISSING IN RANGOON
Thirteenth in the series
Heaven Lake Press (2013) ISBN 978-616-7503-17-2

As foreigners rush into Myanmar with briefcases stuffed
with plans and cash for hotels, shopping malls and high
rises, they discover the old ways die hard. Vincent Calvino's
case is to find a young British-Thai man gone missing in
Myanmar, while his best friend and protector Colonel Pratt
of the Royal Thai Police has an order to cut off the supply
of cold pills from Myanmar used for the methamphetamine
trade in Thailand.

As one of the most noir novels in the Vincent Calvino series,
Missing in Rangoon plays out beneath the moving shadows
of the cross-border drug barons. Pratt and Calvino's lives are
entangled with the invisible forces inside the old regime and
their allies who continue to play by their own set of rules.

"[Moore's] descriptions of Rangoon are excellent. In
particular, he excels at describing the human and social fall-
out that occurs when a poor, isolated country suddenly opens
its borders to the world.... *Missing in Rangoon* is a satisfying
read, a mixture of hard-boiled crime fiction and acute social
observation set in a little known part of Asia."
—Andrew Nette, *Crime Fiction Lover*

"The story is delicious. Calvino gets a missing person's case
that takes him to Myanmar (Burma), drugs are involved, and
the plot takes several wonderful twists that keep the reader
mesmerized... It's Moore at his best... Reading a book
like *Missing in Rangoon* will open up a whole new world
of knowledge that will help the reader to understand the
element in the story that the newspaper—and reporter—
dared not reveal." —*WoWasis Travelblog*

RalfTooten © 2012

Christopher G. Moore is a Canadian novelist and essayist who lives in Bangkok. He has written 25 novels, including the award-winning Vincent Calvino series and the Land of Smiles Trilogy. The German edition of his third Vincent Calvino novel, *Zero Hour in Phnom Penh*, won the German Critics Award (Deutsche Krimi Preis) for International Crime Fiction in 2004 and the Spanish edition of the same novel won the Premier Special Director's Book Award Semana Negra (Spain) in 2007. The second Calvino novel, *Asia Hand,* won the Shamus Award for Best Original Paperback in 2011.

CPSIA information can be obtained at www.ICGtesting.com
Printed in the USA
BVOW01s2329180215

388231BV00009B/484/P